The Mysterious Crown Prince

The Mysterious Crown Prince

Priscila K.

INITIO MACNA

To my brother, Jason K.

For being the first one to read this novel

For the unbreakable sibling bond
we have.

Always.

— PART 1 —

The Royal Phantom

1

My fingers brush halfheartedly over the pages of *The Rules of Royal Attraction*. Only at this time of day, I grow suffocated towards being enclosed in what is actually my favorite space in the whole palace domain of the Twelfth Provincial Region.

All the while I'm flipping each page absent-mindedly, I'm turning my head around in secret. My eyes amble along the rows of bookshelves dyed frost until my field of vision returns back to its focal point. The stony-white staircase was carved like ivy branching into two where continuous stacks circle the whole upper area with matching neutral shade and golden rails, and when my neck stretches higher above, the rest of the ceiling curves to a rounded vault on which thousands of pendant lights hang from the painted blue sky. Like bright stars in broad daylight.

But with my touch of hands sensing that I'm finally reaching the last few chapters, my view immediately comes back to directly beneath.

Here by the cold marble-top desk is where I've been spending the last few months catching up on learning. And by learning, I don't mean Psychology or Criminology – *sadly*.

Running out of patience, I'm cutting my reading-act short as I dare my hands to wrap my cheeks like a bowl and pout like a deflated balloon. I seriously can't wait to get out of this uncomfortable off-the-shoulder yellow ball gown and drown myself in bed. But eventually with a particular brewing vision, I can't help but release an eager, conceited smile.

This may just be me being insensitive, but I can't help to desiderate the sound of the royal trumpet being blown from the Throne Hall downstairs. Because that means, someone needs my help to solve a case.

My help. *Me.*

All of a sudden, a stack of papers smacks me right at the top of my head. Once, then twice.

"Ouch," I shriek as a reflex in the end because it *really* hurts.

Straight away, I rub my head with glaring eyes as it turns to follow the proud culprit's every move. Such as that of her giant gold-pinned bun of hair white and twisted like a winter storm, her long green dress contrastingly bears the unnecessary weight of a giant silver feather that towers beyond her head. Just like how everyone always dresses up so excessively around the palace – myself has been included by force.

"Oh, don't give me that look," Lady Francoise conveys her words with an unbothered expression on her white-powdered face as she calmly takes her seat to my nearest left. In her right hand, the stack of papers conventionally tied with a blue ribbon, which she thereupon not-so-gently throws onto her side of the table.

My Royal Rapport – an utter disappointment, she's clearly shown. I get it.

"If you're by any chance thinking about getting out of your royal lesson by playing detective again," she further says, her hand reaches for the clay teapot and swings it over her empty cup, "don't even bother. You'd wiped the whole Provincial Region clean for the past three years, there has been no criminal activities reported for months. Now, go on. Back to your precious reading."

Back to one of these stupid books, she means.

I want to make a fuss so badly, about *everything* to be exact, but unfortunately for me, I'm more scared of this particular old lady than my own temperament. And so I hastily chicken out – and do as I'm told.

If only she's not *ancient*.

What I mean is, Lady Francoise had even taught my mother *and* her mother (Grandmama), so even *they* are still scared of her too. Not to mention that this elderly basically has the full power when it comes to everything about my education. Makeup sessions, dining etiquette, dancing lessons, and *royal romance* are just some of these nonsense middle-grade subjects that the kingdom has deemed to be compulsory for centuries.

Correspondingly, I continue flipping the pages somewhat furiously that in no time, I'm already reaching towards the end of the book. Even to my own surprise.

Oh, yes!

But right after my fingers mindlessly flip through just the beginning of the last chapter with a precipitous smile, she signals, *not so fast*, by flipping a page back with her free hand. "Read this passage very, very carefully," she distinctly instructs aloud. "Now that you're finally coming of age, this has become the most important part of all." Her big brown eyes keep staring at my face. "This page in particular," she goes on while tapping her pointer finger on the page, "tells you about the powerful neurochemical that triggers an adrenaline release and causes one's heart to beat faster than usual. Also known as… *falling in love.*"

Promptly upon, her face emancipates a bashful smile from whatever pictures in her head I cannot relate, and so I accidentally let out a snort. *Like I care.*

"I see. So you're *still* not taking the matter of your heart seriously." She makes it sound like I need to contemplate gravely on the matter, but my heart only rolls its eyes. "Once it happens, everything is going to change for you at last. The moment you feel the touch, and your heart moving faster than a shooting star. *Believe me.*"

The touch? My heart moving faster than a shooting star?

I can't help but roar with laughter. That sounds so cheesy and lame.

"Enough with this frequent attitude of yours!" she suddenly raises her voice with her big protruding eyes glaring like a hawk, I can't help but be startled.

She can't read minds, can she?

"*This* is exactly what will get *you* in trouble throughout the course of tomorrow's Royal Coming-of-Age Ceremony, I can promise you that," she's still yelling. "And don't even get me started with your chance of getting into the Royal Princess Academy – *realistically speaking.*"

I want to roll my eyes, but I'd say she has the total right to lash out at me since I've most likely already jeopardised her retirement plan in its entirety by, simply, being me. And so I keep quiet and continue pretending to read, all the while I'm forsaking the elegant sitting manners just to clearly get my message across.

I don't give a damn about the ceremony, the academy, and whatever nonsense about the matter of heart.

But out of the blue, she releases a mirthful little smirk and returns to her forced-calm demeanor, which is weird. "Perhaps an extension to our lesson today would be necessary, if you keep slouching on your seat and–"

Shit!

And so without delay, I straighten my back and *act* to very carefully and elegantly read the rest of these stupid pages.

"Well, that always works," she says with a galling smirk, and straight away, she's back to drinking her cup of tea with ease while I'm constantly swallowing in fear. "You may think of me as a mere devil, but I can't stress enough what's at stake here, Princess. For your own good. Especially when the Royal Princess Academy has raised the bar exceptionally to the highest, *only* for this year," she sighs. "The fact that this year is when the Crown Prince turns sixteen too, just like you."

With the cup still in her hands, she unconsciously looks up to the ceiling with a beam from ear to ear. So while I'm still successfully faking my serious-studying appearance with my coordinated gestures, I quickly grip on the opportunity to flip the pages through faster than she realises.

If I'm lucky, I'll be done with this last chapter before her daydream ends.

"Since it will be mandatory for His Royal Highness to physically attend the Royal Prince Academy, as well as it will be customary for only the selective best of the very best of the Royal Academies' freshmen to move to his *mysterious private island,* that means only the kingdom's finest princes and princesses from across the whole wide Kingdom of Oceastarasia will finally get to see the face of the Crown

Prince himself!"

Because *nobody has* – for whatever reason remaining as mysterious, completely enigmatic as the whole idea of him. But anyway, I keep on flicking through the book without her notice.

I'm getting to the last few pages.

"And should you get the invitation," I want to roll my eyes – already such an impossibility, "how great would it be for me– for you!" She quickly corrects herself and clears her throat thereafter, I try to suppress my laugh so badly. "What I really mean is, even if you don't get to marry the Crown Prince, it'd still be an opportunity of a lifetime – for you."

At the same time I flip the book to a close, I say, "Well, at least *he* doesn't need to worry about getting into the Royal Prince Academy," and end it with a chuckle.

In all seriousness, I still meant to say it as a joke, but unfortunately for me, it only sounded funny in my head.

Straight away, Lady Francoise's microbladed brows fall to the middle as she releases a skeptical humph. "Back to our lesson, I suppose," she says as she finally puts down her cup of tea. Thereafter, her arms swing to cross against her chest. "Now tell me, what would your ideal *prince* look like?"

For the millionth time, *not again*. I swear to God, she always asks me this stupid question at the end of every lesson. Every. Single. Lesson.

As always, her crinkly eyes stare gleefully right at my soul, filled with high hopes at first. Only when she notices me slightly drooling with a suppressed laugh, she loudly inhales her anger while closing her eyes and says, "Please don't tell me you're about to say 'one crispy potato gem with a crown on its crunchy top' again."

"I'm sorry," I say while still softly chuckling. And I really don't know what else to say – since she's right.

"We've discussed this multiple times, Your Royal Highness," she finally exhales and opens her eyes. "You have to choose a prince tomorrow. A *real* prince, and *only* a prince." Straight away, she proceeds to massage her temples like she's suddenly got a big headache. "Only rough features of a face, that's all *we* need. Honestly, how hard can it be?"

Well, why doesn't *she* picture it for me instead? Why does she always insist that it needs to come from me? I mean, how would I know if I can't even remember any of their faces?

"Remember that the ceremony is only tomorrow, Your Royal Highness. To – mor – row!" she reiterates, which immediately makes me want to snort. *Tomorrow-me's problem.* "This has always been our concern, you must know that too. This *ignorance* of yours." She has to take a very deep breath before she goes on, "And if you haven't been able to pick one before then–"

"I can always just choose randomly tomorrow, can't

I?" I suggest, with a totally-relaxed manner.

I mean, how hard can *that* be?

"I beg your pardon?" She looks as if her soul has just left her body, her right hand clenching on her chest with disbelief. "Mind you, we're talking about the affairs of the heart here, Princess."

But in response, I bow slightly as I bid my farewell, my body raised with my feet launching for an immediate take-off. Even when her lingering expression distinctly warns me of a great deal of danger, I still take it as a no-stress situation.

"We haven't even got to the part where we discuss the Royal Dating Schemes, which happens *after* you choose a prince to dance with for the ceremony," she shrieks with terror as she follows me to stand, I simply roll my eyes without her notice. "Look!" She flicks her head and frantically waves her hand at the *The Rules of Royal Dating Schemes* book enclosed in a standing gold-lining glass frame that's never been opened – not even once – as if it'd somehow miraculously motivate me. I only give it the side-eye and quietly snort. "What you've been missing, thanks to those *bloody adventures* you'd been up to for the past three years – and I mean, *literally.*"

Oh, please. She could've just said *solving murders.*

The two guards by the door look between me and each other confusedly, but I only signal tiredly with my hand to give way for me to exit, even when I can still perfectly hear Lady Francoise screaming at me purposefully to a pitch behind me, "You have no idea what you're getting yourself into, Your Royal Highness!"

Like I said. Tomorrow-me's problem.

2

Sitting on the ceremonial royal seat made entirely of gold, I'm supposed to practice breathing in the illusive sense of power, except that I'm not. Quite far from it, I've never felt as... powerless.

The moment you feel the touch, and your heart moving faster than a shooting star.

The touch...

My heart moving faster than a shooting star...

Damn it, these stupid words.

This was supposed to be easy, and quick. But now that the time is near, I begin to feel the stress, and I find myself hesitating.

Typical me.

"Your answer, Princess?"

My shoulders jolt abruptly to the piercing sound of the present time, ripping me off my wandering thoughts. Even now, the prince standing right before me still peers at me with great uncertainty. Dressed in yellow silk and two giant gold feathers on his back shoulders, his dark-brown hair shimmers with the chandelier lights above, waiting perplexedly for my response.

Panic rubs cubes of ice all over my skin, regardless of the warm temperature. I must look like an idiot just now.

My eyes are now drifting blankly across the glamorous Festivity Hall of the Twelfth Provincial Region's Reigning Palace, ridiculously spacious, and filled with a handful of princes from across the whole Kingdom of Oceastarasia wearing different styles and colours of feather-incorporated cashmere suit with a sword on their hip.

Back to my screening mode again.

Him. Not him. No heart beating faster than usual for me.

A few look rather excited, but most others seem as disinterested and forced as me – yawning, brushing their suits, checking their nails, moving around their swords – while they're waiting for their turn to formally wish me a happy birthday. And in accordance with the *Dance Courtesy for Royals* book, I have to have my very first dance tonight for the sake of my Royal Rapport.

I have to.

Stupid royal protocol. Stupid royal party. Stupid royal blood.

"Princess Seraphine of the Twelfth Provincial Region," the same prince raises his tone slightly more, his temper still avowedly contained though seemingly to a near pass beyond its limit, which is understandable. "Do I have the honour of your attention?"

My bad. I mean, it's a miracle that he hasn't left, and the others too.

I'm obviously procrastinating.

"Apologies, Prince…" Wait, what did he say his name again? Whoever he is and whichever Provincial Region he's from, I've completely forgotten. Oh, *shit.* Nevermind, then. Let's just skip the part where I'm supposed to formally address him. "You certainly have the honour of my attention without fail," I say. *Lie.*

Subsequently, the prince walks rather dazedly a few steps closer towards me. His head moves slightly forward, his eyes sort of roll to the left and right bewilderingly, though his body manages to keep to his sturdy princely posture the whole time. "Are you… okay?" he whispers, sounding bearably normal without forcing the royal formality this time, appearing utterly confused. "You looked like you… I don't know."

"Never better," I then clear my throat. "Please, you were saying?" I say without guilt remorse, as if I hadn't been ignoring him from the start.

"Right." He walks a few steps back with his eyes still glancing around confusedly. "As I was saying," he clears his throat, "it would be a pleasure of mine, *and* yours," I desperately want to roll my eyes, "for me to have your hand for the dance tonight. You see, I've been invited to attend the Royal Prince Academy," the prince proclaims very loudly. His brows jump up and down repeatedly in the process, then added to his expression is a soft grin as his head whirls briefly past the crowd behind him.

Okay, at least I kind of get him now. *Show-off.*

Afterward, it seems like he wants me to say something, but when I don't, he clears his throat and says, "The invitation is a very big deal, you must know, as everyone here must already perceive – especially to a great number of princes in this entire wide kingdom who have not and are not going to be invited, thus such for half the guests in this hall – I have to say, what a pity."

Pompous ass is what I really want to say. But since Lady Francoise is currently watching somewhere from across the platform resembling a scary ghost, I've decided to back out. So, "Good for you," I give my response sort of lazily. Honestly, I just can't think of anything else to say, other than a bunch of offensive words.

When it looks like he's about to say something again, I immediately bow my head slightly and wave my hand like a windmill. *Next!*

At this point, I just want to quickly and finally get to any one of them who doesn't piss me off as much, pick him for the dance, and get this night over with.

But following various shining and extravagant exhibits of what each prince after the other has brought me as a birthday present, whatever they all say just sounds

exactly the same to me in my head. *I've come with more
gold. Bigger diamond. Much bigger diamond than the one before
me. Happy birthday. Heard of you. Seen you before. Pick me for
the dance. Why? Because I've been invited to the Royal Prince
Academy, that's why. So, would it be me? Pick me now or ask me
later – your choice, of course – but preferably now because I'm
better than anyone else.*

Show-off. Show-off. Show-off. A bunch of show-offs.

But the worst is what comes next, when several
others ask me if I have received my invitation from the
Royal Princess Academy. Maybe because I've been acting
ignorant about theirs. So naturally because of them, I
have to repeatedly admit in public that *I still have not*. So
embarrassing. It's basically no different to saying I'm not
getting in.

Almost everyone replies with the exact same
response: an uncomfortable smile with raising eyebrows.
Except for one. A prince in a dark-green suit with similar
extravagance like the rest, who responds a bit differently.

He holds his head up so high, I almost thought he
was talking to the vaulted ceiling above instead of me.
"Your Royal Rapport," he starts with a judging look, "it
can't be that bad."

A challenge, my temper takes it.

I try not to let out a pathetic smile as I manage to
regain my classic composure, but by countering with all
honesty in my head that it's actually worse than he thinks.

Much, much worse than even a blank page could do any harm.

"It's coming, I'm sure," the same prince in green startlingly reassures, his voice coming out softer. Not sure if he suddenly feels bad or if he just suddenly wants to look nice. "School starts in a week, but you still have time."

Yeah, right, I want to say, but I've decided to just nod silently and leave them be with whatever trifling ruckus they're now raising towards each other.

I mean, let's be real. My Royal Rapport is definitely not for the faint-hearted to read. Lady Francoise should've probably left it blank for my sake *and* hers. If anything, its gaping and blood-soaked contents push off even more prospects–

"Shut your mouth!"

My shoulders jump at the sudden sound of noisy quarrels.

Okay, now what?

"You, shut your mouth! It's our choice not to be invited. *Our* choice! We don't *need* their invitation," ironically, says the prince in the purple suit who has not got the invitation from the Royal Prince Academy – but who am I to judge? "A bunch of blistering arrogants," he adds with something like a low guttural sound in the throat.

"You! Come here, you!" The prince in yellow strides towards him.

So naturally, the two start punching each other. And

in double the time, everyone follows with their fists. Right in front of me – the birthday girl.

Talk about *royal manners*. All I can do now is just sit on the throne with the palm on my cheek. Frowning. Watching all these princes who come to look no different than a bunch of dressed-up rearing pegasus with crowns – with or without an invitation – butting heads against each other until they turn blurry once I begin to yawn.

Well, I give up. Not that I have tried to stop them from fighting, but maybe I just give up on my life in general. On being a princess, going into the prestigious Royal Princess Academy, updating my Royal Rapport with royal-banquet accomplishments, dancing with a prince, *et cetera*. Perhaps, it's not a bad idea to give up my royal title. Be something else, do other stuff. Nothing far from being too idealistic, but also nowhere near being realistic. Like becoming…

Detective Princess Seraphine. Detective Seraphine. *The* Detective Seraphine.

I think I'm smiling.

"So, Princess, which one is it?" My complete awareness is once again brought back into the party without warning, now thanks to the prince in red suit with some kind of tapering flag trimmed with lace on his front rib.

"I beg your pardon?" I ask with a genuine confused expression.

Seriously, I'd rather stay preoccupied with my own thoughts. And I'd much prefer for them to keep fighting among themselves and leave me be.

"Which one among us shall you pick for the dance tonight?" says some prince in a blue suit with scrubby tufts of glittering feathers on both of his shoulders. "We have collectively decided. An answer from you should settle it, once and for all."

"One who is invited to study in the Royal Prince Academy?" The prince in yellow jumps in, followed by the prince in purple. "Or one who isn't?"

And then everyone asks simultaneously, "Who *wins*?"

I see. So now they're trying to shift the burden of their argument to me. Should've expected no less. But the worst is when they are all now just staring at me quietly, all in agreement, waiting for an answer.

All of a sudden, my thoughts just go blank again. I mean, I still can't believe that I'm really supposed to choose one of them to dance with as the highlight of the ceremony. I repeat. *The* highlight of the ceremony.

I swallow loudly down beyond my gland, my heartbeat races.

Shit! I still can't choose. Remember, this should be *easy*. Well, I thought it should've been. So why the hell it isn't, even when the reason couldn't be any clearer.

I don't want to dance with any of them. Heck, I

don't even want to have anything to do with any of them afterward.

For God's sake, just point your finger at some random prince and get this over with! I scream in my head.

I want to slap myself.

Honestly, the stupidity a form of panic could bring. I mean, think about it. The sooner the royal first dance will start, the sooner the ceremony will end too. After that, I can just make some lame excuse to never meet the prince again. Sick. Injury. Worst case scenario, fake my death. *Easy*. So why so much hesitation? Why does it have to take so long for me to decide? It's like I'm sabotaging my own plan. As if deep down, I already have a figure in my head.

Nonsense. I mean, if there is one…

Actually, there is one.

I think.

But when Leon appears unannounced in my head at the moment of urgency, it makes me cringe, and shock, and confused. Regardless, my heart suddenly beats out of control with just a mere image of him. His brown hair, his grey eyes, his captivating smile. All of him.

Once it happens, everything is going to change for you at last.

Falling in love.

With every blink of my eyes I've come to realise, I think this is the first time in my life when it really strikes me – that he's probably the only person I won't mind dancing with.

So, what about now?

What if… I just do it now?

Call him out and choose him for the dance. See what happens.

Even when he's not one of them.

3

For a long moment now, my head has been moving round and round like a lunatic.

Where the hell is Leon?

"He's not here," I finally say subconsciously, my head keeps turning back and forth confusedly. Where else could he possibly be right now?

"Not here?" The prince in purple repeats.

"You mean, none of us is worthy?" The prince in yellow falsely deduces.

Apparently, I've just accidentally caused more misunderstandings between them, so they end up arguing again.

I sigh.

Maybe I should just leave now. Screw the ceremony and the royal first dance and my Royal Rapport and the Royal Princess Academy and all.

Find Leon.

I'm just about to get off my seat, but then it's getting

quite exciting when a bunch of them start pulling out their swords, so I get distracted and decide to linger and watch for a while.

I want to snort. Like they're *ever* going to strike. Their hands are shaking with hesitations, merely bequeathing harmless threats over ethereal shadows.

They're never going to strike.

The Festivity Hall is massive, so my eyes can only wander to a limit across. A shadowy glimpse of two figures with big shining crowns as they are watching, moving rather excitedly, and sort of clapping from side to side. Probably falsely thinking that the princes are drawing their swords for me instead of their big fat ego.

But surprisingly, the couple's excitement seems to breathe out a sense of courage in them. Suddenly, it looks like these princes are really going to poke one another.

I'll see if they ever dare. These bunch of chickens with their golden crowns, looking pathetic.

But when the palace guards suddenly run to stop them from hesitatingly waving their swords in the air, I get bored again and finally make my excuse for the "powder room".

Screw the monarchy. Screw my royal title. Screw Lady Francoise. Screw them all.

I've just leaped to my feet when they're now trying to encourage me to decide with the one present I think is best, followed by their classic interrogative pair of words,

"Who wins?" All the while they're still in their loser-in-battle position. Two hands on the sword confronting the ground. Sweat all over their faces. Each of them. Seriously. *Pathetic.*

I mean, honestly. I highly doubt that my birthday actually *means* something to them. Best gift? I mean, whatever it is, Leon has probably gotten me the best birthday present of all, even when – and especially because – it won't be something shimmering and boring like diamonds and gold.

A gift from Leon would be something money can't even buy.

A case. A skill. A puzzle for me to solve.

His sworn-to-life protection.

So what can I say when I can't even remember anything they've shown me upon? All I remember is a bunch of shining necklaces and bracelets that don't mean anything to me. None of their gifts came across as personal, or if they really know me, or if they really *want* to know me. And so I let out another deep sigh and decide to say whatever is on my mind.

"Whoever wins the sword fight, *I declare*," I answer lazily. Period.

I don't think they'll take it seriously anyway.

I have already turned my back completely and walked away, when suddenly, I smell something familiar from behind me.

Something coppery. Something metallic. Something

like iron.

Blood.

When I turn my head around, it's immediately clear to me that there is no winner, as they're all now laying down in their own pool of blood. It suddenly crosses my mind too that the guards didn't stop them this time, that they all have taken my words as a *royal decree* to let them fight to death for the win.

So now, I'm the only one to blame.

I never meant for all of this to happen. Clearly, I've given way to the tendency of underestimating the weight of my words. I mean, in my defense, I really thought they wouldn't–

You are no human. You have no heart.

I wish *her* voice hadn't come back to me. Not like this. Not right now. Not when I've almost forgotten it. Forgotten *her*.

Feeling guilty, I run back to where they all lie down on the floor. Or maybe because I just desperately need a distraction.

Out of habit, I bend my body down and place my index and third fingers on each of their necks to check their pulse over their carotid artery.

I've seen worse, I think.

No one is dead. Good. And there isn't too much blood splattered in between. But since most of them have tried to grab my right hand in the process, much of their blood has glossed over my skin and dress.

I now look like a scene from a horror movie.

Soon after, a team of royal medics catch up with first aid. So I walk slowly away from the chaos to where the floor is empty. I rest my legs and palms on the ground, then I look up to the ceiling and catch sight of what looks like a thousand light bulbs on twisted golden branches.

I reckon this is where I was supposed to have my very first dance tonight.

I can leave now, but instead, I'm thinking about a lot of things. How my Royal Coming-of-Age Ceremony has easily turned into a *royal bloodbath*. How Lady Francoise is ever going to get this written in my Royal Rapport. How I'm never going to get into the Royal Princess Academy. Down to my least concern, finding the mysterious Crown Prince – a cryptic puzzle I'm never going to solve.

Not sure how many minutes have passed when one of the medics with a ponytail suddenly approaches me.

"The princes," she says. "They are all alive, but in no stage to move properly, or dance."

I know, but I still let out a genuine sigh of relief. Maybe it's a good thing that they all almost died, since none of them is dead anyway.

"But they keep insisting that the dance will still need to go on," she adds. Even her lips sink in confusion.

"What?" I answer furiously.

"They still insist on you choosing one of them. *A*

winner," she says with a frown of uncertainty, now biting her lips.

What in the *hail* of *rain*?

Are they being serious right now? I mean, look at them. They look like a bunch of mummies staring at me with their eyes wide open. I can't even keep track of their expressions. They can barely keep their feet on the ground at once, so how in the world are they going to move their body in order?

"You know what? I'm going to bed," I say as I stand.

These princes. These idiots.

The medic turns her head left and right, still confused. "Your Highness?"

"You tell them, I'm going to bed. They can do whatever they want to do to be the winner. I don't care."

Because it's either this or stabbing myself with a sword.

Early enough, Moyra and the other ladies in waiting come up to me with what seems to be a replica of the dress to what I was wearing, just when I'm rising to my feet. Moyra, in particular, looks very proud as she saunters excitedly in the lead, the layered ruffles follow her mood to sway all over the skirt of her pink ball gown.

"I've got it all covered," she whispers with a big smile. Then she tells me how she's had multiple dresses of the exact same ones made. "Believe it or not, I knew something like this would happen. *A royal bloodbath*," she giggles. "If there's only one princess who could pull off something like this, it's you."

Except, I wasn't even trying – I think.

"Perfect timing," I say, while raising my shoulders apathetically. "I'm supposed to dance with one of these mummies," my smile displays a brutal sarcasm, "but instead, I'm going to bed."

"Excuse me?" Moyra stares at me for a long while. "But–"

I brush her off by walking away immediately. *"Bed,"* I counter sharply.

And find Leon – if he hasn't found me first.

My right foot has barely touched the entrance of my bed chamber when I notice a peculiar small white paper lying in a scuttled angle, like it's being slid over underneath the door from outside in a rush. Moyra acts to stride towards it from behind me, but I immediately stop her with my hand against her chest.

I step out of my heels and walk a couple steps ahead alone.

Both feet on the cold marble floor, I bend down and pick the note myself.

7, West Dungeon
Royal Phantom
Happy birthday

Moyra catches up to me in time and kneels right beside me.

"It looks very suspicious," she says as her head motions slowly towards my face until it blocks the view of the note in my hand completely.

"As it is most curious," I say while gently pushing her on the left cheek as far away from me.

Still admiring the note. The message. The *clues*.

"You're not going, aren't you?" Moyra asks, and takes a huge gulp of air right after. "Please, tell me you're not going, *Your Royal Highness*." And I know how serious Moyra gets when she starts properly addressing me. "You know what? Let us change you to a proper ball gown instead."

I still appear calm but I can't hide the fact that my other hand quivers slightly.

I'm shaking. Shaking with excitement.

Because the note smells of Leon all over.

I don't give Moyra an answer but it's becoming clear when I start making more haste with my pace. Even cooperating with changing my dress obediently without complaint. But as soon as I'm done, I'm going rogue.

Goodbye, mummies.

I'm heading straight towards the West Dungeon.

4

I almost fell as I ran my way down the narrow spiral staircase – this stupid ball gown – but I'm alright.

The palace guards who've been chasing me for quite some time are standing right behind me, but they know better than to restrain me. They carefully keep their distance – eyes on, hands off, waiting for my next move.

The glass heels on my left hand swings back and forth as I gradually gain back composure. It's a good thing that Moyra was willing to compromise, stealthily exchanging the crinoline to a much more loose petticoat underneath the cerulean poofy skirt from my waist to legs; otherwise, I wouldn't have even made it as far as the palace entrance.

I take a very deep breath, before I push the wooden door open and find a bunch of senior commanding officers filling the seats by the long pine table in the middle of the room, leaving a few empty chairs near the wall.

Look at these shocked faces.

They can't believe I've managed to find them here, and I still can't believe they're trying to hide this from me. They all perfectly know how much I've been waiting for this, so naturally, I feel so angry.

"It's a good place to hide, isn't it?" I strangely sound calmer than I'd expected. "Where is it?"

Without waiting for an answer, I drag an empty seat all the way across to the other end, right next to Gaspard – the Commanding General of the Twelfth Battalion of the Royal Military Force – who looks as if my presence has just cut through all his senses. My glittering pump heels land deadly first on the table with a big thump, then I sit myself down and tap my pointy finger repeatedly on the surface.

"Give me the card," I demand.

Everyone stays silent and takes turns to look at each other.

"Princess," Gaspard finally speaks after regaining his consciousness. "The party. The banquet. If the *Prince* knows you're here–"

"Give. Me. The. Card," I raise my voice this time. My crown slips forward in effect and I slap it back with my right fingers, giving everyone else in the room a gasp of surprise. So not princess-like, they must think, but I don't give a crap.

"But His Royal Highness has strictly forewarned. We shall bring you back to the Festivity Hall at once. The ceremony. The princes. The dance–"

"The. Card," I persist.

As though having been forced to raise a white flag, Gaspard sighs and drags towards me the mysterious card comprising a code. It's pink, primrose scented, and signed with a small scale of a full-circle struck by a big crescent shape in the middle.

The Royal Phantom's very own insignia.

And there, right on the center of the silk-coated paper, is the piece of information I have been anxious to read.

The third becomes the first when the other two disagree.

Stand right next to the pillar, and that's when I'll sneak in.

You'll have zero chance the next day, should you not believe me.

Hear this in your lullaby tonight, so my plan would succeed.

The Blue Tiara will once ever be mine eternally.

I now find myself repeating the message in my head.

What in the world does that mean?

"None of us has cracked the code yet. It's been *three hours.*"

I shift my head to the right to where the voice comes from, and then I let out a discreet cheeky smile in response.

I know what he means.

Where have you been?

The corners of his lips are struggling to keep from turning up with great pleasure. Multiple stars of medals hang proudly on his blue army vest, just like the rest, but his shine most brightly among theirs in my eyes – in the same way his presence has always been to me.

It's totally not his fault that I came down here three hours late. As a matter of fact, I'd wished I'd been back in my bedroom lounge much sooner to find his note.

I was right about Leon getting me the best birthday gift of all, even when he doesn't seem to realise it. I mean, if it hadn't been for him sliding a notepaper into my chamber, I wouldn't have even found out about the party here – where I was clearly not invited.

Regardless, my attention saunters back into the note as quick as my adrenaline rises. *The Royal Phantom.* What I would give to catch a mere glimpse of him right in front of me, to reason the face behind the mask. What I would give to touch even the slightest end of his robe with my own two bare hands, see if I could work out what the fabric was made of. Though both deeds would be considered near impossible.

But, seriously. What I would give.

Come to think of it, I don't need to confuse my wants with what I am and what is highest expected of every princess in every Provincial Region of this kingdom:

to marry the Crown Prince. I don't know yet what I'm going to do in the future, and I've always been better known for my unpredictable demeanour, but it's always clear what I want right now.

And right now, I want to catch the Royal Phantom. *Me.*

I want it so bad.

"Princess?" Gaspard distracts me with his eyes wide open. He quickly flicks his eyes at Leon who appears calm, back to me who's now returned from my stupor, sighs in relief, back to Leon, and then back staring at me again. I think he means: *Is she dead? No, she's okay. Is she, really? Alas, what is she still doing here?*

The first time Leon saw this state of mine many years ago, he turned all panically overreacting as if I'd just left my own body. But now I know that he knows, the way he knows that I know, that he's perfectly used to it. Explains why he's only letting out a small chuckle.

"Surely, this room is intolerable for you," Gaspard falsely claims the reason for my unexpected trance. But now that he brings that up, he's right. The walls are bare with nothing but shady white scratches off the grey paint, and some of the floorboards have been pared down to mere sand stones. And what is that smell? Something like an oily rag, or maybe rotten eggs. Everything here is so horrible, I don't think rats could even survive this place. Clearly, this room hasn't been used or cleaned in ages.

"We should all move then," I propose. It's for their own good too. I mean, I know they only chose this place to hide from me in the first place.

"Er… I believe that would not be possible, Princess. You see, all the better rooms are currently… inaccessible." Yeah, right. Clearly, he's still trying very hard to get rid of me. "Shall we escort you back to the palace now? Naturally, we are very concerned." And he's still using it as an excuse.

"I should be fine here. Thank you, Gaspard," I counter respectfully.

"The smell here must be revolting for you, Princess. We – the guards – can simply adjust, but surely, you will not stand for this. Best for you if we escort you back to the comfortable palace and–"

"Don't worry about me. I'll manage," I say as I stare at the message again, then turn the card around with my right fingers.

I hear a tick sound coming from Gaspard tipping his tongue, but I just pretend not to. Shortly after, one of his subordinates enters the room in a hurry, approaches him, and whispers something in his ears. He then looks frightened and whispers back.

I close my eyes in return, trying to get myself free from all these distractions.

The third becomes the first when the other two disagree. What in the world does the Royal Phantom mean? If the third becomes the first, does he mean number three? But if the other two disagree, that could also mean–

Creak.

Argh, damn it. I've lost my focus again.

Now what?

With the sudden sound of the door turning once more, my eyes are enticed to open, my nose tuning into the smell of roasted beans. With this much caffeine at this late hour, no one here's expected to be sleeping tonight.

In total boredom, my sight follows two palace guards distributing the hot drinks by going around the four concrete round pillars.

Stand right next to the pillar. Pillars. What do they all have in common? Tall? Strong? Vertical? But which pillar does the Royal Phantom mean? Could it possibly refer to… a number?

"Alright, that should be everyone," Gaspard tells the whole room.

I've realised everybody's got a cup of coffee but me. Of course. *Obviously.*

Gaspard clears his throat out of the blue, then looks the opposite way and to the ceiling. I'm pretty sure he's covertly letting loose a bit of a smirk too. Another soft message that I shouldn't be here; that the Reigning Prince of the Twelfth Provincial Region has noticed me gone and given them the order to bring me back into the Festivity Hall safely at this instant without restraint; that I'd just fall drowsy at the message and come back to the palace of my own accord.

The Royal Highness knows I don't like being pushed. The last time that happened, they had to secure the whole province just to bring me back into the palace, to Gaspard's sweat and tears.

Well, shame on him, and shame on them, because I don't even like coffee.

Leon slides what's supposed to be his cup towards me, putting me somewhat at ease. It's his way of making a statement, since he perfectly knows all my drink preferences.

I turn my head, expecting to see the usual gentle smile on his clean boyish face, but instead I'm getting a coded turning of grey eyes beneath his brown, messy quiff haircut. It seems Leon really wants to solemnly show everyone in the room that he's on my side – the only one, that is.

Naturally, the others look pissed, including – and especially – Gaspard. Now he seems to realise who's given me the tip about their covert meeting. *His own son.*

Thick skin on the face with no-sorry phase, I choose to gladly stay comfortably in my current seat. What's more, I wrap my arms as a way for me to say I'm not going anywhere. No way. No chance.

No chance.

You'll have zero chance… the next day.
Hear this in your lullaby… tonight.

Suddenly, it hits me.

Of course. It's always been so simple. And so I unwittingly rise and strike the table with both of my hands.

"The Royal Phantom," my voice shivers, "tonight." I suddenly find it harder to breathe. "He's coming… tonight."

The room is immediately filled with gasps. Some are starting to laugh, while some others become petrified.

"But the first eleven cases were never this soon," Gaspard argues. "They all had at least twenty four hours." And yet none of them had managed to break their assigned code in time. "Are you sure, Princess?" He looks at me with a puzzling look.

Back to sitting down, my long dress puckers as I cross my right calf to its left.

Am I sure?

The skirt is undeniably heavy, but not more than my mind has been.

Zero, one, two.

Stand right next to the pillar.

Then I look at the short arrow on my gold ellipse watch.

"In two hours," I say as I close my eyes, then take a really deep breath – *You'll have zero chance the next day* – and let go. My eyes are open when I finally contend with, "I'm sure."

5

Gaspard has been standing and turning the card around very slowly under the hanging light for whatever reason; his loaded gun tangible on the side, his clean head shines. Somehow, it annoys me.

As usual, he doesn't believe me. *He never does.*

"The message," Gaspard murmurs, before making a pointless circle with his right foot. Then, he closes his eyes and turns his head directly at the light above him. "If I recall…"

I feel my patience is gradually slipping away.

"The third becomes the first when the other two disagree," I start repeating out loud from memory. *"Stand right next to the pillar, and that's when I'll sneak in. You'll have zero chance the next day, should you not believe me. Hear this in your lullaby tonight, so my plan would succeed. The Blue Tiara will once ever be mine eternally."*

Seriously, what else does he need? *Do you want me to explain?* I want to say. But I know he doesn't. Every

time I tried to explain my deduction in the past, he
instead asserted the exact opposite of what I'd just said
out of pride, which almost cost us tons of criminals in this
Provincial Region let loose. Took me three long years to get
used to what he'd been doing.

But I'm sixteen now, and so I'm thinking of a
different strategy this time.

"You must see it too now," I say pleasantly. He
sort of nods his head. Good. The least he can do now is
to pretend to understand. "Yes. You see it too, Gaspard.
Wonderful," I try to produce some sort of state of hypnosis.
"He's coming tonight, at twelve."

"Right, right, I see it now, Princess," he nods. I
exhale deeply out of relief. He can even take the credit if he
wants to – as he always did in the end. But instead, he says,
"He is *not* coming tonight."

"What?"

Remember, Seraphine. He's still Leon's father, I repeat in
my head.

"Clearly, he means three days." Gaspard taps the
card with the nail of his right pointer finger at what I
assume is the word *third*.

"Three days?"

Remember, Seraphine. He's still Leon's father, I repeat
much faster.

"*The first… the last two…* In three days at twelve.
No– two."

I try to take a very deep breath at first, as Lady Francoise always taught me.

Words of profanity only in your head, if you can't avoid any, I recall her saying that to me constantly during lessons.

Right. Okay. Words of profanity only stay in my head. *Crap. Shit. Idiot. Dog Poop.* Excuse me. Not out loud this time. I think I've got it.

Next, think about the exact opposite. Pleasant words in the ear only, my dear; and that's how a princess should be – at all times, I recall her lesson again.

Right. Opposite. *Rubbish–* I mean… *Treasure. Perfume. Intelligent. Dogs are cute. Gaspard is not. Gaspard is annoying. Gaspard is full of rubbish.* Damn it, it's not working. *Gaspard is full of shit.*

Oh, shit. Don't let me lose my temper again. I'm sixteen now.

I'm really, really, really trying my best to come up with more pleasant words to say despite my fury boiling hot. But, *uh oh,* it doesn't seem to work anymore this time.

Boiling. It's boiling even more. And then it explodes.

"Gaspard, I've had it with your offhand guesses!" I scream.

There goes my limit.

Unbelievable. This stupid bonehead. And to think that I was starting to feel sorry for him. How he biologically shares a blood with Leon or how he ever became the Commanding General in the first place is still beyond me.

I walk towards him and snatch the card from his hand. "*The third becomes the first when the other two disagree.* He's talking about the first prime number. *Stand right next to the pillar.* That's one. So he means twelve. And he says we'll have *no* chance. He's coming tonight, at midnight!"

"Princess," Gaspard gently rests his hands on my shoulders, "I believe this room is starting to get on your nerves." More like he is. I move my shoulders to try to shake his hands off, but fail. "Perhaps it's time for you to get some rest." He flicks his head to a few chosen guards, giving them signals to escort me back to the palace. "And we should all do too." And then he laughs. He freaking laughs his fat belly out until he snorts.

In response, the other officers look next to each other bemusedly and force themselves to laugh along with him.

"Nevertheless, gentlemen," he snuffles, "I've now solved the code. The Royal Phantom will be coming in three days." Seriously, Gaspard? Why does this keep happening? "Now, now, Princess, let us safely get you back into the Festivity Hall. Leon, if you will."

I swing Gaspard's hands off my shoulders. "No," I steadfastly defy.

I turn around to the others as my last resort, including Leon. I'm swinging the card furiously like it's fanning the heat in me. My brewing impatience promptly bursts into an overflowing cauldron as I shout, "Don't you see? He's coming in two hours! We have no time! Let us hurry!"

At last, with all the quiet response and blank faces I'm getting, I'm completely losing it. "You know what? Nevermind," I bawl. "I'm going to the Crown Chamber myself, and no one is going to stop me!" Then I turn around and stare at Gaspard. "Especially you!" I point at him with the card, his eyes grow blank and wide. "I'm going to prove you wrong. Remember, Gaspard. I always did."

Gaspard's face starts to blow red like a balloon. Mine too, in response. I know he doesn't like it whenever I try to help with a case, and he hates it more when I can solve it.

But, seriously? *Three days*? Surely he could've come up with a better guess, if he had given himself a chance to think with his brain instead of his big fat ego. I mean, *three days*, we might as well deliver the crown ourselves to the Royal Phantom.

"Sir, if I may," Leon finally decides to step in aloud. "I believe Princess Seraphine has a point. And if you may allow me to humbly be on your guard, Sir, *dear Father*," I want to puke, "what do you think the Prince would say to you – the Honourable, the First in Command – if the Royal Phantom would indeed be coming tonight and we haven't taken any measures?"

I get it now. He's going with the kissing-ass approach.

"As I'm sure," he continues, "you're at least more than familiar with the Reigning Prince himself discreetly taking pride in Princess Seraphine's rather… *uncommon* interest…" What's that supposed to mean? "… as much as he's exceedingly concerned about her safety and prospective to be." He then walks a few steps closer towards Gaspard, and whispers, "If only His Royal Highness could at least be informed of such astounding progress, he would be more than grateful."

The way Leon wondrously and peacefully takes care of this idiot of a chief commanding officer – his *dear father* – and in a beguiling way… to a success.

As if Gaspard has just suddenly been bewitched, he walks out of the room in silence without so much as giving me or anyone else a second look, leaving all his subordinates confused. But we all know where he's going. He's going to talk to the Reigning Prince of Douzevoir, the ruler of the Twelfth Provincial Region – my *dear father*.

Little snitch. The one thing Gaspard's actually good at.

I'm getting calmer for some reason, maybe because Gaspard's completely out of the view, but Leon in a flash turns hectic and in full ordering-people mode.

"In two ticks of a clock," he starts shouting, "the Royal Phantom is going to break into the main palace of the Twelfth Provincial Region we call home to steal the Blue Tiara," the crown of blue faceted gemstones, the one my parents say can only be worn in the presence of the King who's bestowed one crown upon each of the Provincial Region, which in the sense of hence also serves as, "a symbol of trust by the King – a symbol of peace, to our dear province."

He glances at me for a split second, and that is even more than enough for me to suddenly feel this surge of energy throughout my whole body. Like my heart begins to palpitate out of havoc. Strange.

"Now that we know what time he's coming, thanks to Her Royal Highness the Princess," he goes on with his speech, and I feel like blushing, "we'll have the upper hand. We will protect *our* crown!"

As if his words are stimulants of stronger caffeine, everyone cheers to gear up. Later on, he announces his plan to catch up with his puerile First-in-Command of a father first, before dispatching the captains and is ready himself to leave.

"We'll be on guard, Princess," Leon takes the time to assure me with a smile and a gentle nod. He then races outside with the rest of the guards, leaving a few to escort me back.

My heart has just skipped a beat again. And again. And again.

This primitive, recalcitrant heart.

But regardless of all that, I'm at peace that at least Leon has taken my words seriously. *He always does.* It's like this huge weight has been lifted off my shoulders.

Suddenly flicking myself back from my wandering thoughts, I quickly grab my heels from the table and start running barefeet. Deep down, I really can't wait to get out of this stinking place of a dungeon.

I'm back on the spiral staircase which seems to grow higher than before as I ascend; and in the intervening moment I'm slowly washing off the putrid smell off my nose, I keep thinking about what the phantom thief is said to look like.

In all his previous fiendish stopovers, he managed to forge witnesses who'd seen him only from a great distance. And they all said the same thing.

A very tall man with a lengthy curled blonde hair tied into the lowest ponytail. A face hidden behind a white smiling-mask revealing only his eyes at a glance. A long black robe with a matching tall hat of that of a squire man. A pair of white opera gloves. Golden braided loops around his shoulders. And, a pair of shining black shoes.

I can't hide my cheeky smile any longer. Will he be exactly as he was painted, or will he be so much more? Either way, I'm going to find out with my very own eyes.

I have to.

A certain amount of people will be trying to stop me, most definitely, but I'll do whatever it takes.

Soon after, determination leads me to white light spots cast by the moon. The dark blue of the sky slowly becomes visible within my sight and the ground's back to level with the soles of my feet as I finally come out of the stone tower.

The smell in the air around forthwith shifts into that of fresh green grass. I stare straight at the side of the main palace building for a sense of resolution. I stand still for a while, catching my breath, and I hear the guards behind me doing the same thing louder.

I almost forgot about them, to be honest, but anyway, "I'm ready," I whisper to myself. "Nothing is going to stop me." No one will, but me.

And so to the guards' dismay, we're immediately back to running.

6

I take pride in my experiences with some of the palace's secret passages. One whoosh through the right wall and I magically disappeared from the hallway.

But what feels like the speed of light as well as incongruously the longest one hour of my life, I've finally found my way back into the main palace and into my bed chamber.

If it hadn't been for avoiding the Festivity Hall where the party is *and* losing all the guards along the way, I'd not have taken the detour.

Finally reaching my wardrobe room, I begin rummaging in total chaos for the obvious combination of soft cottons and linens. Black trench, white shirt, dark grey pants, white running shoes, and an old deep-blue cotton hat that shows a silhouette of the Blue Tiara right in the middle – this region's own icon.

Let me help you, Detective.

Even when I'm in such a hurry like this, I

unwittingly still let out a smile at these venture garbs piling from my chest up to my face. Memories whisper of the nameless town boy whose face remains hazy under the same cap – eyes so soothing like the evergreen forest, and hands that took me out of sight.

Guess I always end up with the exact same outfit for a reason.

The pants are getting so much tighter, and what was my ankle-length is now half my thigh. The shirt fits me just nicely now as it was very comfortably loose.

It seems I've grown so much compared to three years ago when I first sneaked into the nearest town and thus managed to obtain all of these pieces of clothing with the help of that daring suburban boy seemingly my age. I got caught, actually, by the royal guards on the very same day when I ran out of hiding onto a proscenium stage to point my finger at a culprit who was trying to blend in with the audience, so naturally, everyone else found out too. That wasn't at all a moment to regret, other than the fact that I completely lost sight of the boy afterward, who's never to be seen again. I guess it just somehow never crossed my mind that after all the crazy adventures we had had the whole day, he would just completely disappear without a word – just like that. And even when there were always people asking for me to help with a case ever since the news about me solving two different cases in a day found its way into other towns and all the cities across the

Twelfth Provincial Region, and even to my own excitement I'd always accept, all that remains of that suburban boy is this set of clothes he had spontaneously bestowed upon me. Along with the memory.

Now that I'm all perfectly dressed for the pursuit in utter comfort, I hurry down the sparkling golden stairs. My plan is to sneak into the Crown Chamber early and without notice by walking towards the glass-framed exit for an outdoor shortcut.

To a success.

Well, almost.

When I look back briefly, and as I sprint across the palace garden maze, I see Leon and a few other guards follow me from behind. Then I steal a glance at my watch.

Eight minutes.

In less than no time, of what feels like a very high bar of stamina built up over the last three years of my adventures across the region, I've already reached the door to the Crown Chamber.

Seven minutes.

"I need to talk to you first." Leon suddenly stops me from squeezing the knob with a light touch on my arm. *His touch.*

Oh, come on, Seraphine. Seriously? It didn't usually bother me, but now, it gives me some sort of butterflies in my heart. What is wrong with me?

"Don't do anything stupid," he warns. "I'll just be

on the other side of this door, as planned. If he comes–"

"*When* he comes," I suddenly snap and forget everything about all this cheesy feeling in me. Back to my old self again. Good.

"Yes, *when* he comes, just stay where you are and *do not* chase him!"

I instinctively stare at the door.

"Are you listening to me?" He shakes my arms unconsciously. "Do not go after the thief, whatever happens. I repeat. Do not go after him. Do. You. Understand?"

"Alright, I get it," I mutter, looking annoyed.

"I know you, Seraphine," he now speaks in a much lower voice. "Your parents don't even know all the dangerous stuff you've done for the last three years because for some reason, I always chose to omit that from my report; otherwise, they'd not even let you out of your bed chamber tonight. Not to mention–"

But Gaspard suddenly approaches both Leon and me, which immediately gives us a fright. He and the rest of his team have just arrived, so it seems.

At first, Gaspard looks very startled as he notices my presence by the door. But after quickly sneaking a peek at his watch, he only sighs, slightly bows his head at me, and doesn't say anything. Tired of another quarrel, maybe, or that he's somehow believed me, considering the constraint of time.

But me too – tired of another quarrel, if I'm being honest.

Clearly, he and I can never see eye to eye.

Gaspard has his right hand on the knob and pushes the door wide open. He goes right into the Crown Chamber and tells the last guy in his march to leave the gap. Twenty guards – all armed with a rifle – come in with him and start to take position as instructed. Three guards in every room corner, two by each side of the glass case in the middle with Gaspard on the right.

I promptly gather that, unless the Royal Phantom has found a way to knock all twenty guards in one go, he has no chance.

Meanwhile, Leon still speaks of more unnecessary and repetitions of instructions for me to follow. As much as I love to admire his handsome worried face, I feel like this is just wasting both of our time.

By the drive of thrill that the Royal Phantom is coming very soon, my eyes are rolling high and low across the Crown Chamber as Leon's still giving his lecture. I'm not really listening to him as much.

I first observe the ceiling glass that is way up high, followed by Gaspard doing some sort of laughable warm-up stretches and encouraging the others to do the same. And then, I pay more attention to what's behind him.

The Blue Tiara perches on a low glass batten that makes it look like it's floating halfway inside the case. A rare piece of this really big gemstone in the shape of one rounded heart shines from the crown's center a strapping deep blue luminescence, and on each side hemmed in smaller pieces of the same jewel that silhouette the circlet.

As unparalleled as it appears, it is also the last piece of the crown collection that the King himself has bestowed upon the twelve Provincial Regions. So should the Royal Phantom manage to steal it tonight, he'd have the whole set. And for what? What would he do if he did? Keep them? Sell them? Destroy them?

"Do you hear me?" All of a sudden, Leon wrap both of my cheeks with his hands in urgency to turn my head and look him in the eye. I feel my heart beat at a rapid pace, and in an instant, I've forgotten everything about the world.

What is going on with me? I think… I blush. But luckily, he doesn't notice as I'm still entirely sunk in… his touch. His palms are still on my cheeks, making them warmer than they should, and I'm now certain he's doing it unconsciously – out of being worried sick.

But then, there it is. He startles himself and abruptly lets go. And for some reason, I don't like it when he does.

"There's a large window right on the left side of the crown," he says, then abruptly clears his throat. "Hide underneath so you won't be seen. It's small, but I'm sure you can fit in well and see everything just fine. But, do not get close to the Royal Phantom whatever he does. I'm dead serious. So let me repeat." Here we go again. "Do. Not.

Follow. Him!"

"O-K, O-K, I get it." Jeez. "Can I please go inside now?"

Leon follows me a couple steps in.

"Stay where you are!" he warns me again before his head slithers back and he closes the door on me.

I roll my eyes.

Three minutes. I walk slowly, heading to the large window as Leon's instructed.

Curling to my own two knees hiding in the dark deep corner under it, I was shaking, but very, very excited.

Two minutes. Some guards are starting to glance my way. They probably don't think that the great and magnificent Royal Phantom who has so flawlessly stolen the King's eleven noble crowns is not going to notice that someone is hiding under a casement window, though I'd argue that this space is too small for any of them with those rifles on their side. None of them would even fit in here in the first place.

One minute. Then what feels like repercussions after mental exertion, just when the time now is nearest to my prediction, I'm beginning to feel the doubt.

What if… I'm wrong?

Three. Two. One.

The clock suddenly strikes twelve, and the Royal Phantom's straight off appeared right before my eyes like a dream. He's very punctual for a thief, and for that I feel very much relieved.

And then, it has suddenly registered in my brain that I haven't heard anything, not even a vague sound of glass breaking.

Where did he come from?

But what feels like mere half a second after his arrival, all the guards have now turned weak on their knees in a fury of exploding white smoke and they all plunged steadily onto the floor. All at once. Quietly.

What has he done?

Just when I was still trying to work out in my head how he even came in so swiftly without notice, a great amount of white fabric suddenly fills the room like some ribbon tornado and covers all the guards. No one underneath gives any signs of movements.

When did he even manage to knock everyone out, and how?

Everyone but… me.

A sense of relief comes upon me all of a sudden.

He didn't get me? Did he not expect me? Better yet, he doesn't seem to have sensed my presence at all. And so, I've decided to hold my breath and monitor him silently.

Nevertheless, he takes no time for compromise or even a short tour around. At the speed of the wind, he calmly breaks the square glass in front of him with just a touch of his gloved hands. When the alarm rings in response, and Leon and the other guards are coming in, he snatches the crown with the same-old painted smile without any sense of urgency and fires something like a gun up to the ceiling, which releases a long line of black cable that shatters the ceiling glass and pulls him up immediately.

He's insanely efficient and–

But without further thinking, I jolt myself to leap out of my hiding hole and run the hardest I know how. And with an enormous amount of luck, I somehow manage to catch him by surprise when my two hands grab him by the edge of his robe.

This isn't part of my plan, nor his.

The Royal Phantom soars up the long distance only in a very short period of time, so I can only manage to briefly give one last look around the Crown Chamber as we ascend.

I've realised that because of me, all the guards are no longer in the position of shooting. No one seems to be given any instruction, and that's when I notice Leon turning into a carved sculpture with his head facing the sky, just watching me disappear into the broken glass of a night.

Just stay where you are and do not chase him!

Too late.

I'm already flying in the air.

7

After bouncing off the top of the palace ceiling and deplaning sideways, the Royal Phantom and I both drop abruptly onto the roof floor.

It seems that for a moment, he starts panicking and losing his cool as he struggles to swish me away from his robe. As he decides to run regardless, I accidentally slip and sink onto the ground. But quickly after, I come back up to my stand in one push off the air and I run after him with everything that I've got.

I've managed to catch up within a couple of feet close to him, until after about a few hundred meters of running, he reaches the edge of the building, hops onto the low balustrade and… jumps.

I only have about a split second to think, but as if my body acts by instinct instead of fear, I find myself already fluttering in the sky like a wingless bird. I manage to grab the edge of his robe again, but unfortunately on a much lower angle.

I'm desperately holding tight without harness, bouncing past towards the old castle tower and over the fortress walls as the Royal Phantom does. I'm sure he's noticed me still hanging, but he doesn't make any effort to exude me, nor to stop, or even give any sign of ever slowing down – not one second – until beads of sweat start spreading all across my palms and I'm slipping and – uh oh – I'm falling!

The feeling is like seeing a really big light flashing before my eyes in a world that's suddenly turned completely dark. I'm scared to death, because I'm about to die, and I don't think my parents would ever forgive me for being dead. But luckily, and rather surprisingly, the Royal Phantom catches my slipping hands just in time and pulls me up to his side. My hands are back holding tight but onto his middle robe this time, and my nose briskly detects a certain scent I can't fully describe.

Something deep, something earthy, something… unique.

What's more, I still have no idea how he's able to fly. This almost feels like magic, and not. His robe moves with the wind while the moon envelopes our struggle, and I have no choice but to scrape off my long-formed deduction that the loose garment might act as a glider.

Certainly there's no such thing as wizardry or humans with wings, and I don't hear or see anything that resembles a jet pack underneath his robe. So what is this sorcery he's performing?

But then I'm suddenly reminded by a more important thing, when my hat retires from my head and quickly vanishes in absentia towards miniatures of people rushing out in a frenzy. That building is definitely the main palace, and that spot… they must be coming out from the Festivity Hall!

Oh, shit!

They're watching the sky for a glimpse of the one and only Royal Phantom, only to find that there's now two – with me clinging on for dear life to the robe of the most wanted criminal in the whole wide kingdom. There's nothing anyone can do but watch wordlessly. I don't even want to know if my parents are among the crowd; but if they are, I sincerely hope they're not fainting at the view. I mean, from every angle, it really looks like I could plunge to my death at any given moment.

But perhaps owing to the fact that the Royal Phantom has saved my life, I feel perfectly safe. The feeling is like, even if I'm going to slide out again, I know the Royal Phantom is still going to catch me – which is totally preposterous because he is still a *criminal*. And he's got the crown, so what does he have to lose? But he knows I'm never going to let go, obviously, and with the guards following us from below pointing with their guns without shooting because of me, the only way for him to escape comfortably is to keep me by his side until we completely pass the castle ground.

That's it. Maybe that's the only reason he's saved me. He's stuck with me if he wants to live, and he'll need to get rid of me after to keep his identity, or he'll have to find another way out.

But then, almost immediately, he stops his effort to escape right on top of the last curtain walls, ceasing movement on the bricks' edge. Once more, against all my deductions.

My hands slide in effect, but still firmly attached.

He's now standing, staring straight at what I reckon passing through the moat and hills and nearest towns. His two right fingers are clutching the front tip of his hat, all his left slip into his pocket.

Meanwhile, my hands turn rocky on his end fabric with heavier might. I'll never let go. I'm so close! In fact, all this is already a series of miracles happening I thought would only stay in my imagination. So if he wants me gone, he'll have to kill me first.

But somehow, I know he won't.

"The code." He speaks all of a sudden while facing the height beyond. His voice is hoarse, but calm like the wind tonight.

"The code," I repeat, panting as my adrenaline starts catching up. *"The third becomes the first when the other two disagree. Stand right next to the pillar, and that's when I'll sneak in. You'll have zero chance the next day, should you not believe me. Hear this in your lullaby tonight, so my plan would succeed. The Blue Tiara will once ever be mine eternally,"* I swallow. "The first clue is that you wrote 'zero chance' instead of 'no chance'. Include number zero, and the sequence becomes zero, one, and two." Then I inadvertently make a pause.

The dumbfounded effect begins to strike.

I'm having a conversation with the Royal Phantom.

The Royal Phantom.

The Royal Phantom.

Oh. My. God. I cannot believe this.

"Go on, kid," he utters his words softly.

In effect, my heart pounds twice as much. Such a voice. Why is it ever endearing for a freaking phantom thief? And somewhat familiar. Sixteen? Twenties? Forties? Sixties? I don't know. Could be any age in between. I mean, he could even be faking his voice, right? And his age? *Kid* – as if he somehow wants me to straight away believe that he's older than me.

But then I give my head a light shake back to the present time and choose to do as I'm told, as I notice him still waiting for the remainder of my answer patiently. *"The third becomes the first when the other two disagree,"* I repeat again, hands still holding tight to his robe. "You're referring to the first prime number – that is, number two."

Instead of staring at the guards below who are ready to shoot him at any given moment, he's now calmly looking up towards the sky. His right hand swiftly meets the other pocket. I presume the quietness means he still wants me to proceed.

"*Stand right next to the pillar,*" I exhale, and in, then out again. Somehow, I'm beginning to lose my breath. I've just realised that I'd been forgetting to properly breathe since the moment I jumped off that roof, and I've probably long surpassed my stamina limit solely out of pure epinephrine. "You mean to put number two after the pillar," I continue regardless, "which looks plainly like number one. And that becomes twelve."

"And how do you know it's tonight?" I can sense from his shoulders that he's now more intrigued. His head turns slowly at me, our eyes meeting for the very first time. They're pure green, but sparkling emerald when he's just under the moonlight. If only he'd be taking off that mask next.

But then I quickly swallow, trying not to be distracted.

"*You'll have zero chance the next day, should you not believe me. Hear this in your lullaby tonight, so my plan would succeed.* You've never done it this soon. Why?"

"I thought 'the next day' was supposed to be putting one day over tonight's lullaby."

"You always did that," I say, "in your other letters." I swallow again. "I read them every single night for the past three years." Hoping– wishing, for this exact same moment.

I detect a fleeting smile under the mask. "I guess it's

true."

My eyes squint in return. What's true?

"Princess Seraphine," he continues. "The only daughter of Prince Orland of the House of Douzevoir – the Reigning Prince of the Twelfth Provincial Region – and Princess Valerie of the House of Deuxvoir. The only royal bachelorette of the Twelfth Provincial Region, who's been spending most of her time slipping away from the palace for the past three years, constantly putting herself in danger, playing *detective*."

Why is the sudden fun fact?

"I must say, this present time clearly made sense of that thing you did when you were just a baby," he proceeds without request. He begins to giggle uncontrollably, before forcing himself to stop. "Other princesses were choosing gems or crowns or royal garments. You instead went to one of the guards and tried to touch his sword."

My heart jumps.

"Who are you?" I straight away ask. "You were there during the Royal Birth Ceremony?" How? The finding as such drives me to briefly recall everything up to this moment. Whence all the first twelve crowns were distributed not long after I was born. All his letters. His knowledge about the castle, the palace, the crown. His voice. I have to assume, "Are you... one of us?"

A royal guard. A royal staff. A royal blood.

He could be any of these.

No. He must be either one of these.

I hear a bit of chuckle coming from the Royal Phantom. "Brief recognition without pure awareness remains a mere coincidence," he now tries to be philosophical. "But if you must know, perhaps tonight would serve as your reward in my acknowledgment of your… *credentials.*"

Credentials? What's that supposed to mean? Another code?

I was going to ask more questions – in fact, a lot of them. But as if a mind reader, his left hand suddenly moves from inside his pants underneath his cloak and unexpectedly throws away the crown beyond the wall. My damn instinct makes me let go of his fabric and jumps to catch the diadem just in time, with his hands pulling me back by the collar to bring half of my body back safely onto the rim.

"Intelligent, and yet impetuous. Both *will* hurt you someday, kid, if you're not careful."

Is he testing me? I'm about to ask again. But at this exact point of moment, he… floats?

Wait, what?

How?

No human being can possibly levitate over the sky. That just doesn't make any sense at all. This is something neither biology nor physics can explain. Even the guards below seemingly remain static from such a phenomenon before their eyes.

And I'm so close to him. Catching him.

"I've never been beaten before, kid," he says. "And dare I say, by a *Royal Highness*." Both of his hands remain inside his pockets, and he's still floating. What's more, I now hear the guards' running steps reaching towards us from the back.

But why is he still floating? Is he getting ready to fly? I'm not even sure if I can be a hundred percent at present moment right now, as I'm still trying to figure out, how in the world is he doing all this? Since the very beginning, how is any of these even possible? And why now floating? When he was just standing on the edge, why wasn't he floating?

Freaking floating in mid air.

Is this some sort of device that needs charging? But why is there no sound?

And why is no one shooting?

"Let's stop here where we both may lose," he suddenly distracts.

But before I can even utter a single word of response, he flies many meters away from me in a whoosh then swiftly vanishes into another smoke bomb and thin air, while the Blue Tiara is still safely thrust into my hands. Loud noises deriving out of strains of bullets coming from underneath give chase to the shadow who has long gone by the time they've started shooting.

8

The Royal Phantom has now completely disappeared.

For a long moment, half of my right arm still extends beyond the fortress wall, holding the crown out of the threshold. The Blue Tiara could slip away from my hand and crash onto the ground at any given moment now, but I don't seem to be able to move.

Perhaps, I'm being paralysed by the fact that none of these has been making any sense. Who is the Royal Phantom? Have we really met before? Does he know me? Or does that apply to every prince and princess in the kingdom? But why? How was he even capable of flying and staying afloat in mid air? And where the hell is he going to next?

The sound afterward is coming from Leon panicking, making orders, and rushing towards me. Two palace guards who've come approaching look somehow blurry to me, but I notice that one of them is Leon by the voice, who gently lifts me from the back and brings me down to sit on the brick floor as he says, "Are you hurt? Let me know if you are."

"I'm fine," I say as I glance at what's still in my hand. The tiara never lets go out of my grasp, and no one's trying to take it away from me. Not even the guards.

I guess this has become my mission to finish. Mine.

Subsequently, Leon's now screaming a lot of things right at my face but I can only pick up a few like "You're killing me" and "I'll never let you get in trouble again". His both hands are only briefly wrapping my cheeks before he turns his attention to the other guards and decides to immediately let go.

As immediate too, I stop him by the wrist. "Wait," I succinctly say, staring right at his eyes, currently coated with a complete perplexion. We've never been in this situation before.

Well, not exactly.

But, shit! What am I doing?

Though I keep on holding his hand, regardless.

Forget about the guards. There's a string between our eyes, moving words left unspoken. *What if I'd never fall in love with a prince?* If he could understand, if he does – if he wants to. *Where do we go from here?*

Imagine the possibilities.

How quickly a person's heart can change? This moment I feel his touch, my heart moves faster than a shooting star. I'd consider this damn sudden change of hormones some leniency. A *chance* to fall in love. Whatever that cheesy stuff is, however it works.

But as fast too he pisses me off when he turns his head to the guards again and gently swings my fingers off. His slow movement speedily transposes into an aching heart. *Why, Leon?* I'd not mind if he'd hold me longer, or hug me, or embrace me harder at the first squeeze. Wouldn't even give a damn about the people around us. But I guess his strict princess-bodyguard-relationship probity would. *Why do you have to care about what other people think?*

As such, my feelings whirl around quickly into moodiness, all the while he goes on to deliver his speech of disappointment. "Why didn't you listen to me? I told you to stay where you were!"

I get it. What just happened didn't mean anything to him. His heart didn't move faster than a shooting star.

It was only me.

You know what? I don't care anymore. Irrational sentiment tends to override logical sense, and I start to hate myself for it. For being, *feeling* like this – whatever this is. And so, "I'm sorry," I just say concisely, trying to stop Leon from talking.

I'm too tired to argue.

I bring myself to stand, my body automatically keeps rejecting the help he constantly tries to offer. "I'm fine!" I yell, though rather unintentionally.

I can still manage on my own, for now. So I go on walking away.

But that expression of his right now, it's like I've just jarred him on the face.

He's not at fault, I know, but for some reason, I feel like being left alone with only my thoughts. Everything and everyone else becomes an interruption, and outright deep annoyance.

Moving forward, everything seems to be happening a lot faster. I somehow manage to get down the stairs from the top fortress wall with only what's left of my own strength, and I can feel Leon and his subordinates behind me, watching my every move. Likewise as my steps bring me further away from the old castle blocks.

Reaching the edge of the modern palace ground, everyone has just arrived. I guess they're not used to walking this far on foot. My parents are the first ones to hug me – very, very tightly – and for a moment, I thought they wouldn't let go because it's starting to get much harder for me to breathe.

"Seraphine, I cannot believe you!" my father says, his arms stretch to look at me with the same blue eyes like mine.

Accordingly, I can tell from my father's sweaty forehead underneath that he was running. Well, he's obviously not used to it. What's more, he didn't even spare the time to take off his royal crown off his blonde pompadour haircut and his red royal robe. He just chose to jet right out.

"And what are you wearing?" And that's my mother. And she was, too, running, which is super rare. That used to be her top concern whenever scolding me. *A princess should not be running*, I recall her many shouts in the past. She remembers, like, the whole book of *Rules of Being a Princess*, and I'm not even kidding. "That shirt, and that pants, and that– argh, nevermind. It's not like it's the first."

My mother now touches her forehead underneath her crystal-rounded crown, and it seems to start aching. If I didn't know her any better, she almost looked like a silhouette of a ghost, with her green eyes turned teary and her face pale white (all because of me), her silky white dress long, and her lengthy black hair stretched out. The crown on her head even looks a bit crooked in position.

For a split second too, I notice Gaspard's cheering eyes as he sees the Blue Tiara in my hand. He seems to be fully awake now. "We've protected the crown! We were right! It didn't get stolen!" he shouts, to others' cheers.

We, I snort. *Yeah, right*. Says the one who insisted the Royal Phantom was coming in three days. Three. Freaking. Days.

Next on the line of crowd, I see the same amount of boys in the party – still covered with bandages and wound dressings – come forward with a glowing face whichever part is visible.

I could only tell all of them to "get out" with my eyes.

I don't mean to be rude, but I don't have time for this. It may be the adrenaline, the pressure, the disappointment, or maybe just too much thinking on my way here, but I start to feel the worst kind of headache. And as I'm still not able to stop thinking, consequently making the pain feel worse, my mind keeps driving me to forget how to breathe.

All the people start to look like drifting fluffy clouds.

Gradually, spots of lights unfold before me, along with the sound of shutters. I almost forgot about all of these photographers who were supposedly induced to take pretty pictures of me – and how they've now got me in my worst.

I only wave my hands and smile. I've lost my energy to speak completely, then my balance, and shortly after, half of my consciousness.

Moyra offers her right arm to me just in time but I push it away gently.

I don't want to look *weak*.

No.

The Blue Tiara in my hand has to be the world sees me with, I vow. Not me vomiting. Not me passing out. Not me looking defeated – especially, not in front of all these cameras where it could last for a lifetime. And for that to happen, I need to get myself into bed. A – S – A – P.

If I could just reach my chamber in time, I earnestly pray.

At this point, even the cold floor of my bedroom lounge will do.

9

I woke up with a small migraine. Face on the pillow, still in yesternight's unbearable garments.

My palms struggle hard to push against the bed, but somehow, I manage to spin my body in reverse.

When my blurry vision progressively turns to clear, I gaze to my right where the sun sneaks in bleary drops of light through the golden draperies. With this strong refulgence out of the lambency, it must already be past noon. Then I look to my left to see a bunch of today's newspapers as well as a glass of water already beside me. I guess one is to slap me on the cheek, the other to gently stroke it down.

My dry throat longs for a sip of water first but nervously settles for just saliva, while my other hand quickly reaches for the papers.

Thirteen newspapers in total. Twelve as one for every Provincial Region, the other from the Capital Region.

I go for a deep long breath.

Capital, front page first.

Breaking News, it starts. *Royal Phantom Finally Defeated*, the headline reads underneath, followed by its drophead, *The Blue Tiara Remains Safely in the Twelfth Provincial Region*.

Not a total surprise.

What's funny, all the papers have me hanging on the phantom thief's robe for dear life printed two thirds of a page. But since I look more like a tiny blot of black ink there in my opinion, I drink my water in peace.

Okay. So far so good, I think.

But then comes the next part. The paragraphs.

I take all the anxiety into one very loud gulp.

Here we go.

. . . .

Hmmm. So all the papers say various things about me, though they all seem to agree on one thing: how I didn't act like a princess *should*. That part is not really a big deal for me, since I've always known to be – how should I put it – *eccentric* compared to the rest of the eligible princesses, but it's going to be a very big deal for both of my parents, since all of their concerns always come back to how they think I'd not get an invitation to the Royal Princess Academy. Because if there's only one criteria the academy looks for in their potential students, it's how a princess must act like a princess *should* at all times – flawless, opulent, and poise.

Obviously, I'm more than often the total opposite.

I thought that was about it when I reached the end of the first page, but I was wrong. Apparently, I have made it to the second page, and the next, and a few more pages after that. My first case. Some of the very big ones I got myself into within the relevant years. Testimonies from witnesses to all sorts of dangerous stuff I did in the past. A bunch of spiels from a few prisoners I'd put in jail. Journalists draw up statistics as proof that the crime rate in the Twelfth Provincial Region has significantly declined to zero percent within the past three years because of me.

Provincial-crime hero, they all call me.

Nevertheless, how did they even get all of these to print in such a short period of time? I'm honestly more amazed than being surprised or feeling morose at this point.

But if there's one thing I'm not too happy about, it's how I look in all these papers. There isn't a single nice picture of me, as they've only used whatever they got the night before. Whichever visible, my face shows I could puke at any given time.

If only my hat hadn't flown away. How I'm forever grateful that at least I didn't faint until I reached my bed, because that would've been worse. Way worse.

But I don't mind at all with how the crown looks in my hand. In fact, the articles have no choice but to discuss how I became the first to ever solve the Royal Phantom's code and saved the Twelfth Provincial Region's most precious treasure – the last from the King's bestowal crown set and the only one which remains unstolen. Not Gaspard.

I can't say these do not get into my head, despite the hurtful comments they all wrote about me being… the worst princess ever born.

"The worst princess ever born," I mutter.

But then I quickly try to brush it off and bring myself to read the next section.

Well, my outfit seems to receive mixed reviews as well. *So not princess-like, no prince would ever marry.* Like I care. *Cool and mysterious, we kinda like it.* Okay, this one, I kinda like it too. *Very bohemian.* Whatever that means.

But my favorite of all. *Perfect for detective work.*

Detective, I ruminate as I walk out of the bed.

I really like the sound of that.

Moyra finds me just by the door of the bedroom lounge where she's been standing. She slips her head outside, perhaps to talk to one of the guards, then closes the door and makes haste of her feet towards me.

"His and Her Royal Highness will be joining you for lunch," she says. Her encouraging smile below that pair of dark-framed spectacles that wasn't usually there as well as the messy shoulder-length brown hair, however, tells me that my parents are currently in their worst mood.

Oh, no.

But why? I've saved the crown, haven't I? I'm still

alive, aren't I? They hugged me last night, didn't they? I don't see why they need to remain furious. Do they care that much about what the news has been saying about me? Or… is it something else?

In such a way that she can read my mind, Moyra brings me immediately to the shower room where she's prepared some fresh freesia and mulled pears inside a thin glass vase. Only slightly calming me down.

Under the light fall of precipitation, I become half asleep. The water runs through my bare skin without notice.

Where could the Royal Phantom be now?

Beneath the shower rain, my eyes become widened as I begin to really wonder. If the Royal Phantom was indeed part of the royal system, what did his role encompass? Which part of the region? And why?

I guess it's true.

It suddenly hits me.

If he's only heard the rumors, that means he must not be from the Twelfth Provincial Region – if he was letting it slip by accident. And if I could somehow go around the other regions this time, I may be able to really find out.

Right. Let's make that my plan, now that I'm *definitely* not getting into the Royal Princess Academy.

The worst princess ever born.

And so I come out of the shower with some grip on reality instead. My towel's off, and Moyra dresses me up with a long pink dress in the wardrobe room.

As soon as I get out of my bed chamber, Leon's already by the front door. I greet him "hello" with a big smile, feeling somewhat apologetic about last night too, but he instead turns a deaf ear and acts like an ignorant robot.

He's angry, I get it, but what's worse, he chooses to walk behind me instead of the usual next to me. So I pout.

Moyra, knowing this, rushes towards my side and tries to cheer me up with some jokes she's read. As usual.

"Why is six afraid of seven?" Moyra asks.

"What?" I answer moodlessly.

"Why is six afraid of seven?" she repeats.

She knows I like solving riddles and stuff, but come on.

"Because seven ate nine," I give my answer acrimoniously.

"Alright, that was definitely too easy for you," she says as she brushes her chin.

"It's not that it was easy, it's that you've asked me that so many times," I sigh.

"Hmm, maybe I ought to read more riddle books." But then she claps her hands all of a sudden. "You know what? I've got one. *Totally* a new one." She lets out a vexing little smirk. "What kind of music does stainless steel like?"

Okay, I have to admit, this one's really new. So I stop my feet from pacing for a while, shift my elbows to think, and begin to forget about Leon still acting all mercurial behind me.

Stainless steel. What is stainless steel made of? Well, that depends on what kind of stainless steel it is. But regardless of the categories, they're all always made of one component. Chromium. But there's no such thing as chromium music, so maybe that's not the answer. Is stainless steel magnetic, maybe that's the lead? But that, singularly, also depends on its category. In that case, what about… does the material keep bacteria? But people usually say earworm when it comes to music, not ear-bacteria. Although, I've read somewhere that the smooth surface makes it harder for bacterias to attach themselves and multiply. Unless, the word stainless steel is also a diversion, and–

"Princess?" Moyra shakes my shoulders, my face trembles in response. "Oh! Thank God you're alright. It's just… it was as if your body was here… but you were not. I was still worried, though it's happened so many times."

"It was just her in her deep thoughts," Leon interrupts by finally deciding to say something, though not to me. Regardless, I turn my head towards Leon. "So she couldn't listen, because she never does anyway," he explains languidly with rolling eyes, then looks the other way.

"It's funny how you decide to stay mad at me but you're still following me around," I say while still glaring at the side of his face. "Why don't you just stay away from me like a normal angry person does? Come back when you stop being annoying."

"I'm your salaried man-guard. I have no choice, *Your Royal Highness.*"

My eyes draw to the center out of rage as he bends his body afterward. He's perfectly aware that pisses me off the most, *especially* when he's the one that does it. And I know that he knows that I know that he has a choice, *especially* inside the palace. He can just send someone else to guard me from my bed chamber whenever he'd like. He's a freaking leader of a sub-battalion and he's Second-in-Command for a reason. Clearly, he only wants to show me that he just doesn't trust me anymore.

"Fine!" I reply to Leon, before I turn my body and stride away towards the stairs angrily.

I guess he and I won't be talking for a while. But the timing couldn't get any worse than now. Just when I'm about to come to the acceptance that I may want us to be more than friends, he just has to make it so obvious that he doesn't share the same feelings.

Good thing I never confessed. And you know what? I never will!

"So Moyra," I say as I look to my side, but then I quickly shift my face away whenever Leon is visible within my peripheral vision, "I've come to a conclusion that you need to give me at least the specific of what kind of stainless steel–"

"Beg pardon?" Moyra's head spins sideways as we slowly walk down the stairs. "But Princess, the answer is only metal. Metal music. Stainless steels are fans of metal. Get it?" She then lets out a very big laugh while shifting her eyes between me and Leon – still behind me. Obviously, she thinks it's incredibly funny somehow.

"Metal? Of course! How can I be so stupid," I say while nodding to myself. Still not laughing. "Metals are naturally occurring elements that can be found in the earth's crust, and steel is an alloy made from metal."

"Er… Yeah, okay, sure – that's *exactly* why," Moyra says as she scratches her head.

"Can we get a move on, please?" Leon is obviously annoyed by the delay, or maybe he just wants to get away from me as soon as possible.

I only roll my eyes quietly.

He has neither reason nor obligation to stay next to me once I'm eating with my parents anyway.

10

Arriving at the Dining Hall, the high chair is moved for me almost immediately by one of the butlers. I take my usual seat which is diagonal to my father and opposite from where my mother sits. Three-quarters of the long marble top table remains empty, and Leon's already completely gone from sight.

"Good afternoon," I greet with a cheerful and graceful manner.

And to no response. Nothing at all.

The big chandelier on the high ceiling above only illuminates their anxiety which seems to grow as the minute goes by. I mean, what a sight. My father tries to restrain himself from biting his nails while my mother holds her forehead with an epic shaky hand. She even has her elbows on the table and sits in a slightly slouching position, which I believe is strictly forbidden in the *Book of Manners for Princesses*.

So, what about me?

Well, I just can't wait to see what I'll get to put on my plates. I'm starving.

When all the servers come at once, I direct them to scoop a fare from each plate onto mine. Grilled lamb chops, beef steaks, classic marinara spaghetti, some stir-fried greens, and a lot of little hashbrown balls.

When one of the servers asks me if I want a glass of juice to go with those, I just un-botherly answer, "Two, please. One glass of apple juice, and the other, hmmm, oranges!"

Perhaps this could explain why I always have a lot of energy to support my curiosity.

"Maybe if you had listened to me like you did to your stomach," my mother snaps all of a sudden, "you wouldn't have almost died, and the invitation from the Royal Princess Academy would've already come this morning."

When my head turns to look at her, her face only shows a calm expression, though she's butchering the little bacon piece with her knife as she speaks. Afterward, she starts yelling about some of the cases mentioned in the papers, all the dangerous things she couldn't believe I'd done – all she knew nothing about, a lot more she hasn't (she needs not to know) – and yet, not a single word about me saving the region's most precious crown.

For whatever reason, I begin to feel annoyed. Deep breath, then out. I cut one potato ball in half, gracefully get the little piece inside my mouth, slowly chew, and wait to completely swallow before I talk. *Defeat the blade of temper with the sword of elegance.* I got it from the *Book of Manners for Princesses*, I believe. That or Lady Francoise – sometimes I still can't tell the difference.

The thing is, I can hold myself to *act* as a proper princess, just not all the time. Only wherever I feel like it. Because there are side effects – such as now, I have to bring more food to my plate.

I guess keeping calm means burning more energy for me too.

"How can you still eat so much on such an excruciating day like this?" My mother stares at me like I'm some sort of an animal in the zoo.

"Excruciating? Maybe for you," I sedately answer. "And I'm perfectly fine, *thank you for asking*," I burst out sarcasm.

Considering I had almost died and I didn't.

My father inhales deeply then out even deeper as his own preliminary preparation, before my mother begins her shouting. "Of course, you're perfectly fine. You have jumped off a building and clutched yourself at the Royal Phantom's robe. I'm sure you've had such a wonderful time. But did we almost die from a heart attack when you were fluttering in the sky? Were we able to sleep the rest of the night thinking about what the Royal Princess Academy would think about you? And were we so worried about your future that we couldn't even eat anything for breakfast this morning? As a matter of fact, the answer is yes to all of the above. But did you even *think* to ask if both of us were fine? Of course, you didn't. So *thank you for asking*, my dear."

Thereafter, my mother basically murders every bit of food on her plate, and she still hasn't eaten any of it. My father acts the same way, only without the words and the energy.

"Why are you so angry? I'm still alive, aren't I?"

Seriously. When they hugged me so tightly last night, I really thought they wouldn't act like this. Leon included.

"Still alive? STILL. ALIVE?" This time, it's my father's turn to shout. I only continue eating in agitation as I listen. "My dear only daughter, Seraphine!" He then slaps the table at once. "Did you already forget that you'd been running off and going to all those places in the region doing all those dangerous things trying to solve whatever cases for the last three years?"

To think that not even the newspapers have covered half of the level of dangerousness I'd actually gone through. But he, too, needs not to know.

"I even went as far as blowing the royal trumpet to greet in glory the attendance of whoever needed your help," he proceeds. "But even after all that, you *still* didn't care about any of us. Abandoning your princess duty, making contact with the phantom thief–" He abruptly stops himself from screaming further at me as he's momentarily out of breath. "I need a drink," he says to one of the servers on stand-by behind him. My father rests his back on his chair with his fingers on his forehead and says, "One shot of the lemon liqueur will do."

I've heard there are only two bottles of that in the whole world.

The waiter nods without expression, but then my father stops him abruptly from going. "You know what? Make it double." And then he waves his hands in order.

"I've saved the Blue Tiara," I claim without consent. I then take another bite of the hashbrown.

"I beg your pardon?" My father narrows his eyes at me, and at the same time, his drink comes. But he keeps on staring at me, ignoring his glass.

"You forgot to mention that," I munch.

"Don't talk with food in your mouth!" my mother yells. "Honestly. We should have been more strict with you. *I* should've been. Why didn't it cross my mind that you would go after the thief?" she flicks her forehead. "If you had at least just stayed put in the Crown Chamber like Leon had convinced us you'd do, the invitation would've probably arrived right at this very moment."

Jeez. Still about the Royal Princess Academy.

"And let the crown be stolen?" I counter.

"Maybe I'd rather have," she replies audaciously.

I roll my eyes.

"Valerie!" my father snaps before he briskly finishes the whole glass of alcohol in one sip. After that, he releases a deep breath that smells like some pungent lemony ethanol, immediately looking almost high. I raise my eyebrows with the rest of my scathing expression.

"Anyhow, let us all be… sensible," he says, then unintentionally lets out a loud hiccup. "We still have six days until we really know for sure if the invitation is coming, or not–" Another hiccup. A crinkled smile suddenly appears on his face, though his expression gradually changes to a bit hesitant. "But if Seraphine doesn't get the invitation, that just means she won't get married to a prince." He flicks his arms forward and lets out another forced smile.

Well, I'm glad that he's at least willing to compromise to be more realistic this time.

"I mean, she could still marry one of the nobles," he says, grinding his teeth and twisting it upward.

Looks like he'd rather not.

"But since the highest of nobles would also prefer a princess who graduated from the Royal Princess Academy…" But then, he doesn't proceed. He only covers his face with both hands as if he's now imagining a horror scene.

I let out a deep sigh.

If only I had a sister.

In turn, my mother twirls the spaghetti on her plate around with a blank face. I haven't seen her eating anything except playing around with her food. "I guess I should start giving up on my dream that Seraphine would ever marry the Crown Prince," she mumbles.

Me? Marrying the Crown Prince?

My *dear* mother, you have got to be kidding me.

So in response, I unwittingly burst out a chuckle of amusement that eventually turns into a very big laugh. Both are now staring at me like I was insane.

She has very big dreams, I can tell you that. Further than even the stars – and I think, I'd even have more chance flying in space than ever marrying the Crown Prince.

Even funnier when I think about how she herself didn't even marry the Crown Prince back then (now the King), though I heard my father himself was already a great catch, as she was too. I mean, the fact that they had both gotten their invitation *months* before the school even started, and I have not… but let's not rub more salt into the wound.

With immediate effect, I remove myself from the table – still laughing – and walk back upstairs.

Me, marrying the Crown Prince. What a ridiculous idea. For the love of pure imagination, this is what every mother of every princess in every Provincial Region always dreams about – if any of us would ever marry the mysterious Crown Prince.

Good thing I know I won't.

The worst princess ever born.

I mean, realistically speaking, I'd have to get into the Royal Princess Academy first. And we all know that's not going to happen.

11

My two feet reach the library door without realizing.

Lady Francoise, whose only mission in life is to teach me princessy stuff until she can peacefully retire to some small tropical island with clear skies and active volcanoes, lives inside the palace and comes to the library to teach me six days a week, except on Sunday. Today is a Monday, so there she is, already inside.

And not to my own surprise, she looks mad. Like, really really mad. I was going to apologise to her for missing the morning class, but that's probably going to make it worse.

Sigh. Here we go again.

First Leon, then my parents, and now, Lady Francoise.

"Let us start by discussing your future," she says. No other forms of greetings she deems necessary. I haven't even fully sat down yet. "A future without the Royal Princess Academy, should the invitation not be coming by this Saturday evening," she emphasizes.

Well, at least for now, I know what that would be for her. She won't be able to retire as planned for at least another year or ten.

That explains why she looks so sick, like she's about to vomit. She moves towards me a piece of handwritten paper that basically says that for the rest of this week, I can read whatever I want in the library while she drowses in devastation on her chair.

Actually, great!

So I spend the rest of the afternoon session going around the mountainous bookshelves to come up with my own syllabus. I pick up some books that catch my intention for me to sort later on, head back to my seat, and begin drafting.

Monday. Non-fiction. *Crime Scene Reconstruction* by Annalee Zaiker.

Tuesday. Non-fiction. *Science of Ballistics* by Jayden Pierce.

Wednesday. Fiction. The whole series of *Private Ames* by Sir Canon Royce.

Thursday. Non-fiction. *Chemistry of Poisons* by Jazzlyn Fisher.

Friday. Non-fiction. *Mastering Anatomy* by Logan Clarke.

Saturday. Fiction. The whole series of *Detective*

Antoine by Gabrielle Amos.

The perfect syllabus.

91

12

Nothing has changed since the beginning of the week. It's like I've taken everyone else's soul. Gloomy breakfast with my parents, depressing morning lessons with Lady Francoise, gloomy lunch next, then another depressing afternoon session, closed by a gloomy dinner.

By the end of light, I have the rest of the night to myself. This is when I keep myself busy with solving various riddling and puzzling antiques until I'm ready to sleep.

The invitation is not coming, I tell myself before I close my eyes. But for some weird reason, I'm not entirely relieved. Not sad, not even worried, but not that happy about it either.

I wonder why.

Morning comes again as expected. All of a sudden, today is already Saturday.

The moment of truth.

Still no invitation, which apparently for a lucky

few rumored last-picks came right off two days ago and yesterday morning.

Breakfast still gives the same silent joyless atmosphere and the morning lesson feels like I'm reading next to a corpse. Every few minutes, I actually check on Lady Francoise to see if she's still alive. Just in case. I mean, I don't want her to die just because the Royal Princess Academy is not going to invite me in.

"Last day," she whispers to herself before coming back to her dying state. "I wonder what would become of *you*," she heavily sighs as though I'm bringing the world to an end.

I start to wonder how long this new routine filled with devastation is going to last in this palace, especially since I'm pretty sure the invitation is not coming.

Weeks? Or maybe years?

More importantly, she's worried about me? Are the others too, except… me?

And if that's really the case, should I be worried too?

I mean, if anyone asks me if I actually want to go to the Royal Princess Academy or not (not that anyone has), I think the answer would be that I'm indifferent. I don't mind going, but I don't mind not going either. I don't mind marrying a prince, but I don't mind not marrying one either. I don't even really know where my heart currently lies. Not even about Leon. Would I give up my royal title just to be with him? Maybe I would. But would I miss my ass being pampered? Yes, I *definitely* would. So, what do I really want to be then? If I have to choose, would I rather be a detective or a princess? I think… a detective… but can I just be both?

Shit, now I'm beginning to worry too.

But as though the universe is trying to give me some serious signal, I hear the sudden sound of fanfare trumpets blazing through the whole palace from the Throne Hall.

My true calling.

It'd been quiet these past few months, so someone must be here wanting my help with a case. Anyone within this Provincial Region. But could it be anyone from other regions this time? Maybe even the Capital Region!

Finally, perfect timing. Just when I start to really wonder about what I'll do with my life without the Royal Princess Academy.

Detective Princess Seraphine, the title whispers in my head.

Maybe I can really be both.

"Could it be?" Lady Francoise wonders to herself. But with the unanticipated clamour, she suddenly looks so much better.

Not sure what she's expecting instead as she rises from her chair and pats her skirt to unwrinkle. Is she coming, she sets forth? Because if she is, she's definitely testing my patience. I understand that she's old, but she's moving way too slow.

"May I—excuse me." I immediately changed my mind about asking for her permission. I just sprint towards the Throne Hall.

And I'm feeling so excited! So very much. As it has now occurred to me, I have been so bored and desperately in need of a new puzzle to solve. A distraction.

"A princess should not be running, Your Highness!" Lady Francoise screams.

Too late. I already am. And I couldn't care less.

But as soon as I reach the outer entrance, what I see now is *not* what I ever did before. Actually, it's not anything I'd be expecting to see at all.

Close to perhaps fifty guards in total, all dressed in matching cream blazers and trousers along with golden-bordered red sashes and round golden pins on top, come marching towards where my father has just hurriedly sat upon his giant throne, followed by my mother on his left whose seat is only slightly smaller as mine on his right.

After taking my seat, still in confusion, I turn my head to see my parents and they look as sanguinely startled as Lady Francoise who's now caught up and is standing at the side of the platform. She already looks extremely younger, and fabulous, in just mere minutes.

"The King's army," my father whispers, his head turning slightly towards me while still gazing excitedly at the incoming guards. And more of them just keep coming.

"Was this what the Royal Prince Academy sent here when they invited you?" I whisper back.

"Don't be ridiculous," he replies, still with a grin from ear to ear. "The academy never sends anyone as grand as *the King's army*."

So it's not the Royal Princess Academy then? It's about something else besides the invitation, I suppose.

But all of a sudden, my ego boosts and buzzes a gold medal of achievement around my neck in order.

This is already so much better than the Royal Princess Academy.

Detective Princess Seraphine – yes, you can be both.

I picture it again, and I accidentally let out a big dreamy smile.

Just when the last guard enters the hall, the door is closed. My father looks rather excited as if he's expecting a show. And he's right. Out of the blue, half of the guards lift their rifles and throw them in the air. They're performing some sort of a structured army dance, and from time to time, they're screaming some army chants while their weapons are in the air.

I'm getting confused.

Meanwhile, my parents are constantly clapping their hands throughout the show.

After the performance, one of the men who seems to be the leader comes forward.

"Greetings, Your Royal Highnesses," he announces,

before introducing himself as Rayson Batard, the Commanding General of the King's Army. His dark brown hair is pushed behind his ears that have one golden stud of bijouterie on each side. No sign of belly fat underneath that striking armour. Already a much better version of Gaspard.

I lean my body forward without conscious thought.

Could he be the Royal Phantom? I suddenly contemplate.

True that he has a seemingly-similar physique to the Royal Phantom in a glance, and that he's not from the Twelfth Provincial Region. It's within my speculation that the enigmatic thief could be part of the royal guard, if not of royal staff or royal blood. This guy's hair is brown, straight, and short, but it could be only a disguise. And his eyes… are not emerald green. They're more like solid hazel pairs.

I sigh and lean back.

The Commanding General stands before my father, bows, then clears his throat.

"We have come here to bring you a message from the King. Much rather, a *gift*." he says.

My ego once again aims for my perfect kind of glory. I'm envisaging *Personal Investigator to the King, Chief Private Detective of the Kingdom of Oceastarasia*, or maybe even *Commander to the Special Battalion of Catching the Royal Phantom Division*. I'm not even sure yet if those roles actually exist, but they sure do in my imagination.

Meanwhile, the look that my parents have right

now – I don't even know how to describe it. Let's just say, if the sun and my parents compete, they would win by a long mile. Their faces look brighter than even the quasar, they probably don't even care about the Royal Princess Academy anymore.

"The King was very pleased to hear that the Twelfth Provincial Region had managed to defeat the kingdom's enemy, the Royal Phantom, by protecting the Blue Tiara."

Here it comes. My medal of honour. *Heehee.*

"It was His Majesty's intention to send his commendation as soon as Monday morning, if not for concocting bestowals for such inordinate endeavour, a bequest fitting for such esteemed triumph, when it suddenly came to His Majesty's attention that Her Highness Princess Seraphine of the Royal House of Douzevoir had not been admitted into the Royal Princess Academy."

Wait, what? What does that have anything to do with my gift?

"As such–" He momentarily pauses, then opens a white scroll with a hazel-coloured bar. "Princess Seraphine of the Twelfth Provincial Region has been admitted to the Royal Princess Academy, entirely within the Crown Prince's own personal discretion. Congratulations and welcome!"

My father stands, my mother holds her hands over her mouth, and Lady Francoise cries of happiness for she can finally retire.

Meanwhile, I'm still stuck on my seat, staring confusedly at the Commanding General – all the while my head rings to a stagnant trench.

What just happened? Where's my gold medal with the Royal Phantom logo on it? What about my Royal Detective title? What does my gift have anything to do with the Crown Prince? What about the King's army?

"In addition to the invitation…"

And there's more? I haven't even been able to process this yet.

The Commanding General continues spinning the scroll at a leisure pace, then clears his throat before he speaks again. "The Royal Princess Academy has requested for Her Highness Princess Seraphine's immediate departure from the Twelfth Provincial Region."

I have to leave *now*?

"Whereby time is of the essence, Her Highness will be escorted by the King's own conveyance and royal escorts in furtherance of such inconvenience."

And I get to leave with the King's private plane? And His Majesty's own guards?

"Lastly, but most importantly," he continues.

Seriously, there's more? I feel like someone's slapping me continuously with a bouquet of fluffy and soft petals.

But… does this mean I'm *finally* getting my official Royal Detective title?

Again – if there's any.

The Commanding General in effect walks up the platform and comes towards me. His knees balance on the floor mere centimetres away from my feet and his hands sway upon me what seems to be a different kind of scroll with similar color.

"Your Royal Highness' first school assignment from the academy," he announces to the hall with a serious expression.

My what?

"Due tomorrow night," he whispers only to me this time.

WHAT?

— PART 2 —

The Royal Princess Academy

13

My father keeps holding a handkerchief under
his eyes. His feelings are perfectly clear. Meanwhile my
mother's, not as much. One second she would shed a tear,
the next she would ramble in fantasy.

"And in my dream," she still hallucinates *loudly*,
"the Crown Prince comes to find you. The very first prince
you see on arrival." Her arms come up to her face as she
dances on her own. "It's like my dream is coming true!"
she further hypes. I roll my eyes. "You'd better go now."
She then pushes me as such. But the next second comes
and she's hugging me like she's never letting go of me. The
new second afterward, she rambles again and pushes me
towards the black limousine once more.

Seriously, when is she going to make up her mind?

After packing up some of the books from the library
under the guidance of Lady Francoise's thumb fingers
as well as a few others of my choice from my bedroom
bookshelves, the palace servants are still moving back

and forth in between chambers, but mostly with the other hand empty. Same with my parents who suddenly bring themselves going back and forth, directionless with idle hands. They all seemingly look confused as they're not entirely sure what else I need to bring. I mean, all the academy's residential houses already come with deluxe amenities, palatial clothes, designated drivers, a whole lot of culinary team, housekeepers, *et cetera* of everything else no one ever really needs. Perfectly in accordance with what they all say – that if the Royal Academies' student accommodations are compared to the usual worldwide hotel ranking out of five stars, they're an easy ten.

A chaotic moment of silence has passed when my mother suddenly re-appears.

"Leon, make sure you take care of her, as always?" my mother instructs, looking my way. "Even when she never listens." I roll my eyes.

"With my life, always," Leon replies. A faint whoosh of air tells me he's right behind me and slightly bowing. But I try not to turn my head to confirm.

Seriously, why couldn't he just answer with a simple yes and give my heart a break?

One last hug with my parents and a couple of hours later, the black limousine serves its purpose to carry me towards the King's private plane. Even the outside already looks so much grander than my father's. White body with two golden wings is ready to lift me across the oceans to my new home, currently for a yet-determined long.

Additionally, to my own personal surprise, Rayson Batard has changed his outfit to a pilot suit. And so I fix my gaze peculiarly at him.

But in a very casual way, along with a pair of lazy eyes, he just says, "I will be flying the plane."

Okay. *Wow.*

When I get inside the plane, my already-high expectations are just effortlessly surpassed by what I'm seeing. The walls are covered with gemmed draperies, and I'm given a matching velvety mantle as soon as I've come to terms comfortably with my seat. The interior here somehow matches my white silky tops and long pants, along with my ivory cashmere coat.

My gift. This royal treatment fit for a king, merely on my way to school.

The plane's now taking off and I'm seeing the land of the Twelfth Provincial Region turning miniature from above. Everything is so smooth and cushy, I could easily fall asleep if I haven't already got a thousand things to think about.

Who could've predicted? Just a few hours ago, I had set my mind and heart pretty much on a life without the Royal Princess Academy. But now… I'm leaving the Twelfth Provincial Region. I'm flying far away from home. I'm eating mushroom risotto with shaves of white truffle and drinking a glass of cold pinot gris on the King's private plane. All the superior extravagance, and yet, I'm still feeling kind of weird about the whole thing. No sadness. No excitement. Just pure static and… full-on curiosity.

The King's army. The Royal Princess Academy. The King's plane. What's next?

But then abruptly, my train of thoughts stops right at the Leon Station. How do I really feel about him now? Since pretty much we haven't really been talking for days.

I turn my head and look between the small gap next to my seat. Leon's sitting behind me alright, next to Moyra, but even when I make the obvious gesture to catch his attention, he won't look at me.

He won't let me away from his sight, worse yet, he won't look at me either.

It's killing me.

I mean, seriously, why is he still so angry with me? I want to tell him to "grow up". But since he's like two years older than me and I'm not acting any better either, I've decided not to. But then, why am I so bothered by this? He's very important to me, alright. More than a friend? Maybe, I admit. But, I'd not go as far as I've fallen in love with him. Like, how does love feel anyway? I mean, how would I know when I… do? Argh, you know what? I'm thinking this will start giving me a headache soon, so let's move on.

What's Moyra doing?

Moyra, without anticipation, has just fully evolved

into my mother's version of living in fantasy. Very annoying. Why is she choosing this time to be like this? Crown Prince this, Crown Prince that, Reigning Prince this, Reigning Prince that, Handsome Prince this, Handsome Prince that – I wish someone would just give me some ear plugs. I mean, she won't even stop reminding everyone on the plane about my own parents' love story. She would shift her head between guards and flight attendants, telling them how the two first met in the academy and pretty much graduated in time – as in, got married in exactly three years after. I guess if my parents begin to exhibit some sort of new kind of anxiety about me after I've got into the academy, it's if I'd be able to graduate at all, which in my case, could still entirely be an impossibility.

Suddenly, I find it harder to breathe.

When I look out the window to ease my swivet, the plane is now completely above very thick clouds. They remind me of those puffy white cotton balls.

What's with those puffy eyes? I'm suddenly reminded by.

You look like you need somewhere to hide, the boy said.

Let me help you, Detective.

The cloud is obviously the wrong kind of distraction, so I get my hands to move like a pretzel to open the scroll. Let's get some work done, I think.

My very first school assignment from the Royal Princess Academy. It says, written in golden ink, as follows.

If you could only get one wish, what would it be?

You can ask for anything you want, you shall write whatever you truly desire, and one thing will surely be granted — should you pass the threshold point.

May we recommend: a specific that fills up your royal needs.

Let me get this straight. So the very first school assignment is… . it's basically what it is. And, *a specific that fills up your royal needs?* They're not even trying to be as treacly as for us to write "the one thing that fills up our heart" or some other royal bullshit instead.

Unless, it's a trick.

Or that my mind always treats everything like it's a trick.

"Perhaps you could write what His or Her Royal Highness did in the past." I turn my head to find Moyra already poking her head to my side. "His Highness was granted a personalized yellow-gold necklace for Princess Valerie, with her name on it."

Wow, really? I'm getting goosebumps.

That sounds like my father has set his eyes on my mother even before he'd gotten into the academy. But then again, they filled up the three years of their life prior to the academies effectively with ceremony attendances. I'm probably the only royal who had skipped all of the middle-grade banquets – well, both me and the Crown Prince, I guess.

"Her Highness," Moyra continues, "*Rules of Being a Princess* night audiobook."

Come again? And what the hell is a *night* audiobook?

"More importantly, they got full marks on each."

Full marks? You've got to be kidding me.

But, wait.

"And how did you know all these?" I ask curiously.

In response, Moyra brings upon my face a leather-bound book as thick as my thumb. The papers are filled with both my father and my mother's handwriting.

"The only one of its kind in the world," Moyra apprises.

Right on the first couple pages, I see that my parents did write down what Moyra just said. I guess the assignment wasn't a trick after all. They *do* mean royal needs. Something personal. Something extravagant. The more specific it is, the better.

The more you know what you want, the quicker you can get what you need to get what you want. I find myself staring at these words for just a bit longer.

Next, I quickly flip the rest of the pages. All the assignments, mid-terms, and finals for their three years in the academy. At a glance, they all seem so stupid.

I'm so anxious to get to the end that I cause wrinkles

on each and every page I turn.

These lessons. These assignments. These final exams. They've got to be some sort of a joke altogether.

"Written most royally and carefully by His and Her Royal Highness during your *treacherous expeditions,*" Moyra distracts while giving me the eye for the fresh wrinkles on all the pages. In a flash, she closes the book so pretentiously like it's fragile and brings it back to her arms. "His and Her Royal Highness call this," she swings the book front and back, but in a most-royally and carefully way, "*The Royal School Guide for Our Dear Daughter Princess Seraphine.*"

Even the cover says so.

Well, that sounds like an awfully long name (and totally cringy) for a book.

"And they have said that I need to guard this book with my life," she says as she hugs the book to her chest. "My life!" she repeats.

"Okay?" I'm not too sure if the book is worth her life, but anyway. I think I get the gist of it.

Yet still, I have no *royal needs* I can think of but one: *catching the Royal Phantom.* Damn, what I would give for that ever since I came so close to it. But I know they can't give me that.

"So," I ask Moyra, "what would you ask for, then?"

"Me?" She looks startled.

"What would you write?"

"Hmmm." Moyra shuffles her arms and shifts her

head up. "A new riddle book!"

I rest my forehead on my fingers. Why am I not even surprised?

I proffer an impetuous turn with my head to steal a glance at Leon. Once again. I want to ask him – what he'd write, what could his true desire be – but I choose to hold back. He seems pretty content just looking seriously at the clouds, his left palm on his side chin. Don't know what he's seriously thinking.

I recline my seat to about one-fifty degrees and courteously reject the flight attendant's offer to move me into the plane's bedroom.

I close my eyes and come round to the shaft of sunlight on my face. I'm not really planning to sleep, so I just leave these three window covers open.

If I could get an answer to my very first school assignment from the academy as I catch my forty winks…

14

What I thought was mere seconds later turned out to be many hours lapsed. My bare feet brush off the soft carpet like turf-type buffalograss, my espadrilles are nowhere within my sight. The scroll, too, has simply vanished; seemingly had left my lap a long time ago for the nearest table – rolled back to its former look, placed nice and tidy on the center like it's awfully precious.

When I see the three window panes engulfed in sandy-brown screens, I know the reason why.

I sneak a look behind me to find Leon apparently not in his seat. It was just a hunch, so maybe I was wrong. Bright portholes remain where he'd stare blankly at the clouds, while Moyra at hand looks like a cuddly lamb too peaceful to wake. Same as the other guards on the other side, except they're snoring a little.

A few minutes later though, I see Leon coming back from the cockpit.

Still with his coldest tune and attitude, he reaches to

my side and whispers, "The plane's preparing for landing." Continuously, his left arm stretches onto my upper headrest's left as he imparts, "It'll be a mighty change, the pilot warns," all the while he's staring at his window behind me. I guess he's wondering what Rayson means as much as I am.

"Okay?" I whisper back callously. "But who closed my window shades? I wasn't planning on sleeping." My right arm rests on the table to placidly shake and crumple the scroll within my grasp. *This damn assignment.*

He turns his head at me. "I did," he mutters without regret. My hunch was right. "You needed rest."

"Oh?" I flinch just a bit when he suddenly slides the scroll off my palm and places it delicately next to the back of my hand. A man of gesture. "Well..." I swallow, and then I find myself suddenly speaking in the gentlest way possible as I ask, "did you sleep too?"

"No," is his only reply. Sharp and bland.

I roll my eyes at him, but the side of his face only looks expressionless as he leisurely strolls towards the third nearest window shade.

"I was asking you nicely," I snap, my stare at once turns into glare. "An explanation of *why* would be nice," I mutter loudly.

"I was just doing my job. What else do you want me to say?" he replies with a tone as cold as a frozen tundra while calmly and dexterously opening the first blind, then the second next. But when he reaches the one nearest to me, I feel him slowly taking his time.

Or maybe I wish.

Nevertheless, I take cognizance of his eyes sneaking a look at me as he bends his body slightly to carefully open the blind. His cheeks are only a few inches away from mine, though only for a short moment.

If only I could clench my own heart to stop it from beating like this.

Like it's very hard to breathe.

Carefully and without further delay, he kneels just on the sidetable angle and opens the drawer below to reveal my missing pair of shoes. "You need to do your best in the academy from now on," he says as he gently snugs my left foot by the sole into the soft feel of the grain leather comfortably – *his touch, his touch, his touch* – "while I do my best to protect you."

It's so obvious that he's now taking his damn time with my right foot, as it's perfectly clear he knows what it means to do my best in the academy. Get to marry a prince. Not him.

Seriously, he's killing me now.

But for a short second, I'm hesitating to beat my ego – to say I'm sorry for whatever reasons, to ask if we could just go back to how we were. Just for more moments like this. And longer.

Let's see where we can go from here. *Together.*

Right here, right now.

Without the royal title. Without the academy. Without any responsibility.

What can't we do?

My heart may deceive my eyes, but I think he's contemplating the same thing.

But then of course, he acts to quickly get my foot in and immediately moves back to his seat without another word.

As a result, I'm getting annoyed again.

See? This is exactly what I've been complaining about in my head. Whatever this is.

Any distraction will do at this point. Even the puffy clouds.

I rest my elbow on the seat side and take a peek at what's down there now as they get bigger in vision. Almost instantaneously, several things catch my attention – and rather surprisingly.

The one underneath with the long runway could only be the airport. About an-hour's walk up is what seems to be a big suburban town of opulence with profuse grandeur houses; and right in the middle, the tallest building in town. Various areas are divided by rivers and each is surrounded by big fields equipped with seemingly advanced farm technology, and yet there's something about all that still gives a sense of keeping rural.

But further upward, various houses much grander

than the ones before surround two modern palaces of the same size with quite a vast space in between. They're both white with shades of dusty gray in colour and share the same Baroque architecture.

They must be the Royal Academies.

On the left side of both academies and up towards the island's top are green hills and blue mountains that reach beyond the clouds.

But then… there it is.

A massive castle stands profoundly right before the highest mountain, where next surround it, thick walls guard the coastal line which frames the whole island.

It could only be… where the mysterious Crown Prince lives… couldn't it?

But I'm still so mesmerised, I can't even look away.

What seems to be the highest, brightest, and conspicuous of everything else built by men is also the most secluded place in the island. What's more, it looks like it's made of glass entirely. But the castle somehow doesn't speak of pretentiousness to me, not as much of its reticent transparency. Almost like… it was solely made to hide, and to protect – nothing else.

Somehow, I feel it in my heart that there's more to this castle than what meets the eye from high above. Like it could speak to me, a faithful representation of his personality. I just can't point out what it is yet that makes me feel this way, or what the right words are.

Perhaps, something but a normal glass is anything but a gabby reason. A flawless glass that is stronger than steel and speeding bullets. Strong and grand, imposing the maker's upscale permanence. I mean, if one could only tattle.

But as the massive structure ceaselessly catches the light by day, its whole surface seemingly reflects the incoming to appear sort of unseen. Like a giant looking glass, it's easily becoming the most beautiful castle I've ever seen in my entire life.

Far from grand of what it was built, and yet fails in self-effacing.

Indescribable to the eyes and heart, even more so clear of hiding.

Well, whatever kind of peculiar glass it may be, it has worked to magically enchant me, and so I drive myself on the rare occasion to take a picture. See if I can map the layout from the top and figure where everything is on paper later on.

But… it doesn't work.

My phone only captures as far as an empty giant space of a stagnant blue sky.

Why?

I shift my eyes back to the window and the castle's right there, peer back into my phone and… it's completely gone.

Okay, now I get it. Not only that the castle's made of

glass, the whole massive structure itself is a giant freaking mirror. When glass should refract through the aircraft, the mirror reflects it from the surface – and that must be why I'd been feeling sort of unease with the glass concept.

A whole lot of indestructible mirrors, I can only hope.

Needless to say, I have come to greatly wonder what it's all about, just as though I'm completely drawn to a new dazzling puzzle.

Giant mirror. Keeping invisible. Tacit veil. Secluded whereabouts. Everything is so unforeseen, what could possibly be his motive? His physique? His mere personality? What is he hiding? What does he really look like? Why is he so difficult to understand?

Why is he being so damn mysterious?

But all of a sudden, the Crown Prince's castle's gone from my view entirely, and I have to brace myself for landing. Fortunately, it's smooth. I don't remember much turbulence when the plane was taking off either, so I guess Rayson has proved himself a very skilled pilot.

Touchdown airport, a line of happy and graceful groups of people have formed to greet all of us on arrival. But what surprises me the most is that they respectfully bow for courtesy and proudly introduce themselves as "commoners", telling me that they'll go back to their crops and livestock soon after. Because no matter how I see it, they all look like royals to me. Even the clothes they're all wearing are almost the exact same ones as me – evident in the eyes that they're made of the best material, not coming off as flashy but timeless. Not even the nobles could often dress and act this royalty so casually and humbly.

Is this really a commoner's town? I seriously doubt it.

But Rayson and the other King's royal guards only indifferently bid their farewell as they head on to prepare the plane for their next flight back to the Capital Region. They don't look so astonished so I guess they've all been here before; thus, the warning.

Meanwhile, Moyra and Leon as well as the rest of our entourage of most-trusted guards keep looking to their left and right, still very much surprised and utterly confused about what constitutes our surroundings. I mean, the current view is definitely as perplexing as it is completely out of the ordinary.

Why are there no cars? Why are there so many horses? And is that a golden-painted four-wheeled closed carriage with red curtains on its windows I'm seeing? A freaking carriage on a horse? Which year do they think they all live here?

On my way walking to where the carriage is, I take in with my thoughts the new sensation this place has to summon. It's like I'm being transported into another universe, or a time machine where you get to bring back some of the technological properties from the future. Green pastures and mountains circle around the fresh air that I breathe, and there's an aptitude of complete serenity in mind I can't really describe. It feels so unpretentious and archaic here, the sudden appearance comes into sight some sort of predilection for the mystique figure on my part when it didn't. What's behind the indecipherable mist, this obscure silhouette figure of the heir to the throne?

I have now become totally intrigued.

15

Before I take the hand of the footman to get me into the carriage, the friendly royal-like commoners ask Leon and the other guards that come with us if they can *ride* instead. They nod, then walk confidently to choose their horses.

Leon settles for a seal-brown kind. He seamlessly jumps right on top when immediately after, he directs the other guards to follow his steps and follow my carriage from behind. *So hot.* But I immediately pretend that I've just not said that in my head.

Inside the carriage, I'm unperturbed by the unstable excursion as the horses speed at a canter. I was expecting a funny smell as the books tend to talk about the mammal's strong odour penetrating the wood and iron, but quite the contrary, it smells more like beautiful lemon trees in here. And the cushions are so comfortable, I feel no different to falling asleep on the King's plane.

Shortly after, Moyra offers to hold the scroll for

me, which I'm still unconsciously holding on to. I choose to let it stay with me, but give her my phone instead. Who knows, I may get a sudden idea of my "royal needs" along the way. Such as comprehension.

Me in a carriage and Leon on the horse.

I know I've been a princess my whole life, but somehow, today I really feel like I am. Something about this place being reversed in time that brings the susceptibility in me.

Maybe this is exactly what I really need. I mean, this does boggle the mind, and I do love my mind being boggled.

On my horse-and-carriage way through town, I pass by what looks to me are various big communes similar to nobles. Their houses look like they're made of strong wood and best golden paint, while their fields look colourful with a variety of seasonal crops. Every few blocks of land, there are taverns, bookshops, bakeries, local markets, and so many others that seemingly only supply essential leisure.

All the town folks look so happy and relaxed. They wave at this carriage moving by, and when they do, I feel this great excursion to wave back without any sense of insistence, even when they can't really see me beneath the slightly opened curtain.

Something about this place has definitely changed something in me.

And, the level of curiosity that I have about the

Crown Prince.

I mean, he must have done something here. A very-good thing, I think.

Maybe the people here have even met him in person. Which gets me even more curious. What has he done, or more like, what has he been doing so well? At such a young age?

And what does he look like?

Somehow, now I begin to wonder if he really is as handsome as he is *presumed* to be. Mind you, I never did.

Reaching the academy's residential houses complex, I ultimately notice some upgrades, but not as much. The houses are in different sizes, and despite being fancy, they're nowhere near flashy. The architecture tells more of timeless ornaments instead of being extravagant, as they are strong and sturdy for practical reasons.

But just as we get closest to the hillside, our carriage is stopped by a group of Royal Academies' staff. They all look very welcoming though with appearing fragments of uneasiness.

What gives?

A middle-aged man comes forward and introduces himself as the Counsellor while my mind is still wandering around. In my head, I can't help but compare this male of a stranger to the physiques of the Royal Phantom I've met. Again.

The man is with short black hair, wearing a long

white coat with golden buttons where his right chest reads a golden "RPA" symbol. And his eyes are grey.

Not him. Again.

But suddenly I realise, I forgot to pay attention to what he's been saying. What did he say his name again? Edgar? Edward? Allen? Oh, well. Let's just call him the Counsellor for now.

Feeling guilty, I force myself to listen to him more closely this time.

"Now, the initial size of the house hinges upon the number of *royal points* you've collected for the past three years; in other words, your *royal grade*," he instructs.

"Royal grade?" I think aloud.

"From the lowest to highest: Bronze, Silver, and Gold. The royal points are derived, converted, and accumulated from your Royal Rapport, which permutes into your royal grade." His eyes meander uncomfortably. "Look, Your Royal Highness," he sighs, "I'd like you to brace yourself on what lies ahead."

"Right?" I utter with confusion.

The Counsellor smiles awkwardly, bows, and then directs my carriage in very little steps.

And finally, we're here. A two-floor structure made of golden lumber, stone, and thatch combined.

As much as it looks incredibly entrancing, it seems like it's the kind that's being haunted. The paint is all vanishing and rusty, all the whites have turned darker in shades, and most of the wooden lines have been stretched out inward.

Now I get why the staff was more or less appalled. I guess none of my "uncommon interests" count as admissible royal points.

But if I'm being honest, I don't think it's entirely that bad. I mean, if I don't compare it to the other houses.

"This may be– *is* the worst mansion on the land." And then he has to make that part so damn clear. "I don't even know why this house was ever built in the first place," the Counsellor swallows audibly. "But let me assure you," he stares deeply into my eyes with teary eyes, "I have no right to share your current royal grade to anyone, Your Royal Highness."

I chuckle wryly at his seemingly-empathetic remarks. As much as I want to appreciate the gesture, it seems to me like there's no need. I mean, how can it not be that obvious? Anyone can definitely tell without asking. Bottom of the bronze, or even lower than that. A minus maybe, if the system allows.

Though he raised a good point.

So why was this house even built in the first place?

"If I may give just a little bit of *pourboire*, Your Royal Highness," he now whispers, "May I suggest that this is *when* your royal need comes in?"

The way he waves his hands – if a fire alarm could live and breathe as a person.

"Just write a wish," he suggests as he reluctantly brings me closer to the house entrance. "Say, another house." And then he tops it all with a repeated nod and a big concerned smile.

Good tip, I guess. But, no complaints from me.

Strangely, I already like it here, and I don't feel like moving at all. My adrenaline pumps as tonight I'll be testing the existing theoretical postulations whether ghosts really do exist. I mean, I've been wanting to.

Guess I don't even need the scroll in the first place.

Leon jumps out of the horse and takes measures with the other guards to catch up with me. But then, coming out of nowhere, this very tall guy with long white hair tied into a medium-height ponytail and long black tuxedo appears from the back of the front door and stops all the guards from coming in with only his eyes and hand gestures. He looks like he could be in his fifties, maybe even sixties.

"The Butler. He never speaks, comes with the house," the Counsellor informs me. He then turns his body towards Leon and waves his right hand. "Just follow what he says. He means well for the house." he instructs.

I give a curious observation at the Butler.

Could he be the Royal Phantom?

He looks as tall as the Royal Phantom. Plus, he *never* speaks. He won't or he can't? But then as quickly too, I've come to the conclusion that he can't be the Royal Phantom.

Despite his long black hair if it was coloured yellow *and* his similar green eyes, somehow I didn't get the sense that the Royal Phantom could be this old.

No, I don't think it's him.

However, another thought – or more like a revelation – comes to me. Is this how my mind is going to behave every time? I seem to have been doing this since Rayson first appeared before me. Scrutinising every male stranger looking so similar to Royal Phantom in physique even when they're not.

But when I finally get out of my thinking stupor, I come to notice that Leon's been trying to go against the Butler's wish. In turn, Leon gives me a hard stare, like he *needs* to shadow me around regardless even when I'm inside the house.

Well, sadly for Leon, I don't feel like pleasing him, so I choose to piss him off by instructing him to wait outside with the other guards while I'm inside this potential ghost house.

"But, Princess–"

"You're my *salaried man-guard*," I cut his boring reason short. "You said that yourself. So you have no choice when I say so, *General*." Wait. What do his subordinates actually call him? "I mean, *Captain*. I mean, *Commander*," I try to correct, but keep failing. "I mean… You know what? Whatever you are, other than a *friend*." I even end up closing the front door with my own two hands, not waiting

for Leon to respond, and I think everybody gasps when
I just casually let myself in – except for the Butler whose
expression remains as blank as everything about him.

Remind me again why I'm so angry at Leon?
Honestly, I don't even know anymore. Lately, it's come to
my attention that my emotion has been… roller-coaster
ride… weird. Especially when it comes to Leon.

But, anyway.

After briefly calming my head down, I take my time
to look around. From the entrance hall, the hallway in the
center is divided by two stairs that merge the mezzanine
balcony on top.

But at the right side of the interval, I see a peculiar
tall figure. Someone. A man, I think, sort of standing with
his back on the wall and his arms enveloped against his
chest. It's quite dark in here so I can't really see him clearly,
though somehow, I can tell that the shadow of his face is
currently facing me, and that his somewhat slick attire is
the exact opposite of pitch-black in colour.

A shade of cryptic snowfall.

"Ah, you! You, boy. Perfect timing," The Counsellor
speaks loudly toward the stranger male, his lower feet are
forced to elevate. "The Servant Boy. Comes with the house
too," he whispers to me swiftly, before turning his head
back towards whoever he calls the Servant Boy. "Please,
go to the market for fresh ingredients – *now*! Whatever's
left. Her Royal Highness will need to have her dinner in an

hour or two," he screams. "And quick!" He claps his hands when thereafter, the Servant Boy unhurriedly, moving almost lazily, takes one step forward facing us – still in the completely dark shadow, stands sturdy on his feet, and bows vaguely before he disappears.

A butler. A servant boy. More extras I don't need.

Walking further inside and around the first floor, the Counselor still non-stop babbles about a thousand reasons why I should leave the house immediately. Meanwhile, Moyra's been all too quiet that I start to worry. But as soon as we all reach the second floor where the bedrooms are, emerges from inside her this sudden drive to be in charge that she starts giving instructions to several maids (also come with the house) to make the house as clean as the King's feet.

"And there's not much in the house, as the number of things made available inside apparently come with the size of the house," the Counsellor suggests another frailty.

"I'm happy with the house," I heavily sigh as I respond. I've really lost count on how many times he has said all the bad things about the house or told me to move out. "It's small, but cosy, and I can use a bit of adventure at home," I say all the while I'm turning my head around with a big smile.

"Even my residence is bigger than this, Your Royal Highness, and definitely more of a *royal appropriate for a banquet*," he stresses, my eyes can't help but squint at the last few words. "If I were you to write the assignment, perhaps a five-story mansion? You must have noticed several on your way here. They are usually reserved for *Gold* students, but that's what the first assignment is for. I believe there's one still available." He flicks his pointer finger in the air. "You can only go higher from the worst, so it may even get you a full mark, for recognising a royal needs only the best! And let me assure you once more that you will *need* a better house. I simply cannot be any clearer than this." He nods at the white scroll in my hand and beams smugly.

Seriously? What's his deal pushing me away from this house? I feel like getting away from him now.

Not sure if Moyra is doing it on purpose, but she subsequently confronts him directly to ask a bunch of hygiene questions about the house and thus manages to distract him completely.

And so I use the opportunity to slip away.

No phone. No blank scroll. With only my thoughts.

I'm going out.

16

I've decided to run away to town – by walking.

Actually, I've been curious to walk around it since I first passed it by. The coachman's about to get on his boots but I tell him to rest. I just feel like walking the distance before dinner time.

Leon does not speak nor pout nor even condemn. He just follows me quietly with little footsteps from behind, not asking me anything. And he doesn't even take any of the other guards with him – just the way I want it.

I feel bad now somehow. Maybe I was too harsh on him in front of everybody. I mean, he was just trying to keep me as safe as possible. And why the sudden mention about the "salaried man-guard" coming from me? That was like… from days ago. Why all of a sudden that came across again just now? Argh, I'm so confused with myself. I don't get any of these. I feel like solving a murder case is so much easier than trying to understand my own feelings, *and* others.

Why does a human's heart have to be so… I don't know… complicated?

As I just keep on walking, my two feet have suddenly brought me to the town entrance. Has it really been that long? I've been preoccupied with my own thoughts, unquestionably.

I just still feel so perplexed.

Actually, let me be straightforward with myself. Do I want Leon as more than a friend? Or do I just want him back as a friend? The way we used to be. The way my heart was like. No drama. No blushing. No boundless heart beating. Just me and Leon, platonic.

Maybe that's the right word. *Platonic.*

"Yes, *photonic.*"

I suddenly hear a voice of a boy seemingly my age. Wearing his silky brown suit, he's standing on a small platform in front of a group of people who seem curious and attentive to hearing more about his blaring speech.

In particular, there's a lady in a green dress whose expression displays that she's been charmed by his word of science, or maybe just the boy.

"It's the physical science of light," the same boy goes on. "In a manner of speaking, manipulation of light, and that's what beholds the Crown Prince's Castle!"

"Oh, do shut up, Isaac," another boy yells among the crowd. But he's wearing a similar brown suit too. "Or should I say, Prince of the Fifth Provincial Region?"

"Just helium off, Prince Humbert of the Sixth Provincial Region," Prince Isaac shouts.

"Well, you should plutonium blast out of here!" Prince Humbert shouts back.

Thereupon, the both of them continue to argue with all the elements from the periodic table. Literally.

I shake my head and giggle. Guess I've just found two princes my age who were not in my Royal Coming-of-Age Ceremony, since I'm pretty sure they would've fought with chemistry sets instead of swords.

Actually, now I start to wonder where they are. The *mummies*, I mean.

But all of a sudden, I accidentally bump into a girl in a pink puffy dress.

"Ouch!" She covers her head with a beige silky scarf and her eyes with big sunglasses. Her lips seem to be messily smeared with something brown. "Oh, I'm so sorry! Please excuse me," she says in a hurry. Both of her hands are holding tight to a small cotton rucksack full of something that releases a crisp tone, like it's made of aluminum and plastic. No, from the sound, there are lots of it. More like candy wrappers. Chocolate lollies!

The peculiar girl looks to the left and right, and in an instant I notice a group of ladies in waiting and guards I don't recognise who look like they're looking for someone. A princess. "Once again, I am so sorry," she says as she notices them too and hastily flees on foot.

I haven't even said I'm sorry too.

Nevertheless, I can't help but laugh again.

Guess there are some royals I can feasibly bear.

Though it seems, I have spoken way too soon.

Out of the blue, walking from far away across are a bunch of princes who are with bandages and plain-sight swords, still recovering from their fight wounds.

The mummies!

Shit. I must hide now.

But as if a light blazes down from the vault of heaven, a big burning object strikes from the sky above. The trajectory is abnormally vertical and it hits the ground a few feet away from where I stand.

And so I run towards it as fast as the others trying to get away from it.

As I'm getting closer, it's burning still, and I immediately recognise the fixture. The size. The possible weight. The sense of proportion. The flaming suit of broadened shoulders. *No movement.*

It's the burning body of a dead man.

I try to cohere into what's beneath the fire even when it pains my eyelids. The body is beyond crushed and the face has become unrecognisable, so I'm thinking, the best that I can do now is to focus on what else is apparent before the ashes.

Anything at all.

First, I'll try to figure out how long the man's been

dead – but I can't. I would be able to if there wasn't any fire because I'd need to touch the body. Plus, I still have so many things to learn about it.

In the past three years, there was always someone helping me in this particular department. Experts such as forensic pathologists, some random people who were giving me clues inadvertently, or even witnesses and suspects who just happened to have some forensic knowledge of some sort. But there's no one else here.

Alright. It's risky, but I'll just have to skip it.

Next. The victim's physiognomy or any physical evidence to the eye.

His hair. Yellow. Actually, a bit brown, maybe? Something seems a bit off, but anyway, I'd better move on. I need to be quick. His attire. White shirt on a red suit, or maybe velvet. His hands. His left hand. Formed knuckle. And is that blood? Why does it look so bloody?

But, wait.

There's something on his chest, standing firm straddling in between. A knife's stuck in the heart with a small pink-glossy sheet visible right on top of it, only it appears inflammable. I mean, it should take about eight seconds for a normal printed paper to burn, add thirty seconds for a paper as thick as something like the Royal Phantom's card–

The Royal Phantom's card.

Right. That card. Of course. Why does it oddly look

so similar? The colour, the shape, and everything. And if
that really is what could be the Royal Phantom's insignia
below… But it's too far away for me to be able to see it from
here, let alone the message.

You know what? I'm going to have to come even
closer.

But suddenly, a brush of soft fingers softly touches
my right arm, stopping me from walking much further.

Leon? I think.

"Stand back," he says.

Except… that voice… it's not him.

My eyes slowly roll in motion to follow the trace,
starting off a long-sleeve garment of white seemingly made
of the finest silk, then rather out of place, a grocery basket
full of greens on the other hand.

He's so tall that I have to look up to his face. And his
face…

The same time something throbs my heart
insistently, Lady Francoise's voice immediately rings in my
head.

Honestly, how hard can it be?

This. I think I've finally found my answer.

His whole face *is* the damn answer.

I have never seen a man more handsome and
beautiful.

I mean, where do I even begin? His short hair –
bright and yellow – reminds me of a winter aconite. His

skin looks delicately smooth like an oval plate of sweet yoghurt. And his eyes–

But I could barely peer into the sparkling details as he swiftly turns his head towards the body and says, "I believe the man's been dead for at least three hours."

As immediate as I was mesmerised by him, as quickly too his words brought me back to my deducing awareness. So my head turns to look at the body again and asks most curiously, "How do you know that?"

"Rough patches appear to show on his neck. See that?" He points with a finger that has taken part in caressing my skin. "They only appear within thirty minutes of death. But with that level of darkness in color, I'd say three to four hours." Then, his finger moves gracefully as per his words of explanation. "But do you see his hand? It looks like it's just starting to stiff. Rigor mortis should appear two to three hours after death."

"So he'd been strangled to death about two to three hours ago, but he was only set on fire minutes before his body was pushed to the ground," I think loudly, still looking at the body.

"And how do you know that?" he asks me inquisitively.

"The shape of those dark purplish patches on his neck you mentioned. Then his state of burn. Based on how his epidermis is currently ardent, he's not yet reaching third degree. And concludingly, there's no blood splatter on his chest. I'd say, he was stabbed after he was murdered."

"I see," he says, nodding his head. "So, what do we do now?"

We? Okay. Alright.

"I'd say… we try to analyse the body as much as we can here until the firemen arrive. Try to not leave any evidence prone to ashes behind. What do you think?"

Right after, my head turns to face him again, only this time to particularly look into his shining-green eyes more closely, which look even brighter with the flame extremely close by.

A familiar green. No. A *very* familiar green.

Wait.

Who's this guy?

And why does he seem so familiar?

Bright eyes gaze at me like two constellations at bay. "I'd say, sounds good," he says with a soft smile.

And that smile. *Especially* that smile.

I've seen it before, I think. Or at least, I felt it beyond the mask.

Barely a week ago.

17

Of course. The first day I'm here, murder happens.

But now that the firemen have come and clear out the priority issue, my mind moves on to the next.

Seriously, who's this guy?

I'm totally distracted from this point on. My eyes cannot stop staring at him, just as much as he's still looking at the burnt body.

Height as tall as the Royal Phantom. Hair the exact same yellow, eyes as emerald-green as his. The only thing contradictory is that he seems to be exactly the same age as me, though there's something about his countenance that speaks of a fully-fledged maturity.

Go on, kid.

Still, overall, this guy ticks almost all the boxes to get me very suspicious about him being the Royal Phantom.

You know what? He really could be.

"Who are you?" I firmly ask with my arms crossed.

At least, I need to hear his voice again without the

sound of fire burning, to really weigh up how different it is compared to the Royal Phantom's I heard that night.

Still with the basket of greens on his right hand, he shifts his body innocently towards me. "I'm the Servant Boy," he directly replies, and then simply bows – though a bit more respectfully this time.

Different voice but with the same soothing tone.

No, he could still be faking it.

"Who are you?" I repeat with my eyes blazing, fiercer than ever. I want to pierce his mind.

I'm waiting for him to accidentally say the word "kid" even though it makes way more sense that we're perfectly the same age.

He empties his hand to the ground then bows again. "To be more precise, I'm *your* Servant Boy, Your Royal Highness." Then he picks up the basket and stands.

"That, I already know," I say.

"You do? How?" His emerald-green eyes spark with curiosity. "You barely saw me just now." He seems to forget to formally address me, but *like I care.*

"You're the only one with a basket filled with withering fresh greens. But more importantly, back to my question. Who?" I bring my face as close as possible to his, so that no one else is listening. "Are?" Closer. "You?" Too close – our nose basically almost touches, we could kiss. I even notice him swallowing in panic. But, I still don't give a damn.

"What do you–"

"Are you the Royal Phantom?" I interrupt.

In response, his cheeks only shimmer in pink. No answer. So I bring my face even closer to his now. Our lips now basically half an inch away from each other, but again. I. Don't. Care. I just need to know the truth. So, "Are you?" I reiterate.

Out of the blue, I notice Leon running towards me as he's calling out to me from behind. But when I turn, I realise that he's not alone. He's… he's… he's with…

"Gaspard?" I scream in shock.

"Who, milady Your Royal Highness?" Yellow-moustache Gaspard answers me as he's still out of breath from running. He then looks to his left and right and then left and right again.

"You… Gaspard?" I'm starting to think that I'm wrong. I look at Leon and he shakes his head quietly while squinting his eyes.

"Me, milady Your Royal Highness? For it is only I, Rainpard, the Chief Police in town," he answers, then bows to me ninety degrees low.

Wow. Well, he's *definitely* not Gaspard, I can now tell as much.

But I wonder now if Gaspard has a brother, though Leon doesn't say anything. Not that we're currently on speaking terms either.

Following his gesture, all the police officers who

were running with him are now bending their upper body towards me too.

"Now, milady Your Royal Highness, what's your order?" Rainpard asks, still bending his body low.

"My what?" My mouth stays open to the disbelief. "And could you all please stop bowing?"

Giving respect is one thing, but overly doing it is just plain annoying.

"I must say, Your Royal Highness, I am a really big fan." Rainpard blushes, then hands to me while bowing again, a bunch of newspapers.

I sigh. Who even carries this stuff around?

"Your order is my *royal command*, Your Royal Highness," he says, then bows his head again. For God's sake. He was clearly not listening.

I look at Leon and he shrugs his shoulders. Then I look at the Royal Phantom– I mean, the Servant Boy – for now. Whatever on my face he's smiling about, I'm just relieved that he's still here.

I'm not letting him get away this time.

"You see, Your Royal Highness," Rainpard continues, "We don't get many cases around here. None, actually," Rainpard chuckles uncomfortably.

"Okay?" I give my answer hesitantly. I guess he's not been very busy.

But then I see Rainpard and all his subordinates still looking at me with what I presume some sort of high expectations. Like they're waiting… for my order.

Right. Just do what I usually do. Except, I've realised now that what I usually did was to defy police and guards who weren't letting me in the case – not actually being in charge. And because of that, I'm now pumped, but also scared. "I guess, I'm really in charge now?" I corroborate, more for myself.

I browse for many pairs of eyes around and find Rainpard along with his men nod excitedly.

I inhale deeply, then exhale.

Isn't this what I've always wanted? Crime Investigator. Chief Detective. Whatever is similar. And if I ever want to know if I'm really up for the job of my dream, I should just use this golden opportunity to really step up. Take courage and just do it. But honestly, I'm so nervous, and somehow I'm afraid of messing up.

And so I try to calm my head down with presumptions. Facts, more importantly. And logic. I mean, you can't go wrong with facts *and* logic, right? So let's say I'm in charge…

Wait, what am I thinking? I really *am* in charge.

Okay. Breathe in. Breathe out.

What would a *real* detective do?

There are steps, measures, responsibilities–

Responsibilities.

Oh, boy. Okay. Calm down, Seraphine.

On the right spur of moment, Leon walks towards

me and stands just on my side.

"Do you want me to take the lead?" he offers.

But, he's asking. Like, really asking.

So, he's giving me a chance too?

I swallow. "Do you think I could—"

"I think you're ready," he cuts my hesitation short, and then lets out a smile that really warms my heart. "Besides, I'm better at staying just beside you. Making sure you're safe, that's what I do best. Not solving puzzles and crime."

My heartbeat moves beyond progressive.

I can't help but smile back at him, and I think we're back to where we were now. Warm. Conversation. Encouragement. Comfort. Trust. *A friend*. And that's what I really need from him right now.

So I close my eyes. Inhale deeply, exhale again. Then I open my eyes.

"Okay, first thing first," I begin. "We need to secure the scene. You," I randomly point at one of Rainpard's men, "Set a barrier and don't let anyone come close to the body." The man nods cheerfully and moves on to the task I'm giving him.

"Next, a few of you need to ask around. Find some witnesses and see if there's anyone missing. Let's go with… you, you, you there behind him, then you, you – yes, you – and… you." All at random who've got their hands empty.

Similarly, they happily accept and off they go.

"Now, the rest of you," I make a circle with my fingers at some of the men who are bringing their kit, "come with me to scan the scene and collect some evidence." My feet take charge and I lead them towards where the body still lays. "Oh, I almost forgot." I stop for a moment. "This is very important. One of you should go find a doctor and bring him here. Let's go with… you." I take my chances with randomly pointing fingers once more. Always choose the one with the empty hand. "Okay, go!"

The man jumps up, being excited, then circles around for a bit before he goes to where he thinks is the right direction.

Well, at least if the doctor never comes, I know who else to blame besides myself.

18

Even as I walk towards the crime scene, I still look around for the Servant Boy.

He's walking behind Leon, Rainpard, and the others. He's not trying to run away, so it seems. I'm glad, but I'm still worried – in such a way that I feel the need to keep him very close to me at all times.

And that's when I've finally decided to call him out to walk by my side, and when I do, I notice Leon squinting his eyes with scepticism.

Well, I'll just tell him all about it later when we get home.

Reaching to where it happened, everything else's been burnt very badly with only a few things remaining distinguishable.

I move my eyes around the body first.

The first thing I notice is the knife and the card that's stuck with it against the body's chest. After some of them are done taking pictures for evidence, I'm about to take the card with my hand until I realise I haven't got any handkerchief or glove with me.

But without delay, the Servant Boy glides with his fingers a pair of white gloves right in front of my face.

"Let me help you, Detective," he says.

I stare confusedly at his smiling face while still letting my expression clearly show that he very much remains under my suspicion radar. "Who brings out a pair of white gloves around, if he's not the Royal Phantom?" I say with a slightly louder voice, since he's just next to me.

He lets out a chuckle before he answers, "A real gentleman."

"That's for a handkerchief," I say.

"And I'll have you know that a real gentleman always brings a pair of gloves to ready himself even for a dance at any time, Your Royal Highness, among many other things," he replies nonchalantly. "So really, the concept applies rather universally."

"Whatever," I give my response rudely the same time I grab the pair of gloves briskly from his hand.

Seriously, this guy. Is he challenging me or something? I'd better not let him out of my sight until I'm entirely sure. *Keep your enemies closer*, they say.

I put on the gloves and lower my body to begin the evidence extraction. Just like what I'd thought, the card is indeed signed with the Royal Phantom's insignia.

I shift my head upward to take a glimpse at the

Servant Boy's face but he doesn't show any alarming reaction to it.

"Recognise this?" I ask.

He sighs. "If you mean if I had written it, I'll have you know that I didn't. I can assure you." He looks really serious as he puts down his basket of greens and bends his knees beside me.

"Sure you can," I say while shrugging with sarcasm.

He sighs again while managing to keep his smile perfectly constant and beautiful as a picturesque painting of snow rain under the sun. "Let's read it, shall we?"

Now we both have our faces on the same line and look at the card closely together. There's almost no space in between our cheeks, but none of us seems to mind at the moment – or even care.

The heart of the real Crown Prince is what I really want.

"That's it? Where's the code? Damn it!" he suddenly snaps at himself.

I stare at the side of him in disbelief, looking perplexed.

Is this some kind of acting he's trying to perform? Why is he looking so frustrated instead?

But, I have to admit that even he has a point. This message seems… extremely odd. And probably for the same reason as the Servant Boy.

Which reminds me.

"Why does it say the *real* Crown Prince?" I think out loud.

And why the heart of the Crown Prince?

"Oh no!" Rainpard suddenly screams from the back of my head. My shoulders leap in shock, I almost fall on top of the dead body. Luckily, the Servant Boy instinctively catches me in time with his arm and lets go leisurely with a smile. "You don't think… it's the Crown Prince, do you, milady Your Royal Highness?"

I rub my ears in fortuitous annoyance, then stand and turn my body around. "And why did you say that? You certainly have seen the Crown Prince, haven't you? I mean, you live here," I say.

Although, no one can really see anyone beyond that dead body's unrecognisable face.

"No, milady Your Royal Highness. I, too, have not. *No one has.*" He shakes his head like a tornado.

"No one has?" I repeat after him. "Are you serious? Not even a glimpse on when he arrived or went out?" I raise my eyebrows.

"Not a soul, no. The Crown Prince only keeps to himself inside the castle. Not even sure how he's got around in and out of the island. But he'd always send his royal knight to read his decree." *The Crown Prince's army.* "That's why nobody's ever seen the Crown Prince, milady Your Royal Highness. And to be honest with you," he comes closer to my right ear as he starts to really whisper in secret, "sometimes I'm not even sure if the Crown Prince really lives here."

"Why are you whispering?" I start to whisper too.

"Well, the thing is, the Crown Prince may not be here, but his *eyes* and *ears* always are." He speaks very quietly. "*Everywhere*," he emphasizes. He then looks around in fear.

I'm getting more and more confused. "What are you talking about?" And what is he scared about? "You're not making any sense. You know what?" I stop whispering. "I'd like to make a request to see the Crown Prince. For the sake of the investigation, of course." I clear my throat for an impacting effect. "If this was the Crown Prince, this would be a big problem, wouldn't it? An heir apparent to the monarch, *dead*?" I perilously dare. "I sure hope he's not."

Rainpard and his men move their hands up and down repeatedly like I need to shush myself. My eyebrows lower themselves in confusion.

A sudden loud noise like thunder racing towards me from behind is more than enough for me to think over my actions. "*Ahem*," someone suddenly clears his throat so loudly.

"Should I... turn around?" I ask Rainpard hesitantly, my eyebrows furrow in concern.

I think... I'm scared.

In response, Rainpard nods while closing his eyes,

almost sobbing.

When I turn my body around, I see a tall man with short curly brown hair and hazel eyes, covered in silver plate armor, riding on a black horse. And he's not alone. In fact, about fifty other guards with similar heavy metal armor are with him. *The Crown Prince's army.*

I swallow as he jumps off his horse. For someone who didn't even flinch when seeing the dead body on fire thrown from the sky, I'm actually frightened to make eye contact with the man before me. Plus, I have to look up just to reach his chin as he's insanely big and tall.

As much as he seems to be awfully important around here, something about him looks vicious, dangerous. Is it the claw marks on his right cheek? If not, the scorch mark on his left? Or maybe just the idea of what this guy had been through to get to where he is now.

To protect the Crown Prince?

The scary man in full knight armour takes his time to carefully circle his eyes around me and my surroundings before the dead body. Almost like he's looking for something – or someone, and then back to me.

"Princess Seraphine of the Twelfth Provincial Region. Your Royal Highness," he says.

Oh, shit! He already knows me. I'm probably already on his naughty list. But then the unexpected happens afterward when he gracefully bows just a nod low.

"Let me promise you," his eyes still glaring at my

soul, "that the Crown Prince is perfectly safe and sound in our protective care. You shall not be worried."

Well, that doesn't sound convincing. And the way they just got here that quick out of nowhere?

"Regardless," whatever his name is, "I need evidence." I then awkwardly clear my throat. Still scared, still acting to remain brave. "Could I please… show my respect to the Crown Prince in person?" I ask while looking towards the castle.

Not going to lie, I've been curious about what's inside there too.

"That won't be necessary, Your Highness. *For now.*"

For now? What does he mean?

"That should be all, I believe," he says, before making a turn to go back to his horse.

"Wait!" I shout, before I immediately swallow. Well, curiosity definitely comes before my fear, but since it's already come out, I might as well continue. "May I ask why no one has ever seen the Crown Prince before, hmm, Sir Knight?"

I'm not sure what to call him. Mind you, I've skipped a lot of my princess lessons whereas the ones I did attend don't tend to stay in my mind for long.

But to my own surprise, the scary man lets out a soft laugh, and when he does, he doesn't look as scary as he was before.

"Yves Thevenet, Your Highness. And to answer your

question. Well, what can I say? A man always has his own reason," he smiles again.

"But he needs to make attendance in the Royal Prince Academy, does he not?" I tilt my head.

I need to verify that the Crown Prince does have a time limit with his hiding.

"Correct. That means, when it's time, you may be able to catch sight of him in the academy. *When it's time,*" he reiterates – whatever that means. "In the meantime, I'd suggest you stop waiting for the doctor who's still getting lost on his way here." And of course, he already knows about that. Why am I not surprised? Eyes and ears of the mysterious Crown Prince everywhere. "Once he comes, he will still need to fly the body out for further autopsy where he'll be able to confirm the dead body's identity. After that, you may then proceed with your so-called investigation again."

"But that could take weeks, or maybe months, just to get the DNA analysis done," I protest.

"Then *solving murder* would have to wait," his voice roars like big thunder. "I'd suggest you focus on your study first, Your Royal Highness." Then he flicks his head at Rainpard with a very serious look. "Rainpard, I leave you to it."

In response, Rainpad and his men perform their classic ninety-degree bow and only stop once all the royal knights are out of sight.

19

I walk home with a much stronger curiosity about the mysterious Crown Prince. For a long hour there, I've even totally forgotten about the murder or even the Royal Phantom.

But when the door opens to the interior, what my house is now totally baffles me. This almost feels like I'm back in the Palace of the Twelfth Provincial Region.

When the door is closed, I notice that the Butler is not the one who opened it.

Where is he?

Moyra greets me with a very tired but proud face, her dust mop still hanging tightly on her shoulder.

"You know, they all said it'd be impossible." The Counsellor, she means? "But I'd say, nothing is impossible to clean should Moyra be directing it."

"Wow, I must say, this looks entirely beyond my expectation. Really great job, Moyra!" I give her a high five, to which she responds energetically with a little jump.

"And who's this?" Moyra accidentally bumps into my shoulders but she doesn't even notice. Her focus is being totally captivated by someone standing behind me. The Servant Boy. "Enchanted to meet you, Sir…"

That's right. I haven't even got to know his name. I just straight away accused him of being the Royal Phantom.

"Reon," he replies with his soft, classic, picturesque smile. "The Servant Boy," he adds.

Reon.

Wait. Reon?

Damn it. Why does his name have to sound like Leon?

"Reon, the Servant Boy," she hums. "I'm Moyra, *the Servant Girl,*" she says while still shaking his hand continually and blinking her eyes repeatedly. I sigh.

"I think that's too long for a handshake," I interrupt.

"Oh, right. I'm sorry, Reon." She very slowly lets go of his hand. I roll my eyes.

"What's that in your basket, Reon?" She asks with a very girly voice.

Somehow, I find it annoying. *Very* annoying.

"It's for dinner," he says. "It's probably a bit too late for Her Royal Highness, but I'll have it with the chef right away."

I look at the big clock and it shows seven o'clock.

"I'm skipping dinner," I announce. "I'm going to the library."

"Oh, for your assignment, of course? Due tomorrow night," Moyra reminds me.

Shit! I've totally forgotten all about it.

"Right. Right, you are." I then give out a cynical laugh. "Where is that scroll?" I look around in total blankness. I've totally forgotten where I put it.

"Here," Moyra takes the scroll out of her deep left pocket and gives it to me with a giant smirk. "Lucky for you, I caught sight of it when you just left it on one of the small decor tables."

Seriously, what can I do without Moyra, the Servant Girl – a new title she's bestowed upon herself.

"Are you coming with me?" I ask her.

"Oh, I shall not, Princess. I haven't even started to clear the second floor yet! Your bedroom must be as spotless as it was back in the palace!" she shouts in panic.

I roll my eyes. "There's really no need. I can live with a bit of dust."

"Certainly not! You know what? If I start now, your room will be done just at the right time when you're going to bed. Although, I can't say the same thing about the other rooms. Oh, what I must do!"

"Off you go, then," I say to Moyra, to which she immediately runs as fast as a bolt. Then I shift my gaze towards Leon. "You're coming with me?"

"I'd love to," he says, "but I must attend to the other guards first. Substantially with the murder in town, we will now need to secure the perimeter inside and out, discuss additional protective plans for your safety in the house, not to mention–"

"Alright, I get it," I sigh. "You can leave now." I can tell Leon's feeling all edgy, imagining a thousand scenarios that I could be in danger. "I'll be fine," I assure him. "No one's going to murder me with you and the guards here."

"Certainly. Not on my watch," he says confidently, then does the unnecessary bowing, and immediately off he goes too.

Sigh. Why is everyone around me always so busy? Even back in the palace too.

And so I walk to the library by myself. All alone.

Arriving at the library, I've noticed that this space is the house's priority. As much as the other rooms are slightly more than decent for living, here is where everything else was built around.

Located right in the center of the mansion, it heightens the whole area to the top where its walls are filled with books. The ceiling is filled with interior lights that illuminate the whole spots in balance. I could just move my bed and sleep right at this spot, but it doesn't seem like Moyra and her team have done much of their cleaning here.

I stroll around the walls for something that would catch my attention. Anything that would help me to solve the murder case earlier. And so I choose to settle for two. *DNA Analysis* by Yannis Vermeersch and *Rigor Mortis* by

Loris Depoorter.

But all of a sudden, I hear the sound of a small trumpet. *A royal decree,* I think. There's no clock in the library so I can't tell exactly how long I've been here. Maybe two hours have passed.

So I put the book *DNA Analysis* back on the shelf and I leave the other on the table next to the scroll I've been disregarding – still. I then walk out and arrive near the mansion entrance to find that I'm the last to arrive.

Coming forward to the center of the room is not the same scary knight from earlier, though all the rest behind him dress the same. Still the Crown Prince's army, I presume.

"I hereby announce the King's Proclamation," the guard announces.

The King?

"All loyal subjects of His Imperial Majesty whose residence are currently permanent in the Crown Prince's Island are hereby notified by the royal proclamation that in conjunction with the recent brutal murder case in the town square, it is upon this hour onward that everyone is forbidden to leave their assigned premises until the six sharp of the first morning on the new Monday. The only exception is the Crown Prince's army to collect in due course the first assignment assigned by the Royal Prince Academy as well as the Royal Princess Academy, in addition to the Provincial Region's royal guards in charge."

Damn it. They still care about that stupid assignment.

"That is all, by royal command of the King."

As fast as they come in with the announcement is as fast as they leave the premise too. While everyone else is immediately back to what they were doing, I unwittingly sneak a look at the Servant Boy when apparently, he does at me too.

On his hand is something on a tray enclosed with a metal cloche.

20

When I walk back towards the library, I notice that someone is walking behind me. As I go in, I've realised now that it's the Servant Boy.

Reon.

"I'm only here to fill your sustenance needs," he says with a surrendering kind of gesture and expression, waving his occupied hands in the air as if I was about to choke him to death or something.

I only sigh to indicate that I'm not some kind of sociopath, if that's what he thinks of me. Not even sure if he's only joking.

Thereafter, he puts the tray on the other side of the table and opens the cover – with a little chuckle, I notice. But what comes more as a surprise to me is how there are two plates instead of one. Each has the same cut of steak and fresh greens as the sides – the ones from his basket earlier, I'd presume.

"There are two?" I ask.

"Only if you want some company. Otherwise, I can leave," he says while placing a plate in front of me. Somehow, his tone comes out a bit weird towards the end, and as usual, he's forgetting to formally address me again. *To my delight.*

"You haven't eaten too?" I ask as he's slowly walking away.

"I wasn't very hungry," he briefly answers.

Not sure what his expression looks like as I'm only seeing the back of his head now. But for some reason, I find his answer rather comforting, even though there's a strong possibility that he's the Royal Phantom and is only trying to manipulate me – or poison me. Nonetheless, it doesn't mean that I can't try to manipulate him back, or risk myself being poisoned. Leon's here anyway. Somewhere. Out there. He always manages to keep me safe somehow. And so, I've decided to take up the challenge.

I'll take your bait, I smirk. *Keep your enemies closer.*

"You can have it with me. I don't mind. I'm just reading here," I say.

Still trying to keep my stare tight on him like a leash, I pick up one of the books with my left hand while my right just brushing the steak aimlessly. At times, my eyes manage to sneak a look at his gorgeous face – still too magnificent and dangerously close to becoming an obsession. But I focus on working out what he's doing or trying to do.

Why is he really here? What's his motive? And why does he look so calm?

But like his eyes are that of a hawk, he takes notice and abruptly makes his way to stand next to me. What is he going to do?

"Here, Your Highness. Let me," he says as his fingers brush mine, taking the fork off my hand so delicately.

Thump. Thump. Thump.

With his other hand proceeds to the knife on the side of the plate afterward, he neatly cuts my steak into little pieces. "Now, you can go on reading without brushing your steak."

Thump thump thump thump thump thump thump thump thump thump…

Quiet, my maniacal beating heart! I rapidly yell in my head at my stupid cardiac organ. I want to slap myself, but luckily, the idea only remains in my head. For now.

After he finishes organizing the pieces of steak on my plate, he takes his plate to sit across from me. "You wouldn't mind, would you?"

"Not at all. Help yourself," I say, trying to sound as unbothered as I can be.

Trying.

As a matter of fluke, this is just the perfect angle to watch him closely. Although, I'd say that's quite extraordinary for a servant boy, considering it took Moyra and Leon long enough to sit on the same table with me, let alone asking for it.

A friend.

"*Rigor Mortis*," he says, looking at the book in my hand. "I'd say the author has proven her theory right this evening."

"She says it right here." I flip a couple pages back, and then quote, "*Rigor mortis appears approximately two to three hours after death–*"

"*–starting with the muscles of the face, progressing to the limbs over the next few hours, and in completion at length between six to eight hours after death,*" he quotes back with the exact same words, then goes on to take a bite at his steak in the most proper way.

The way he's eating… I can't help but observe. That's extremely elegant for a servant boy. But more importantly… "You've read this?"

He waits to swallow, and then says, "Only ten times for now."

Ten times? TEN TIMES? No wonder he could help me analyze the body earlier.

"That sounds a bit disturbing," I say, every word laced with sarcasm.

And hot.

Jeez. Stop it, Seraphine! He could be the Royal Phantom, manipulating you!

What is wrong with me all of a sudden? My heart

suddenly feels… funny again. Like it's just grown wings and flown like a butterfly in mere split seconds.

Don't take the bait! I scream to myself in my head. *Only pretend to take the bait!*

"It is as disturbing as the fact that it is much less than the number of murders happening out there," he goes on. "They need to stop." He looks down on his plate, pondering something sad, I think.

In response, I continue my reading silently because I don't really know what to say or react in situations like this. Back to my own thoughts.

Which region exactly does he mean?

But as if unbothered, he goes off to find a book on his own and comes back to his seat with a choice. The Servant Boy then opens the book and reads it calmly. I sneak a look. *Private Ames: A Scandal in Balthazar* by Sir Canon Royce.

Damn it. Why does he have to choose that one? Now I wonder how many times he's read that one too. I feel like closing my book and having some discussions with him. No, Seraphine, no! Maybe he already knows and that's exactly what he's going for. To manipulate you even more. But, how could he know? It's not like we've met anytime long before the recent week. Anyway, I'd better shut up and keep my distance from him while at the same time keeping him up close to me at all times.

Close to me?

At all times?

Damn it, why does that sound so cheesy now? And why does he have to resemble the Royal Phantom so much? I mean, he's the perfect companion. The most perfect so far, maybe. He lets me do my own thing in silence, he doesn't make a noise while I'm at it, and yet he's still here with me. Plus, he reads this kind of book too. Damn it. That's hot. That's *very* hot. But, damn it! Why can't he just be a normal Servant Boy? Because I think we could've been really great friends… or maybe even more than friends… Argh, stop it, Seraphine, you idiot! What are you even thinking?

"Is something the matter? Why are you… shaking your head?" he asks me curiously.

Oh. My. God.

I didn't even realise that I was shaking my head.

"Nothing," I say, even though I can feel the extreme warmness on both of my cheeks from this deep embarrassment. How did I not even realise that I was shaking my head? Seriously, I think I'm going crazy. Because of him. You know what? I need to get away from him. As soon as possible. And so I announce, "I'm going to bed," while raising my body to stand. "Will I be seeing you tomorrow morning?" I ask in subconscious, after which I want to slap myself in realization.

"I mean, just in case you really *are* the Royal Phantom and thinking of running away from here, and not because I care about you being here or not here, because

I don't. I'm not even sure why I said 'will I be seeing you tomorrow morning?'" I let out a small pathetic laugh. "I mean, I don't even care if it's in the morning or night that I'll be seeing you. I mean, if I am to know in the morning, that would be great, because it will just give me some extra peace before the evening comes. But certainly not because I care about you. I mean, I only care about if my hypothesis is true or not, whether I'm being right or wrong. That's all."

I'm suddenly losing my breath. It's like I've just rapped. Seriously, I should've just held my tongue.

The Servant Boy in response lets out an uncontrollable laugh. Very loud, without restraint, and yet it remains a strong allure. The kind that only he can pull off so charmingly. "You'll see me first thing tomorrow morning. How does that sound?" He then gives a simpering smile. "Just nice that tomorrow is the perfect day to do it."

"Okay?" I've come to agree suspiciously. Although, I have to admit. It does give me some sense of peace.

"Well, in that case, I bid you goodnight, Princess Seraphine."

He stands then bows so gracefully.

"And you… Reon," I reply bashfully then try to slightly lower my head just as elegantly.

I turn my body around and really try my best to walk calmly out of the library door. But then afterward, I'm immediately running to get to the second floor, only to be

reminded on the way that I definitely totally blushed when
I said his name aloud for the very first time. *Reon*.

21

When I close my eyes before bed, I think about how I could keep them on the Servant Boy without actually being next to him. I mean, at best, I need to stay as far away from him… before whatever this is I'm feeling gets worse, or spins me out of control.

So when the morning comes, I'm settling for the plan to send either Moyra or Leon out to check on the Servant Boy's existence in the house. That is after I'll let them know about my Royal Phantom suspicion that I forgot to tell them both, since they had been so busy.

I bet they've probably already started to imagine things about me and the Servant Boy after our read-and-meal session together late at night in the library. Moyra would be acting like my mother or Lady Francoise, how I'd seem to be falling in love with just about anyone other than a prince. Then, there's Leon; if he's put together what he'd seen back in the town square. I mean, looking back, it almost appeared as if I was about to *kiss* the Servant

Boy, when I was really only trying to get the truth out of him. But surely Leon wouldn't misunderstand? He hasn't got the time to ask me anything about it but he probably already has a lot of questions lingering in mind – if he hasn't interrogated the Servant Boy himself first. He's my protector, after all.

When someone knocks on the door, I expect that Moyra will be coming in with my breakfast in bed.

Imagine the horror on my face when I find Reon– I mean, the Servant Boy, walking towards the bed with my early meal in his full white attire, same as yesterday.

By instinct, I hurriedly swing my hand for the neatly-folded navy-blue silky robe on my bedside table and cover my white dress pajamas with it.

What the hell is he doing in my room?

Well, at least he made good on his words. He is indeed the first person I'm seeing this morning. Not even Leon, whose unexpected presence wouldn't surprise me as much.

Merely seconds after, however, I see Leon go straight for almost breaking my bedroom door.

"What are you doing?" he bellows menacingly even beyond the passageway. "It is *not* your duty to get Her Highness' morning meal! It should either be the First Lady in Waiting, or the maids, or on some very special occasions, *me*." And by very special occasion, Leon must mean whenever it was our adventure time back in the Twelfth

Provincial Region.

"My deep apology," the Servant Boy says, though it doesn't look like he regrets it. "Although, it has come to the agreement between me and Her Royal Highness that we will be seeing each other first thing in the morning. Isn't that right, Princess?" The Servant Boy shifts his head towards me with an innocent smile.

Meanwhile, Leon stares at me with a creasing forehead. "Is this true?"

Suddenly, I panic. "Well... yes... but–"

"As now it's been confirmed, we'd better let Her Royal Highness carry on with her morning routine, shall we?" The Servant Boy proceeds with placing the covered tray on a table near the wall. He then gently leads Leon out of my bedroom and says, "Your concern is much appreciated," before closing the door as noiseless as Leon has been left petrified behind it.

Is it just me or the Servant Boy looks to be in a hurry?

"What have you done?" I interrogate the Servant Boy as he approaches. "You're twisting my words!"

Quite the manipulative Royal Phantom, even when I'm still waiting for him to blurt out the word "kid".

"If you don't slowly but hurry with your meal, then we will have less time to sneak into the Crown Prince's castle." The Servant Boy eagerly but patiently picks up then prepares my breakfast on top of my bed.

"The… what? We're going to what? Where? But how are we even going to–"

Without notice, he hastily but gently puts a spoon of warm pea soup into my mouth. But the one thing that makes me completely lost for words is how his left fingers press lightly on my chin while his right feeds me, then brush delicately against the spill around my lips.

The sheer audacity.

If I hadn't been so tongue-tied, I'd have blurted out something about a handkerchief, or some royal protocol, but it's already too late now. My heart is beating rapidly in the most frantic way, I only remain speechless.

"You heard me," he says. "We're going to sneak into the mysterious Crown Prince's castle, from *here*."

22

I always knew that there was something special about this library. It's just the idea of a secret passage to the Crown Prince's castle leading from here was never in my way of thinking at the time, let alone now to process. And the fact that the Butler is here willingly to assist me and the Servant Boy is even more unexpected, considering it's so hard for him to have Leon and the other guards walking around inside the house, even when they've agreed with the time limit he's set upon them.

"Allow me," the Butler says. His voice is like a deep soothing narrator for bedtime stories.

"He speaks!" I cheer quietly towards the Servant Boy.

"He does, only when he thinks it's necessary," he whispers.

The Butler walks to one of the walls – the one in the direction where you can see the sun rise. He picks up one of the books on the second highest row and fifth from the left, then pushes the wood partition behind the empty space.

Following his effort, half of the bookshelf wall opens to a narrow passageway about two meters wide and three meters tall.

When the Servant Boy and I step into the small corridor, I realise that the Butler stays where he is, so I make a little detour and sneak just my head out into the library.

"You're not coming?" I ask.

"I'll be here, Your Royal Highness," the Butler answers, then bows.

As only the two of us walk down further into what seems to be an underground tunnel, I ask the Servant Boy again the same question I've asked many times before. "Who are you?" For perhaps more than a dozen times, if not already hundreds and thousands in my mind. "How do you even–"

"The Butler and I, we are sort of the caretaker of this mansion. And this place, as unsightly as it appears from the outside, is only to hide the true reason why it was built in the first place. A secret passageway."

I nod in silence while my eyes scan the area, but I'm thinking, *you know, if I just happen to die here, no one would know.*

I stare at the back of the Servant Boy as I carefully move my feet behind him, but then I realise, it looks like it'd be easier for me to kill him from here than the other way around. And so I've decided to let the presumption slide.

After what seems like a very long walk down then up then down then up again, we reach a long ladder seemingly towards the surface. "The Crown Prince's castle," I whisper while grinning. *Yes!*

The Servant Boy climbs up first to try to move around the wheel to open the cover. But before he disappears from view, it doesn't seem like he's expecting anyone to be just on the other side, like I would. So now I'm thinking about all the possibilities of who he could be, considering he doesn't seem to worry at all about being caught.

Let's say that I'm not already fixated by the idea that he may be the Royal Phantom, of which I already am, so what are the chances that he could also be the–

"There," he says excitedly.

I choose to brush the thought off for now, then I lift my arms and legs one at a time up towards the circle light.

I won't ever say unless I'm one hundred percent sure.

From down here, what's up there looks too bright to be the interior of an empty room of a castle; unless there are people around, which makes total sense since everybody is supposed to be inside their house.

A few climbs away from the exit, I feel more unsure if we're not going to be caught. Or does he want *me* to get caught? Is that the whole point? I mean, why does it look so bright? And why did he decide to show me this secret passage in the first place?

Although, it sounds awfully quiet up there. Either the guards are expecting us, or… "Are we alone?" I try to scream as softly as I can. "It's the King's decree. I don't want to mess with the King," I say. History books have implied enough so. Only a complete idiot would dare to mess with any of the Kings, who had all retained and defeated more than enough enemies, turned their land into protectorates now known as Provincial Regions. So even as naturally rebellious as I am, I still don't want to be on *our* King's bad side, who, just like all his great ancestors, is widely known as being awfully strict about his royal decree and terribly merciless to his disobedient royal subjects. I mean, I don't want to die an insufferable death just because I stupidly get caught snooping around the Crown Prince's castle for fun. Even I have to admit, that would be a very stupid reason to die.

"Yes. Come on up," he reassures.

"Alright. I still don't trust you but I will," I scream softly.

This curiosity in me may very well become the death of me someday.

As soon as I reach, I feel the breeze of fresh air. It's the kind of smell after the rain. Wet moss and earthy wind of scent fill up my nose to make clear to me of where we are.

We're on the hill.

"This is *not* the Crown Prince's castle," I complain. I look around at what seems to be the entrance to a deep forest. "You said we were going to sneak into the Crown Prince's castle!"

"I never said that we would sneak from the inside," he shrugs. I'm still staring at him in complete disappointment. "What? You thought I was the Crown Prince or something?" he snorts.

Blood rushes rising up to my cheeks. Luckily I never blurted it out, otherwise I would've sounded so stupid.

This is exactly why I always need to be one hundred percent sure.

"Alright, it's almost seven o'clock," he informs. "We're just in time. Look!"

The Servant Boy turns my shoulders one hundred eighty degrees around into the view of three mountainous sparkling diamonds that look into the ocean, except they're not just some gigantic gemstones. What's more, there's something inside it that almost looks apparent beneath.

"Wow," I say under my breath. And as the sun rises at a certain angle directly towards it, what's inside becomes visible to the eyes. "I think that's the library right there," I say as my pointer finger draws a straight line in the air.

"And that's the first thing you see? How predictable," he answers while shaking with guffaw, to which response I let out my laugh in a gleeful way.

"Okay, what about that? Is that a kitchen?" My right pointy finger rises slowly with the sunlight as it forms another line and upturns.

"You tell me," he says. "And what's that next to it?"

"That? That's probably just a dining room," I say.

"Not the one next to it?"

"That's probably one of the dining rooms too."

"Why does there have to be more than one dining room?" he asks peculiarly.

"Well, the palace back home has separate dining rooms based on certain occasions, types of royals, types of guests, various royal staff, and blah blah blah." Even I don't see the point of this. "So I'm guessing it's the same for the Crown Prince's castle. Mind you, we even have a Dining Hall. Very unnecessary, if you ask me."

"I see. So that's why they're all around the kitchen," he nods his head.

I consider his way of reply. Is he being serious right now?

"What about that one?" he asks again.

"Where exactly? I can't tell." I'm now seeing about five to six rooms at the same time, while the library and the kitchen-like below have just turned back into a concealed glass.

In response, he moves my pointy finger while his left palm still rests on my shoulder. *The nerve of him*, I think – but still, I don't yet complain aloud. If he was one of the mummies, I'd have probably already punched him in the face for sure. But even now I can feel his soft breath next to my right ear and… I don't even mind. Screw social status for now. "There. Do you see it now?"

"I don't know. Looks spacious. Probably the Festivity Hall." I swallow.

"I see. Is that where people dance?" he asks.

"Yes," I languish. He tilts his head in confusion. "I'm sorry. I didn't mean it that way. I mean, yes, that is where. Such as a Royal Coming-of-Age Ceremony. That kind of event." The most recent I can think of, since I skipped all of the other royal parties for the last three years. My Royal Rapport is technically a blank page.

"If I ask you a personal question now…" I can sense his gland swallowing.

"What sort of question?" My eyes are still stuck on the scientifically-magical castle, but I tilt my head just a bit.

"About the dance," he says. "Your dance."

I think, where do I even start? The boring conversation? The unintentional massacre? Or the one where I didn't get to dance because I chose to fly with the Royal Phantom– him, presumably? Anyway, what does he really want to know?

"Did you get to choose a prince during the ceremony?" he asks further. "The news has never really said anything about what was actually happening in your ceremony."

"No, I did not." Then the image of those mummies comes to mind and I immediately shiver. "Thank God, I didn't."

"Why?" he asks.

"Well, I didn't see any prince that I wanted to dance with, that's why." And the sword fights. But then I think about how I thought of Leon that night. "Maybe I never will. I don't know."

"So you don't care whether you're going to dance with a prince or a commoner?" he asks.

"I don't know." I pause. "It doesn't matter, I think." But then my eyes squint with peculiarity without his knowledge. What's with the sudden nosiness?

"What about the Crown Prince?" he asks again. "What if he suddenly reveals himself and asks you for a dance in front of everybody?"

He must be talking about the Crown Prince's upcoming Royal Coming-of-Age Ceremony, which is probably the single biggest thing everyone's been talking about in the whole kingdom for the past year. Naturally, he'd want a sip of inside information too. But… "Why does it matter?" I ask curiously.

That's quite a strange circumstance as an imagination. I never even thought of it before. *The worst princess ever born.*

"Well, for a start, you look like the kind who would dismiss the Crown Prince's offer to dance in public. And that would be an embarrassment to the whole monarch, wouldn't it?"

In response, I accidentally let out a chortle I didn't manage to suppress. "I mean, if he turns out to be sort of a jerk, I definitely will." *The worst princess ever born.* But then I shake my head slightly. Back to the case. "You know what, about the Crown Prince, has no one really ever seen him before here? Not even a single soul? What about any of his royal knights?" All of a sudden, I'm reminded of that scary guy on the black horse.

"I suppose if anyone truly knows about the Crown Prince's identity besides the King, it has to be the Royal Knight Commander," he extrapolates.

Straight away, I go straight into my deep-thinking mode.

The Crown Prince. The *mysterious* Crown Prince. No one has ever seen him before. *The heart of the real Crown Prince is what I really want.* The Royal Phantom. Murder. The man with a red-velvet suit. Burnt. The Royal Knight Commander – that has got to be that scary guy on the black horse, Yves Thevenet, right? The town folks seem to think that he's the only one who knows about the Crown Prince. And everyone on the island is terrified of him. But say, he had killed the real Crown Prince, turned a random boy into the future king-to-be, changed his face, brainwashed him into his little puppet, and then someday, he'd manage to rule the whole kingdom when the fake Crown Prince took over the throne. Who's going to know? But, if that's what really happened, why threw the body out in public and in such a dramatic way? Wouldn't it be safer to just dispose of the body quietly so the King would never find out? When the King himself has sent the royal proclamation, that's already a threat by itself to be suspected. So what is it? I guess the real problem is, we'll never truly know until the body has been fully identified. Who is that body? But that will take weeks, maybe months. Maybe that's why the body had to be burnt in the first place. Such a delay will buy a lot of time for the real killer to let loose, or worse, make the rest of his or her plan come true. That's it. *A delay.* That's got to be it. That means now, I just need to buy some of the time back by keeping my eyes and ears open too. *Like the Crown Prince.* And maybe that's what he's been doing – if he's still alive.

Alright. I think I've set myself a plan.

Starting tomorrow, at school, meeting the Crown Prince in person will be my mission. I'll barge into the Royal Prince Academy if I have to.

Now, where was I with the Crown Prince's castle?

"Back from your deep thoughts?" The Servant Boy welcomes my return from my stupor.

In response, I raise my eyebrows. Did he just–

However, soon after, my attention flips side quickly as the inside view of the Crown Prince's castle has turned invisible under the looking glass. Completely. It's turned back to being as concealed as opposed to everything around it is visible on its Brobdingnagian-like mirror.

"Where is it gone?" I panic.

"We only got a minute," he says. "And one minute has passed."

"Well, can we go again tomorrow?" My eyes spark with anticipation.

"We can – except, we cannot." He then gently turns my body towards where the academies are. I sigh. "Besides, this place is always packed with people around this hour when they go foraging, so only today we could go through this tunnel. It would be very odd if people see us coming out of the bushes, don't you think?"

"I guess you're right," I say as I look down on the ground. Then I turn my body towards the forest. "And that means, no one is going foraging today, right?" I ask with sparkling eyes.

"True. What are you suggesting?"

"Well, are we going there now?" I ask. "Because I think we should." I literally jump out of excitement.

"We can, if you want to; though, I don't think it's quite suitable for a princess," he says while raising his eyebrows.

"Then it makes perfect sense because I'm not a princess," I say sarcastically. *The worst princess ever born.* I guess it's just about time that I fully embrace it.

"Well then, take it that I'm not a prince, shall we go

explore?" he says with a big happy grin.

Going to a strange forest with the Royal Phantom alone? Sounds like a very bad idea to begin with.

Regardless, my eyes beam with light as I nod my head repeatedly.

23

As we saunter down the forest, I take in the refreshing air and twirl around. I'm enjoying every moment, I even dance a little as I walk.

"Sometimes I feel like I should've been born in the woods instead of a royal palace," I say.

"That's strange, considering that's where I was born."

"You were born in the woods?" I stop my pace and grasp his shoulders with my hands abruptly. Which gets me to notice. He smells like the forest too.

But as I've just realised what I'm doing, I immediately let go.

"Sixteen years ago, I was," he laughs. He then puts his hands in his pockets, his whole head turns slightly red in the process.

"This wood?"

"Not this wood," he clears this throat. "It's… somewhere far away from here."

"Where?" I ask curiously.

"Near where the Capital Region is now. I believe the kingdom had just barely survived a deleterious attack from the enemy, so my birth itself was a miracle in a sense." I detect sadness trying so hard not to burn his eyes, but it shows.

"Oh, right. I remember that part in History," I reply. "Someone had been trying to kill the King from the inside. I think that was just a few months before I was born, and even then the kingdom was still recovering. I guess you could call it efficiency that they got to compile the royal birth ceremony of all the princes and princesses who were born that year. I'd say, just like your birth, it was a blessing in disguise."

After expressing my own opinion, weirdly I feel like asking more questions. Which day of the month? Where is that wood exactly? What was the process like? When did he move to this island? Why? And where is his family? But Lady Francoise's full hard-on empathy training reminds me that I should keep my mouth shut if I have too many questions to ask in my mind.

But in contrast to my own thoughts, the Servant Boy lets out a genuine laugh. What's so funny about what I've just said? I don't get it.

"Let's move on with our expedition," he says, after finishing his laugh. "There are still so many things here that I want to show you."

"Like what?" I'm intrigued.

"Okay. Primary but not necessary, have you ever done foraging before?"

No, I think. Solving murder cases may indeed require me some overnight trips in the past, but never a need for foraging – or at least, not on my part. Leon would never allow me to.

"Does it matter?" I ask.

"Because we may need to prepare for ourselves some lunch should we decide to stay longer here."

I suddenly hear Lady Francoise say, *A princess never prepares her own meal.* I think that was either from the *Book of Manners for Princesses* or *Rules of Being a Princess.*

The Servant Boy seemingly tries to work out what I think inquisitively. "It's more than fine if you don't prefer to. We can always go back to the mansion for–"

"No! Let's forage." I start screaming like a kid would. Leon's not here, so would I pass on a golden opportunity like this? Hell, no! "I want to do some foraging!" Then I walk past him further deeper to the forest even though I have no idea how foraging is done or where we should go.

I notice the Servant Boy giggles from behind me. "On your right, Princess," he says as I'm going left, and so I walk backward steadily to change my course while covering the right side of my face, and then I slow my pace on the correct path until he's next on my side again.

I hear him softly laughing again. Why do I manage to keep embarrassing myself in front of him?

"Are we going to cut some trees?" I ask, trying to look cool. "Because we may need some axes in that case, which I am quite familiar with of using." That, though I only have the experience holding for scientific purposes. Not within Lady Francoise's field of study, of course.

"Whatever that for?" He asks me with an unfeigned smile and ludicrously big emerald-green eyes.

"I mean, for lunch. You mean we're going to cook, right? Don't we need woods for that? And maybe a big rock? Like a fireplace?" My eyes widen innocently as I enquire. Because that's what seems logical to me. I mean, I've never cooked if one doesn't take a poison as food – again, for scientific purposes. But that's what you'd need, right?

In turn, he rolls his body to his stomach, highly amused. I look at him with a peculiar face. What did I say again that sounded so funny to him?

"Branches just fine, Princess. And some fallen woods should be lying around. And no big rock. I repeat, no big rock!" he instructs.

"Okay, okay, I get it. No big rock," I reply with a shrug on my shoulders.

Subsequently, we're able to pick a location of his choice to gather some branches for our natural stove. The perfect spot is surrounded by tall trees and flourishing green bushes. Right in the middle, there are three tree stumps forming a loop, with two are of similar size, just nice for our table and two congenial seats for lunch.

Next, the Servant Boy teaches me all different kinds of plants and flowers in the forest – which one is edible, which one is poisonous. He is quite the botanist, which is nowhere near close to my lack of expertise, and that is on top of his proven anatomy proficiency. There are little moments when my stupidity overcomes my inexperience, such as the time I ask if we're going to catch some fish for lunch where the sea is just on the other side of the Crown Prince's castle far away from here. The Servant Boy laughs uncontrollably and teaches me to catch some rabbits instead.

I turn ecstatic when the fireplace– I mean, the campfire, blazes from the branches; although, the Servant Boy did most of the work while I was just watching his face– I mean, watching him turn the flame flicker to firm.

This also brings me back to the past, when Leon did most of the hard work too like today. Little moments like this makes me wonder what he's doing now back in the mansion. But when the Servant Boy waves at me my first grilled rabbit in a tiny-branch skewer, I can't help but be distracted back to the present minute.

I can't remember the last time I had such a great conversation and a good time with someone. The feeling is like for many hours, I'm allowing myself to forget about

the idea of the Servant Boy being the Royal Phantom
completely.

No. Not the Servant Boy. *Reon*.

24

When the early evening is about to come, Reon suggests that it's time for us to get back to the mansion, to my own dismay. I feel like staying here a bit longer but the thought of Leon could barge into the library at any second he'd realise I was missing scares me more than the thought of being bored. So we walk back to where we came, climb down the tunnel, hike up and down once more until we reach the library again.

Arriving, we find the Butler is peacefully killing his time by doing some reading. I guess since he's been so relaxed, Leon hasn't broken into the library just yet.

In a very efficient way, once taking notice of our presence, the Butler unhurriedly places the book back into the shelf, then arranges the systematic back on to close the entrance. Back on the table, I also see two covered plates and one empty with crumbs, which I presume was supposed to be my lunch and Reon's.

"Help yourself," the Butler says.

Well, fortunately, I've got a big appetite. So it's now as if the three of us had been in the library, having lunch and reading books all along. Just the three of us.

Moments after, I hear the trumpet being blown again. And when I coincidentally catch sight of the scroll on the other table, it's clicked.

"Shit!" I scream, which is totally not appropriate for a princess to say. "I forgot about my school assignment!"

In a frantic way, I run towards the said-table and roll out the scroll all the while I'm still standing. I read it over, over, and over again.

If you could only get one wish, what would it be?

You can ask for anything you want, you shall write whatever you truly desire, and one thing will surely be granted – should you pass the threshold point.

May we recommend: a specific that fills up your royal needs.

"Royal need," I mumble anxiously, my palms resting on the table. "What is my royal need?" I start to move my right leg repeatedly. Whenever Lady Francoise saw this during our private princess lessons, she would smack my thigh so hard with a book. "Argh, I still don't get it!" I shout.

I push the top of my head with both hands.

I know the Counsellor kept insisting on me getting

an upgraded house, and I was planning to fill that out in a moment of urgency such as this. But now, even more than when I already did before, I really don't feel like moving at all. No. I *have* to stay here, no matter the cost, now that I know about the secret passageway. So there goes my backup answer into the drain, my last resort.

I keep trying to think about what I feel I really need right now. As a royal. My royal need.

"It says 'royal needs'." All of a sudden, Reon is standing next to my right. His green eyes focus on the scroll, his arms shuffle against his chest, his body soars high like a tower.

That reminds me. I haven't even thought of getting my butt onto the seat and I don't think I even have time for that.

Meanwhile, the Butler stays where he's been, giving the two of us some space to talk in private again.

"Whatever," I say briefly, then go back to my panic mode.

"What are you thinking?" he asks.

"DNA results from the murdered victim in town, if I'm being honest."

And to that, Reon can't help but laugh again.

"I'm being serious," I'm perturbed. "I have no idea what to write."

"Well, that is not exactly a royal need, is it?" he says, and then he laughs again.

So not helping.

Think, Seraphine. Think.

"What would you write?" I ask him, since Moyra's answer sounds ridiculous – but I'm so desperate that I'm actually considering it.

"Let's see. Picture I'm a prince. I live in a palace. I have people to attend to me. And that means, I already have everything I need: food, water, clothing, and shelter. What difference does it make to a commoner?"

"I don't know. What makes it royal, I guess? Power. Ruler. Palace. Castle. Status. Hereditary right. Responsibility–"

"Responsibility," Reon repeats. "When you think of a royal as *just* a human being, what else do you think they need?"

"Nothing, I guess?" I tilt my head and squint my eyes.

What the hell is he talking about?

"If not in different circumstances, the royal *needs* to attend to what the people need, and nothing else," he propounds. "A royal *needs* to fulfill such a responsibility."

That is… groundbreakingly… the perfect answer.

I find myself staring into Reon's emerald-green eyes for the longest time, as his to the bluest of mine. Is he always this handsome? Not to mention he's incredibly wise, then the unnecessary extension, *for a servant boy* – and, *he's right.*

On top of that, it's in this exact same moment that I realise, maybe the fact that I can't think of anything else is the answer.

Nothing. Or, *nothing else.*

I gain back my composure and hold my head up high with the scroll in my hand. I roll it on my way to the mansion entrance where the guards are waiting to collect my assignment. It's enclosed like new just when I reach.

"Here you go," I say, in front of the same amount of people as when the King's decree came. Reon may be somewhere behind me, hidden, watching from against the wall, maybe even smiling too.

After the guard leaves, Moyra approaches me – still with her cleaning tools on her hand – and whispers, "What did you write, Princess?"

Two seconds later, Leon whispers into my other ear. "I was just about to suggest: extra guards from home for more protection. But you weren't coming out of the library. So, what did you write?"

"Nothing," I say.

"Nothing? What do you mean?" Both Leon and Moyra ask with the exact same words at the exact same time, their tone losing total composure. They look at each other for a second out of surprise, then shift their head back at me.

"It means," I reply calmly, "I leave it blank."

The royal needs *to attend to what the people need, and*

nothing else.

So, nothing. And nothing else.

25

The heart of the real Crown Prince is what I really want.

I hear the voice in my dream, but it's not the Royal Phantom's. Even within my unconscious mind, I don't think he's the killer. And maybe due to some swayed prejudice over Reon, I don't think of him to be the Royal Phantom anymore. No. More like, now, I don't want him to be.

I'd like Reon to stay a mere servant boy.

He's so much more than just a servant boy, I now hear my own voice say. *So much more.*

When I suddenly wake up, the outdoor sound rises with the sun. It's not as quiet as yesterday morning. No one has been to get out, until the six sharp of Monday morning comes – that is, the first day of school. *Today.*

I grab all thirteen newspapers that are already laying on my side table. For some reason, the words about the murder in the town square have gotten out throughout the whole wide kingdom due to the King's royal decree.

I see Gaspard– I mean, Rainpard on the first page with a dubious face and his two fragile thumbs up hanging, but I'm glad that he's smart enough to have not said anything about the Royal Phantom's card.

Rainpard, I leave you to it.

I wonder which side he's actually on.

Regardless, some journalists seem to have pointed out that the Royal Phantom was involved, due to how the body was falling from the sky.

Could the phantom thief be a murderer this time? it says, since he's the only one so far who's managed to make flying look so easy. As if he'd easily move on from the twelve sets of crowns to one heart of the Crown Prince.

Consequently, some suspected that the King's royal decree to lock all of us in the house on Sunday was to ensure the process of moving the Crown Prince back to the Capital Region smoothly. But I don't buy it. Not even for one second. I mean, isn't he supposed to make an appearance at school today?

Plus, this whole thing about the Royal Phantom being the murderer they're all going with, I'm not buying it either.

The Royal Phantom is not the murderer and I will prove it.

I can't believe I've just said that in my head.

But the door suddenly opens to Moyra with the usual breakfast tray on the bed. I flip the newspaper and put it back on my side of the bed.

After I'm done with all the meal, she waits for me to wash my body, then attends to put on heavy make-up on my face and a formal white ball gown with golden embroideries on my body as well as a pair of matching slingback heels on my feet.

Next, she rolls up to my elbow a pair of two long gloves in white as a finishing touch. "I know you don't like it, but sadly, the whole look is your *school uniform*," she says. "And now, let's do your hair. Let's see." She's now reading the instructions. "They require a high ponytail, braided this way, then this nice little crown on top."

I look at myself in the mirror and I have no idea who in the world is in there.

"Do you mean I have to dress like this every single day?"

"Six days a week, unfortunately. We've already got the other five sets ready for you. Oh, gosh. You don't think they're trying to make all the princesses look the same, do you?" Moyra then continues doing my hair as she shakes her head.

Sigh. I'm already hating school.

Once I'm ready, the door opens again to find Leon ready to accompany me to the Royal Princess Academy. He looks a bit startled as he sees the super-significantly-transformed me.

"Don't even think about it," I warn Leon.

"I'm not," he giggles, and so I glare at him. "Anyway, the carriage is ready for you, Princess," he says. "I think the horse misses me."

"Sure it does. Even I'm already missing Lady Francoise," I reply. Ironic to say, but it's true. As hard as she was to me, at least she wasn't as *military* as this academy.

Leon snorts and walks beside me. *He walks beside me again*, I think, and so I can't help but beam with ease. I've got my friend back, at least.

When I reach the mansion entrance, I see Reon is wearing a slightly different outfit and is bringing on his shoulder a tiny golden cabinet of what seems to be a covered mountain of school supplies. He's already smiling at me in the gentlest way, his eyes follow my pace as I walk slowly down the stairs.

"Please don't tell me he's going to school with Her Highness," Leon protests at the Counsellor who I've just noticed has been standing right next to that fake small tree on the left side of the entrance.

It seems Leon's already hating Reon's presence, even when he hasn't said anything.

"*The Servant Boy is to assist any prince or princess as they're serving their royal duty in the academies by carrying their educational supplies,*" he reads from what comes across as a guide book for the Royal Academies staff. "It's only an antecedent in both Royal Academies. I don't see a problem," he adds.

"That's something *I* can do," Leon argues, then strides towards Reon only to stand in front of him. "Besides, there's something about you that seems fishy," he says in a lower voice, but I can still hear him.

"Such as?" Reon replies, but his voice sounds a bit different. Like deeper, and fierce, instead of the usual benign.

Reon stands firm on his ground and glares at Leon right back. It's not against the kismet how they're both just perfectly the same height, as their stare forms a terrifying horizontal static.

"Such as, you're constantly stepping over the line. The Princess may never think of the need for such boundaries, but you need to know your place, *Servant Boy*."

"I know perfectly where I stand," Reon replies with full confidence.

Leon brings his face closer frontward. "If the Butler hadn't been in the library with the two of you yesterday, I'd have broken the door into pieces. Don't even get me started with the breakfast episode, which will never happen again on my watch. Now, hand me over Her Royal Highness' school essentials."

"Please, gentlemen, the time is ticking," the Counsellor says as he walks speedily and separates the two with his hands, as far away as he can until his arms are in full stretch. "We are almost late, for which I'm going to be blamed for, of which I will be able to blame no one."

Except, I know who to blame. The Royal Princess Academy for requiring all the students to put some photoshoot-like make-up on and braid their hair in such a complicated way.

"I'd say, just let the servant boy do his duty, while you do yours. Stick to the guide." The Counsellor shifts his head back and forth between left and right. "As a royal guard, young boy, you are allowed to stand at close proximity. Now, as for you, *Servant Boy*," his tone changes slightly to disdain, "I don't know what's been going on in here, but you are only to assist the Princess and nothing else." The Counsellor now taps the book repeatedly with his hand. "I stick to the customary." He then points at both Leon and Reon in noticeable anger, his precious book almost slips. "You two stick to your duty."

The Counsellor then shifts his body towards Leon, and his tone changes back to normal. "I believe the same case will follow with other princes and princesses. The more a princess adheres to the rule, the better her grade will be. Thus, there should be no trivial problems such as this. Now let us all walk to the carriage. We cannot be late!"

The Counsellor claps his hands and directs me to my transport while Leon and Reon walk dazedly behind us. "Now, Your Royal Highness, you will be sitting in this second carriage right here." The same extravagant golden carriage that brought me from the airport. "You will have all the large space to yourself." The footman immediately opens the door to the carriage, but I choose to stick to my ground.

Instead, I proceed to watch the Counsellor as he saunters towards the others.

"The servant boy will sit with me in the first carriage." He points to his way of transport looking cosy with its wooden panels plainly painted white. "Now, Servant Boy, I will be telling you all the things you need to know to assist Princess Seraphine during her study. Remember, *I* need her to marry a prince, otherwise *I* will lose my job," he shrieks. I swallow in effect. "As for the royal guards… Well, you can ride your horses whatever manners you like. Now, come along, and off we go!" The Counsellor in a way is surprised that I'm still outside and so he forcefully pushes my back to quickly get into the carriage.

"I sure hope the princess will get the attention of at least one of the princes in the academy, for *my* sake," I hear the Counsellor loudly mumbles after closing the door to the carriage himself, leaving the footman perplexed.

I roll my eyes. But at the same time, I feel so sorry for him for being assigned to me. He may want to start looking for another job, I think.

The worst princess ever born.

But in no time now. Passing better houses. Passing much better houses. Passing the hills. And then, I see we're coming into a short enclosed garden wall followed by a beautiful school gate in gold that can only fit about two carriages at a time in width.

What feels like the shortest time but it's not, we've finally arrived at the building with a sign that says "Royal Princess Academy". Everything looks the same as what I've seen in a glance from above, except for cemented embroideries around each of the windows with their red and golden tapestries.

And right across on the building's left side has to be the Royal Prince Academy.

The footman opens my carriage and almost immediately after, the Counsellor takes charge to walk me into the school. I take a glance at Leon and Reon behind me – both look even colder than the Antarctic.

I'm only a few steps away from the school entrance, but I can already see about hundreds of people right before me as the giant golden door stays open. Based on their uniforms, all include princesses plus their royal guards and servant boys. All in the same categories dress the same, even the royal academy staff too.

This really feels like the military, and I bet they place great emphasis on discipline – which is definitely not my strongest forte.

I walk as my head moves around. When I look up, the hallway ceiling rockets into the very top. Different rooms encompass the large area in layers of stairs, almost looking like the library at this-island home with rooms as its bookshelves and doors as books.

Soon enough, every group's Counsellor directs each of us into one of the rooms far across, which turns out to be a very big hall. There's a big stage in front of… one… four… six… twenty four chairs with a very wide gap in between, as I finish counting. What's more is that each row of seats is in different colors. Deep brown at the very back. Silver and gold next. And then white at the very front – so uniquely sparkling, it illuminates with the light.

"Now, Your Highness, could you please stand over there, until the headmistress calls your name to your seat." The Counsellor points at where the other princesses already start lining in the middle of the hall, standing like they're waiting to be seated instead of dancing in a ballroom."

Whatever happens, don't forget to smile," he twirls his fingers gracefully around his cheeks, "and bows," he lowers his head.

But almost like lightning strikes, he's beyond appalled to see me only watching him with a blank face. "Show me your smile, Your Highness." I turn both corners of my mouth upward by the force of my mind. "Then bow," he says as he presses both my shoulders, "and spread your wings." The Counsellor moves his hands against the pants under his coat as if he was wearing a skirt. "Spread your wings, Your Royal Highness." And so I do as I'm forcefully told, just to make him stop talking. "Great. Alright, you're ready. Off you go, Princess. And don't forget. Smile, bow, then spread your wings."

I roll my eyes as I turn my body and force my feet to walk to where the line is.

Seriously, this is so lame. Why do we have to present ourselves to each other like this? Why can't we just go to class straight away?

26

As I now wait among a long row of creepy dolls
(that sadly includes me), I notice that the princess right next
to me is the same girl that bumped into me the other day.
The chocolate-candy princess. And it's not because of her
face, considering we're all now currently looking the same.
Rather, it's the little smudges of chocolate on her upper
skirt.

A few people come up on stage to place a new
podium stand right in the middle, then quickly run away
as if they were invisible. Subsequently, a middle-aged lady
comes on the stage and stands at a lofty height. Wearing a
long golden dress made of heavy-weight fabrics, her two
giant inward curls on both sides to customarily match her
outfit.

Everyone stays silent like they're holding their
breath. If Yves Thevenet is as scary as his scars, this woman
is as terrifying as her demeanour.

The lady introduces herself as Princess Prudence

Delafosse, the Headmistress, before going on with the things to know. First, she mentions something about each class having its own restroom. Second, the servant boys must put our school supplies in the Cabinet Room. There are four Cabinet Rooms, of which one to go will depend on the class their princess is assigned to. In addition, Princess Prudence specifically describes the location of the Cabinet Room as completely intentional, meaning, the servant boys cannot be seen running around the palace, which brings her next point to be about the royal guards, of whom they can only be on stand-by outside of the academy building.

Finally, she announces that she will begin calling our names to our seats.

"I believe you are already familiar with our kingdom's royal grade scheme, which officially starts for every prince and princess the moment they turn thirteen. May I remind you that your attendance and contribution to every royal banquet and ceremonial festivities for the last three years have been effectively remarked on your Royal Rapport, that you get to be here this morning. The finest and foremost of all the princesses in the whole Kingdom of Oceastarasia."

Glad to be reminded that for the past three years too, I had been doing nothing of its merit to accumulate it.

"The class you're assigned to will be *quite* similar to your current royal grade. If I say Bronze before your name, that means you belong in Class Bronze. So on, and so forth. I take it now that no one is as oblivious as I am being understood. Nevertheless, I will forthwith commence. Bronze."

I guess she starts with the lowest of the hierarchy first. That means, my name is up next.

"Princess Amelia of the Tenth Provincial Region."

Alright, maybe not the lowest of the lowest, since she's not calling my name.

"Bronze. Princess Cyrille of the Fourth Provincial Region."

Okay, maybe it's in alphabetical order.

"Bronze. Princess Noemie of the Seventh Provincial Region."

Regardless, I'm expecting my name to be called soon.

After a few minutes have passed and three more names have been called that are not mine, she finally pauses then says that she's moving on to the next class.

Wait. What about me?

"Silver. Princess Rachelle of the Eleventh Provincial Region."

Silver? I move my head around.

We're now up to Silver? Did I hear it wrongly?

"Silver. Princess Anastasia of the Third Provincial Region."

She did say Silver.

This can't be happening. I can't be in Silver class. It's

impossible.

Remember my student house.

"Silver. Princess Laurine of the Ninth Provincial Region."

Remember what the Counsellor said.

"Silver. Princess Romaine of the Sixth Provincial Region."

The worst princess ever born.

Regardless, a couple more names for Class Silver have been called but it's still not mine.

I'm so confused.

"Gold."

Gold? We're now already in Gold?

"Princess Georgette of the Second Provincial Region."

Oh, wait. I know her. That's one of my distant relatives. And she definitely has way more royal points than me, I can assure you, considering how she's more like the opposite of me – attending all the royal parties ever existed in and out of the region while I was too busy looking at multiple dead bodies.

 As such, my mind can't even bother to listen to the other called names anymore. This is so bizarre. There is no way I could be in Bronze, nor Silver, and now, Gold?

"At last," Princess Prudence exhales and sends out a big smile, "We have now come to… Diamond."

Diamond? What the hell is a Diamond?

What is going on?

I look behind me to all the guards and servant boys and they're all now moving their heads to the left and right, just as confused. I see the seated princesses are now even whispering next to each other.

"Let's begin," Princess Prudence announces with a big smile.

As the headmistress calls out the Class Diamond names, I try to pay more attention to their names *and* their Provincial Regions this time.

Princess Ghyslaine from the First Provincial Region, who looks kind of snobby as she smirks at the other eighteen princesses in the back row before taking her seat.

Princess Leonie from the Third Provincial Region, who looks kind of sassy as she literally yawns on stage while her left palm gently taps on her both lips.

Princess Orianne of the Fourth Provincial Region, who looks very familiar to me. Who could she be? Oh! I think she's that girl who cheered the most for that periodic-table prince back in town.

Then Princess Coralie of the Ninth Provincial Region, who takes her longest, sweetest time to come down the little stairs. I suspect something about her heels doesn't feel right, but anyway. Even Princess Prudence starts looking at her watch. She's that slow at the moment.

In the meanwhile, I take in that the chocolate-candy princess is the only one still standing besides me, and she looks as perplexed.

"Hey, do you know anything about being a Diamond?" she asks quietly, her head tilted towards me but her eyes are still looking at the stage.

"No, I do not," I whisper back.

"This is strange," she says. "I know I'm a Gold, but I've never heard anything about a Diamond royal status."

Well, at least she knows she's a Gold. Good for her. I mean, I don't even know where I stand, because I thought I was even less than a Bronze before coming here. And to be honest, I don't even really know what it means to be a Gold Princess, moreover a Diamond one. What's the special perk?

"Diamond. Princess Melodie of the Eleventh Provincial Region," Princess Prudence calls.

"Oh my God, that's me," the chocolate-candy princess mutters.

She looks a bit clumsy and panicky when her name is called but as soon as she reaches the stage, she's a totally different person. Poise. Mature. Sophisticated. She smiles at Princess Prudence, little bow, then the audience, bigger bow, and finishes it flawlessly as she makes her way to her seat. But surprisingly, she then turns her head and looks my way with a smile while her right arm cheers modestly.

I guess… she believes that it's my turn next, since there's no other princess left standing but me.

"And finally, the very last Diamond of the year.

Princess Seraphine of the Twelfth Provincial Region."

I swallow my nervousness deep to my gland and begin my trudge. In the meanwhile in my head, I keep thinking. There's no way in heaven nor earth nor hell that I could be honored with the Gold royal status, moreover selected as a Diamond – whatever that means. But, here I am. Pacing my steps carefully on my way to the stage as one. Up the mini stairs slowly, trying to move more gracefully. And I'm thinking, maybe I'll follow what Melodie did. So I try to make eye contact with Princess Prudence, smile – *don't forget to smile*, the Counsellor said – then bow. Her expression doesn't show that she's impressed with me, but I'm going to disregard that and shift my body towards the audience. I smile, then – what the Counsellor has said – spread my wings and bow.

Everything turns out to work out O-K even as I reach my Diamond seat, and to my own surprise, it's literally covered with diamonds. But more surprising for me, that I didn't trip, as no one did either. So far so good.

"Next on my list to discuss with every one of you on the seats – our honorary students. You must have already been wondering. Why do we have a Class Diamond this year? A very special class, I might add; and such a divine reflection of the highest royal grade, only when the Crown Prince is present in the academy."

Every princess looks to their left and right, including me. There's a rustling sound coming out of

Princess Prudence's lips.

"The secret will be out in the following second for the very first time from my lips. For the last three years, the Crown Prince had been exploring the whole wide kingdom for what would be his most suitable wife in his eyes. As such, the Crown Prince has *personally* handpicked six of you – regardless of your royal grade, it seems," I feel her eyes look specifically right at me, "of now the highest regarded princesses assorted into Class Diamond. In other words, those who are considered befitting to the role of Queen Consort, His Royal Highness' future wife."

Everyone in the hall now either gasps or howls in shock.

So the Crown Prince had been on a searching-for-wife expedition for the last three years, in secret? That explains why Gaspard– I mean, Rainpard, thought the Crown Prince didn't even live in his castle here – because he didn't! I wonder what the Crown Prince sees in each of the six of us – and why the hell did he pick me too? *The worst princess ever born.* Is it just to prove a pity point or something? Have we even met before?

But then I think, what are the chances that the mysterious Crown Prince turns out to be… the *real* Royal Phantom?

"And now. The following will apply to everyone, regardless of your assigned class. Your lessons structure in the Royal Princess Academy," Princess Prudence continues her speech, but everyone else is still loudly whispering. "If you could all please, be silent!" she screams, and the hall immediately turns into a graveyard. She then straight away goes back to business; doesn't even give us enough time to process the news. "School days are Monday to Saturday. There are going to be two classes in one day. Morning and afternoon. And as for your timetable; Counsellors, if you please."

The footsteps are coming from each of the assigned counselors. When mine comes, he hands me a thick glossy paper printed with my schedule. "I'm so proud of you," he whispers, and then he gives me the biggest smile he's ever shown to me so far.

When he leaves, I read the agenda in my hands.

Diamond Class
Princess Seraphine of the Twelfth Provincial Region

Monday
Morning Class: Finest Table Manner
Afternoon Class: Impeccable Etiquette Lessons

Tuesday
Morning Class: Absolute Beauty Treatment
Afternoon Class: Ultimate Beauty Maintenance

Wednesday
Morning Class: Elegant Fashion Appropriation
Afternoon Class: Precious Jewelry Selection

Thursday
Morning Class: Royal Attraction Decorum
Afternoon Class: Royal Dating Schemes

Friday
Morning Class: Planning a Royal Banquet
Afternoon Class: Dancing with a Prince

Saturday
Morning Class: Inevitable Marriage Proposal
Afternoon Class: The Crown Prince's Royal Coming-of-Age Ceremony

If I hadn't read *The Royal School Guide for Our Dear Daughter Princess Seraphine*, I would've probably suffered from a heart attack right here, right now. I mean, what's even the difference between *Absolute Beauty Treatment* and *Ultimate Beauty Maintenance*? They both sound exactly the same to me. And don't even get me started with the Saturday classes.

"There will be one assignment for each school semester, which includes the one that has been given to you. You'll be notified of which class is responsible for the topic of each as a *surprise*."

I roll my eyes. Does it even matter at this point?

"His Royal Highness The Crown Prince's Royal Coming-of-Age Ceremony will encompass the mid-term examination." I knew it. Somehow, I've already had the feeling. "The rule is simple. You must dance with a prince during the ceremony. Should one of you get to be picked by His Royal Highness The Crown Prince for a dance, it'll be an immediate result for the highest grade of the batch. Grade A. Meanwhile, Grade B for future reigning prince positions, and Grade C for other prince titles. And remember this. Should you choose to dance with a commoner, you will be considered as failing your mid-term examination. I don't need to remind you of the fatality resulting from such an act of breach of the book of *Rules of Being a Princess*."

Whatever.

"As for the final exam, you may all have already expected this – that by the end of this school year, one of you will be chosen by a prince to take your hand in marriage."

In… *what*?! I know a princess should not be allowed to curse, but, shit! This soon?

"Moving along to the next curriculum. Should you pass this school year, your next syllabus will be individually tailored based on the status and hierarchy of the prince by whom you have been chosen – reigning or passive of the Provincial Region, or in this very special year, the heir apparent to our kingdom monarch – in when the relationship should unfortunately come to a fail by the end of the year, there will no longer be an engagement ceremony, and grave repercussions to such non-fulfillment will be subjected to primary accusations."

Oh, shit.

"As such, you may be requested to repeat the school year, and in some terrible cases, return to your Provincial Region home in ignominy and have your birth status revoked."

Double shit. I could even lose my title by failing?

After all that information, it's like my mind goes blank. I think Princess Prudence is now talking about some special condition for this rare event when a princess is chosen by more than one prince, but I'm not even listening anymore because there is no way in hell that I would even be able to get one prince to want to marry me.

The worst princess ever born.

Sigh. It'd be much easier if I could just pick Leon.

But then, I think again, why not?

Him, or the Servant Boy. Either way, I'm screwed.

"At last, I sincerely welcome you all to the Royal Princess Academy."

27

By the end of Princess Prudence's speech, I've almost lost all of my consciousness on my seat. Too much information. I find it easier to memorise the whole chapter of *Blood Spatter Analysis* than even all this.

Some of the princesses are feeling bummed that the school orientation had to fill up the whole Monday, thereby replacing classes *Finest Table Manner* and *Impeccable Etiquette Lessons*, which are apparently the favorites of many. But I'm just glad when the headmistress says we get to go home once the evening almost comes.

I can't even really put my focus on what happens after Princess Prudence's groundbreakingly informative speech. All the teachers now come up on stage and say a thing or a hundred about what their class encompasses, but my mind still draws blank for the whole session on top of a thousand other things on my mind.

My royal grade is now somewhat superior to Gold? I'm one of the candidates for the role of Queen Consort?

And a prince has to propose to me by the end of the school year, otherwise I fail? This is all too ridiculous beyond limit.

When the last teacher speaks her ending diction, the evening at last approaches.

It's now time to leave.

Finally, because now I can finally begin to sneak a look at the mysterious Crown Prince next building.

See if he makes his attendance today.

Apparently, I'm not the only one who's thinking about it. All the princesses are now seemingly marching altogether in a graceful speedwalk out and towards the Royal Prince Academy.

The building layout of the Royal Prince Academy is horrifyingly the same as the Royal Princess Academy, and so everyone knows exactly where to go. Straight into the right hall with a faster speed.

What is royal patience when the royal target is near.

"It was hard to keep on your right, but look at me managing," Melodie suddenly whispers beside me, still catching up on her own breath. I didn't even notice that she'd been next to me all along. "What do you think the Crown Prince will look like?" She tiptoes by the long window.

But out of the blue, a man comes out of the door with force. Think Princess Prudence, but the man version, except for his long glossy silver hair. And for his age, he sure remains faithful to the royal skincare routine to keep his face as smooth as a baby, as for every prince in this academy would. Kind of reminds me of my father too, with his porcelain skin and all. Plus, I'm willing to bet my golden carriage – that's not even mine – that he is the Headmaster of the Royal Prince Academy.

"I may need to have a word with Princess Prudence about all of your behavior. This is, unexpectedly, very unacceptable for princesses like yourself," he comments.

"Princess Ghyslaine of the First Provincial Region, Class Diamond, Your Highness." Ghyslaine then bows and spreads her wings. "Forgive me, Most Respectable Prince Providence. We are only to attest if the Crown Prince is indeed of attendance, as he is required – as His Grace has carefully chosen *me* to be his suitable bride."

I hear Leonie snort. "Chosen, my fellow Diamond princess? Not as such as you have been triaged among the six of us?"

Prince Providence clears his throat. "Please, Your Royal Highnesses. Due to the brutality of the recent murder in town, the Crown Prince will remain in hide of his true identity. I can assure you that your learning will not be affected by such circumstances. If all of you may now go to your assigned royal residences," he instructs. "Royal Guards, if you could please escort your princesses."

In complete obedience and total despair – just like the rest, I follow Leon to my carriage. While my left palm is still in the footman's right hand, I move my head around, searching for Reon, my servant boy.

"Where is he?" I ask Leon.

"Where is who?"

"The Servant Boy," I say.

In response, Leon's face turns down and displays annoyance.

"He'd left, as such for the other servant boys too after you'd been assigned to your seat. They're only to assist the princesses with carrying your school supplies in the morning, then off back home to serve in the house. That's what the Counsellor says," he explains while his right fingers move over the horse's body with seemingly gentle pressure. It seems to calm him down gradually. "They're not like the royal guards, who are to stay with the princesses at school at all times. Making sure of safety."

He then fixes his stare solely at me, as if he wants me to agree with him about something.

28

Reaching home, I find the Butler opening the door for me.

"Where's Reon?" I ask in a haste, before Leon approaches very soon.

As a reply, the Butler only flicks his head towards where the library is.

Stepping my feet inside the library, I find Reon reading a book titled *Fundamentals of Forensic Pathology*. All these books he's been reading, I notice, it's like he's been studying to become a forensic doctor or something.

When he realises my presence, however, he calmly closes the book, stands, then bows.

"How is school, Your Highness?" He asks as he moves the seat for me to sit. Right across where he was.

Long story short, I tell him everything, and then more from my deep-reasoning stupor. "And so I was thinking, what if the Crown Prince is the *real* Royal Phantom? He'd been going around the kingdom in secret for the past three years. Maybe sometime during he got bored, and so he thought, since he'd been hiding his identity anyway, he'd just do this Royal-Phantom thing before his *daddy* the King got him to attend school. But then the murder happened, right? Someone *claiming* to be him murdered this man who maybe was pretending to be him too. So now he's back into hiding again, because as unlucky as he is, someone who knows him also turns out to be this murder freak. What do you think?"

What to me is a very unexpected reason, Reon lets out a loud guffaw. I open my mouth unconsciously as an act of disbelief.

"What is this with you and the Royal Phantom?" he says while shaking his head. "First, you thought I was the Royal Phantom. And now, you think the Crown Prince is the Royal Phantom. Which reminds me. You still haven't fully explained why you thought I was this mysterious phantom thief."

"Well…" Should I say it was his beautiful emerald-green eyes? His height? What about his white gloves? "You know what, it doesn't matter. Anyway, so, what do you think?"

"Well, I think you should now maybe start considering the chance that the Crown Prince may ask for your hand to dance."

"What? That's what you've picked up? I mean, what do you think about my theory? I know it's still mere supposition." I'm still lacking that dead man's identity and if strangulation was really his cause of death, before I can be more sure. But since the victim looked about the same age as me–

And then it hits me. My hands smack the top of the table all of a sudden, Reon flinches out of surprise.

"I need to start limiting the suspects at school," I say. "I have this feeling that one of the students did it." I rub my chin in the meanwhile. "You heard what Rainpard said, that there were no cases before we all arrived."

"But what are you going to do? Start interrogating the whole school?"

"That's exactly what I'm going to do. Starting with the princesses in my own class."

29

When the next morning comes, I wake up earlier than usual to get ready and reach the class. Arriving, I see a lot of girls that's about the same number of princesses running around the building. Who are they?

"Ah. The royal academy assistants. They're the ones in charge of moving the students' school supplies between the Cabinet Room and different classes," the Counsellors says while pointing at them, as if he has just read my mind.

Next, the Counsellor brings me to this very large indoor area called the Beauty Hall. The space is filled with six large benches that form a row. The left part is a basin station, middle is skincare, whereas the right is filled with all the make-up tools. I guess this is where I'll be spending the rest of my morning and afternoon, attending classes with the name as stupid as *Absolute Beauty Treatment* and *Ultimate Beauty Maintenance*. I already want to puke.

Shortly after, our teacher comes and introduces herself as Lady La Merina.

I don't remember much about her face from yesterday as all the Beauty teachers look the same with all their porcelain-white make-up, but I do remember her hair. Who doesn't, when her hair is as tall as half of the floor's height. Her bright yellow hair towers in braids to the top and is covered with a lot of round-cut diamonds, which I presume are real as they're all shining so brightly with the chandelier above.

I wonder how she gets into every door. She must experience being stuck on the door ceiling at least once in her life.

But the morning class is as stupid as its name too.

First, they make us meditate in front of the water basin. I mean, who does that? Then, they tell us to wash all of our make-up off. So I urge myself to do some protesting.

"With all due respect, Teacher Lady La Merina, but why didn't you just tell us yesterday to just not wear our makeup this morning?" I ask in front of the class.

As much as I wasn't really listening much to what she said yesterday, I would've remembered something like this – or more like, I was hoping she would.

"Good question, Princess Seraphine. Why, oh, why, which answer is, perhaps I forgot." she sings. Sings!

I roll my eyes.

Next time, I'll just keep my mouth shut.

30

The morning class is now done – thank God – after which we have put toner on our face, several different serums with complicated brands and names, some face oil of which part of substance accidentally got into my tongue, moisturiser which flower smell I actually enjoy, and lastly, some type of powder sunscreen.

So next, each of our counselors directs us into some sort of dining hall for all princesses from every class to have lunch.

Our table is divided into four separate long tables of three chairs on each side. My seat, thankfully, is next to Melodie; but unfortunately, Ghyslaine is just sitting across from me.

I know I said confidently yesterday that I'd start interrogating them, but oh my, I don't even know where to begin. And to be honest, I'm very nervous. Terrified, even. At this moment that I've realised, I don't even know how to properly make friends with anybody. I skipped all of the royal parties for the past three years, and I probably had more contact with the dead than the living.

What should I do? What should I say?

Suddenly, I find the air feels colder, and my palms all sweaty.

"Now, I remember!" Orianne sitting on my very left edge of the table suddenly shouts. "You're that Princess Seraphine! The one that almost caught the Royal Phantom!"

"You've just realised that now?" Sassy Leonie retorts, then begins to cut her steak.

"I didn't recognise her because of that make-up, silly!" Orianne replies.

"Well, there's such a thing as recognising one's name *and* her Provincial Region," Leonie scolds, then takes a fork of sliced steak into her mouth. Brutally, and elegantly.

"Nonetheless; Seraphine, you're famous! Like, no one does that. Let me rephrase. No princess *ever* does that," Coralie says. "And I don't mean it, like, in a bad way. But like, hey, maybe that's why the Crown Prince chose you too."

"Tsk. Please. The Crown Prince was just messing around. He told me so," Ghyslaine responds while cutting her steak with her head up high. She's not even looking at her steak, and not even at my face; more like, whatever is on top of my head.

"HE TOLD YOU SO?" Every other princess on the table, except for me, screams at her.

"The Crown Prince told you so? The mysterious Crown Prince who's never ever been seen by anyone before?" Melodie tries to clarify the bombshell.

"Perfectly like so," she answers calmly, then chews her slice of steak elegantly with her eyes closed. "He even said he was going to *propose* to me in the second year. So yeah, you're looking at the future Queen Consort, my fellow *Diamond* princesses." In particular, Ghyslaine is glaring at Leonie, but she only snorts when she notices.

"What is he like?" Coralie asks excitedly.

"Where do I even start," Ghyslaine taps her right cheek repeatedly with her fingers. "Tall. *Very* tall." Check for Royal Phantom. "His hair is like the sun. Bright and yellow." Another check. "And his eyes." My heart's pounding. Please say green. I don't care if he's set his eyes on Ghyslaine for marriage. I don't care if she's going to marry the Crown Prince in the third year of school. I don't even care about her being crowned Queen Consort. All I care about is getting a closure on this Royal Phantom and town murder-mystery on my end. So, green. Please, for the love of God, say green. "Like the leaves falling from the trees. Beautiful green." Bingo! "And he's always in this red-velvet silky suit." Red-velvet silky suit? Are you kidding me? That sounds exactly like the dead man's attire!

Straight off, I have this instant courage boiled in me.

"Can we meet him?" I ask.

I mean, this is perfect. Just perfect. I can't believe

I've hit the jackpot this quick.

"Why?" Ghyslaine replies in a sceptical manner while looking at me with the eyes of a challenger. "So you can *steal* him from me?"

"Excuse me?" I repel.

"I don't think she means that, Ghyslaine," Melodie promptly defends me, which is quite unexpected for me. "She did say *we*. So, can *we* meet him?"

I can't help but smile a little at Melodie, to which she returns with a brighter kind.

"I don't see a reason *why* you all should." Ghyslaine takes another bite of steak without mercy.

"Okay, to start. How do you know he's the real deal? I mean, how are you even certain that he's not a fake?" Leonie argues.

Good point.

"He is *not* a fake, okay? I have you know that he has every reason to be the real Crown Prince, I can assure you. Nevertheless, I find no reason to let any of you see him. Besides, he has to protect his identity. You see, someone was trying to kill him."

"KILL HIM?" the other four princesses scream again. I want to sigh.

"That murder in town on Saturday. Do any of you even know the details?" Ghyslaine asks sarcastically.

Surely after this, she'll try to prove that she knows all the details directly from the Crown Prince, her face shows.

"I heard it from my servant boy who was just running some errands in town," Leonie says. "He said it was horrible. Someone fell from the building while burning or something."

"I saw it with my own eyes!" Melodie shrieks. "Only he wasn't falling from any building. It was more like he was falling from the sky! I ran as far away as I could when it happened." With her chocolate-candy bag, if I may add.

I look at Orianne, expecting her to jump in with her part of the story, since I know she was in town too. But to my surprise, her face shifts to pale and she turns all quiet. *Why?* I wonder.

"Ha! I knew it. All of you don't even know anything yet. Now I can prove to you that my Crown Prince is the real deal. He told me he knew who the body was."

"WHAT?" Now I'm screaming along with the other four princesses.

Ghyslaine moves her face as close to the center proudly, ready to whisper, as we all do too. "The Crown Prince said, someone's been trying to kill him, and the body was a commoner covering for him. To be precise, one of his *servant boys.*"

Of course. Now that explains it.

The heart of the real Crown Prince is what I really want.

And no one's supposed to know what's in the card

but me, Reon, Rainpard, and his men. So Ghyslaine could be right. Maybe this Crown Prince *is* the real deal.

I've made up my mind that I really need to speak with him. I have to verify. This may speed up solving the murder case much earlier than I thought it would.

"Anyway," Ghyslaine brings her head back to good posture. "That's all you're getting from me. I just wanted to prove that my Crown Prince *is* the real deal. Now, there's no reason I should bring all of you along with me to see him."

No! I scream in my head. This is the only chance. Somehow, I have to be able to convince her otherwise. But how? What should I say? The truth? That I just want to confirm if he's the real Royal Phantom? Wait. What if… that's it.

This time, I bring my face forward to the center, to which everyone else on the table is quick to follow.

"You know how I've met the Royal Phantom with my own eyes? Even come as close as being stuck with him flying mid air?" I say. Everyone nods, including Ghyslaine. "Well, what if I say to you that I think the Crown Prince may be the Royal Phantom?"

Ghyslaine gasps the loudest. "You really think so?" she whispers back.

"That's why I need to see him. I can't be sure until I speak with him, or at the very least, I need to hear his voice," I say. The other four princesses hum and nod repeatedly in support of my plan.

"Okay. Say he really is. What if he's dangerous? I can't tell my guards. I sneaked out every night to meet him in the back of my house, just like we always did for the last seven days. If I tell the guards, they're going to put a barrier on it," Ghyslaine sobs in panic.

"That's why the others are coming too," I say. Everyone else but Ghyslaine nods again excitedly.

"Okay. I guess… you're all coming into my house for dinner… tonight."

Alright!

31

After school ends around early evening, all of us make a pact to go into Ghyslaine's school *mansion* and keep the plan only between the six of us, pretending that we're going for some *girls' night in.* For some reason, Leon is very happy for me.

"Well, this will be the first. You're hanging out with your *friends*," he says as he walks me to my carriage.

"I wouldn't say *friends* yet, Leon," I say. "'Classmates' is more like it."

"I mean, you never know," he smirks. "This could be good for you."

I shrug my shoulders.

I honestly don't know what to expect about friendship, other than the matter of solving the case.

But at least her five-story mansion is way better to look at than mine – all decorated with much grander curios and fresh paint. Plus, there seems to be no ghosts around here.

Although, the dinner atmosphere at Ghyslaine's imposing residence is as cold as our dessert of chocolate ice cream cake with sheep's milk mousse.

I don't think it should be anyone's fault that everyone is feeling pretty tense, except for the host herself. Everyone on the table is on their best look, but me – to Ghyslaine's own disdain. Other than me, they're all with their make-up on, wearing their best dresses tight on the waist with corsets. In contrast, I'm wearing a casual black silky long sleeve and dark pants with no make-up at all.

Where my priority lies is clear as day.

"I knew you were all going to seduce the Crown Prince – *my* prince! Except for you, Seraphine. It's so obvious to me that you're just here for detective work," Ghyslaine says.

Thanks, I guess?

"All's fair in love and game," Leonie says. She then drinks her red wine with total poise.

"So, when is he coming?" Melodie asks.

"In about thirty minutes," Ghyslaine answers hesitantly. "Anyway, how are you all going to protect me with those dresses? Seraphine, can you fight?"

"Don't worry. I know a bit of martial arts," I answer.

I really do. I guess you could say I've learned a thing or two from Leon. He said that at least with my state of no-stranger-for-danger when it comes to solving crime, *he* needed to be prepared for the worst. And apparently, I'm not entirely bad at it, though not super good at it either.

"*A bit* doesn't convince me, Seraphine," Ghyslaine flutters her shoulders. I roll my eyes. "Anyway, I just hope that you're wrong – that the Crown Prince is not the Royal Phantom."

"So, what are we going to do for thirty minutes in the meantime?" Orianne asks.

That reminds me. I need to ask her about what she saw in town that murderous evening. Something that seems to have even managed to shake her until now.

"I don't know," Coralie says. "Girls' talk?"

"Oh, I know!" Ghyslaine jumps a little. "Let's talk about who's asked you for a dance when you attended any prince's coming-to-age ceremony, and who you've asked in your own ceremony. And then, what you did on the date afterwards. Okay, I'll go first. All the princes in and surrounding my region *obviously* asked for my hand, and not a single one didn't. I rejected most of them, of course. And when I did accept, they would take me to the garden to show me flowers that they thought would resemble me, have the whole space of a fine dining restaurant for a romantic dinner, and clear the whole shopping center for me to shop. A perfect date for the perfect princess," she blushes and touches both her cheeks.

"Same for me, actually," Coralie says. "About the date, I mean. Isn't that the procedure from that book? What's it called again?"

"The Rules of Royal Dating Schemes," Leonie answers then yawns. "Every prince always takes their ideas of dating from that book. It's so boring. I even made some of the princes cry because I just kept ignoring them during, then I just left them in the middle of the date."

I have to say that I'm not totally surprised. As expected from the sassy princess, I'd say.

"I always told any of my dates to bring chocolate. That's always been my request. But then one time, this Prince from the Seventh Provincial Region – Kitburry is his name – brought me to this place filled with sculptures of just chocolate. Just chocolate! It's not even anywhere in our school book. At the end of the day, we just ate all the sculptures until we were full while we were laughing. Oh, and he's here! In the Royal Prince Academy! You know what? I don't even care about the Crown Prince anymore." Melodie suddenly goes under her upper dress and struggles to pull out her corset. We're all so surprised. That's really unexpected, especially from a princess with a Gold – now Diamond – royal grade. "Anyway, you've got my point," she rests both her arms on her thighs as she fails to take out the corset. "I'm going to marry Prince Kitburry, for love!"

"Me too!" Orianne suddenly stands, both her hands smack hard on the dining table. "I only have my eyes for one prince. One prince! My Prince Isaac of the Fifth Provincial Region. He's the smartest man I've ever met

in my entire life. I asked him for a dance first during my
ceremony. When we danced, he said I was the first princess
he ever danced with, and then he asked me that very same
night if I could dance with him at his ceremony because
he'd rather allocate his other time for his scientific research.
And when we danced at his ceremony, he suggested that
he'd propose to me so he could save even more time for
science. Oh! And the best part is, for our date, he even
let me watch him do experiments in his lab for the whole
day. So romantic!" She now dances with her palms on her
cheeks. "Melodie! Help me with the corset, and then you'll
help me."

Melodie cheers and then runs immediately to help
Orianne take off her corset.

"F this. I'm letting go of the corset too," Leonie
shouts. And did she just say 'f'? "Coralie, you help me."

"Okay, as long as you help me too," Coralie replies,
and then runs to where Leonie is. *A princess should not be
running,* I recall Lady Francoise saying. But none of that
seems to currently matter here.

"Whatever. As long as *you girls* don't end up with
my prince. Oh, this corset." Ghyslaine then rests her feet on
the chair next to her and bends her upper body backward.

That's right. *Girls.* I guess we're just being girls
at the moment. Not princesses. The *Book of Manners for
Princesses* is out the window for now.

I'm actually quite enjoying this. Just listening to

whatever stories they have. Observing whatever funny things they do. They're being who they really are. I don't even think I've ever spent any time with a bunch of girls this long, let alone fellow princesses.

But then suddenly, they're all looking at me.

"Well, Seraphine?" Coralie asks as she momentarily stops pulling Leonie's corset strings.

"Yes?" I answer.

"What's your story?" Melodie asks curiously.

I mean, where do I even start? The one when I skipped all the royal ceremonies for the past three years? The sword fights on my own ceremony? The part where I've never danced with a prince? Or the fact that I've never been on a date?

"I… I've never danced with anyone before," I've decided to answer briefly. Simple and short, so I don't have to elaborate.

"WHAT?" Everyone stops whatever they're doing and screams in surprise.

"You mean… so you've never been on a date before? Ever?" Orianne tries to confirm.

"Did no prince ever pick you for a dance?" Ghyslaine asks.

"What about your own Royal Coming-of-Age Ceremony?" Melodie presses.

"That… I… was… busy," I give my answer sort of hesitantly. I really don't feel like explaining. More like, I'm *lazy*, because it'll be too long to even elucidate.

"Busy with what?" Leonie asks with her usual gangster tone.

"The cases! Of course!" Melodie answers for me. "Remember the newspapers? That… for the past three years, Seraphine had been on the road in her region. You know, solving murders and stuff. And on the night of her own ceremony, she left to stop the Royal Phantom with her own bare hands."

I shrug my shoulders to neither confirm nor deny.

As long as I don't have to explain myself.

"I'll have you know what my very trustworthy source has told me." Everyone can already tell that Orianne must mean Prince Isaac. "There are still two Diamond Princes who haven't yet had their coming-of-age ceremonies. They will have no choice but to have them here. And as my incredible and wonderful source of intel is also a Diamond Prince, he was able to credibly verify these two princes' Diamond royal grade. Seraphine, what do you think?" Orienne asks.

"About what?" I ask with a face that shows genuine confusion.

"About being on a date with one of them, of course!" Orianne claps her hands. "Forget the other royal grades. One of these two Diamond Princes is going to invite you to his coming-of-age ceremony, ask you for a dance, and then, you're going to have your very first date! Oh, so romantic!" She seems to be excited about this. Even more than me.

"Don't I have to have met them first in any other royal parties to make the acquaintance before I could actually be invited?" I argue. Considering I don't even have any prince as a friend – the mummies excluded.

"You know no one? No prince?" Coralie asks.

"You five are the only royals I know," I answer with all honesty.

Unexpectedly, they come to my seat silently and hug me in response – more surprisingly, even Ghyslaine and Leonie too. What is this sudden warmth I've never felt before from my fellow royals?

But when they all start to squish me, I begin to regret it.

"We'll make sure you'll have your very first date very soon," Melodie says, her arms still circling on my shoulders. Everyone else nods repeatedly.

"Do you have a type?" Orianne asks.

"Who are the two Diamond Princes, do you know?" Leonie asks Orianne.

"Oh!" Orianne shouts. "The two of them are–"

"Girls, I don't mean to ruin this moment or whatever, but the thirty minutes are up. I think my Crown Prince should be arriving soon," Ghyslaine says.

So shortly moments after, we find ourselves trying to sneak into the back of Ghyslaine's five-story mansion.

It's not easy with all the six of us trying to hide ourselves in the hallway, pass the library, then pass a few other rooms until we reach the exit door. Afterward, we take turns to run into the garden wall. Ghyslaine goes first to let us know which door, to which we follow one at a time.

After we've succeeded with our quiet march, five of us hide, bend our knees beneath the bushes while Ghyslaine stands in the middle of what looks like a secret garden. The area is filled with flowers, and in the middle there's a long white bench and table.

A short moment after, a figure comes closer in darkness.

"He's coming!" Coralie shrieks but barely manages to suppress the pitch.

"Shhhhh!" Everyone else warns Coralie.

Slowly the man is appearing in light. Very tall with short yellow hair, just as Ghyslain has described. We're all holding our breath as his face is about to become clear under the moonlight.

I'm now focusing on where his eyes may be. *Green*, I expect. Then, his voice.

"Ghyslaine, my Queen," I hear the Crown Prince speak.

Or, so I thought.

He's now only inches away from Ghyslaine as he kneels and kisses the back of her hand.

I definitely recognise this voice. Very, very vividly.

His face is not as clear, but I'm sure. There's no doubt in my mind.

I know this guy.

It's *him*, alright.

32

Without alert, I stand and reveal myself from the bushes, to which the others confusedly but still immediately follow.

"Stop it right there!" I shout.

I saunter towards where Ghyslaine is. She moves her head towards me, flabbergasted, while the man – *that man* – immediately turns into a sculpture with his one knee still on the ground.

He definitely recognises my voice too.

"*Shit!*" the man blurts out.

I let out a winning chuckle. It's *him* alright.

His face becomes much and much clearer as I'm getting very close, but I don't even feel the need to verify anymore. I've seen this face – unfortunately, many times before.

"What is it, Seraphine? Is he really the Royal Phantom?" Ghyslaine shakes in fear while the man's still holding her hand hostage.

"Even worse," I reply.

"What do you mean?" Leonie says as she and the other girls are catching up behind me. Melodie's hands have been stuck on my shoulders like glue.

I walk much closer to the man who's now just seeing me with disbelief. Fear wraps his soul as he trembles, and as his skin starts to perspire, he turns ignorance to make eye contact. So now that I'm only inches away from him, I bend my knees to level with his countenance.

"He's my cousin," I announce.

"He's your WHAT?" Everyone screams.

I raise my body to stand while shaking my head to disbelief.

"Ladies, meet Prince Jerome of the Second Provincial Region."

Jerome grits his teeth and covers both his ears with his palms as all the princesses shout, "You're not the Crown Prince?"

I don't know how they all manage to keep being synchronized.

Moments after, we find ourselves sitting on the bench with the fake Crown Prince. Meanwhile, Jerome keeps looking at the table, feeling helpless.

"Seriously," I say, "after all this time, you're still trying to pretend to be somebody else you're not."

King. Fairy. Dragon. Even his own royal guard once. You name it. He always got caught in the end, of course, except no one really knew how he managed to get the timing right in between. He said he'd been following them, but no one even suspected it. Not even his own royal guard, who was supposed to be following *him*.

And it's not like he hasn't got anything to be proud about. He's the next Reigning Prince of the Second Provincial Region, for God's sake. Why does he always have to act like a freaking stalker? So embarrassing.

Everyone now stares at Jerome like they want to rip his head off, especially Ghyslaine. Actually, maybe she really would, the way how red her face is right now.

"I can't believe you lied to me!" she yells. She's not even crying, just complete anger in full throttle. "I thought you were more than just a prince!"

"A Diamond Prince, I'll have you know. I'm even on the same grade with the Crown Prince, among the four other princes of course," Jerome argues. "But yes, I'll admit my grave mistake. I'm deeply sorry to have disappointed you, my Queen," he sobs.

"Disappointed me? Even worse. You're embarrassing me!" Ghyslain shouts.

I don't mean to be on Jerome's side, but she was indeed the one who bragged about knowing and marrying the Crown Prince and stuff. But anyway…

"Nevertheless, everything about my feelings are true, Princess. There's only you in my heart. Even when you didn't choose me at your Royal Coming-of-Age

Ceremony, due to which I constantly sobbed in my bed for weeks." Jerome tries to caress Ghyslain's right hand but she flicks that hand so hard in the air, he almost falls onto the ground.

"I didn't even remember you at all," Ghyslain turns her head to the other side with her hands folded.

"Exactly my point, my Queen. Imagine my excitement when you mistook me as the Crown Prince," Jerome ripostes.

"Hold on," Melodie interrupts. "I'm confused. So is he or is he not the Royal Phantom?"

"No," I say. "He's *definitely* not the Royal Phantom, I can assure you." He may have yellow hair and green eyes too, but even the short and chubby Gaspard would've been a more convincing phantom thief than him. "But I do have a question for you, Jerome. How do you even know about the card?"

"The card? What card?" He looks perplexed.

"You mean, you don't know about any card on the murdered victim?" I ask.

"No. I've never seen any cards," he says with a very perplexed look.

"So… how do you know about the body being a commoner? Moreover a servant boy covering for the Crown Prince," I ask very curiously. The other princesses move their heads closer to Jerome, and he turns blushing.

Jerome then clears his throat, ready to tell a story,

thinking that it'll be enough to make up for what he's done.

"Well, so here's what really happened." He closes his eyes, then opens and moves them around all of us.

"So here I was, Monday morning," he says. "My first day on the island. *Bored to death.*" I roll my eyes. "After they assigned me to this five-story mansion just down the road, I thought, why don't I go to town and find something fun to do?"

Was everyone here assigned a five-story mansion but me?

"Something like *what*?" Ghyslain asks with a ferocious tone.

"Something like… finding someone to impersonate because I was bored?" Jerome's eyes and mouth clench upward. He then tries to make Ghyslain look him in the eye, to an epic failure.

"Anyway, continue," I say impatiently.

"Yes, sorry. As I said, I was going to town and then I saw this peculiar boy – dark brown hair, green eyes – holding this basket full of meat. He just left this butchery shop. And so I thought. Okay. Maybe he's a servant boy. And then I thought again. Wait. I've never been a servant boy before."

I roll my eyes again. Typical Jerome.

"And so you followed him?" Leonie says with a lazy tone and eyes.

"And so I did," he replies sheepishly. Everyone else

now rolls their eyes.

"Anyway. Okay. Where was I? Right. Following the servant boy. But then he was acting so peculiarly. Guess where he went after the butcher."

"Where?" Melodie asks enthusiastically.

"The tailor!" Jerome answers with the same level of energy. Both his palms form a fist and he smacks them onto the table.

"The tailor?" Melodie gasps.

"Yes! And so I eavesdropped, and apparently, he was running some errand by this Sir Knight Yves or whoever – to pick up a suit." That scary royal knight. I should've known. "Guess whose suit?" he asks.

Nobody answers, including Melodie who frowns her forehead to think. I bet it's the Crown Prince's, but I don't feel like entertaining him like Melodie.

"The Crown Prince's!" Jerome screams exuberantly, to everyone else's gasps. I roll my eyes again. "Red-velvet silky jacket and pants – *divine* with a touch of what I think was the finest mulberry silk. I must say, the Crown Prince got some very high taste."

Red-velvet suit. The dead man's suit.

"And so I walked up to the tailor and said, 'Make me the finest red-velvet suit fit for the finest prince!' Something like that," he reenacts aloud dramatically.

"And then, what happened next?" I ask.

"Naturally, I left the tailor shop in a hurry to catch

up with the servant boy and followed him again. Guess where he was going." Jerome raises his eyebrows over and over again.

"Where?" Melodie shouts.

"The Crown Prince's castle!" he immediately answers.

"F me," Leonie says.

Maybe I ought to ask her later what she really means by 'f'.

"So, did you manage to go into the castle?" I ask.

"Sadly, I did not," he sighs. "I was thinking to, but then I saw this scary man with all sorts of injuries on his face riding on his black horse. He was guarding the gate when the servant boy came."

Yves.

"And so I waited by the trees nearby. A couple of hours later, I saw the servant boy come out of the gate. Only his hair had suddenly turned yellow and he wasn't dressed the same anymore. He was wearing *the* red-velvet suit!"

Everyone gasps, including me.

"And then what happened?" Coralie asks.

"Well, next, he was on his way to the academy. The Royal Prince Academy. Only, he wasn't alone. The scary knight guy and a few other guards were with him too. And so of course, I followed them. Up the stairs a few minutes afterward, we reached the Headmaster's office. Only our Headmaster Prince Providence, the scary knight, and the servant boy came inside the office. And that's when I finally got to fulfill my destiny to pretend to be the servant boy! I reckoned there would be no harm done since it looked like *he* was pretending to be the Crown Prince," he shrugs his shoulders.

"And so," he goes on, "while I was pretending to do some servant boy stuff, I slipped through the royal guards and sneaked into the office to confirm my suspicion. I was right. The servant boy was trying to act like the Crown Prince no one had ever met before. But it seemed that Prince Providence already knew that he wasn't the Crown Prince. He said something like he wasn't too sure anyone wouldn't notice that he wasn't actually the Crown Prince if he was to go to school as His Royal Highness instead."

Everyone draws their breath heavily.

"Why, did they say? Why did he have to pretend to be the Crown Prince? Where was the real one?" I ask.

Has someone already tried to kill him before? How many times? Since when?

The heart of the real Crown Prince is what I really want.

"I think they mentioned something like someone or some people had been trying to *kill* the Crown Prince – since *birth*. For unknown, various reasons." Everyone starts to gasp at the reveal of the fact, me somehow just a little. "The scary knight wasn't sure if the time was right for His Royal Highness to reveal his face to the public; at least, not until he was ready to take over the throne. Meanwhile,

Prince Providence was worried about some customary law. He said the Crown Prince needed to make attendance at least once a month, otherwise the academy had to fail him, even if he was the future king," he answers.

Suddenly, I feel so sorry for the Crown Prince. I mean, seriously, someone's been trying to kill him since birth? And so he's not some kind of anti-social who simply hates people? I begin to think about what life has been for him to live in such fear. No wonder he's never been seen – not even once. I guess being *mysterious* has been keeping him safe from harm.

If he's actually still alive.

But once-a-month attendance? Damn. Now I feel like being the Crown Prince. That sounds like a really big compromise, considering we *royal-peasants* have to make a total attendance of at least ninety-nine percent for every school year. And to be honest, I think I'd rather risk being killed than having to go to this stupid school. Every. Single. Week.

"And in terms of the Crown Prince's whereabouts, apparently no one knows. Not even the Crown Prince's army. The scary knight said something like, '*As long as the Royal Knight Commander is with the Crown Prince, no one needs to worry. His Royal Highness will be safe.*' Something like that," Jerome tries to mimic Yves' voice.

Wait. So Yves is not even the Royal Knight Commander? So, who is?

"Anyway, that's all you can get from me. I mean, after that, it's a plain road. I followed them back into the castle, tried to sneak past the gate this time – which I did – but then I got caught when I was about to sneak past the entrance. And when they found out I was a student in the academy, they escorted me back respectfully out of the gate." Jerome now turns towards Ghyslaine. "And that's when you saw me, my Queen. You thought I was the Crown Prince because I seemed to get out of the Crown Prince's castle from the inside. And that's when I thought… I've never been the Crown Prince before. Okay, Jerome. You are now the Crown Prince." He then shows a pity smile.

But to think that Jerome has even managed to retrieve such an important piece of information, and only because he was simply… bored… and an idiot. I'd better push him with more questions. Maybe he actually knows more than he thinks.

"Anyway, Jerome. Let's fast forward to the day the murder in town happened," I demand. "Where were you?" I ask, since Ghyslaine said Jerome was always with the red-velvet suit. I mean, regardless of how seriously annoying Jerome can be, I'd much prefer for him to be alive than being dead. He's part of the family, after all, not to mention a future reigning prince.

"Funny thing. I was on my way to town when I suddenly noticed him walking by himself," he says. "Him, as in, *you know who* who became *you know what*."

"What time was it? Do you remember?" I ask.

"Sometime in the afternoon, I believe," he answers while scratching his head.

Three to four hours before the dead man fell from the sky. That fits the timeline.

"And then, what did you do afterward?" Leonie asks.

"Well, I thought, *Bad timing*. And then I went back home," he says, shrugging his shoulders so casually as if the event doesn't take into account the fact that he was *almost killed*.

Oh my God, he really could have been. Oh, Jerome…

Well, anyway. Lucky for him.

But thanks to Jerome (very unexpectedly), now I don't really have to wait until the DNA Analysis is done. Starting tomorrow, I think I can start my investigation again.

Yeay!

But then I think, wait. I'm still missing something.

Oh, that's right!

On the spur of the moment, I've realised that Orianne has been awfully quiet again, just like this afternoon. I'm sure she had some stories to tell as a witness, but somehow she acted like she wasn't even there. Just listening. Her eyes showed like she was uneasy too. And so, I'm thinking about what I should say to lure her into talking.

"By the way, Orianne, I think I saw you in town that evening too. I happened to see you with two other princes, talking about some elements in the periodic table," I say while moving my body forward, looking straight into her eyes with a big fake appearing-innocent smile.

"You did?" She seems surprised.

"So you were in town too?" Melodie asks. *Bingo*.

"Why didn't you say so?" Coralie jumps in. *Another bingo*.

About time. For the sake of the investigation to proceed.

Orianne looks around perplexed as all the attention has now suddenly turned to her. Thereupon, she turns jumpy and sighs. "Argh! Alright. I know what you're thinking. I must have something to hide."

"So, do you?" Leonie asks.

"Oh, I do," Orianne sobs.

Everyone's now waiting for Orianne to finish crying. Once she calms down, she prepares her breath to start with her story.

"Well… I think… I had bumped into the murderer before it all happened."

"WHAT?" Everyone screams, including me.

"Did you see his face?" I ask.

"No, but I accidentally glanced upon a knife on his right waist. I mean, who brings a knife like that, right?

And when that happened, and everyone was talking about a man burning with a knife stuck in his chest, well… you know," Orianne starts crying.

"What was he wearing?" I ask further.

"I don't know. Like everybody else around me? Brown jacket with white shirt and brown pants. I mean, even Isaac and Humbert dressed like that too. And then… that's all." Orianne's eyes move to the left and right.

She's still hiding something.

"What else?" I ask.

"What do you mean, what else?" She blinks her eyes, then looks up to the sky suspiciously.

And so I think to myself. If she's still hiding something, it would either be about her, which seems unlikely, or the person she truly cares about.

Prince Isaac.

"Do you think… Prince Isaac has something to do with it?" I ask.

Tough call. She might hate me for this, but I have no choice.

"Excuse me? My Prince… has something to do with *it*?" Orianne's face suddenly turns red just like when Ghyslaine was mad at Jerome – still is. Then, she loses control. "Certainly not! I can't believe you've just said that, Seraphine. The murderer just smelled like Isaac, that's all!" Orianne immediately slaps her mouth with both of her hands as she's realised what she's just said.

"Smells like him?" My palms collide with the table as I respond.

I stand right away. My instinct brings me to walk to where Jerome sits, then sniffs his coat.

"What in the world? What are you doing?" Jerome shouts.

"Investigate," I reply briefly, then I shift my head towards Orianne. "Orianne, I need you to do something for me. It may clear your prince charming's name," I order bluntly.

"Please don't tell me you want me to sniff his jacket too." Orianne squints her eyes.

"Yes, I do. Come, quickly!" I say impatiently.

Orianne frowns but stands and complies anyway. "This better clear my prince's name, or else," she yells, then she does the sniffing.

"So? Is it the same?" I ask eagerly.

She sniffs again, then sniffs, and sniffs, and sniffs again. Her eyebrows gradually stir to meet. "I think so, but… not really. Oh, wait. Okay. The guy with the knife… there's… something else." She sniffs once more. "It's this smell… plus… something else."

"Something else? Something else like what?" I ask intensely. This could really be the key to solving the murder.

"Something like…" She sniffs again. "Something like…" She sniffs and sniffs again. "Like… something I had smelled before in Isaac's lab. Argh! I can't recall." She pulls back then rubs her nose continually. "I'm done sniffing," she announces.

"So the potential culprit smelled something like Isaac," I say, about which Orianne looks annoyed. "Are you really sure the guy with the knife wasn't your Prince Isaac?"

"I have told you, Seraphine. Isaac has nothing to do with the murder. You want proof? I didn't get my eyes off of Isaac, okay? Not even for one second. So he couldn't possibly do such a hideous thing. No way. And I'm not lying!" she screams furiously, and then she starts crying.

"Seraphine, have more sympathy, will you?" Coralie walks to where Orianne stands – still next to me – and embraces her shoulders.

Did I do something wrong? I'm confused.

All the princesses are now looking at me like I did, but… what did I even do?

I was just asking questions, wasn't I? Merely an inquiry to the derivatives of facts.

What's so wrong with that?

33

Tuesday night, I try to find Leon and Moyra. I manage to, but they say they have very important things to do – one to keep me extra safe, the other to keep the house extra clean. I feel like since we've both come to the island, they've both become extremely busy, and thus, can only spare no time to actually have a conversation with me. And so I search for and find Reon reading in the house library afterward. Again.

At least, there's him now, I think. He somehow always has enough hours to spend time with me.

Like so, immediately I share very excitedly about the groundbreaking progress of the case.

"So I'm thinking, one of these princes must be the murderer. Although, it could be the headmaster or the royal knight too. Nevertheless, I'm still missing some clues. About where the Crown Prince's servant boy was killed and how the culprit made the body fall out of the sky. By the way, speaking of servant boys, how many do you think they have in the castle?" I ask.

"Well, every house should only have one, as one is already more than enough, in my opinion," he replies with a nonchalant shrug on the shoulder. "But what interests me the most, is how your friends are going to set you up on a date with another prince?"

"They're not my *friends*. Well, at least, not anymore," I say in a low voice. I think for some reason, I feel rather affected by it, but then I quickly brush it off with the murder case in mind. "Anyway, that's not important. What's important is that, since we now sort of already know about the body's identity, I'm thinking, *we* should talk to the butcher, talk to the tailor, then follow that Yves knight. Skip my class. Skip your chores. We can just fake a disease or something," I suggest with happy and eager nods.

I mean, imagine. With his forensic knowledge and my deductive mind, we'll be unstoppable!

The perfect partner.

"I'd say that could jeopardise all the findings that you've got so far," he replies. Mirrors suddenly shatter in the back of my mind. "The murderer might find out that you were getting on to them. Remember, Princess. This case is on a very different level compared to every case you'd ever faced for the past three years. They're targeting the Crown Prince, pretending to be the Royal Phantom."

Pretending?

"The whole kingdom is at stake," he interrupts my thoughts as he steadily goes on, I unwittingly flick my eyes back solely into his. Bright pair of emerald orbs. Beautiful and enchanting. "So we need to make the investigation process extremely subtle." He sighs before he ends the brief silence. "I believe we need to solve this case with more *patience.*"

"And what a wonderful coincidence that patience is also where I'm lacking – among many others." I throw myself into the seat next to him. "I'm not fit to be a princess. I'm not fit to handle a big murder case such as this. What am I to do, really," I sigh.

"Princess, I've never had any doubt in my mind that you've got everything you need to solve this case."

Reon then holds both of my palms gently, as unexpected. They're warm, like how my cheeks feel.

What is this, again? My heart suddenly cannot stop beating rapidly. I can't think logically. Not with his skin touching on mine like this.

"My full confidence in your ability is what I'm willing to proffer to you, everlastingly. I've seen all the princesses from all around the kingdom. You're... *special.*"

If sweet words are a curse.

"Forever, in my eyes," he adds.

His eyes. Damn it!

"Always remember that," he adds while still looking deeply into my eyes. His emerald-green pair of sights, still and always a vision.

The perfect illusion.

"And so, I'd say, we'll go to town normally on Sunday, just like every other student will. And then, we'll do your favorite thing in the world. *Investigate*."

I nod silently, like I'm in a trance.

To all things, but one.

34

I choose to listen to Reon to patiently wait for Sunday to come. In the meantime, he has made it his personal mission to ease my pain of waiting by doing activities together.

My evening routine after school has now become spending time with Reon in the library. After dinner, we go to the secret passage as we watch the dark forest brighten faintly by the stars in the sky. No other people around us.

Now and then beneath the firmament, I try to steal a glance at Reon, my servant boy. Both of our palms form four pillars down to the grass on the ground, his head looks up with a beautiful smile that I can only describe succinctly in my mind as a real vision. At this point, I may not even care if he turns out to be the Royal Phantom, since I'm already starting to think… if he verily means any harm… if I've indeed become oblivious…

Damn it, what is he hiding?

But whenever I go to sleep at night, I keep seeing

Reon under the stars. I wonder if this counts as having a crush or *falling in love*. I still don't really know the difference.

Why does he keep appearing in my mind these days?

Then the morning comes, and suddenly I see Moyra with my dress on her right hand and make-up tools on her left as I open my eyes. And when I leave my bedroom, Leon's already in the hallway to greet me.

Leon. Reon.

And then I go back to being confused again.

Cold air fills the air around the classes this Wednesday and Thursday. Only Melodie still smiles at me from time to time, but even she chooses to stay as far away from me. Whenever lunch time comes, I still sit on my usual seat next to them, but they don't even talk to me. At least, not really.

Once in a while though, they would ask me something like, "So, Seraphine? Anything you'd like to say to Orianne?" or say something like, "We're waiting, Seraphine." Orianne's eyes would then stare right at me, gleaming with tears again.

I really have no idea what they mean. What do they want me to say to Orianne? I investigated, I asked Orianne very important questions, but then she got all sensitive and cried and angry; and since I haven't really got any more questions about her Prince Isaac so far, I just leave her be.

Maybe if Orianne happened to have some more clues about the case, only then I'd know what to say to her. It's their fault for being so complicated anyway – or am I the one who's making it so?

Meanwhile, classes are still dreadful.

Elegant Fashion Appropriation is actually not that bad, considering we're all just doing a mix-and-match of different styles from the latest royal formal and casual clothes. Except when they let out the crinoline, which I still hate to my bone.

Hooped petticoats should not be legal.

What's more, when the teacher Lady Valentine, whose appearance is pink with glitters all the way from her hair down to the skin of her feet except for her royal staff uniform, makes us do that runway thing at the end of the class, I just feel so awkward.

Precious Jewelry Selection, however, is boring as hell. The only two things I remember about this class is that the Bijouterie Hall is so bright and sparkling with thousands of gemstones that we all need to come in wearing the uniform sunglasses, which are these gigantic dark glasses with two big diamonds on each edge – specially constructed by the teacher Lady Tiffany. Very heavy both on the eyes and the head.

Royal Attraction Decorum and *Royal Dating Schemes*, in the meanwhile, are more informative, in my opinion. The middle-aged teacher, who looks almost like Prince

Providence with his long yellow hair, is apparently Prince
Hugo of the Tenth Provincial Region, whose original
residence is within the Capital Region and whose life
is solely dedicated to teaching. Most of his lecture is all
about theories and presentation slides that show subtle
signs when a prince is interested in a princess, and various
examples of how they would take us on a date after the
dance.

During both classes, I notice that the other five
princesses sometimes gaze at me, looking like they're about
to say something excitedly to me, but then immediately
change their mind.

Well, I guess it's for the best, since I'm not even
really listening.

But once in a while, Prince Hugo would release
new information about the princes' protocol that manages
to catch my attention. And since he's a prince himself, we
can be sure that the information is from the most credible
source.

I manage to compile some of the few fascinating
points in my head.

Every prince, such as him, is apparently tasked
with a secret *royal expedition* tailored to their needs and
preferences, starting at their thirteen years of age. Now
this explains how my father had set his eyes on my mother
since the beginning of the school year, and why the Crown
Prince had gone away from this island too.

Once a princess decides on a prince to dance with on her Royal Coming-of-Age Ceremony, the prince will then be allowed to take her on a date. When the prince decides on the same princess to dance with during his own Royal Coming-of-Age Ceremony, they're bound to be engaged in the future by the customary law of *royal commitment*.

I guess that means Orianne is already one step ahead closer towards graduation, and that's why she's so upset. I was basically accusing her *fiancé* of horrible murder.

In some cases when the princess has accepted more than one or two hands in dance, all the princes may still try to win her heart until she formally chooses. In what would be considered a very steadfast endeavour, the prince may declare a *royal promise* to never marry anyone else but the princess. A worst case scenario for the princess who doesn't reciprocate the same feeling. Apparently, this is what happened to Sir Hugo, and unfortunately for him, the princess subjected to his promise still chose to marry somebody else anyway, so that's why he's never betrothed. Everyone else in the class exhales in ache, but the teacher's response is only a soft-hearted smile saying that it's only for the best and that he's never been happier as long as *his* princess is.

I guess you could say our teacher is definitely the most hopeless-romantic guy in the world. Maybe that's why he's the best person to teach these two classes.

But there's something else interesting he's told us.

"Only for Class Diamond," he says excitedly, his right pointy finger strikes his lips. "It's about the Crown Prince."

Everyone in the class, including me, immediately moves our head forward and brushes our few hair strands off our ears.

"The Crown Prince is scheduled to make an appearance within the next few days."

35

Today is now Friday, and based on the timetable, we'll have *Planning a Royal Banquet* in the morning and *Dancing with a Prince* this afternoon.

I already want to cry, even by the sound of the name of these classes.

What sort of nonsense do I have to put up with today?

The footman opens the carriage, and I don't feel like going out, so he just awkwardly stands while moving his head left and right, waiting for the Counsellor to arrive in panic.

When I see him approaching, I tiredly jump out while ignoring the footman's hand and force my both feet to walk into the building. "It's not you, it's me," I tap the footman's left shoulder.

"Now, this afternoon class will be in the Ballroom," the Counsellor says while trying to hide little giggles. For some reason, he's looking way happier than usual.

"Oh, Your Highness, I can no longer hide my excitement anymore. I've just found out this morning myself. Wait until you see who's going to be your dance partner!" he says rapidly. "But I can't say anything further. I'm not allowed. Oh, you must make haste to the morning class! Make it faster for the afternoon to come! Before I burst into little bubbles of joy!" He then dances on his own leaving me in front of the Festivity Hall as I look at him with confusion.

My dance partner?

The Festivity Hall here is as big as the one back home, and almost everything looks the same, including the big chandelier on top of the dance floor – or maybe it's just standard for every palace. What's more, I can see six empty tables are already set for the *Planning a Royal Banquet* lesson and on each table is placed one book titled *The Only Guide for Preparing a Royal Banquet in the Most Acceptable Way.*

Apparently, the Headmistress Princess Prudence herself is the teacher for this class. Everyone swallows in fear. Without long introduction, she strolls around the tables, and as she approaches one, she assigns a princess to where she currently points her fingers.

I'm called last. Table number six.

"Planning a royal banquet is a princess' ultimate and sacrosanct duty. It essentially sets the face and future of one's royal family," she starts, her head held up so high. "You should have started at least one of your own within the last three years of your life as part of your princess lesson, as you have earned your place here."

Not this princess.

Ironic as it may sound, the Royal Phantom is
probably the one who got me to earn this seat.

"You may have noticed that none of the other
teachers have given you any new assignment aloud or
revealed the first part," she continues.

She's right. So I guess the first school assignment is
either from this class or the next.

"And so I shall be the first one," she announces.
Everyone gasps. "A *new* assignment. After our lesson today,
you will be expected to promptly start planning your own
royal banquet."

Is she being serious? I don't have time for this.
I have a murder case to investigate. That hasn't even
included the fact that I'm the only one in this class that has
never done it before.

I don't even know where to start.

"By the end of this school year, you will be holding
a royal banquet at your own assigned premises," she cuts
to the chase. For some reason, Princess Prudence stares
at me when saying the last few words. "Every student
in the academy will be invited, and the theme you have
determined for your royal banquet as well as your guests'
impressions of your effort by the end of the night will form
part of your grade for the assignment."

Everyone now seems to be holding their breath,

including me.

"Now, let's begin our lessons," she instructs with an incandescent tone. "And if I see any of you taking light of my class and not writing anything down, she will have to find me in my office after class."

Somehow, I feel her eyes are staring directly into my soul. Again.

During the class, I go as far as writing *everything* down to avoid the chance of being called into her office.

Theme. Mansion (or ghost house). Invitations. Formal royal attire (must be with crinoline underneath). Dominant colors for decorations (preferably two). Full course menu (hors-d'oeuvres, amuse-bouche, soup, appetizer, salad, fish, main course, palate cleanser, second main course, cheese course, dessert and mignardise).

When the bell rings, I let out a deep exhale and massage my writing wrist for a reset.

But regardless of writing everything down and not taking light of her lesson, Princess Prudence stops me from going my way into the Dining Hall. "Princess Seraphine of the Twelfth Provincial Region. If you could please follow me into my office."

The other princesses stop moving their feet out of surprise and watch as I walk behind Princess Prudence.

What did I do?

Arriving at her office on the top floor, the great ceiling narrows in shape with the turret roofs. The walls are bright in white and golden ornaments.

I move my eyes around the office as I'm heading towards the seat across from hers. Remembering the very similar layout between the Royal Prince and Royal Princess Academies, I wonder where Jerome was able to sneak in when he was eavesdropping that day.

Then I see a narrow hall on the side which connects to a door outside.

I'm thinking, Jerome must be hell of a very good spy to not be caught. I guess you could say, my respect for him has increased significantly today.

"Please, Princess Seraphine." Princess Prudence's wave of hand directs me to my seat. No smile. Just a very serious face. "Now, you must be wondering why I am calling you into my office. I must ease your burden quickly by letting you know that we will be discussing a different matter of sorts than our class this morning. First on my agenda," she opens her book, "Have you ever met the Crown Prince?"

"No," I answer with all honesty.

"Alright," she nods. She then proceeds to write something down. "Second, do you think the Crown Prince might have met *you*?" She looks at me with her eyes squinting in idiosyncrasy.

"No?" This time, I answer with ambiguity. What difference does that make?

"Hmm," she lets out, but it doesn't follow with

another word. Afterward, she goes straight into writing
something again. "Third. Do you think you know why
the Crown Prince has chosen you among the six? You see,
we had just begun finalising the process of assigning our
students to class on that dreadful Saturday. Believe me, the
reasonings for the other five princesses are as clear as the
diamond itself, due to their Gold royal grade. And as clear
as their patterns in contrast to you being the only one in
your… circumstances…" She must mean my royal grade
is even lower than Bronze. "You must understand my
grave concern, should the reason be that the Crown Prince
may have set his eyes on you as the future Queen Consort,
regardless."

"WHAT?" I scream. Princess Prudence raises her
eyebrows. "Excuse me, Princess Prudence," I correct. "I
mean, I beg your pardon?" I say it in a much poise and
polite way this time.

This doesn't even make any sense to me at all.

Princess Prudence clears her throat. "Right. As such,
I need to make sure you graduate from the academy as the
top of the class. Just in case. For the King and the Crown
Prince's sake. Which brings me to my next question. Why
did you leave your first school assignment empty?"

I swallow. What am I supposed to say? That I don't
have any royal need I can think of but catching the Royal
Phantom? And this particular desire of mine is not even for
the sake of the King or the whole kingdom? You could say,

it's just for the sake of my curiosity. So… what should I say? But then suddenly, I remember what Reon said.

"If not in different circumstances, the royal needs to attend to what the people need, and nothing else," I quote Reon. "I simply leave it empty because I have consented to myself that all of my royal needs have already been fulfilled, as it is time for me to return to the people's needs," I bluff, then I clear my throat.

Okay, I think, *not bad*, coming from me, even when I couldn't have pulled it off without Reon.

Princess Prudence seems perplexed with my answer – as in, Reon's. She stares deeply into my eyes, and in the process, she closes the book in her hands.

No more questions.

"Well, if you had written 'five-story mansion' as Edgar had so *plainly* suggested, we would've been able to give you a full mark. But now, I'm contemplating." She then squints her eyes at me. "But perhaps I may not have to worry as much, since you leaving it empty turned out to be a blessing in disguise for your next class."

I'm not sure I'm following what she means by that. A blessing in disguise? Next class?

But at least, now I can confirm the name of my counselor. Edgar. I almost thought it was Allen that I had heard. Thank God I hadn't mentioned it aloud.

"Now, for *our* lunch," she announces.

I tilt my head, confused, when Princess Prudence

suddenly waves a small bell on her table, after which the royal academy assistants immediately come with two covered plates.

During the meal, Princess Prudence keeps pointing out what I should do and don't. I guess you could say I've now received the *Finest Table Manner* lesson in advance.

But it's so annoying to be told what to do. I only believe in the practicality of doing things, so when she tells me to patiently cut the small peas in half before eating, I can't help but struggle. She gives me these eyes when the peas start flying around. I mean, who cut all their little peas in half? This feels like such a waste of time.

I can't believe I'm saying this, but now, I just can't wait to get to *Dancing with a Prince*.

36

The afternoon class today is happening in the same Festivity Hall, except all the tables have now gone and there are some guys waiting with my fellow classmates.

Princes from the Royal Prince Academy?

Anyway, this may be why the Counsellor – Edgar – is so excited. I may get to dance with a prince today. Maybe he sees Leon and Reon as a threat, without knowing that I'm already thinking of declining the Crown Prince's hands for a dance.

I mean, what does he expect? That every princess in the kingdom wants to marry him just because he's the *Crown Prince*? Well, not *this* princess.

Jerome, my stupid cousin, is there too among the scattered rest, which makes it that they must all be the Diamond Princes. One, two, three, four, five.

Five? Why is there only five?

Where's the Crown Prince?

Jerome and Melodie are looking like the extraverted

ones, trying to gather everyone into one big group, which they have succeeded.

"Cousin!" Jerome suddenly screams. "Over here!"

Argh, *shit*. You know what? I'll just ignore him. Besides, I don't feel like the other girls… would want me there.

Surprisingly, Melodie comes out of the group and approaches me.

"Are you alright?" Melodie asks.

"Yes," I say. Why should I not be?

"The others were worried about you too," she says as she's now basically pulling my arms to drag me into the group.

They were all worried about me? Worried about what? But that seems unlikely – the part where they all worried about me.

As I'm now standing with everyone, I try to observe all the other princes closely.

I wonder which one could have the attributes to pull the murder off.

But for a short moment, I sigh in relief. At least none of them are – you know – *the mummies*. Two are the periodic-table princes, Isaac and Humbert. Isaac looks like he's been preoccupied by his own mind whereas Humbert looks like he's just annoyed all the time – kind of like Leonie but male version. Then there's one that looks a bit chubby, and judging from the smudges of chocolate on his pants, this must be Prince Kitburry. And then finally, there's the other one that I don't recognise. But for some reason, he keeps staring at me with a dampened smile.

"So, Seraphine, why don't you say something to the princes?" Orianne asks while smiling and blinking her eyes repeatedly at me.

Why is she acting like that? Like we're *friends*, I think. I mean, I thought she hated me.

I can't believe you've just said that, Seraphine.

I look at the other princesses and I become more confused. I don't understand. Why are they all smiling at me? And what do they want me to say?

"Say something, Seraphine, go on!" Coralie says.

I look at Coralie in a baffle.

Seraphine, have more sympathy, will you? I remember her saying that to me just the other night, sounding so angry.

"Just be yourself," Melodie encourages me with a big smile and her hands sort of push me towards the princes by my shoulders.

I swallow.

Just be yourself.

I guess… I'll just say whatever's in my mind then. Right.

"Then… I'll start with you." I face the two periodic-table princes. "You're Prince Humbert," I point my finger at him, then move it to his right. "You're Prince Isaac. By the way, I will need to smell your jacket later," I say bluntly.

I think I speak at a faster speed than usual too. Am I nervous? Anyway, proceed.

"Next, you," I point at who I believe is Prince Kitburry. "There are smudges of chocolates on your pants," I point at the smudges, "so you must be Prince Kitburry. And now, you," I now face the stranger prince. Handsome – *very* handsome, actually – with short black hair, blue eyes, and on his two earlobes are placed two gold solid-round earrings. "I haven't heard about your name, so I can't say anything other than you love your roses. The scratches on your elbows and the two petals on the edges of your right shoe say so." And then, the very last one. "Oh, and hi, Jerome." I can't believe I've managed to say all of these within one breath.

But, silence. No response, except if I take into account all the princesses' mouths that are currently wide open.

What's the matter? My face now conveys discombobulated expressions towards the girls. They did say they wanted me so say something. There you go.

Leonie sighs. "Okay. We should've probably said, 'Seraphine, introduce yourself so at least one of them would remember your name and take your hand for a dance. Don't investigate.' Or something like that."

Ghyslaine flicks her head. "I should've seen this coming, considering you've never even had your first date.

This," she moves her pointy finger in the air forming a curved shape at my forehead, "is what will never get you your first date. Do you understand?"

Jerome, in response, laughs at me. "Okay, as her cousin, I can vouch that she's not a lunatic. She's just being–"

"A *detective*. Princess Seraphine." The handsome stranger-prince saunters towards me. He then reaches for my right palm. "Prince Florian of the Eighth Provincial Region. Forgive me." And now, he kisses the back of my hand.

I think my heart has just skipped a beat.
Not again.
But, "We meet again," he says.
Huh?
The other princesses are now acting in a very strange way. Their hands look like they're now punching the air towards the ceiling, they're hugging each other, and they're constantly smiling cheerfully – even Leonie and Ghyslaine included.

"I'm sorry, I don't think we've met," I say bluntly.
It's true. I really don't think so.
I hear the other princesses groan and so I stare at them again confusedly. But seriously, I really don't think I've ever seen him before in my life. He can't be one of the mummies, can he? I mean, with a face and gentle-demeanor like this, I wouldn't say I'd have not thought about picking

him to dance with me for formality sake.

"One of my trips to your region a couple years back, as I was on a… mission," he clears his throat. "But I believe you were in one of your *cases*. You were barging into this flower shop and asking questions about some petals on a murder victim. I came to your rescue with an answer. You said 'thank you' and then you just left."

Okay, now that he's mentioned it that way, that really sounds like me.

"And what is this your friends were saying about you've never been on a date?" he asks rather curiously as he walks up to me closer, I have to retreat a couple steps behind.

But all of a sudden, all the lights are off. I'm thinking, another murder? Only straight after, the chandelier lights are back on and a classic ballad instrumental starts to play.

In a very quick move, two people – one male and one female – jump off from the second floor and land safely with a graceful dancing pose. The male is in a black-and-red dancing robe and the female with a formal ball gown of similar color.

I've got to say, that's actually pretty impressive despite looking very dangerous.

"Diamond Classes of both, welcome!" Both of them shout with their hands up high, afterward bow, then dance again. They look very energetic.

Subsequently, they introduce themselves as Fabien and Fabienne as they dance.

Why am I not surprised?

"Dancing is a matter of connecting one's true *desire* over another. See what I did there?" Fabienne chuckles. "That's right! Your very first school assignment here… is from us!"

"From us!" Fabien repeats.

I roll my eyes.

"Now, we have determined each of your dance partners based on the answers you've all given." Fabienne's eyes move slowly around all of us. "We will be reading them to you, to which you should come forward to the dance floor and meet your companion for the twirl."

"The twirl!" Fabien repeats.

The lights are suddenly turned off again, and then it goes back to shine only on Fabienne, forming a spotlight as the music starts.

Oh, God. Please don't tell me this is going to turn into a musical.

"If you could only get one wish, what would it be?" Fabienne starts singing. *"You can ask for anything you want, you shall write whatever you truly desire, and one thing will surely be granted – should you pass the threshold point. May we recommend: a specific that fills up your royal needs."*

Damn it. Why do I have to be right this time?

Fabien and Fabienne are dancing again with now

two spotlights following them around.

If I was wearing a watch, I would definitely look at my wrist. I just want to get this class done and over with.

"At last, lady princesses and gentle princes. The moment you have all been waiting for." Fabien gives Fabienne a scroll for her to read. "The first pair! The princess first." She then pauses for momentum, then goes on singing again. "A fountain full of chocolate. Princess Melodie of the Eleventh Provincial Region!"

Melodie walks a few steps forward. She looks a bit unsure as the spotlight shines just on her. "And now, for the prince. It's Fabien's turn to sing. A swimming pool of chocolate. Prince Kitburry of the Seventh Provincial Region!" The spotlight now adds to two, shining on Kitburry as he walks towards Melodie confusedly. But then the lights are turned off once more and now moving back to shine only on Fabienne again.

"The second pair! Protective gears and first aid kits for chemical explosions. Princess Orianne of the Fourth Provincial Region!"

This one is going to be a no-brainer.

"A laboratory space filled with…"

Fabien swiftly grabs the scroll from Fabienne, then takes in a very deep breath, before he starts rapping. "… science equipment things! I'll also write some other things here just to be clear. Funnels. Beakers. pH meters. Pipettes. Goggles. Fire extinguisher. Glassware. Hot plates.

Incubators. Freezers. Mixers. Agitators. Scales. Centrifuges. Bunsen burners. Okay, I think that's it. Oh, wait! I'll also need some lab gloves, plus two or three coats too. Prince Isaac of the Fifth Provincial Region!"

As Fabien collapses on the dance floor, running out of breath, Fabienne approaches him to grab the other scroll herself. "The third pair! The brightest diamond necklace in the whole world. Princess Ghyslaine of the First Provincial Region!"

"Well, I already have one. I just thought I could need another one," Ghyslaine mumbles stridently as the spotlight follows her.

"A special gogglegear that can see through even the brightest sun and the darkest sky." Fabien seems to have now recovered. "Prince Jerome of the Second Provincial Region!"

"What? This is unacceptable!" Ghyslaine complains as sunshine Jerome walks happily towards her. After both of their spotlights are off, I can still hear the faint sound from Ghyslaine keeps protesting as the music volume goes up.

"The fourth pair! F this, F my life. If you're curious to know what the F is, it simply means austerely *fabulous*. Princess Leonie of the Third Provincial Region!"

"For everyone including my best bud to shut the F up. P.S. F means *fabulate*. Prince Humbert of the Sixth Provincial Region!"

"And now, we've come to the fifth pair!" Fabienne sings.

"The fifth pair!" Fabien repeats.

"A garden filled with fruits and vegetables. Princess Coralie of the Ninth Provincial Region!" Fabienne sings again.

Fabien takes over. "A royal-asscher rose, the most beautiful and rarest flower of all. One of its kind, of whom I desire to be with for the rest of my life. Prince Florian, Eighth Provincial Region!"

For some reason, Florian shifts a look at me and looks disappointed.

"And now the sixth pair," Fabienne sings in a whispery voice. "The last pair."

"The last pair!" Fabienne sings and *shouts*.

Now I get it. Instantly, this makes sense of all the questions Princess Prudence was asking me.

Well, I guess it's my turn now. And since he's a no show, I just hope that means I can go home early – since I have no one to dance with.

"Nothing," Fabienne sings in a much lower voice.

"Nothing?" Fabienne sings, still shouting.

"They both say nothing."

"They both say nothing?"

"They both wrote nothing."

"They both wrote nothing?"

"Princess Seraphine of the Twelfth Provincial

Region… and… Prince Gregorius the Crown Prince."

Their song suddenly ends with only one spotlight in the room, shining right at my face. I can still hear everyone else's loud gasping voice.

Subsequently, all the lights are completely turned on again. Everyone is still looking at me with their mouths wide open.

Only Fabienne approaches me. She lets out a smile and gently rests both of her palms on my shoulders. "I'm sorry that His Royal Highness is a no show. It's as expected as to what currently the state of matter is. But be assured that we have been thinking about this. You will act as an audience here in the meantime throughout the duration of the class."

Great! I think. Although, it'd be much better if I could just go home now.

"However," she continues, "We're still thinking of alternatives to find a suitable partner for you. After all, all the princes have been chosen as each of their dance partners, a princess. If you could just wait here after the class, I can promise you we'll try everything we can to get your proper lesson covered today."

Great, I sigh.

As the official dancing lesson is about to start for everyone else, I sit on the side as I've been ordered to watch how the dance works in accordance with the book *Dance Courtesy for Royals*. I think Lady Francoise already taught me this sometime ago but I just couldn't care less.

Fabien starts the lesson by asking the princes to bring out their gloves from their pockets before the dancing really begins.

"Just as his handkerchief, a gentle-prince always brings his own pair of gloves," Fabien says. It suddenly reminds me of how I once accused Reon as a Royal Phantom because of it. "Now, princes, I want you to close your eyes. Think of a place. Anywhere but this hall. Somewhere, out there. Under the sun. Beneath the stars. Think about the fresh scent of grass just passing through your nostrils. Only when it's vivid in your mind, you may then open your eyes and see the beauty right before you. And now, bow for courtesy, ask for your princess' hands, and start to dance."

For some reason, I pay attention. I guess because this is just a class, there's no date obligation involved, but I do now understand more about the importance of chemistry between the two people. One truly desires. Royal needs. Both of us filled the assignment with *nothing*.

If I was right in the first place…

But suddenly, the class ends and all the others start walking to where I sit. They all say they feel sad for me and will wait with me, but I say I couldn't care less about it.

All I can think about now is how I *need* to sniff on Isaac's jacket. But when I'm just about to do it, Fabien and Fabienne ask them to leave.

And so I continue to wait in the Festivity Hall, all by myself, as I'm told.

37

This is really drawing in my impatience. How long have I been sitting here? An hour and a half, at least.

Out of boredom, I go out of the building to see Leon and the other guards from back home waiting for me. I tell Leon in private about everything that's happened as I rest my back on the outer wall of the academy, standing. He's almost speechless from the shock, but then he manages to put some words back on his tongue.

"Maybe the Crown Prince has seen something in you, the same thing that I have been seeing. All I can take is that there's a high chance that you'd be the future Queen Consort for the whole kingdom," he says with a big smile. But there's something about his tone that feels different. Almost like… he's not entirely happy about it.

"Well, what if I don't want to? For a start, because of him, I'm stuck here in this school until further notice. This is really annoying," I grumble.

"I tell you what? How about I wait with you inside?

I'm not sure if it's allowed, but maybe they could make some exceptions. You know what? They *should*. I don't like the idea of you waiting all by yourself in the hall," he complains.

This guy is always about safety and protocols, but I smile regardless and say, "Sounds great!"

All the students seem to have already gone home, so it feels like there's just me and Leon sitting here in the hall. I start telling him about everything from the start, except about the secret passageway moments. He seems to find it funny that I'd been accusing Reon as the Royal Phantom, but he tells me not to disregard it completely.

"If there's anything I've learned for the past three years, it's that you have a good instinct when it comes to mysteries like this. And also a bad memory when it comes to anything else other than puzzles and clues. Am I right?" he laughs.

"I'm not even the best at that – *yet*. I'm still learning," I say while moving my legs back and forth.

"Well, you're already the best *detective* to me. You were just born... *different*," he smiles.

Afterward, there's a long pause.

My head looks up then around the hall. "You know, this almost feels like we're back home."

"I know," he says while now looking around the hall too. "I wish I'd seen the princes who fought for you then," he laughs.

"Fought for *themselves*," I retort. "There's a difference. They didn't care about me. They only cared about who was winning."

"Well, I think, they were fighting for your attention too. You just didn't see it. You know, you never really consider the effect you can have on people. All the princes out there… I'm sure they find you really charming, and attractive, not to mention extraordinary."

I snort. "And weird, and cold, and *bloody*," I say. "I bet the Crown Prince accidentally chose me in his sleep," I joke.

"See? This is exactly what I'm talking about," Leon instead takes it seriously. I can feel his temper rising for whatever reasons. "Why didn't it ever occur to you that the Crown Prince may have seen something in you the second you were chosen as one of the Diamond Princesses? Even the headmistress could see it. *I* could see it too. You're hopelessly clueless when it comes to other people's feelings!" He rubs his hair from the top to near the back of his neck, before he goes on again. "Whenever you talk about the Crown Prince, I feel like it's always about the killer or the Royal Phantom for you – and about any other princes for that matter. Do you know how I've been putting extra hours to not just secure the premises but look for any potential that the Crown Prince might be watching you? Because I just have this *feeling*. And you know what else I've found? The eyes of the Crown Prince's royal knights are always around *us*." Just like that, the percentage has suddenly gone up. "But even if I had told you that, not even for one second you'd ever think about whether the Crown Prince has been watching you all this time. Maybe he's even fallen for you. I know *I have*."

Leon suddenly stops every movement in his body. Sweats are suddenly pouring all over his face. His eyes have enlarged to his consternation – so have mine.

"What did you just say?" I ask.

I know what I've heard. I just still can't believe it.

Leon pushes his upper body forward to hunch. His elbows rest on his thighs and both of his palms stand against his whole face.

There's a long pause again. A very long pause. But I choose to let us be, until he's ready.

"I'd promised myself to bring this to my grave," he says in a very quiet voice. "Even when I really, really tried by giving us some space. I thought… Princess, I…" and then we're back to silence.

"I was looking for you when I was about to choose someone to dance with during my ceremony," I say. My legs are still moving back and forth, my eyes are looking at my skirt. "I was thinking, if I were to dance with someone that night, I'd only want to dance with you."

For some reason, I'm sort of hoping he'd ask me to dance right here, right now. But I know he won't.

I just know.

Leon gets his hands off his face and shifts his head to look at me. "But… that doesn't make any sense. You were supposed to dance with a *prince*," he says.

"That's the thing," I say. "Maybe… I just didn't care. I never care. You know, lately, I've even been thinking if I should just give up my royal status and not marry a prince," I say in a very relaxed manner. Half joking, but that also means I'm half serious.

Leon suddenly turns into my parents' mode. "Certainly not, Princess! That… That is simply out of the question. You shall only marry a prince!"

I stare at Leon perplexedly. I could've sworn my parents would've said just the same thing, except my father would also cry hysterically. And so I laugh.

"This is not a funny matter, Princess. I know my place. I always make sure I do. And I can assure you, that my feelings towards you will not stand in any way of my duty to protect you, nor even you marrying any prince, which I will do everything in my power to assist," he declares. "And what is taking so long?" Leon comes back to feeling so agitated about the wait. "What are they even doing now? Making a princess wait should be a crime," he says.

In response, I laugh again. It's funny how, even after all that, we can still be like this. If anything, it's like we're back to exactly what we were. Just friends, or maybe even more. Closer.

"I guess they're still struggling to find me a dance partner for class. They did say all the princes were taken. I guess they just have to fly one in," I joke.

Leon, apparently, completely misses the point of me being just kidding. "Well, that will not do. How long do you think they're going to make one fly here? I'm going to try to do something about this. You just wait here, Princess. I will do everything in my power to bring you home safely and sound before dinner time," he vows.

Leon then stands, bows, and immediately goes out of the door. And now, I'm all alone again.

"You could just stay here and wait with me, you know. That will do," I mutter to myself.

But Leon does what he always does.

I swing my legs back and forth against the chair once more. I know I'm not supposed to do this. Not very princess-like. Against the sacred *Book of Manners for Princesses* for sure. But, whatever. I just don't care anymore. There are more important things to me now. Such as, to think that Leon has just confessed to me – by *accident*. And to also think that… I don't feel the urge to reciprocate. Is it because of–

"I thought he said he didn't like the idea of you waiting all by yourself in the hall," I suddenly hear Reon's voice.

I chuckle. Is it getting this worse that he now starts speaking in my head during the day? But, it really did sound like he wasn't just in my head. Completely different compared to whenever I just talk in my head – which I do all the time. So am I just turning crazy?

When the door is suddenly wide open to a very familiar shadow on the floor, I let out a deep breath to express my relief. *Leon*, I think? Except, he's not.

Wait. He's– Has it gotten so much worse than I've started… hallucinating?

"Re–Reon?" I stutter. "Is that really you?"

When he's now standing right in front of me, I know it's really him alright.

"What are you doing here?" I ask.

"It's been two hours late, and you haven't come home. Not even the royal guards. I guess you could say… that I was worried," he answers, blushing.

He's now wearing the exact outfit the first time we met. White silky long-sleeve shirt and pants. But this time, his hands are empty.

Out of the blue, I'm so glad that every commoner here dresses and behaves gracefully like a royal. No one could really tell the difference.

I neither can nor care.

"So, how much longer do you think you're going to be here?"

"I guess I'm stuck here until the teacher finds me someone to have a dance with," I say in exasperation. "When did you arrive?"

Reon doesn't answer my question and instead, he just saunters down into the middle of the hall with his hands crossed on his back. His head is now looking at the ceiling and around the upper walls.

That natural princely behaviour.

"If I ask for your hand to dance, what would you say, Your Royal Highness?" he asks while looking right at me from afar, his hands making a cross on his back.

Reon is asking me to dance.

The audacity, no more.

"I swear I'm not the Royal Phantom, but I just happen to bring a pair of gloves." His smile under the dim chandelier lights has just uplifted his level of handsomeness by a billion.

Honestly, I don't even want to care anymore.

Who he really is. One hundred percent.

So I've decided to just go with my instinct by walking towards him. Very slowly.

"Just a pair of gloves? No handkerchief?" I tease.

I'll go with my feelings this time. And no-brainer, with that gorgeous face of his.

"Why? Do you think you will need a handkerchief to dance?" He giggles splendidly.

"I could fall, and cry, and then I will need the handkerchief," I say.

I'm just a couple meters away from him now.

"Well then, consider that I don't have any with me.

In fact, I will make sure you won't need one."

He takes out his gloves and starts wearing them. His right arm stretches to ready pull me in, while his face gleams in complete patience and anticipation. Very prince-like.

Centimetres away.

"I take your hand, alright," I chuckle.

Inches away.

He laughs and shakes his head a little. "That should be my line," he says. He's pulling me in now. "Princess Seraphine, allow me to take your hand and lead you through this."

Our hands have now come together as one. Gently and slowly, he moves my left hand to his chest. I'm feeling his heartbeat. Reon's heartbeat. It's quickened to the point of being fast and irregular, just like mine, but his bearing still keeps to poise and composure. I haul my head up to assess his breathing, searching for a sign of even a slight of trepidation, but that just gets us to stare at each other for the longest time.

He's just perfect.

I totally forgot what I was supposed to do.

"Forgive me," he says, before he moves his right hand to my waist.

My heart is beating at the speed of a tornado, but for some reason, I'm still managing to act calm – though *barely*. I think I'm starting to tremble a little, but his left hand grips my right to stabilize. He balances me. No. More like, he complements me – case or no cases. Heck, I'm not even thinking about the murder case right now.

What was it that I was supposed to do with the case?

Both of our feet now move very slowly without music. I want to keep staring at his eyes, but I find myself looking down on the floor most of the time to avoid my heels stepping into his shoes.

"Guess it really shows that I had never danced with anyone before," I say while focusing on our shoes. "If we don't count my governess, that is."

"Well, right now, you're dancing with my feet," he complains. But then gently, he lets go of his right hand to gently bring my chin up – so that our eyes meet again. This cheeky buggard.

He's just perfect. Everything he does is.

"And now, you're dancing with me again," he says. But I'm beginning to worry about our feet again. "It's okay," he speaks softly while his touch slightly presses on the skin of my chin one more time. "Just feel the steps. Follow my lead, and let me worry about our feet."

I try my best to follow. It's working. And it feels so much better now, because this way, I have all the excuse in the world to keep looking at him. Just him.

Just Reon.

"See, you've got it. Now, I'm going to try to spin

you. Lift you up a bit. Ready?" he offers.

I nod calmly but with fireworks of excitement in my heart. And then he does. I feel the sudden warmth in my body, maybe even a little bit of goosebumps. It's not logical that I can and cannot breathe at the same time. Not even science would be able to explain this. But I want him to do it again. And as if he could read my mind, he does it again.

He's just perfect. Everything he does is. I keep repeating in my head.

"I think you're already much better than the Diamond Princes in my class just now," I say.

It's the truth. Isaac was dancing like his mind was brewing some chemicals on his glass beaker. Humbert, strangely, was looking like he was so afraid to step on Leonie's feet the whole time that he continuously did. Kitburry seemed to focus more on secretly sneaking out chocolate lollies to Melodie than actually dancing. Jerome was constantly being beaten by Ghyslaine that it looked more like a one-sided fight. And Florian… Well, it just looked like he couldn't keep his eyes on Coralie.

Reon shakes his head and laughs again. "Well, you've never danced with another prince before. It's all just from the book, really," he says, trying to be humble.

"Another prince? But, you're not even a prince, aren't you?" I say, but I'm still turning my eyes suspiciously.

Though I've always had this feeling, I think.

"True," he says slowly and hesitantly. "I'm Reon, the

servant boy. Only, a servant boy."

"Unless–Whoops!" I suddenly panic. I accidentally step on one of his feet and lose my balance, but luckily, Reon is quick to catch my back. "Sorry," I say.

"I've got you. Like I said."

"Luckily I didn't do that in public," I blurt.

"Imagine. What would they say," he says as he smiles.

"That I'm the worst princess ever born," I giggle.

Suddenly, there's a momentary pause. Maybe I shouldn't have joked about that.

"How did you feel when you read it?" Suddenly, the air around him turns serious.

We're still moving, dancing at a slow pace. At ease. No hurry. Just maneuvering.

"Well, I don't really know, actually." Let me think. "Maybe I was a bit sad at first, but then I came to slowly accept that maybe I was, maybe I wasn't. Leon said I was just born… *different*."

"Well, for once, I agree with your *bodyguard*," he sighs before rolling his eyes. "I hope you never take it to heart when they're saying something like that about you. It never matters what they all say. What truly matters is what you think about yourself. And the people who love you. I've learned it the hard way."

Our eyes lock as he tries to move my waist for a light spin on the floor. He does it so gently and gracefully,

I'm not even feeling anxious anymore. I just know he will never let me fall.

Just like the Royal Phantom.

"And you didn't slip," he laughs.

"Right, I didn't," I laugh too. "Maybe I'm ready to dance in public now."

I've learned it the hard way, he said. Still lingers in my head.

"Speaking of dancing in public, I hope you don't take me as rude as I have to admit I was. I was just by the door when Leon… said those things. Everything, actually," he sounds a bit reluctant. I wonder how much is… *everything*. "You were really thinking about dancing with him in your ceremony? In front of everyone?"

"I… was. I did," I say hesitantly.

"Were you… are you…"

His eyes briefly depart from me. We're still slow dancing with no music, but that's just about it.

"What were you going to ask me?" I ask, trying to get him to look me in the eye again.

"Well…" he dawdles, "how do you feel about… him?" He's now biting his lips.

"I… honestly don't know," I tell the truth. "I thought I… but then…" I try to be very careful with my words as I'm looking at him. I don't want to *accidentally blurt out* like Leon did. "You know what? I think Leon's right about this. What did he say again? That I was hopelessly–"

"– clueless when it comes to other people's feelings," we end up saying it together.

"Right," I chuckle. Well, now I'm sure he definitely knows about Leon's confession. "I guess one of those people includes me." I shrug my shoulders.

"Well, I guess we should start working on that," he laughs.

"I know right, since Leon hasn't," I snort, my gaze drifting sideways. "It's about time that someone would help me in that department. I thought Leon was supposed to, but then he'd start talking about protection and boundaries and whatever." I roll my eyes.

"In that case, let me help you, Detective."

Immediately, I let go of his hands and start pulling away. Reon looks very startled.

"That's the *third*."

Reon stares at me confusedly. "I beg your pardon?"

"Second, when you gave me your glove last Saturday. And first," I breathe in deeply then out, "when I first sneaked out of the palace back home. You're that town boy I first met three years ago."

Reon fixes his gaze at me, but he neither seems startled nor confused this time. Not even as much as being in panic. He just looks like he's thinking. Very carefully.

It almost appears to me like he's been expecting this.

He closes his eyes. Now, it's his turn to exhale

deeply and out.

"Are you sure this is only the third time we've met?" he challenges.

This time, I'm the one who looks startled and confused. And panicking.

38

That day, I had just turned thirteen. The August leaves were at their brightest green when I managed to slip out of the palace with what I thought was the worst clothes I'd got. A long dress made of silk that had turned faded white all over.

I was always told that the town was dangerous and filled with people who committed crimes, but I still went anyway. Maybe I had thought that I had to see them for myself – the royal subjects, my father had just told me, I was destined by birth to rule upon.

When I first arrived, everyone was still looking at me like I didn't belong. My ugliest dress was still too good to blend in with the judging crowd. As spontaneous and immediate, I kept catching the attention of anyone who saw me passing by, as they were giving me a pair of tired, yellow eyes. I had never really felt like I was in danger before, but at that time, I really thought that any of them would definitely *kill* me for my dress, and so as fast as I could, I found myself hurrying my pace even when no one was chasing me.

I was very, very scared.

I hid myself in an empty alley that could barely fit my width. Next to me was a half-broken glass window as my sole entertainment.

I was planning to wait there until someone from the palace would get me back home safely. Leon, to be exact. He was only fifteen but he was my only hope. If there was anyone who could find me, who could protect me, it was only him. Always.

After a long while, I watched the small window closely as I was scared *and* bored. I came to realise that it was someone's house, and the owner was this old lady wearing a brown ragged dress. About a minute later, I saw a lady with glasses walking into the living room. A few minutes afterward, a man. And then a few minutes after that, another lady.

As it turned out, they were her children and they all had come empty handed.

One of the ladies poured water into the owner's cup, then the man set out cookies on the plate while the other lady with glasses kept massaging the old lady's neck.

One minute. The owner suddenly fell to her death, along with her cup. Both ladies screamed and the man looked horrified. A couple of policemen who just happened to be nearby immediately barged in, along with the people around the neighborhood who ended up watching from outside the door.

Two minutes. I rubbed mud and dirt all over my face and dress, then came out of my shell to look at the body closely.

Three minutes. The policemen were about to get me out of the room just when I said, "Poison. Potassium cyanide. Foam started bursting from her mouth." They said it'd normally take days to get it analysed, but I ignored them at a stroke. I got up, subsequently sat on one of the chairs and just stared at all three suspects without moving my eyes elsewhere.

Four minutes. They all looked at me so bewilderingly, not knowing I was just simply in my *deep thoughts.* A bunch of strangers shook my shoulders as a result. They were worried as I hadn't moved my body at all, as if maybe I had accidentally ingested the poison myself, however it might be.

And then, *five minutes.* I came out of my trance. "I'm alright. I was just thinking," I said. "So now, I know who the killer is," I announced. I pointed at the lady with glasses. "She rubbed the poison on her neck. And she's about to die too."

Witnesses professed my face showed no emotion as I said it.

I solved the case in exactly five minutes, but when the murderer fell dead before me, I was forced to dismiss my quick reward. It didn't digest within me why she killed someone and then killed herself at the same time.

Her siblings were holding her as the killer was dying, but she looked right at me while saying her last words, "You are no human. You have no heart."

When I looked around, everyone stared at me like she was right. *Even when she was the killer*, I thought. And so I ran back into the alley and sobbed.

Is this what they all think of me? And the worst part is, I believed she was right.

But then came this town boy who looked as dirty and muddy as me with his light and long black coat, white shirt, dark grey pants, white running shoes, and deep-blue low cotton hat that shows a silhouette of the Blue Tiara right in the middle – all have now become mine.

"What's with those puffy eyes?" he said. I looked up, then drove myself to sniff back the tears. "You look like you need somewhere to hide," he said with a sparkling smile, his skin looked almost glittered. "Let me help you, Detective," he offered while reaching out his hand to me.

And so the memory flashed before my eyes and ended as quickly.

"Another deep thought," he reminds me.

"That's why you knew," I gather as I briefly recall our first moment looking at the Crown Prince's castle. "But you were gone," I say. "After that day, you never came back."

"For the past three years, I never left."

His words jolt me out of breath in an instant. "What do you mean you never left?"

He starts his explanation with a sigh. "Exactly that. I was constantly around. You were just always accusing me of something. Just like what you did now, with the Royal Phantom. I have to say, you have the worst memory when it comes to people's faces," he argues.

"I *never* forget a face," I retort.

"True, except when they're no longer important for a case or when you think they all look the same. Whenever they're not relevant to you anymore, you just discard them from your memory. Something about your eyes that see people – and the world, for that matter – differently and the same. I am the living proof of that," he shrugs his shoulders.

I roll my eyes. That stings but only because he's right, as much as he's the only one who's ever pointed that out loud.

"But you never came forward." I still try to fight back. "Why didn't you?"

"That's because… I was hiding," he tries to explain. "I was always in some sort of disguise. I couldn't risk getting my true identity known. But at the same time, I wanted you to recognise me, same as now. It's been so hard to keep the balance. That's why I was always trying to leave you a hint. Risking everything, wondering if today would be the day you would recognise me. For the past three years. Every. Single. Case."

We stare at each other in silence for a short while.

"True identity, you say?" I contend.

He sighs in consternation. "And that's the only thing you've picked up?" He then rubs his forehead all the way to the back of his head with frustration. "If I must directly answer, *yes*. But I've made a *promise* not to tell. You know what that means, *Detective*."

A *royal promise*, I think, and that I have to figure it out myself; though, I have this feeling that, "I know." I swallow deep. "I believe I know who you are."

Reon stares at me in both calmness and anticipation.

Say it, his eyes convey the words so clearly.

I mean, I'd be lying if I say I've never thought of it. I only keep away from the signs because even the mere idea of it still sounds beyond incomprehensible. I'm not even a hundred percent sure yet. And I don't want to sound stupid and delusional, if I happen to be wrong about… "You're the–"

The royal trumpets are suddenly played just outside the hall.

This is just the worst timing ever.

But beyond our own kind of surprise, Prince Providence, Princess Prudence, Leon, and all the teachers come into the Festivity Hall in a haste. They look like they'd been running, which they weren't supposed to, manner-wise – except for Leon.

Princess Prudence walks hurriedly towards me and abruptly stands in between me and Reon that he has to step back, as if he's not of any importance. She then puts both of her hands on my shoulders and lets out a grin from ear to ear. "The Crown Prince… is here," she proclaims happily, though her voice alarmingly trembles.

Well… in that case… What in the world could make her so anxious, she's disregarding someone *that* important behind her?

"I know," I say, then I squint my eyes at Reon. But what catches me on the hop is how perplexed he's looking at me right now. Then I shift my gaze back at Princess Prudence, and now, she's just looking at the door.

Wait. I'm confused. I thought *he* was the–

But what comes distractingly after is the Crown Prince's army with that Yves guy leading at the front, followed by a guy who wears a mask, looks, acts, and dresses almost exactly like… the Royal Phantom. I repeat. *The* Royal Phantom. Only without the long hair.

Everyone else, except me and Reon, are now bowing before him as he passes them.

Wait. Now I'm *really* confused.

This Royal-Phantom guy is now walking with sure steps towards me, staring deeply right at me while disregarding the people who are now keeping to bend their upper bodies for him.

As he now stands right before me, I study his face with squinted eyes.

Those eyes – they're emerald green and sparklingly beautiful. A perfect match to both the Royal Phantom and… Reon too.

Who the hell is this guy?

As fast as lightning, I turn my head to the right again to see what Reon's up to, and to my own surprise, he's now bowing to the guy with the mask too.

Now, I'm the only one who doesn't show respect to whoever this is.

This… Royal Phantom? No. The *real* Royal Phantom wouldn't be this stupid… would he?

"Princess Seraphine of the Twelfth Provincial Region," he says while eerily nodding to himself. But his voice… very different from the Royal Phantom. This one sounds more like a blistering schmuck. And he doesn't even say the word *kid*. "I believe we have some lessons to attend."

Fabien and Fabienne suddenly come towards the back of the dance floor in a haste and bow as they wait for further instruction, then they leave to give me and this strange guy some space.

"Who are you?" I ask. "You cannot be… the Crown Prince?" or the Royal Phantom?

And then I look at Reon again.

Still. *Nothingness.*

That's a stupid question and a stupid statement coming out of my mouth, I know, but I think someone just has to say it out loud.

Everyone else is now just looking to their left and right. In contrast, this Royal-Phantom guy bursts out a very loud laugh, and as such, the other subjects in the hall feel pressured to laugh with him, as they eventually do.

Kind of reminds me of Gaspard, if he was my age and taller with a much flatter belly and seemingly perfect facial features.

But I look to my right again and Reon is still bowing respectfully at him too. He's not laughing, but he's also not saying anything.

He can't be serious? I mean, I really thought *he* was the–

"I've heard a lot about you." I'm back staring at this Royal-Phantom guy in effect. "In fact, I've read *everything* about you. Forgive me, Princess, for making my presence very difficult to grasp, but I do hope that this is worth the wait. After all, I've broken all the protocols just to see you. *I have to.*" This strange guy now reaches for my right hand and kisses the back of it. "Prince Gregorius, the Crown Prince."

Did I just... cringe?

And did he really just say the Crown Prince?

The freaking Crown Prince of the Kingdom of Oceastarasia?

"I see you've now turned speechless with my unexpected attendance," he giggles. "Is that your signal for us to start with our lesson, my *dear* Princess?"

Yep. I've definitely just cringed. *Again.*

This Crown-Prince guy thereafter claps his hands in the air as a signal in such a way that very much irritates me. Everyone else but the teachers is now leaving as he's silently ordered them to, including Reon.

My Reon, I think.

But he's not looking back.

In turn, Fabien and Fabienne start giving out instructions in such a tone and gesture that are much too polite than what I have witnessed in class this afternoon.

The Crown Prince acts respectfully and gracefully, except when he just pulls my hands and grabs my waist without permission, as we start dancing.

I can tell one of us is very excited about this, and it's definitely not me.

"I must tell you, I've never danced with a fellow royal before," he blurts.

"That makes two of us," I reply, but my eyes are still looking at the door.

"Do people usually talk while doing this?" he asks.

I raise my eyebrows. What is that supposed to mean?

This mysterious Crown Prince turns out to be a pain in the ass, as he proves to be very chatty too. Something about him being stuck in the castle. Something about him being jet lagged. Something about a horse. Something about him being trapped in his gigantic bedroom of an immersive game arcade. And then, something about his way of choosing *his* Diamonds.

"And so I told my father that this princess in the newspaper must be one of *my* Diamonds." Words keep coming out of his mouth, to my dismay. "You are so beautiful and smart and fearless and passionate as you are *sensational*." I raise my eyebrows at the last word. And yes, I've definitely just cringed again – and literally shivered. "When they told me about your Royal Rapport, my father just had to make the decree to consider *all* your murder-mystery adventures as royal convertible points. And, *voilà!* Suddenly, you've turned into as bright as a diamond, because of *me*!"

For once, now I know why some people want to kill him. I even want to grab a knife and take out his heart myself.

But if this joker of a guy is the real Crown Prince, then what about Reon? What's his true identity? And what about the fake Royal Phantom? The real murderer. And what about the real Royal Phantom? Is *he* even the real Royal Phantom?

I suddenly want to scratch my head so badly.

PART 3

The
Crown Prince

39

By some miracle, two hours have suddenly passed. But then the worst happens when the Crown Prince *orders* me to come to have dinner with him in his castle.

Well, at the very least, I get to have a look from the inside.

And then, I can tell Reon all about it tonight.

The Crown Prince's castle inner space is surprisingly not as grand as his big mouth is. On the contrary to his personality, it's the ultimate definition of humble luxury. Just the finest of materials and decorations with a defined purpose. Something that fits Reon more, in my opinion, but maybe that's just because I'm still pissed off that I was wrong again.

This joker of a Crown Prince is supposedly taking me on a personal tour around his own home, except that he doesn't even know anything about his castle at all. Yves in particular seems to know way more about the castle than him.

Looking at Leon's contorted face confirms that my growing vexation is not the result of any biases. In fact, if his feelings towards me stay true, I bet he's now thinking that I'm better off marrying him than the Crown Prince himself.

The rooms in the castle are mostly functional too, except for the Crown Prince's own bedroom, which apparently literally is an immersive game arcade. But what's really strange is how his bedroom is located underground. My instinct tells me there's definitely something fishy about this.

"My Princess, are you okay? You look like you're sick," he asks.

"I'm fine," I say coldly. "And stop saying 'My Princess'." Makes me want to vomit. "Just call me Seraphine."

"And you're *spicy* too," he says. "I must say… I like it."

I can't help but display the ultimate cringeness all over my face. I even have to fling my shoulders and shake out the abominable.

"Can we just move on to dinner, *quick*?" I ask rather impolitely.

At least, now I don't have to act like I respect him, because I *don't*. I just feel like walking on his face all over with my heels, even though he's the Crown Prince.

"But I still have so many rooms that I want to show

you, and it's all because my castle is so big, like the moon. Oh please, you should at least let me bring you to one more room," he says as he spins his hands in the air pointing nowhere.

You've got to be kidding me. He *cannot* be the future king – ruler of half of this world, for God's sake. My inner thought says maybe I have to kill this guy myself to save the whole kingdom from ruin. But maybe, that's the murderer's true motive; though suddenly, I don't feel the same contempt.

Still, why does the killer have to pretend to be the Royal Phantom?

Which reminds me.

"By the way…" I've finally decided to swallow my pride in order to initiate a conversation with this joker of a Crown Prince for the sake of the investigation. "Why are you dressing like that?"

"Like what, Seraphine?" He looks happy and confused at the same time.

"Like… the Royal Phantom."

"Oh, you mean the *great* phantom thief?" My brows furrowed in perplexity. "Why, only because I'm his biggest fan!" he answers cheerfully. "It's one of the reasons I decided to come back. I heard rumors that he was here in town!"

My mouth opens to a shock.

This… He's… Oh my God.

Was here in town to kill you, alright! I want to scream.

Even Leon looks astonishingly bewildered too, like he's about to trip and accidentally swing his sword at the Crown Prince. And I think I notice Yves stridently sighing in extreme fatigue, I genuinely start to feel sorry for him.

"But he's been stealing from your father – *the King* – may I remind you?" I shake my head.

Unbelievable. This guy. This Crown Prince. This *clown*, a future king.

"So? Why does it matter?" He shrugs his shoulders.

God, please save us all.

"But I must say…" What else can he possibly add to my current disbelief? "I think I'm your biggest fan now. That night you almost caught the Royal Phantom, I was so impressed I couldn't stop jumping on the bed!" Naturally, that explains why he's now jumping like a lunatic. "But I'm also glad that he managed to run away."

I just shake my head. I don't even know what to say anymore, even within my own brain.

Suddenly, I just feel so tired. This guy is draining *a lot* of my energy because he's just… so… incredibly… How do I put it nicely?… A world-class idiot.

"Can you show me the library? And then we have dinner, and then I go home," I plan out aloud. I just want to go home as quickly now. Get as far away from him.

Back to Reon.

The Crown Prince doesn't even seem to realise that,

technically, I've just given him orders, when it's supposed to be the other way around.

I let out a deep exhale again.

This guy is no leader. This guy is no future-king material. Heck, he will *definitely* bring the kingdom to ruin when he takes the throne. So now, I'm curious. What has he been doing besides locking himself and playing in his arcade game bedroom? What about his secret expedition? Who's actually the Royal Knight Commander, if it's not Yves? Why hasn't the King done anything to discipline this pathetic little joke that is his own flesh and blood? I mean, despite his formidable fury, the King is also known to be strong and fierce and loyal and wise. So why can't he implement the same values to his beloved son? Is His Imperial Majesty so worried about his son's safety that he'd just rather lock him in a gigantic bedroom filled with superior gaming gadgets? Out of love for his only son?

I keep on contemplating in my brain as we walk towards what should be the library. As expected, we've gotten lost for the hundredth time, he has to ask Yves again for the location. I roll my eyes.

But the best part about this tour is probably the library. As it is similar to the one in the mansion, it's even bigger and more enchanting than how it appears on the outside in that magical one minute.

It also somehow reminds me of how I always hang out with Reon in the library.

I miss Reon. He would even do just well as a reigning prince. Plus, he'd probably be a much better fit to be the next king than this guy. *The royal needs to attend to what the people need, and nothing else.* No. Reon's *definitely* a much better fit, even if he's not of royal blood. He's even better than all of us.

Which brings me back to this question.

Who is Reon if he's neither the mysterious Crown Prince nor the Royal Phantom?

As we *finally* get to one of the big dining rooms, the Crown Prince eventually lets go of his mask as he's ready himself to eat.

Being awfully shocked is not even close to what I'm feeling. With the exact same yellow hair and emerald-green eyes, he really reminds me of Reon – except in regards to everything else. And so I find myself keep staring at Gregorius as he's telling more of his nonsense stories while waving his golden spoon in the air like a kid.

I have to admit. The Crown Prince is… kind of nice to look at. In fact, I'd say he's way too handsome for his chowderhead. Almost as magnificently enchanting as Reon by the look, so imagine if he doesn't talk…

I want to slap myself.

No. Freaking. Way.

I cannot ever fall for this guy. No, more like, I *refuse* to fall in love with him, even when he is the Crown Prince.

40

I come home to find Reon in the library, reading as usual. Only this time, the Butler chooses to keep an eye on both of us very closely *at all times,* which is super annoying.

Reon and I, while we're fortunately still allowed to sit next to each other, only pretend that we're reading. The Butler is on his seat right across from us, pretending to read too.

"Can we go somewhere private?" I whisper while trying to subtly cover my whole face with the book in my hands.

I couldn't risk getting my true identity known.

I really want to get to the bottom of this.

"Unfortunately no, Princess," he whispers back. "You see, I'm under a *tight watch*." He flicks his head towards the Butler while shifting his book closer towards me.

"Why?" I ask. I raise my book slightly higher. "He's only a butler. Unless… he's *not* a butler."

"I can assure you, Your Royal Highness, that I am indeed just a butler. *Your* butler."

My shoulders immediately jump in effect. I turn my head towards my posterior very slowly. The Butler's hands cross on his back with the book he was "reading" and he gazes upon me so ferociously.

I'm so shocked. How did he even get behind me so fast and without notice?

Like a shadow moving.

I want to talk back, but there's something about his persona that instantly makes my throat dry. I look at Reon and he just shrugs his shoulders coolly and chooses to stay quiet.

So I give in and continue reading my book quietly with Reon still right beside me doing the same thing.

As long as we're still allowed to spend time together, I think.

And for now, I can only hope that he doesn't turn out to be the *enemy*.

That one percent still remains in my head, as always.

41

When the next morning comes, I've realised that I haven't even been sleeping. Instead, I've been trying to recall everything from when the Royal Phantom first broke into my home up to this day.

What am I missing here? There's definitely something that's been juggling in my mind, but what is it?

I feel like ever since that night, all my deductions have been overturned. Something doesn't sit right with me. Solving cases is not as easy and quick anymore, though I still love every second of it.

Compared to how straightforward the case was always to me back home, it's either my deductive skills have become cloudy and rusty or that Reon's right. I'm not dealing with what the news calls *provincial crimes* anymore.

When Moyra comes into my room with my uniform, I ponder about what to expect at school. Today, we'll have: *Inevitable Marriage Proposal* in the morning and *The Crown Prince's Royal Coming-of-Age Ceremony* in the afternoon.

I sigh. I just can't wait to get to town tomorrow.

The morning class feels like the very-boring version of Prince Hugo's, and so I managed to try to catch up on my sleep. I don't even notice the teacher at all, except that she kind of reminds me of Lady Francoise in a glance, and her voice sounds so much like a lullaby to me.

The class is finally over and I wake up feeling more refreshed.

When all counselors suddenly usher every princess from every class into the Festivity Hall in the Royal Prince Academy for the afternoon class, I suddenly develop a bad feeling. And my instinct is proven right when I see this idiot Gregorius the Crown Prince.

Shit.

This joker. What is he doing here? Doesn't he only need to go to class once a month for his own safety?

What's worse than my imagination, his mask is on his hand instead, so naturally, everyone now has seen his face. And what's even worse than worst, he's been standing in the middle of the crowd, talking proudly about our dance and dinner yesterday.

Seriously, this guy is just the worst.

As if his presence alone is not enough to make me feel miserable, half of the mummies are here too. They look like they make up the rest of the Bronze, Silver, and Gold classes in the Royal Prince Academy. They're all now listening very carefully to Gregorius as if he's a priest delivering a sermon.

I'd better get away as far as I can from them.

"Oh, my Princess is here!" Gregorius shouts all of a sudden.

Double shit.

Gregorius makes haste to approach me, surprising all the mummies, and then, he proceeds to right away kiss my hand. *Disgusting.* So naturally, all the other princesses are now either shocked or crying, and the mummies are back to fighting with each other again for whatever reason.

Chaos is what's behind the Crown Prince, and he doesn't even get the slightest clue.

"Why are you here? You just went to class yesterday, didn't you?" I whisper.

"Well, they told me I didn't need to, but you see, I'm *bored*." I only roll my eyes in response. I don't feel like talking to him unless it's between life and death. "By the way, why are we whispering, and who are these beautiful ladies next to you?"

"My classmates."

"Of course." He strolls his eyes around them. No more whispering. "My other *Diamonds*," he says as he approaches them one by one with the same treatment.

Big talker. Attention seeker. Playboy syndrome.

Is there anything else nice about him other than his face?

But when Gregorius' attention is on my classmates,

it's suddenly the mummies' turn to come at me. I feel the
storm of questions and assertions coming my way as their
swords are still in each other's throat.

I've never felt this much relief in class when I see
the teachers coming. Actually, not just one or two teachers,
but every one of them turns out to be included in this class.
Even both Prince Providence and Princess Prudence are
present.

Special class, alright, and all for this joker of a future
king.

The teachers now start ushering the students in
the middle of the dance floor while the royal academy
assistants arrange their seats. Gregorius is placed on a seat
where a diamond on the ring would be, right under the big
chandelier. Ghyslaine has basically just flown like a rocket
to take her seat right next to Gregorius, followed by Coralie
in the same motion.

During the whole class, I can't help but notice that
they both keep holding onto Gregorius – Coralie on his
left arm, Ghyslaine on his right. Somehow, they manage to
keep him in his posture unintentionally. At the same time,
all the other princesses from every class are trying their best
to get his attention while the mummies force themselves
to fit in among the circle. Actually, it looks like they're all
competing for his attention now, which he seems to very
much enjoy. I hope this will last throughout the school year
and that this is the sign he'll pick another princess to play

with so he stops bothering me.

The only princesses besides me that don't seem to care about Gregorius at all are Melodie, Orianne, and Leonie. So we're all now just standing on the side of the crowd instead of sitting down, separating ourselves from all that Crown-Prince madness currently going on at the moment.

Florian is the first prince to come to my side, all the while the teachers are asking questions to Gregorius about which decoration he likes, what color is his favorite, so on and so forth. Afterward, the other Diamond princes follow Florian to the side. I guess they're all as bored since this class only talks about Gregorius and no one else.

Now, it's almost like we're making ourselves a completely separate group. *The Outliers*. Kitburry can't stop giving chocolate lollies to Melodie. Humbert looks much different as he keeps smiling and blushing while standing next to Leonie, whereas she's as cold as always. Both Jerome and Florian are nearest to me, currently whispering to each other about something. Meanwhile, Orianne looks like she willingly listens to Isaac giving speeches about elements and their atomic numbers.

When I see Isaac, I suddenly remember about the case again.

Like… something I had smelled before in Isaac's lab.

Florian's about to say something to me just when I get too excited and move my feet to talk to Isaac straight away.

I stand right in front of Isaac and say, "By the way, I need to smell your jacket."

Isaac turns to look at me but rather calmly, unlike the others. Almost like, he's been expecting me to say that.

"Orianne has told me," he says as he stretches both his arms confidently. "Very interesting points. I'd very much like to assist." And then he spreads his arms wide open and says, "Come. *Smell.*"

Humbert shakes his head speechlessly.

Not exactly the response I was expecting from Isaac but… "Okay?"

And so I sniff Isaac's jacket shoulder.

"You smell like Jerome. That means, whatever it was that Orianne smelled that day, is something that remains in your lab," I say while brushing my chin with my right fingers.

"Good point," Isaac says. "Well, in my lab back home, I have funnels, beakers, ph–"

"Alright," I interrupt. I don't need him to *rap*. "Well, can we go to your lab here instead?"

"That is what I have been asking. Repeatedly. But the school keeps saying it wouldn't be until mid-term that everyone could have their wishes sorted. Something about *fairness*," Isaac sighs.

"Mid-term? But that's in four months! What am I supposed to do in the meantime with no lead?" I grunt loudly.

"I know! I miss my laboratory so much," Isaac replies with the same energy. "I strongly condemn that they don't do Chemistry Lessons here in the academy. It's so quiet here, with no explosions," he further complains.

"That's the whole point, since people like you would burn the whole school," Leonie heckles, which makes Humbert keep smiling at her, like he's just found the girl of his dreams – or better yet, his *match*. It also seems like he's about to clap his hands proudly, before Leonie smacks him to the belly.

"Humbert, for the thousandth time, stop it with the glistening. You look stupid!" Leonie suddenly yells.

Almost immediately, Humbert looks down on the floor, but then he continues doing it again. So Leonie rolls her eyes and leaves him as so, and as she does, Humbert immediately follows to catch up to her like a puppy.

"By the way, talking about mid-term, they've just now decided on the date for the Crown Prince's Royal Coming-of-Age Ceremony. It's around the same time too. The last month of the year." I guess Melodie's the only one who still tries to keep up with this stupid class.

"Isn't that great?" Jerome says. "That means after mid-term, we'll have no more of this class! I can definitely use the rest of my Saturday afternoon for something much better to do. I mean, look at that." Jerome stares at Gregorius cynically. He holds his breath every time he sees

Ghyslaine squeezing the Crown Prince's arm.

Not sure why, but I think I've accidentally noticed something behind Gregorius. Something unnatural. Something shining. Something's not at the right place. Something like a lever and a string. And then all the way up to the chandelier, something that's not supposed to be there.

Something deadly.

Almost by instinct, I choose to immediately run to where Gregorius sits.

"My princess, Seraphine! You've come to see me at last!" he greets from afar.

"Be quiet," I wave my pointy finger in the air. "And don't move."

"What is it, Seraphine?" Gregorius looks nervous but in a happy way.

"I need the others to leave me and the Crown Prince alone," I say to the others while my focus remains on what's behind and above him.

I can hear Gregorius giggles in excitement.

He has no idea what's coming.

"You can just say that you're jealous!" Ghyslain shouts.

I roll my eyes. I don't have time for this.

"Ghyslaine, Coralie, I need you and the others to stay away at least outside the dancing floor circle, if you still want to *live*. Do you understand?" I glare at them furiously. They're slowly getting it. "NOW!" I scream.

As if my words are part of the King's decree, both of them quickly do as I say. Coralie ushers the princesses while Ghyslaine the princes.

Gregorius begins to look frightened. "What is it, Seraphine?" he repeats with a dying tone. "I thought you were going to kiss me."

My mouth instantly opens to forceful emission off my stomach. I really feel like vomiting – and I'd rather gobble down my own vomit than going anywhere near his lips.

But when I notice him about to stand, I push his chest so hard, he thoughtlessly keeps to his seat. I don't have time to respond to my wince either.

"If you get up from your seat now, we're *both* going to die," I warn. "Do you understand?"

Gregorius nods shakily in silence.

Everyone now stands just on the border of the dance floor, if not further away. All the teachers, royal academy assistants, as well as princes and princesses talk to each other in confusion.

"Princess Seraphine, what is going on? This is not a proper way a princess should behave!" I hear Princess Prudence scream. "A princess should not make the first move. *The Rules of Royal Attraction!*"

But I completely ignore her, and I roll my eyes quietly in response.

I try to keep to my head even when she constantly yells about the rest of The Rules of Royal Attraction chapters, on top of the rest of the crowd chattering loudly. Focusing on what's in front of me, I can think like it's now just the two of us in here.

A small part of me hates how I'm currently being misunderstood, but I think whatever happens afterward will be sufficient enough to explain my reasons.

If I can make it in time. No. *We.*

I'm standing on the side of the chair with my left hand resting on Gregorius' chest and my right roaming freely up in the air. And then I feel it. Painted to be invisible in the eye. One that cuts like string and holds like steel. The piano wire circles from his collar all the way to the chandelier above, slanted towards the ceiling just a bit. The way it was cleverly set up to chop his head off as soon as he gets up, or, for the chandelier to fall and hit him in the head should he try to cut the string out.

When did the killer manage to get this set up? Right after he sat down?

You know what? This is not the time to linger on my deduction.

Not yet.

"How fast can you run?" I ask Gregorius.

"I– I– I don't know," he starts stuttering. "M-m-maybe not q-q-quick enough? W-w-what are you t-t-thinking?"

"I'm thinking really hard about how to get both of us out of here alive."

He looks touched by what I've just said.

Well, as much as I don't like him, I still don't want him to die. At least, not on my watch.

"Did you notice anyone around you touching your collars or your upper robe?" I ask. It could only be the teachers, the royal academy staff, or the students. Ghyslaine and Coralie included.

"N-n-n-no, I don't t-t-think. I didn't n-n-notice a-a-a-a-anything s-s-strange," he stutters even worse, sounding more scared than ever. "W-w-what is g-g-going on? A-a-am I r-r-really going to d-d-die?" He starts breathing irregularly fast.

"Listen," I stare at him in the eyes, "You're not going to die as long as I'm here because I'm not going to let you. Now, just keep calm and let me think. And stop stuttering! Get yourself together. You're the freaking Crown Prince."

Gregorius nods softly and rapidly. My left hand on his chest confirms that his heart slowly manages to come to stabilize. His palms, though, keep shaking on his thighs.

I look around his head then on his robe.

"This robe that you're wearing. Do you know if the collar part is adjustable?" I ask, because the string only circles around his uniform jacket collar, and his robe collar looks tight underneath it.

"W-w-well…"

"I said stop stuttering!" I yell.

I didn't really mean to, but anyway.

"Okay, sorry!" he shouts back in panic. He takes a deep breath in then out. "I mean… it's designed to match my neck without the uniform. I guess… I hope so?"

I let go of my left hand to move to Gregorius' collar, along with my other hand. He swallows so hard but tries his best to keep calm as per my instruction. I inhale first, then try to carefully swap the string to go over the robe collar instead. I only exhale when it seems to work.

"I think I've got it. But you have to run as quickly as you can after I switch it. Understand?"

He nods. "Understand," he repeats. "Just let me know when. I believe you. I have to," he grabs my arms while shaking. I feel his pain.

"Don't worry," I say rather softly – not with my usual condescending tone. "You're going to be fine. We're going to be."

If anything, I can't leave him now since my fingers are now keeping balance of the string's circle width.

If he dies, I die.

Very slowly, I bend my body slightly and try to enlarge the circle while staring at the chandelier. Gregorius suddenly becomes curious, and so he tries to move his head to look all the way up. But when I hear a pitchy voice from up there, I stop all movements immediately.

"Don't move your head! I think if you had looked

up, it would've chopped your head off too," I blurt out.

"Would've WHAT?" Gregorius screams.

Oh, shit. I forgot. *Oops.*

Gregorius now turns all panic that I have no choice but to kick his right calf with my left foot. So not princess-like, but I have no choice. "Don't move!" I yell.

I shift my goggled eyes back around the chandelier. There's something in the center attached to it, like a big white brick or some sort, and it centers the engineering behind the trick. It's almost the same principle as the guillotine; except, instead of a wooden bottom frame, it's made of piano wire. And if my guess is true, there's a bomb in there too to time the drop. Either way, it's set to chop his head as the chandelier falls.

When I manage to enlarge the circle without letting the brick-thing to fall down, I force my body to stay firm. If I move less than a centimetre width, the chandelier will definitely fall right away.

"Now, stay calm and try to slowly slide your head down off the string. Once it almost passes your eyes, let me know, because after that, I need to enlarge this string a bit more so that your head can go through; but that also means, that chandelier on top will fall down as soon as I do. Understand?" I instruct.

Gregorius nods just so then tries to slowly slide his body down.

"It's on my nose now," he informs with a shaky

voice.

"Okay, you're ready?" I ask.

"No, but I guess I have to," his voice still quivers, if not more.

"Hey," I say softly. He now tries to turn his eyes to me without moving his head. "You're going to be okay," I try to speak with the calmest voice and gentlest smile I can.

"You're so beautiful," he says.

I roll my eyes. Every time he talks.

"Remember. Run as fast as you can. Ready? In three… two…"

"Wait!" he screams. "In one or zero?"

"Which one do you prefer?" I sigh.

"Zero. No, wait! One, because I want to get out of here as soon as I can. One."

"Okay. I will start again. In *one*, okay? Ready?"

Gregorius nods while closing his eyes.

"Three… Two… One!"

Gregorius and I are now running as fast as our breath can catch up. Behind us, there are sounds of crashing and exploding, but we can't let any of that stop us until we get out of the dancing floor.

The set-up was definitely to make sure that Gregorius was either chopped or toasted. But thanks to all of those disasters in view, I'm free from any obligation to explain what I was doing and why.

At the very last moment, we manage to slide out of

the floor girth. As soon as that happens, the Crown Prince's army barges inside the hall only to find that they're too late but with zero casualties in the aftermath. It's not looking good for them that Gregorius keeps holding my arms and doesn't want to let go, even when they're trying to make him to.

"Someone just tried to kill His Royal Highness the Crown Prince!" Prince Providence bellows out with rage. "This is unacceptable. I thought the area had been scanned and secured."

"It has, I can assure you," Yves replies rather calmly, regardless of the murder attempt. "And to think that it's skipped our attention proves something."

"What does that mean?" Princess Prudence asks.

"It means," I say, "someone here was trying to kill the Crown Prince."

Everyone already gasps in a complete shock, but I'm not even finished. "And they will go as far as killing the other students too."

And this is only the end of my first week of school.

42

Sunday has finally come so it's finally time to investigate– I mean, explore the town with Reon.

Yeay!

But considering the fatality of yesterday's murder attempt at school, I can't all be too happy.

The true culprit is indeed a very dangerous being. So much so that they're willing to go as far as killing innocent people around. So now I'm thinking, Reon's right. I need to be extra careful with my current investigation. More subtle. Perhaps make it look like I'm not even trying.

Since the whole island is filled with people who dress like royalties, I've decided to wear the outfit I wore when I caught my cousin Jerome in action. I guess you could say, it's the perfect disguise to blend in as one of the town folks.

After getting ready, I immediately make my way into the library to meet with Reon. Not so surprised to see him with the same all-silky-white outfit looking charming as he always does, but now, we just look like zebras. He's in all white and I'm in all black.

When we come out into the living room, the Butler is now in a different outfit – one that looks like he's going out to town to chill. All casual, but still in black and white, which complements our zebra look even more.

The Butler doesn't even make it as subtle as Leon that he's following us very closely even when we're passing the town gate. He's walking inches away behind us and keeps it to the exact same distance. Leon hasn't complained so far but I think he doesn't like Reon walking beside me while he's right next to the Butler behind.

"Why is he watching us again?" I whisper to Reon, sounding very much annoyed.

Obviously, I'm talking about the Butler.

"He insists on being with us– me, at all times," Reon whispers back.

"And why is that?" I ask with a cynical tone.

"Because I'm just a butler, Royal Highness," the Butler answers on behalf of Reon right at the back of my head.

Reon shrugs his shoulders again in hopelessness while I roll my eyes.

Seriously, this is ridiculous. I can't even have a normal conversation with Reon anymore because of him. Even Leon would at least give me some space even when he doesn't want to.

Again. I'm thinking of talking back. No butler does that. Ever! If anything, he acts more like a bodyguard now. But there's something about his persona that chickens out my courage. Like he's someone you don't want to mess with. So I just let him be with his "butler" duty.

Reaching the town square where most of the activities are, everything seems to be back to normal. What's more, I see familiar faces from our newly-formed *The Outliers* group.

Coralie and Ghyslaine wave their hands and immediately push their way towards me. But all are with their best dresses and suits, so now I just look like I'm not one of them.

Actually, great!

As they reach, they all cannot stop looking at Reon.

"*Damn*, who's this?" Leonie asks me but doesn't bother to wait for my response. She immediately takes a couple steps forward to where Reon stands. "May I know who you are, Your Grace?" she asks so politely, and she even curtsies a little.

I think this is the first time I see Leonie acting like this. Like she actually respects someone for the very first time in her life. But then I take a brief look at Humbert and now, he just looks so sad.

"I'm the servant boy at Her Royal Highness Princess Seraphine's current residence, Your Royal Highness," Reon answers, then bows with his right hand on his chest. Acting so bewitching as ever, no matter what he does.

"Servant boy?" Everyone suddenly repeats in shock.

Why are they so surprised?

Melodie drags me a bit further away from the others.

"*Damn*," she copies Leonie, "You've got the hottest one of all," Melodie whispers.

"He's alright," I whisper back, though my heart secretly agrees.

"Are you kidding me? I mean, look at mine." She tilts her head towards her servant boy who's standing in the back of the group, and so I shift a look. Her servant boy is tall and rangy with red freckles on both cheeks. "Now, look at the others." I move my head around all the others behind each of their royals. This is giving me Gaspard-Rainpard stranger-cistron again that I get goosebumps all over. Their servant boys are only with different hair and eye colours as well as whether they wear glasses or not. Why do they all look almost exactly the same except for Reon?

"Now you can see that everyone definitely thinks your servant boy is more than alright." She tilts her head around again. "See? More are coming to see him right now!"

And she's right. I didn't really focus on seeing the princesses from the other classes, but they're all now like, gazing at Reon. *My* Reon. They're all even smiling at him and trying to get his attention, while he's now just busy himself staring at the sky without any clear reason.

"They all think he's a prince too," Melodie whispers again. "Are you sure he's just a servant boy? He looks more like… a prince in disguise to me. A very *charming* one," she adds, while her eyes keep going back and forth between me and Reon, seamlessly drawn into him like he's a tower of chocolate, until her facial expression suddenly changes to worry. "You don't think… he's a *spy*… do you?"

But then our conversation is cut short when Reon approaches me. He gently bows at Melodie, making her somehow speechless and stands back on her own accord, before he leans towards my ear.

"The Butler says it's not a good idea for me to stay. What do you think I should do?" he whispers.

As soon as I hear him saying "The Butler", I find myself moving my head left and right unconsciously. Traumatized – I have been, apparently. But, the Butler's not here. He's actually still way over there. Funny how he lets Reon come by himself to talk to me in private this time.

A perfect time to suggest Reon otherwise.

But then, I unconsciously take a brief look at the other princesses whose eyes are still locked just at Reon. For whatever reason, I don't like it. I'm not sure what I'm feeling, but it makes me drawn to the idea of punching them in the eyes for just doing that, which is really beyond ridiculous.

"You know what? I agree with the Butler. I think

you need to go home as soon as you possibly can. Maybe run, even," I recommend, looking very serious. My head nods repeatedly in support.

Reon looks at me so bewilderingly, as if he was never expecting the answer. "You really think so? But, what about the butcher and the tailor? We only have Sunday to ask them together. I thought I should show you around first at least," he says.

For the first time in my life, I feel like my priority has switched. My old self would definitely not care about the other princesses looking at him so intensely or whatever, and then we would just go ahead with the plan to get more clues. But my current self… I can't say the same thing about her anymore.

"Why don't you let me worry about that while you'll be home safely?" I suggest.

Safe from all these prying eyes, I mean.

"Are you really sure?" he asks again. "It doesn't feel right for me to leave you here. I haven't even shown you around the shops. And there are several I'd really like you to visit–"

"Yes, yes, I'm sure." I rush and push Reon's back so he moves his feet to where the Butler is. "My friends are here anyway. Don't worry about me," I say.

And I can't believe I've just blurted out the word "friends". This could be the first one for me.

"Where is he going, Seraphine?" Coralie asks.

"He still has many chores to do back home," I say. Although, I don't even know what else his chores are besides carrying my school supplies and reading in the library for fun.

"Right. Many chores," Reon repeats confusedly. "I'm going to excuse myself, Your Highness," he bows to me. After that, he briefly looks at the crowd and bows at them.

I hear the other princesses hum as he leaves calmly. I only roll my eyes.

"He walks like a prince, and he's a total gentleman too," I hear Coralie say.

"Is it just me or does he look quite familiar?" Ghyslain says, which draws my attention. "Like he's been in my dream," she answers herself with a sheepish smile. And so I roll my eyes again.

I find myself watching Reon quietly from behind with the others as he's disappearing from view. He turns and looks at me a couple times – he's somehow still not sure if I really want him to leave – but I wave my hand and assert in my expression that I'll be fine.

"You have to bring him to the next Royal Coming-of-Age Ceremony we're all going! The other princesses don't know that he's just a servant boy. That would take their attention away entirely and we could have all the princes to ourselves!" Coralie suggests with repeated nods to herself.

"I won't be going," to whoever's royal sweet-sixteen party they're talking about. I mean, I haven't even received any invitation–

"My dear cousin," Jerome shouts out of nowhere, and that's when I notice him dividing the sea of princesses with his stride, trying so hard to look cool as he does. "What a coincidence to find you here. You see, I was just about to drop by your house. Here." Jerome acts to bow and hand me a white envelope with two golden royal seals, but my body remains ignorant. "*Our* Royal Coming-of-Age Ceremony." Jerome then looks to his left and right. "Florian, where are you?" he starts yelling. "We talked about this yesterday. This is supposed to be *the* moment. *Our* moment!"

Florian walks obediently but gracefully towards his side, looking a bit shy.

"Anyway, Seraphine," Jerome continues, "I'll have you know that *this*," he swings the envelope next to his face, "has truly never been done before. Two Diamond Princes. The biggest party of the decade. Needless to say, this will be on par with the Crown Prince's Royal Coming-of-Age Ceremony. So yes, I am a *genius*. And no, the Crown Prince will not be invited. I'm thinking about his safety, of course, and ours."

All of a sudden, all the other princesses from my class approach me and drag me away from the princes, while Jerome's still talking to himself among the crowd.

"Anyway, Seraphine, this could be your chance!" Orianne says with a high-pitch voice in the end.

"Your first dance! Your first date!" Coralie says in excitement.

"Don't think about Jerome, because, *eeeeww*, but Florian is definitely available. And my heart says he has his eyes on you!" Ghyslaine says.

"Wait, but he was supposed to be my prince! Oh wait, I'd rather have the Crown Prince. Seraphine, you can have Florian." Orianne shrugs her shoulders.

Though I'm not so sure if that's a good idea. I think if I have to, I'll choose Florian. But, anyway. It's her life.

"Okay, regardless, it's happening in two months. That's so little time, but we can definitely make it work if we meet *every Sunday* in town for some shopping and makeovers. How's that?" Melodie plans.

"No," I answer briefly.

"No?" Everyone questions in shock.

"But, why?" Melodie asks.

They're all now staring at me with puppy eyes.

"Because," I sigh, "I want to use my Sunday to do some *investigation*. I don't have time for this dance, date, whatever," I say. Although, for some reason, I don't hate the entire idea of being around my classmates. I mean, I hate the idea of shopping and makeovers, but spending time with the girls? Surprisingly, not so much.

"And this is why you're still *single*," Leonie retorts.

"Okay, how about this, Seraphine?" Melodie proffers. "Let's try today first. We'll ditch the princes, and then we go around the shops in town while doing some of your 'investigation'. How's that?"

"It really still sounds like shopping and makeovers to me, the way you say it," I counter with reasonable judgment.

"Oh, come on, Seraphine!" they urge in sync.

I sigh and roll my eyes. "Fine. As long as you girls let me do my own thing."

They're all now hugging me while jumping. I feel weird, but I think… in a good way.

"Okay, let's officially start our very first girls' day out! Where are we going first?" Ghyslain then answers to herself. "I'm thinking, we should go to the jewelry shop first. *Match the dress to the jewelry, not the other way around, my mother always says.*" I can definitely tell that this is her favorite activity to do.

I'm actually thinking: the butcher first, the tailor next, and then go home. But for some reason, I just choose to play along. It'll be a more thorough investigation if I talk to the other shop owners too, perhaps. And it'll definitely look more *subtle*.

As if, I'm only going shopping with my friends.

The perfect illusion.

43

Reaching the first shop, I thought we'd be here for about ten minutes and then we'd be able to move on to the next. But no, I was wrong.

Completely wrong about everything.

First of all, the owners who are husband and wife, Sir Peridot and Lady Ruby, don't shimmer with all the jewelry in the shop like I thought they would. In fact, Lady Ruby only wears a small red pear-shaped gemstone necklace while Sir Peridot has none at all on him. I ask them why, and they answer that they only fancy the gemstones in the eyes, not so much on the skin.

Secondly, the shop itself reminds me of the Bijouterie Hall in the academy, as opposed to what I thought would be just a small room from the outside. The owner takes us to this underground level where apparently, this is where the real shop is. What's up there is simply just an entrance room.

Thirdly, I've learned that the shop also supplies to

the academy. It makes perfect sense why they all look so familiar.

Fourthly, the process reminds me of the boring Wednesday afternoon class, only beyond the hours. Everyone else is just doing what exactly we're supposed to in class, except this time it's in entirety of their own accord – well, except me. I'm so bored, I just get myself a seat on the comfortable sofa in the middle of the room while watching all of them playing mix and match with all the jewelry.

Fifthly, is how some of the shop visitors talk about how they saw Yves and his men had been circling around the town around the same time after when Jerome saw the victim going towards the town before he was murdered. I began to calculate how this could relate to the current murder investigation.

And then, the last but definitely not the very least.

What happens next is that Lady Ruby suddenly approaches and brings me to a separate room that's hidden behind the counter.

The walls are filled with glass squares, each with a different kind of gemstone inside. A peculiar book sleeps slanted upward on a stand within a giant cabinet hollow right in the middle. The cover is made of glass material with a really big diamond on top. The existence of the book itself makes me so scared I'm going to break the book if I accidentally let it fall, because I really want to touch it. No.

More like, I really want to read it.

"I know if the jewelries don't interest you, this will. They don't have this in any libraries out there. Only here," Lady Ruby says.

One of a kind book? Count me in anytime! No matter the topic.

"Who else has been here?" I ask.

"Very good question – just as I've been informed," she says.

I look at her confusedly. What does she mean?

As if she's read my mind, she explains, "You see, not every shop owner has been blessed with such a duty to serve as the Kingdom of Oceastarasia's *Secret Keeper*. This book is one of those secrets."

"Wait. If this is supposed to be a secret, why are you telling me this? Isn't that a breach against your duty?"

"It would be, unless part of the monarch thinks otherwise," she smiles. "That reminds me," she says, before leaving me alone in the room. When she's back, she hands me a silver box with beautiful ornaments engraved right on its border. "This should match the others like a set, as they are all one of its kind," she winks.

Thank God that my friends think I've bought whatever's in the box so I don't have to explain myself.

Lady Ruby doesn't make an emphasis for me to keep everything a secret, but I reckon that's what I'm supposed to do. Besides, I think keeping my mouth shut is one of my strongest fortes.

44

When I get home, I immediately go to my bedroom to open the box. My eyes quickly widen at the first sight of the beauty inside.

Countless blue diamonds cling to a glittering silver shape as a necklace and a pair of earrings. I've never seen anything like this before.

Next, I bring myself to the library again. Reon's already there reading his forensic book as usual, but as soon as I enter, he closes the book and asks about my day. I tell him everything that's happened, though I choose to emit the part with the secret room while I glance at the Butler across from us when doing so.

Reon seems to be listening but he seems to be less responsive than usual, so I ask him what's the matter. He stands to look at the blocked secret passageway, shifts a look at the Butler, and then back at me.

"The Butler thinks it's not a good idea for me to be seen by the other students *just yet.*"

Just yet? What does he mean? And why isn't he looking at me?

"What I'm saying is, that means it's no longer a good idea for me to be seen running around the town. What I meant to say is…" When he suddenly loses his control of words, he takes in some air into his dry throat before clearing it, while looking so nervous for whatever reason that I've come to raise my eyebrows. "If you could spend your Sunday with your friends while I'm here in the library, and then we talk about our days when you get back, and have dinner together while we read some books…"

That usual poise of his gradually fades as he turns garrulous, but the Butler doesn't even try to stop him. Creases begin to form on his forehead as he now mutters, "I know what you must be thinking. What is going on? Who am I if not possibly the most dangerous man for having to hide as much? Why is it that I always act like I have no other choice? If I am not the Royal Phantom, then who am I? If I am not the Crown Prince, then who am I? If I am but a threat to the kingdom, then who am I? So the option was either for me to leave this island for a while…"

Reon leaving? *No.* Anything but not having *my* forensic companion with me. *My* Reon. So I raise my body and walk slowly towards him.

His mind is so all over the place right now, he doesn't even notice me approaching. "But I've insisted that that's not even an option, that I want to stay. *I have to,*" he's still talking non-stop. My eyes are blinking with a glitter of hope. "Which brings us back to the condition that I'm no longer be able to accompany you on–"

"Okay, stop." I quickly brush my pointer finger on top of Reon's lips. He seems startled, but also a bit glad. "First thing's first, I agree with the Butler. I think you really need to stay in this mansion, if that's what's best for you."

I probably mean what's best for *me* actually, since now I don't have to worry about the other princesses preying their eyes on him.

"You do? You're not… angry?" he asks curiously.

"Angry? No. Why would I be? Circumstances we must adjust to, that's all." I raise my shoulders casually. "Besides, as long as you're not leaving, that's good enough for me."

"But when it comes to my true identity, since I've *promised*–"

"Well, since you've *promised*," I interrupt, "I understand too. You don't have to worry. It's probably more fun for me if I can figure it out myself." I let out a big smirk. It's like having a really big puzzle in the house. "I just need to know what I need to know, for now." And let *me* do the solving.

Reon stares at me with a glistening pair of eyes, I almost think he's about to cry. But as if a full amount of courage has suddenly been built in him in such short notice, he forthwith pulls me into his arms without hesitation, not caring if I'm going to return it. My face is placed by motion to cover his chest, and I find both of my arms automatically clench on his back as he wraps my shoulder. His right palm acts like shelter around my head and I feel his fingers gently caressing every strand. Every breath he takes speaks of every relief, but for some reason, so as mine, for a different ground.

But I find my arms hold on to him even tighter.

I still don't understand this *feeling*.

As long as he's here, that's all that matters to me, I think.

But I start wondering if this is what love is. Being an idiot, and a selfish prick.

The love for puzzles and mysteries.

"You have no idea how glad I am to have found you. I *promise* you," Reon says gently. "When the time is right, you will know everything about me."

"Okay?" I furrow my brows in uncertainty. "Although, I have to say, there's still one thing that's stuck in my mind that doesn't feel right."

Reon stretches his arms to look me in the eyes while his palms rest on my shoulders, waiting.

I shift my head towards the Butler instead. "Him," I say. "What's *his* real name? I feel weird that I have to keep calling him 'the Butler' when I perfectly know in my heart that he is *not* a butler."

I now even bravely squint my eyes at him. All of a

sudden, I'm not so afraid anymore.

Reon and the Butler exchange a look, and for some reason, they're now just laughing non-stop. Even the Butler loses his halcyon control.

"This is not a funny matter," I say as I slowly push Reon's arms off of me. I feel annoyed that they're both now just basically tickling themselves in the stomach. *Still.*

"I see why you've set your eyes on this one for the past three years," the Butler blurts out calmly.

Huh?

"What does that even mean?" I ask curiously.

The Butler clears his throat. Reon blushes and drags his stare away from me. "Unfortunately, *little Princess*, it's time for you to go to bed. Please allow me to fulfill my duty in this house as your *loyal Butler* by walking you to your room."

Even as we reach my bedroom door, the Butler still insists that I keep calling him the Butler. Except this time, he's let out more smiles in a minute than he has in a long week.

45

The second week of school starts and ends with no murderous incident, since Gregorius ultimately chooses to cocoon inside the castle for the duration. *Thank God.* I guess he's been pretty shaken that he's decided on going to school once a month as planned.

Apart from that, lessons are as boring as usual.

Finest Table Manner and *Impeccable Etiquette Lessons* turn out to be even worse than my imagination. First, the teacher who I call in my head as Princess-Prudence Wannabe Number One makes us sit on this one big round table in the Festivity Hall. I was hoping that this would be the occasion when I get to enjoy some food during classes, sort of like watching television while eating, but they're giving us fake food instead. They look really pretty, alright, and *real*, but they're just made of erasers.

I mean, what the hell?

Next in the afternoon, another teacher who seems to be the sister of the morning class' teacher, let's call her

Princess-Prudence Wannabe Number Two, makes the royal academy assistants to bring us a lot of books. My heart leaps, thinking this would be a reading session, only to find out that we have to walk around the hall with books on top of our head. One book for level one, two books for level two, three books for level three.

Surprisingly, I've managed to pass level one, but not level two yet by the end of the class.

Tuesday, Wednesday, Thursday, and Friday morning lessons go as the previous week. Not much different. And when Friday afternoon comes, I'm told that I no longer have to stay late after class to wait for a replacement, as long as I keep my focus on watching the teachers' instructions and the others incorporating them in the dance, since Gregorius won't be coming today as well.

As much as he's incredibly annoying, I still feel sorry for him. Just like the King, he has to live in fear of death and betrayal for the rest of his life. Tough life.

At times during class, I find myself looking at the now-fixed chandelier, only to find that it's now good as new without any bomb and murder tricks. But I'm glad that later, I'll get to spend my evening with Reon as we used to, now that the Butler trusts me enough to leave Reon alone with me again.

Going back home from school has now become the most exciting time for me. Before dinner time, Reon and I always stay in the library, and afterward, we sneak out through the secret tunnel to sit under the stars when he'll always make sure to walk me back into the front of my bedroom before Moyra comes to check on me. The repetition has been so perfectly daring, and how I've come to adore what has now become *our* routine every time the night passes by.

But what I hadn't come to expect is how Leon has now slowly turned into the Butler as he starts giving me warnings to stop having dinner with Reon in the library. He's utterly suspicious, I can tell. After all, he has really good instincts when it comes to where I am.

On most of the days now, Leon would go as far as trying to barge into the library, though somehow, the Butler has been strong enough to keep the door closed without breaking. One night, Reon and I accidentally caught the view of the Butler who had been guarding the door with just the side of his shoulder. His right hand was holding a book with a steady cup of tea on his left. After Reon had closed the secret passageway, the Butler swiftly unguarded the door the exact same time Leon struck himself into the library, when afterward, the other guards behind him bumped into his back straight away as they followed him. It was hilarious.

Then three Sundays have now passed, but I've only managed to investigate four shops in total. Thanks to all the other princesses in my class who now happen to be *my friends*.

Although, by spending a whole day in one shop, I've actually been getting a lot of intel from both the shop owners and visitors. Not to mention the mysterious special gifts I keep receiving as a result, after they've revealed themselves to me as the Kingdom of Oceastarasia's *secret keepers*, just because I don't pay attention to what they're selling.

The second Sunday when we all go to this dress shop, some of the visitors talk about how they saw three peculiar middle-aged figures at three different times asking for a desperate change of clothes that particular Saturday. When they say the individuals looked middle-aged and claimed to be royals, I can only think of three people: Princess Prudence, Prince Providence, and Prince Hugo. But what interests me the most is why they needed a change of clothes just moments before the body dropped dead from the sky. And so I think about this throughout the shopping session.

Could the murderer be one of them instead?

Obviously, since my objective is not really looking for a new dress, I sit on the sofa as always, waiting for my friends to finish with their shopping. Once in a while they come to where I sit and ask how they look, about which I just raise my two thumbs up in the air regardless, and then go back to being bored. That's when the shop owner, Lady Charlotte, asks me to go to the secret room behind the counter, shows me a book the size of a door with a dress in a glass case as its cover, and gives me a box with a one-of-a-kind dress matching the jewelry set.

Next on the third Sunday and the fourth, we all go to a shop with all the shoes, whereas the latter is what sells all the skincare. I don't receive much intel here but I do meet two more of the kingdom's secret keepers' awesome secret books and two more one-of-a-kind gifts. One is a box of matching shoes, which is not really a surprise, but I can't say the same thing about the other present as it contains a peculiar masquerade mask that's covered in white diamonds.

46

Today is now the first Friday of the month again.

It's come as a bit of surprise to me that Gregorius is not wearing his Royal Phantom robe as much as he chooses today's afternoon class to mark his monthly attendance; though this time, Yves and the rest of the Crown Prince's army stand on each side of the hall, watching like a hawk.

I thought with his flirty demeanor, he'd much prefer tomorrow's class when he'd be able to get all the attention from other princesses too, but then I think again, maybe not as much considering he almost got his head chopped off just the other month.

As annoying as he's always been, I never expected that the first thing he'd do as soon as he saw me was to cling to my arm, as he's now doing. The others are very surprised, but I see Jerome laughing so hard that his back hits the floor on where he still continues laughing. Ghyslaine and Coralie look very angry and so in effect, while still staring fiercely at me, they keep pointing their fingers at Florian who looks a bit down for some reason.

I struggle to shake my shoulders to make Gregorius get off of me, hoping that I won't disappoint Ghyslaine and Coralie any further. Sad to say, the Crown Prince always manages to stick; but, I haven't given up just yet.

"Let go!" I shout. "And stop looking at the chandelier! There's nothing up there, I've made sure of it." I really have.

"Oh, thank God. Why didn't you tell me that earlier? Now I feel much safer. That chandelier has been haunting me in my sleep. It talks, even," he shivers. And he's still clenching on me, regardless.

"Alright, I get it. Now, let go of my arm. You're safe now." I still manage to tap the back of his hand gently, even when what I really want to do is scratch it to bleed.

"I'm scared, Seraphine. Very, very scared. Like, I really don't want to die," he shrieks.

"Stop it!" I yell. "You're embarrassing me. The class hasn't even started yet."

"I know, but I've been imagining my head being chopped off ever since that awful, dreadful Saturday! That's when I thought, why don't I just choose to attend the class where you can be with me all the time? *Skin to skin.*"

I only sigh. He's so gross.

"I'd been having this crazy anxiety ever since I left for school this afternoon," he goes on. "But when I see you, it's like I'm back in my arcade bedroom. Safe and sound."

Gregorius proceeds to rub his cheek near the elbow part of my glove. I can't help but feel disgusted and so I unintentionally push him too hard onto the floor on the spur of the moment. I've got to say, it looks pretty bad when he hits his back and his whole army quickly runs towards him, so I start to feel kind of bad. But when he gets to stand up so quickly without apparent lingering pain and manages to get into my arm again with stronger joy that I was strong enough to push him, I wish I'd pushed him even harder, he'd have been knocked unconscious.

As soon as we start dancing for the lesson, Gregorius swiftly turns much calmer than before, and so unfortunately for me, he's now back to being chatty as always.

"And then I was thinking, what if you sort of become… my girlfriend?"

"No."

"I'll choose you for a dance?"

"No."

"We'll go on a date?"

"No."

"I'll make you the Queen Consort? We can even marry now if you want."

"Hell no!" I yell. Is he crazy?

"Alright, I see. If being exclusive is what you're looking for, then I think… I can do it," he swallows. That's not supposed to be hard, I think, if one really wants to marry for *love*. More and more red flags. "As long as you're with me, Seraphine, I'll do my best." He simpers and raises his eyebrows repeatedly.

I shake my head to disbelief.

This guy. He wants to marry me just so I can be his bodyguard.

"Still. NO!" I shout even louder. "In fact, I'd much prefer for you to see another girl. You see those two princesses over there?" I point at Ghyslaine and Coralie. I've just realised that they've been looking at Gregorius and so when he looks at them, they immediately push Jerome and Florian off to the floor, then bow and smile at this joker guy of a Crown Prince. "See? Ghyslaine and Coralie are obviously head over heels for you. So why don't you just choose one of them?"

Sorry, Ghyslaine and Coralie.

"Are those what their names are? They're incredibly gorgeous, and *sexy*," he says excitedly while waving at them and raising his eyebrows repeatedly.

I roll my eyes. *Playboy. Pervert.* Seriously, he's so disgusting. I mean, he didn't even remember their names when they'd been clinging to his arms last month.

"But, no." He suddenly shakes his head. "I want you, Seraphine. In fact, I want you to be next to me all the time. Something about you makes me feel safe."

"I'm not your servant and I'm not your bodyguard," I give my answer bluntly. "Besides, you have the whole army behind you. You'll be fine."

"No, I don't mean that. I mean, okay, I'm sorry, maybe I said it wrongly. How do I put this? I love you? I cannot live without you? So, will you marry me, and protect me for the rest of my life?" He then lets out puppy eyes.

"No," I sigh. "Anyway, I think next time you should choose the Saturday afternoon class. I'll be there too." Except, I don't need to be this close to him and we won't be dancing. And the other princesses will be there to distract him, which is perfect.

"There's no point when my royal ceremony has been planned all along anyway. I don't even need to do anything except to attend."

Really? I find that quite strange considering we've only been talking about what his favorite things may be in that class. But then, I didn't have to do anything with my own ceremony too, so I guess that makes sense.

"Besides," he adds, "I feel much safer if you're this close to me. That said, will you spend the rest of your life by my side?"

"I've told you no. It's still a no, and it will always be a no."

I roll my eyes.

Stubborn as hell. Seriously, this guy just doesn't want to listen.

"But I feel like I could die anytime you're not with

me. I'm seriously scared for my life, Seraphine. So will you *please* marry me?"

"Will you please just stop? It's annoying! You're annoying!" This selfish brat of a Crown Prince. Honestly, I just can't deal with him anymore. "I… have a thing with another prince, okay? How's that?" I bluff. Or not. I don't even know anymore.

"Who?" We abruptly stop dancing as he looks around the hall. "Someone here? Another Diamond Prince?"

"No– yes!" The idea has suddenly come to me. "You know what?" I pull Gregorius' hands towards where Coralie and Florian are. "Him." I point at Florian's face.

In turn, Florian looks really confused, but he stays quiet.

"Him? You choose a future reigning prince over *me*? The Crown Prince? The future King of the whole Kingdom of Oceastarasia?" Gregorius screams to a disbelief.

Now everyone can hear him. Mr. Drama Queen. Idiot Prince.

"Yes." Without a doubt. "So, why don't you take Coralie's hands," I say as I push Gregorius' palm off mine and pull Coralie's onto his. She screams in silence and repeatedly moves her mouth saying thank you. "Now, bye!" I then take Florian's hand, pull him away from where Gregorius suddenly turns petrified, then abruptly put his other hand onto my waist and my other hand on his shoulder.

I finally can breathe in complete relief.

"I'm really sorry to take Coralie away from you, but I just can't stand that annoying joker anymore. It was either you or Jerome," I say.

"Not at all, Seraphine. My pleasure, believe me. In fact, if I'm being honest, I had thought of this, only it was me pulling you away from him – not this." He then starts laughing.

Startlingly, he's very charming when he does, and so I can't help but chuckle. And when his earrings shimmer beneath the chandelier lights, something lightens up in me too. I'm not sure what this feeling means.

"By the way," he asks, "Why do you want to get away from him so badly? What did he do that awfully bothered you?"

I sigh. "I don't even know where to begin." Because *everything* about Gregorius bothers me.

"We have a lot of time."

I sigh again. "Well, for a start, he asked me to marry him."

"WHAT?" Florian screams unintentionally. "I'm deeply sorry," he moves closer to whisper. "I mean, I beg your pardon?" His eyes still widen in disbelief.

"He's not being serious, I'm sure."

Florian then steals a glance at Gregorius. "I don't think so. He's… still looking at us. With vicious eyes."

That joker still manages to make me feel uncomfortable even from far away. Unbelievable.

"Don't mind him." I roll my eyes.

"Never do." Florian giggles. "Anyway, you keep impressing me over and over. First, you solve murder cases. Second, you have a really bad memory when it comes to people's faces. And now, you've just casually let go of the opportunity of being a queen." Florian keeps shaking his head with his tongue tics.

"I never care about being a queen. As you've probably noticed, I'm more of a… *detective* kind of princess." I don't even know what that means.

"I'd say that fits you most perfectly," he smiles so charmingly, like a bright star. "Say, Detective Princess Seraphine, are you coming to my Royal Coming-of-Age Ceremony?" And then he sighs. "Sorry, I mean, Jerome and I."

I start chuckling. "Why did you even agree to that?"

"I don't know. I guess, you know, he's your cousin, and so maybe I thought, you would definitely come to your cousin's royal sweet-sixteen party now, wouldn't you?"

Florian then tries to twirl me subtly as the teachers have just directed. I raise my right arm and manage to spin my feet to work. Either Reon has really taught me well, or Florian and I have really good chemistry too.

"I see. So now you're blaming it all on me," I joke.

"Pretty much," he replies with that same charming

smile of his. I can honestly look at a painting of his face for hours, if I have nothing better to do.

He then tries to twirl me again. It has now become an effortless move on our part. This lesson feels so easy, but I keep wondering if it's because I'm dancing with him.

"By the way, is it true that you've never been on a date?" he asks.

"Oh, right. You asked me that during our first class."

"You remember our conversation, but not my face. Real kind, you are," he jokes.

Another twirl.

"Oh, come on. Did I say sorry? Well, if I haven't, I'm sorry, okay?" I laugh. "And for the record, you're not the only living proof of that."

I am the living proof of that, I suddenly recall.

Out of the blue, I'm wondering. What is Reon doing now while I'm dancing with a handsome prince? Should I be telling him this? I mean, what am I to him? And what is he to me? What does my heart say? But then I quickly shake my head and revert my attention back to Florian.

"Are you… okay?" he asks. "For a second there, you look like… I'm not sure. Like you're not here, even though you're here."

"It's me in my deep thoughts. Sorry to have frightened you. It's just one of my *deep* habits."

Somehow, talking to Florian feels so easy. Kind of like with Leon and Reon.

"Not at all. I'd say that's just one of your charms. One of many others," he smiles. "Anyway, would you like to hear what I was saying? We could change to a new topic too if you'd like."

"Yes, of course." I was just about to ask. "What did you say?"

"I was saying, I wonder how many princes out there you've unwittingly forgotten during your many cases for the past three years. I've heard you're even quite popular among the other classes too. Something about a sword fight. They're even still fighting from time to time in the academy. I don't think they've had their winner yet, though. Prince Providence always comes just in time before one of them almost dies."

"Really?" I seriously doubt that. "Well, I just call them *mummies* in my head. I mean, they were just annoying. Just like the Crown Prince."

In response, Florian can't help but lose himself to laugh as loud as he can, we have to stop dancing for a moment. His palms come for support on his thighs as he finds it necessary to bend his body frontward. Consequently, I've come to chuckle in a maze.

"Okay, we need to stop laughing," I say, while still trying to do it myself.

"I'm sorry. I can't remember the last time I laughed this hard. Must be many years ago," he says with a little bit of chuckling remains. "Anyway, the Crown Prince looks really mad now. What should we do?" He keeps to a half-suppressed laugh this time.

"Just ignore him. Worst case scenario, I'm pulling Ghyslaine away from Jerome for the rest of the class so he can have two princesses for himself. But then I'll have Jerome to deal with," I sigh.

"Well, Ghyslaine surely has a type. I wonder who'll win." He chuckles.

"I know, right?" I laugh. "Prince Jerome the Future Reigning Prince of the Second Provincial Region versus Prince Gregorius the Future King. Now, that's a real competition."

"I'd bet on Jerome. Poor guy has only had his eyes on Ghyslaine since day one. My only job as his friend now is to prevent him from blurting any *royal promise* to only marry Ghyslaine. I don't think he'd be able to take it as well as Prince Hugo did."

"Well, now I'm rooting for Gregorius and Coralie," I laugh, when afterward, he laughs again.

It's now been like this. We're just chatting and laughing throughout the dance.

Until suddenly…

"Gregorius is walking to Fabien and Fabienne now." Florian signals by nodding his head to the side with his mesmerising blue eyes. Even from far away, Gregorius still manages to distract us.

"What is he doing?" I look at Gregorius whispering

something to the teachers while staring angrily at us.

"You reckon he asks to switch dancing partners for the rest of the school year? Because that's what I'm planning to do after the class. I'm sure Coralie will be much happier with this new arrangement too. She always complains that I don't grow vegetables."

Unfortunately, Florian's reckon is wrong. Gregorius apparently complains about me going rogue by switching partners without "mutual consent," he specifically says. So now, he asks the teachers to switch us back.

Florian, Coralie, and I insist on keeping the new arrangement, but Fabien and Fabienne choose to side with Gregorius, since he's the Crown Prince.

There's still half the duration of the class left and I'm back to slow dancing with Gregorius again. I sigh.

"I've never been rejected before," Gregorius says in a grumpy way.

"Get over it." I roll my eyes.

I then shift my view at Florian when apparently he does at me too. He nods his head towards Coralie who's still looking at Gregorius while sobbing. And so I try to mimic my face to imitate her. We both end up giggling at each other.

"Okay, I get it," Gregorius speaks with irritation. "You two don't have to make it so *obvious*."

"We're not trying to," I say. We really aren't.

"I don't like it, Seraphine. I think I'm… *jealous*," he

infers.

"Not my problem."

"I'm serious, Seraphine. I'm *jealous*," he whispers.
I roll my eyes. "I feel like, if you're not here with me, I'm
going to *die*."

"That's not even remotely close to being jealous,"
I snort. "Sounds to me like you're just scared to die, that's
all."

"Well, what do you want me to do? Do you want
me to die? The kingdom to have no other heir?" He
starts panicking. "You cannot leave me, Seraphine. I'll do
anything. You know what? Once we get married, I'll take
the throne and you'll be the Queen. A Queen, Seraphine!
I'm literally giving this away to you. Only you! So, will you
please marry me? And protect me for the rest of my life?"

Gregorius suddenly moves like he's about to kneel.
And then, he really does. So as quick as lightning, I pull
him to stand.

We're now back to slow dancing again, as instructed
by the teachers.

I really hate touching him.

"I'm not going to be your Queen Bodyguard for the
rest of our life, okay? So can you please stop talking about
marriage? You're making me want to vomit."

"Okay. How about, you'll be my Princess
Bodyguard for the rest of our school years? We'll start from
there first."

"I'm not going to be your Princess Bodyguard for the rest of our school years!" I yell. "Gregorius, this is ridiculous. I'm telling you this for your own good. I'm not sure if you've known about this since you've been too busy playing video games in your arcade bedroom, but the academy rule is, you're supposed to choose someone to marry by the end of the school year, and in my opinion, you're ought to marry someone you *love*, not a *bodyguard*."

That's pretty funny, coming from me.

But for some reason, I suddenly think about Leon.

"And I love *you*!" Gregorius abruptly confesses, which I'm one hundred percent sure he doesn't mean. I sigh and roll my eyes again for the hundredth, thousandth, millionth of time whenever I'm with him. "And that's why, I'm going to choose you during our final exam."

"You *what*?"

Gregorius immediately slaps his mouth with both of his palms. We stop our dancing all at once.

"You're not serious! Take it back, Gregorius. I said, take it back!" I say while trying to pull his hands away from his lips.

"No! And that's final!" And now he's back to covering his lips.

Once in a while, he lets slip his tongue to mock me. I've had it with him.

In the process that I'm still trying to pull out his hands from his mouth, I suddenly realise a red dot on his forehead. In what seems like within the split of a second, I push Gregorius's body to the side as hard as I can. In an instant, a bullet that was aiming for his head crashes onto the floor instead.

Consequently, my body falls right on top of his. In reflex, I act to cover him by resting my body on top of his, at the same time both of my arms wrap around his head. Meanwhile, Yves and all of his men stand guard in where Gregorius and I fell.

I roll over and feel the momentum of Gregorius' panting on my butt cheeks. As soon as Yves screams "clear", I stand as immediately as I can.

Gross!

"The more reason I'm proposing to you, *still*," Gregorius says. Only this time, he looks and sounds calmer and happier than the other day he almost lost his head. But then straight away, his expression turns to disappointment. "Obviously, you're doing a better job than *them*." Gregorius points at Yves and his men with pure annoyance.

I want to make a joke that maybe one of them is trying to kill him for the sake of the kingdom, but luckily I've managed to restrain myself for I'm sure he'd not feel safe in his castle and would do more annoying things to get me to guard him the whole day and night. Such as living in the castle with him, or worse, sleeping in the same room as him.

Suddenly, I get goosebumps all over.

47

The fifth week of the school finally ends with the highlight being Gregorius the Crown Prince almost died. *Again*.

Today is now Sunday.

So far on my list, I still have eight shops to visit before Jerome and Florian's Royal Coming-of-Age Ceremony.

Florian.

There's something about Florian that makes my heart smile. Maybe something like Leon. Something like Reon. Anyway, I'm still not entirely sure what's happening inside my heart. At the moment, it's total chaos and fireworks at the same time.

But the worst part is how I've been keeping my brief moments with Florian a secret from Reon, even though I've developed this habit to comfortably not leave aside any details about my school day. Besides, Reon always says how he really wants to know what's happened to me at school and such. He's once said that he wants to feel as if he's with me in every class by listening to my stories. So now, I feel like I've done something wrong even when I don't tell him any lies.

From the fifth to eleventh Sunday's girls' night out, I've come to a much much different, more desperate kind of resolution. There are no more one-of-a-kind gifts and secret rooms, and the only intel I've gathered from the visitors is how some of them saw a peculiar object flying in the sky before the body dropped from the sky, and how they think the Royal Phantom was behind it all. But I have a feeling that this could be very important for the investigation.

Within the same period during the first Friday of the third school month, Gregorius has almost become a dead body again. This time, the killer tries to shoot an arrow at his heart while we're fighting in the middle of the dance like last time (he's still insisting on the proposal thing). Luckily, I take in the sound of the swing just in time to flinch and push us onto the other side of the floor.

What's even worse this time, if I had failed to distinguish the sound, I would have died too.

Regardless, I get to notice something else. The target area has somehow changed. I mean, it's still Gregorius the Crown Prince, but instead of the head, it's now reverted back to the heart again.

The body back in the town square was killed by the neck, then finished on the heart post-mortem. The second attempt was entirely targeted on his entire head. The third one was also a shot straight to his forehead. So now, why did the killer only target his heart? What does it mean? Is this some kind of statement or are there more than one killer now?

Urgh. I feel like messing up my hair so badly.

48

When Sunday of the twelfth school week finally comes, I insist on going to the butcher shop first. I've put up with their shopping agenda that lasted for the whole Sunday *each* for the past eleven weeks, so my argument is, today is only fair if we get to cater mine, which is solely for the murder investigation.

"But tonight is Jerome and Florian's Royal Coming-of-Age Ceremony! I don't want to smell like meat," Ghyslaine complains.

"Raw meat. There's a difference," Leonie retorts calmly.

"You girls can do your thing, I'll do mine. I'll be fine, really," I say.

Honestly, I'd probably be better off doing this alone.

"No!" Everyone abruptly shouts.

"We need to make sure you finish this as soon as possible, so that you'll have time to prepare for tonight," Orianne says.

"Besides, I have a feeling you may want to skip tonight's party for the sake of the investigation. Or worse, coming with this same outfit you've been wearing for the past three months. *This.*" Leonie points from my head down to my toe. She then shakes her head while touching her forehead.

"Don't even get me started with the running boots," Ghyslaine says while shaking her head too.

"And the hair," Melodie says.

"And the no make-up," Coralie says.

And now, they all deeply sigh while looking at me.

"You know what, let's go to the butcher shop *now*. The faster we finish this, the sooner we can shower and get ready for the party. How's that?" I say. My turn to sigh this time.

"Okay!" They're all now hugging me while jumping up and down again.

Reaching the butcher shop, my friends are hesitant to enter at first, but they end up entering while pinching their nose.

"Stop it! You're embarrassing me," I say. "Have any of you ever been to a butcher shop before?"

They shake their heads. I sigh.

"Have you?" Coralie asks, still pinching her nose.

"Yes, she has, silly! In the newspapers, one of the cases she solved a year ago is the one where the butcher ended up being the murderer," Ghyslaine explains, to my own big surprise.

"Since when did you read through her cases?" Melodie asks.

"More like, since when did she read a newspaper," Leonie snorts.

"I'll have you know that I've made myself fully informed of one of my best friends' accomplishments, which I am very proud of," Ghyslaine says. For a brief moment, she suddenly turns into a statue as she's realised what she's just said.

"Wait. Did you just say that we're… your best friends?" Leonie softly chuckles.

"She definitely did!" Orianne lets out a hearty laugh.

Ghyslaine's face instantly turns all red. "Well, I'll have you know how lucky you are to even be considered a friend of mine, let alone a selected few of the very *best*. But it's fine if you don't think the same. I don't need any of you." She then pouts.

"Come on, we love you too, even though you're snobby and rude and annoying," Leonie says, and then abruptly hugs her. Afterward, the others join her too, followed by me the second-last after Melodie forcefully pushes me into the solid circle of human arms – before she dives towards us herself.

So now, Ghyslaine looks like she's about to cry.

"Well, you've definitely never had a best friend

before," Leonie smirks.

"Shut up!" Ghyslaine shouts, but with a smile.

"To be honest, you girls are my first best friends too," Melodie says.

"Me too," Orianne says.

"Me three," Coralie says.

"Me four, I guess," Leonie shrugs her shoulders.

"Anyway, let's move on with Seraphine's investigation before she gets mad again," Melodie says.

"Wait! I haven't even said 'me five'," I say.

In response, they're all laughing.

"Seraphine, you don't even need to say it. We already know that," Orianne says.

"That's jumping to a conclusion without assertion," I say.

"And let's jump to whatever investigation you want to do. Let's go!" Leonie orders, her right arm swings like a commander in the lead.

The meat shop is almost like the other elegant shops with all kinds of meat placed on a beautiful wall rack made of glass in the most aesthetic way. I can't help but be impressed by how sophisticated the interior looks – for a meat shop.

Right in the middle behind one of the glass counters, the owner is now attending to a few customers. We then try to quietly listen to what they're talking about while pretending to look around the display case for some random meat.

"I told him this could be dangerous, that this is not the first time it happened," the owner says. "To think that he was so excited to start working in the Crown Prince's castle."

Say *what*?

"Poor boy. It's not confirmed yet but I think it's really him. I haven't seen him around again," the customer says.

"It *is* him! Let me tell you, he hasn't been here again since that Saturday three months ago. But nobody would believe me, just because he was one of the servant boys for the academy's student mansion."

The student mansion?

"You know, Sir Mignon, I heard there were similar cases since long ago, back in the Capital Region. The Crown Prince was presumed to be the sole target, ever since he was born, but the King was adamant to keep it a secret," the customer says.

Well, that confirms a lot of things now.

"That's why I tried to warn him the first time. There was never any murder here, so maybe that was why he felt safe."

"I guess this time, they chose to stab the boy's heart. Poor Reon."

I see. So the victim's name is Reon.

Wait. Reon? REON?

For one long second, I feel my heart stop.

This doesn't make any sense at all. Is this just another Reon or *my* Reon?

But… were there even two Reon in the first place?

"Seraphine, isn't that your Incredibly Handsome and Tremendously Charming Servant Boy?" Coralie whispers with the other girls crowd towards us.

That's an awful long nickname, but *okay*, since every pair of words is right.

"Coincidence is all it is," I say, while trying to convince myself it is.

Reon, who are you? Is your name even really Reon?

"Right. It has got to be." Melodie then lets out an uncomfortable smile.

She must already think that Reon is a spy.

Maybe he is.

"Are any of your servant boys called Reon?" I ask.

I guess I'm still in denial.

"Well, mine's Sergion," Melodie answers.

"Mine's Gaeyon," Leonie says.

"Mine's Darion," Coralie says.

"Mine's Marion, I think," Orianne says.

"I can't remember mine, but I'm pretty sure it's not Reon," Ghyslaine says.

"Anyway, I think it's time we go to the next shop. The tailor," I instruct.

Everyone nods.

49

Walking to the tailor shop, my mind tries to repeat every recent conversation we've eavesdropped for clues, but it always stops whenever the butcher's voice speaks in my head. *Poor Reon.*

As much as I want to countermand the possibility, my instinct tells me that this has got to do with the case. Reon's name. And *my* Reon.

Reaching the tailor shop, we try to do the same modus. That is, trying to pretend to look around while listening to the conversation. This is how I've always done it for the past eleven weeks, and I guess you could say that my best friends are all quick learners. Each of them is a natural, and they all seem to enjoy this too.

The tailor shop looks almost like the dress shop we went to on Sunday of the second week of school, but here, there are also a bunch of garment samples in the glass cases and measuring tapes on both the wall rack and the ceiling.

The ceiling part is probably for decoration or storage

or both.

"Yes! Based on the fabric. It's one of a kind, which is the only one the monarch would ever go for. The best type of silk in the whole world. No one other than the monarch ever orders that in particular. I'd say, from his age, he was trying to fill in for the real Crown Prince. Maybe tried to make him go to school on behalf of His Majesty," the owner says.

"That's definitely strange," the customer nods. "And you know what else is strange? I saw something on the day *that* happened. It was the cloud moving the other way around. I told a few people around me and they saw it too. The next thing we knew, the poor boy fell out of the sky like a meteor."

"But you know what's even weirder?" the owner says. "One of my customers the other day said he accidentally bumped into a young woman wearing a man's clothes with a knife on her waist."

Now every one of us looks at Orianne. She seems baffled by the news and she walks very slowly to gather with all of us.

"Orianne, you said it was a *man* that you saw," I ask.

"It *was* a man! I think."

"You think?" we all whisper, though very loudly.

"Well, now that they said it like that, I don't know. But for some reason, I was sure it was a man with a knife I bumped into. Not a woman. *Oh, no.* Maybe I was wrong.

I mean, it could be, now that I think about it. *Argh,* I can't remember a thing!"

As Orianne covers her face, Coralie comes to her shoulders and taps her back gently.

"So now, what do we do?" Melodie asks, unsure.

They're all now looking at me.

"Get ready for the party?" I reply confusedly.

"No!" Everyone says.

"What about the investigation?" Melodie asks. Everyone else nods in sync.

"Correct me if I'm wrong, but doesn't it mean that one of the princesses could've done it too?" Leonie asks. Everyone but me gasps.

"But, does that mean we should exclude Princess Prudence?" Ghyslaine asks.

"It's like we're going back to the start," Melodie grunts.

"Okay. Is there anything on the body that the culprit may have accidentally dropped? If it was one of the princesses, like, I don't know. Maybe glitter or something?" Coralie suggests.

"Like I would *stare* at a dead body," Ghyslaine chuckles.

Leonie jumps in. "Well, if there's anyone among us who would choose to get close to the body instead of running away from it, and she just happened to be in town that day, that could only be…"

Now everyone's looking at me.

"I can't tell," I say. "Just in case one of you is the culprit."

And then I pause for a moment.

I shouldn't have said that, should I?

Oh, shit.

Well, I guess they're going to hate me again. That wouldn't be the first.

"You know, if I hadn't gotten to know Seraphine like I have now, I think I'd have been so angry. But somehow, I don't feel hurt anymore," Orianne says.

"Same here," Coralie says. "That's just Seraphine being Seraphine."

"Classic Seraphine, I'd call it," Leonie says.

"Okay, Detective Seraphine, we understand. Now please, can we all proceed with our getting-ready party before going to the real party?" Melodie tangles her arm around mine.

"Wait. You girls are not angry again?" I ask.

"Hah! That's funny. Hilarious, even," Leonie says.

"We're your best friends, Seraphine," Ghyslaine says as she tangles her arm around my other arm. "We know you're just being honest. That's actually one of the reasons why I feel I can trust you. Just say the word and I'll believe you. It reminds me of that day you saved the Crown Prince. It made me think I should've known better the first time you said it."

"Well…" I'm still quite shocked. Dumbfounded, even. But, happy too. "I guess…" I swallow deeply. "Regardless of whether any of you did it, as I can't still fully scrap that idea out of my head at the moment, I'll still *royal-promise* that I will try my best to protect every single one of you, especially if there's anyone who happens to want to murder any of you." And I think I'm blushing too.

"Oh, no, girls. I think… I really want to cry… of happiness," Melodie taps the skin under her eyes.

"Damn you, Seraphine! You make me melt." Leonie taps under her eyes too.

"That is so gory, but also very sweet." Orianne already cries.

"You girls, she *royal-promise!*" Coralie already cries too.

"Okay, you know what," Ghyslaine sniffs, "I'd say we make a royal promise too. That we'll stay best friends forever no matter what. What do you say?"

"How about we say it together?" Melodie asks. "*We royal-promise. How's that?*"

"Sounds good," Leonie says.

"Okay, ready?" Ghyslaine says. We now wave all of our hands into the circle. "In three, two, one."

"*We royal-promise!*" they scream happily as we raise our right hand towards the sky. Me too.

50

Everyone's bringing to Ghyslaine's house lots of dresses hanging in multiple racks, boxes of jewelry, and different varieties of shoes filling a couple of long cabinets from home. Meanwhile, I've only got one each.

They're not the ones that are "one of a kind", but each of these three boxes was handpicked by the shop owners themselves after they showed me out of their secret room. They all said they'd bring out my rare blue eyes almost the same way the special boxes would, whatever that means.

Once everyone's ready, we all look at each other bemusedly as we all seem to be in the uncoincidental colour code of the rainbow. Ghyslaine in red, Orianne in green, Coralie in yellow, Melodie in pink, Leonie in purple, and I'm in blue. But then we all laugh and proceed to our individual carriage with the help of our footmen.

Our carriages bring us into the Royal Prince Academy. The school itself has transformed into what seems to me like a "spy getting lost in the magical forest" kind of theme, with hanging gliders and flying foxes on the ceiling as well as an exhibition of exotic flowers on the ground.

Going further into the Festivity Hall, it's more obvious that literally half of both personalities combined into an equal distribution of colour madness in and out. Jerome represents chaos in both black and red while Florian peacefulness in green and yellow, but somehow, the decorations manage to balance each other out.

Jerome and Florian are sitting on their own throne chairs on a platform which are just next to each other. It looks like the order is the same, only this time, I'm the one who needs to formally present myself to the birthday boys.

Jerome looks the most excited when it's Ghyslaine's turn to wish him a happy birthday, so much so that he almost jumps off his seat. But when Ghyslaine presents herself, she does it in a way that ignores Jerome entirely. She holds her head insanely up high and turns away from the queue while seemingly closing her eyes.

In what seems to be a natural effect, Jerome raises himself from the chair and chases her while leaving his birthday buddy behind. It's more than obvious who Jerome's decided on to be his dancing partner for the night. Correspondingly, Florian looks vacantly at Jerome running away but then lets out a deep exhale and decides straight away to leave him be.

The lucky last in the queue just happens to be me now, so it seems. The thing is, I wasn't supposed to, but right in the middle of it, I felt like wanting to pee and so I left my queue, which was just in front of Melodie.

When I come back from the restroom, however, everyone's staring at me. I breathe in a huge gulp of air as I walk towards the platform.

Am I too late for something?

On the way, I pass by my best friends only to find them acting very weird. They're jumping on and off their tiptoes and waving their pointer fingers at the stage where Florian is all by himself.

He seems to have left his throne empty and stands just right in front of the stage. He's also constantly smiling.

When I reach the front of the platform, I do a quick curtsy, and then I wish him a happy birthday. Now that that's off my list, I immediately make my way to where my friends are – that is until Florian suddenly screams, "Wait!"

I stop but I don't turn around straight away. I look at where the girls are first, perhaps unconsciously hoping for their instruction on what I should do next.

They're now moving their fingers into a circle and mouth something like *turn around*.

Okay? I'll turn my body around then.

But as soon as I do, Florian's already catching up to me and now standing right in front of me. He offers his hand like so, but I just stare at him in confusion.

This… Is this what I think it is?

"Princess Seraphine of the Twelfth Provincial Region, it would give me, Prince Florian of the Eighth Provincial Region, the greatest honour if you would humbly take only my hand for tonight as I have only had my eyes on you from the moment you step into that flower shop the first time we met two years ago," he says, which I presume in accordance with the *Dance Courtesy for Royals* book, because it sounds so formal.

I swallow deeply. My heart is beating like crazy but I'm still not sure if it's the nervousness or something else.

The entire two academies are watching me. The teachers. The counselors (I'm pretty sure the one that is still clapping the loudest is Edgar). The royal academy assistants. The mummies. My best friends. The other princesses. Too many eyes are watching for what could be my very first dance in public.

What's worse, I can't seem to move my hands. They're both still glued to the side of my dress. I think I'm sweating beneath the gloves.

This is ridiculous. Why am I suddenly acting like this now?

Florian turns his expression to being puzzled, and then walks a couple of steps even closer to me. We're standing so close to each other now, we can basically feel each other's breathing.

"Seraphine, what's the matter? You… don't want to

dance?" he asks in a quiet voice, sounding down of sorts.

"Yes… No… I don't know. I'm sorry. I think… I'm scared," I whisper.

In response, Florian laughs softly, which somehow eases my panic and makes me sort of want to chuckle.

"What?" I ask while still trying to suppress my laugh.

"I'm sorry. It's just, I found it very funny how you're not afraid of bullets, you're not afraid of arrows, and you're not even afraid of seeing dead bodies, but somehow, you're scared of… what are you scared of now, exactly?"

"I don't know. Like, they're watching, and you're like, asking me for a dance, in public. Are you being serious right now?"

"I don't know how to be more serious than following the *Dance Courtesy for Royals* book," he giggles. *I knew it!* "But you know what? Let me try this one more time." Only this time, he's not asking. Instead, his right hand is already reaching for my left. Our hands are now hanging up in the air together like a braid. "How's this?" he asks.

"It's O-K, I guess," I say. Still nervous, though.

Slowly but gently, he's now taking my other hand and putting it on his chest. "How's this?" he asks again.

"I can feel your heart beating."

"What do you find? Actually, nevermind that. What's the science behind this, *Detective*?"

Now that he wants me to put it that way…

"Well, it's already more than ten beats now. If your heart keeps beating like this, it will exceed the normal resting rate by three times as much. Why is your heart beating so fast?" Then suddenly, I'm reminded by my own heart beating at the same speed just a few seconds ago. Only I've come to a calm when I try to think of the science behind it.

Florian chuckles. "I think you're back to your normal self now, Detective," he says. "And to respond to your question, the answer is *you*. You make my heart beat so fast."

Now, I find my heart beating so fast again.

Seriously, what is wrong with me? First Leon, then Reon, and now… Florian.

I am so confused.

But I'm definitely blushing right now, and he can definitely tell.

Suddenly, my mind races to nothing. Not in deep thoughts. Not in conjecture. Just… blank.

Once I've come back to my senses, we're already dancing in the middle of the dance floor. We follow the series of steps as the music plays. We talk, we dance, we laugh, and he spins me from time to time with ease. It's like we're back in the *Dancing with a Prince* lesson, us getting away from Gregorius, hanging out while pirouetting once in a while. And the best part is, we cannot stop laughing throughout the night.

Since tomorrow is school day, Prince Providence and Princess Prudence make the announcement for us to go home. Our counselors approach us and are ready to usher us back into the carriage.

Edgar looks so happy to see me and Florian, and he can't stop singing all the way to his carriage.

Wait until he knows that I've rejected the Crown Prince's offer to be the next Queen Consort.

Nevertheless, I find myself smiling in my carriage at times on the way home.

Not too sure what I'm being happy about.

The talk? The dance? Or… Florian?

51

Arriving home, I'm shocked to find Reon pushing his back on the wall right next to my bedroom door. With his right hand on his chin as he stares at the floor, he looks like his mind is completely preoccupied with something.

A gorgeous sculpture.

So much so that he doesn't even realise that I'm approaching.

"Reon," I say softly.

Poor Reon. But then I brush it off straight away.

"Princess, you're back. I'm deeply sorry. I didn't realise you were," he responds as he stands abruptly.

"It's okay. Why are you here?" I ask.

"I… don't know," he sounds confused. "I guess, I was just worried, but at the same time, I knew you were just having a good time, and that's what truly matters. Did you have a good time?"

"I… did," I give my answer sort of hesitantly. It's now my turn to look at the floor. "I… One of the princes asked me to dance, and… we did."

Somehow, I'm scared to look Reon in the eyes. Not sure why. Maybe I shouldn't have said that. Though, maybe I should. I mean, by *logic*, there's nothing wrong with that.

So why does it feel so wrong to say it?

At the same time, there's this silence that I don't know how to break. Maybe I'll just wait. But then I realise, it's been too long of a pause.

When I look up, Reon's back is pushing the wall again. Only this time, his head is up, his arms are wrapped against his chest, and his eyes are closed.

"Reon, is something wrong?" I ask with a worried face.

"No. Nothing for you to be concerned about," he abruptly opens his eyes and answers with a smile. A different kind of smile. I can't really tell at the moment. "Now, I should be happy for you. How was the dance? Was he treating you well?"

"He was alright," I say. "We danced in the class before. Funny story…"

Stupid-me proceed to eventually fill in the details I'd missed. The Crown Prince's proposal. This constant laugh with Florian. Everything.

"Well, this Florian," seemingly the only thing he's picked up from the long story, "sounds like a gentleman. So in that part, I'm glad you were treated the way you're supposed to be treated. *One of a kind*," he says.

"Yeah, right," I say.

"You are the only detective among all the princesses in the whole wide kingdom after all," he smiles.

"But you know what? I bet Jerome makes a very good spy. I bet the others too, in their own way," I say with a soft chuckle. Good spy. *Good*. "Anyway, I think I'm getting sleepy. Moyra's probably bored to death waiting for me. I'll see you tomorrow morning before my class?"

"As you always will, Princess," he says. But this time, Reon takes my hand and kisses the back of it. So gently. So smoothly. So… irresistibly endearing that I can't stop myself from blushing. Why is the sudden move?

"I bid you goodnight, Princess. I'm happy that you are," he says, before opening the door for me.

Just at the very last moment, however, I catch a glimpse of a very sad pair of emerald eyes before he closes the door on me.

52

The next morning in class, the girls cannot stop talking about Florian and me, I have to constantly roll my eyes.

"You're going to have your very first date!" Orianne says.

"Like I said, I don't care," I retort with annoyance. "I just want your Isaac to get his own lab as soon as possible so we can get more clues about the true culprit."

This investigation has really been testing my patience.

"Oh, come on, Seraphine. Still about the case?" Orianne complains.

"It's always about the case for her," Ghyslaine rolls her eyes.

"Well, now we need to talk about you and Jerome," Coralie says. "What was that yesterday when you two were about to ki–"

"SHUT IT!" Ghyslaine suddenly screams.

"What?" I say in a complete shock. "What happened?"

"Well, Seraphine, since you were too busy yourself – laughing non-stop with the charming Florian, of course you didn't notice that Ghyslaine and Jerome had 'a moment' there when they were dancing," Leonie chuckles. "I think… they're *in love*."

Next, Leonie tries to keep brushing Ghyslaine's cheeks to her disdain. And then Melodie joins Leonie, followed by Orianne and Coralie.

"I think someone's getting proposed next year," Coralie says, winking at Ghyslaine.

"I'll have you know that I've made myself perfectly clear with Jerome. That if the Crown Prince asks for me, I will say yes for the sake of the kingdom. But if not, then… Anyway, Jerome is nothing but a back-up!"

"Whatever you say. Although, it's pretty clear to me that you've been in love with him the whole time. You're just too proud to admit it!" Leonie says. "You know what? I'm willing to bet that even if the Crown Prince chooses you, you'll still back out and choose Jerome at the last minute. And then, I can have the Crown Prince to myself. I guess now you're looking at the next Queen Consort." Leonie flicks her hair.

"Well, the same goes to you. Humbert's head over heels for you, and as much as you've been yelling at him the whole time, I can see that you're in love with him too. Seeing how so *passionately* you two were dancing yesterday."

Ghyslaine now mimics Leonie's blushing movement the other night, and they're now running around the space trying to chase each other. So not-princess like, but none of us cares. I can hardly see the difference between the royal grades now.

"Seriously, why can't you two just be normal like me and Melodie? See how happy we are now as we're just being honest with our princes as they are with us too. It's called *mutual affection*, get it?" Orianne says.

"Well, regardless, at least you all have your princes now. But what about me? The Crown Prince doesn't even seem to care that much about me," Coralie sighs.

"When the princess doesn't seem to reciprocate, the prince may then risk everything for the one he truly wants for a hand in marriage. The Rules of Royal Attraction says so," Melodie quotes. "Maybe it applies to a princess too."

Is it? I have no clue, since I was just acting like I was reading it the whole time.

"But you were dancing with that prince with a bandage all over," Orianne says to Coralie. "What about him?"

"I don't know. I was just choosing randomly. They're all covered with bandages, after all." Coralie shrugs her shoulders. *The mummies.* "But I guess I'll know as soon as he finds me for a date."

"Speaking of date – the sooner he comes, the more he wants you. My lots of experiences tell me as much," Ghyslaine says, and then smirks and raises her eyebrows repeatedly at me.

53

Reaching home, I wash myself and then go to the library to meet with Reon as part of my daily routine, after which we'll have our usual dinner together among books.

I find Reon reading in the library, waiting for me. A bunch of medical books make two towers on both sides of his table.

But this time, our conversation is interrupted pretty early by the sudden visit of Florian, which really surprises me.

Florian stands with a bouquet of blue roses in my living room, briefly looking perplexed by the condition of the house. But he quickly gets over it as soon as he sees me approaching.

"I thought the flowers would match your eyes. I was right," he says while charmingly stretches his occupied right hand towards me.

I suddenly hear something like the library door has just been closed.

"What are you doing here?" I ask as I receive to hold the flowers in my arms confusedly.

"I should probably ask you the same question. What are *you* doing here? You're one of the Diamond Princesses. Surely they will be able to accommodate you with a much better house," he comments in genuine pity.

"It's fine. Besides, I really like it here," I say. Mainly thinking about the secret passageway.

"You really do?" He sounds really surprised.

I nod my head while smiling.

"You never fail to surprise me. You must know that," he says.

I shrug my shoulders. "I guess, back to my question. What are you doing here in my house?"

"Well," he says, "I thought…" his cheeks turn red all of a sudden, "I'd take you out for a date."

"Now?" I say; surprisingly, not sounding so surprised, about what could be my very first date.

I'm not sure why, but my heart doesn't take the concept as something completely new. Almost like… I've been there before, which doesn't make any sense.

"Well, yes. I was thinking we could go to a restaurant in town to have dinner together."

Urgh. Sounds *boring*. Please don't tell me he's thinking to abide by *The Rules of Royal Dating Schemes* book. And that just reminds me of how boring the Thursday afternoon class is.

Honestly, I'd much prefer to eat while reading in the library, and then sneak out of the passageway into the hill underneath the stars. But at the same time, I don't feel like rejecting his offer.

Why? I'm still not so sure either.

"Well…" I'm trying to think of a polite way to reject his offer. "I'm actually feeling like eating here. Would you like to join me?" But instead, I end up inviting him for dinner.

But he's probably going to say no, since he was judging this house so badly.

"I'd love to!" he screams in excitement.

"You would?" I say confusedly. "Anyway, I always have my dinner in the library these days. Unless you'd much prefer the dining ro–"

"Library sounds good to me," he nods energetically. "Besides, I may pick up a book for myself too. Something to do with gardening and flowers."

So now Florian and I are waiting for dinner to be served in the library while we're both reading. Only this time, two pairs of eyes are watching like a murderous hawk.

Leon and Reon.

Leon keeps using his royal-guard-duty card. Every time Florian moves his hands towards the back of my chair, he'll appear so suddenly behind us. He's turned into the Butler completely, and even the Butler's looking so relaxed

– just chilling, sitting in the corner while calmly reading his book.

What is wrong with Leon? I thought he said he wanted me to marry a prince. So why is he even acting like this?

Meanwhile, Reon is with his serving-the-house card, saying he'll need to clean this part of the table, or that part of the shelves – everywhere near me and Florian.

Actually, it'd have been fine if it wasn't so bad the way he does it. I mean, it looks to me like he's never done any cleaning his entire life.

But the universe has seemingly decided to give me another trial in life.

Who else but Gregorius has to be standing in my living room with Yves and half of his men.

If I had known, I would've stayed in the library and begged Reon to open the secret passageway.

Although, there's something very different about the Crown Prince. Almost like he's not a fan of the Royal Phantom anymore because he dresses like a prince normally does – without the Royal Phantom black robe.

Dare I say, even though I still don't like him, he actually looks way much better when he appears decent like this.

And incredibly handsome when he doesn't talk.

"Well, if you marry me now, you can move to the castle effective immediately."

And then he has to talk.

"After that, what? I have to be the new Yves and scan the castle every morning and night?" I'd rather sleep in the forest.

"On the contrary. That way, we can travel around the kingdom in public. With you by my side, I will not need to be scared of going out again."

"Just keep playing your video games in your giant arcade bedroom," I sigh.

"That's the thing. Ever since I met you, I think… I'm getting bored of video games. Or maybe ever since I'm getting bored of video games…"

I roll my eyes. This guy can never really tell what's inside his mind and heart, can he? *Kinda like me.* I immediately shiver. *No way.* "Anyway, why are you here?"

"Well… the thing is, I've been having this feeling that someone's been watching the castle from the sky. Every time I pass by the big windows in the hallways, I feel like something's coming to my face like they're about to attack me – with something so shiny that makes me want to close my eyes."

I roll my eyes again. "That's just the sunlight. Your castle is made of glass, remember?"

Idiot.

"No, it's different! The feeling is like when that bullet was about to crush my forehead, before you saved me! Only this time, I felt it, and… oh! There's even another one. Surely, you need to know."

"Like what?" I ask rudely, but I'm still curious to know.

"Yves, tell her, please," he instructs.

Yves steps forward and looks into my eyes with full hesitation. "We found these inside His Royal Highness the Crown Prince's pocket after both murder attempts happened."

Two cards. Pink. Glossy. Primrose scented. The crescent-shape signatory. Signed by the Royal Phantom. But the messages between the two are different. One is the same as before, and the other is different.

The heart of the Crown Prince to replace the one you took from me.

And it says the Crown Prince. Not the *real* Crown Prince.

And who does the killer mean by *you*?

"The one you're reading is from the first murder attempt," Yves explains.

"See, Seraphine? The Royal Phantom has been trying to kill me! *The* Royal Phantom! And he can fly, Seraphine! So can you tell now why I'm so scared and why you're my only hope?"

I sigh while rolling my eyes. "First of all, no human can fly." I can't explain how the Royal Phantom did it just yet, but it must be something that science can explain. "And secondly, why didn't you tell me about this?" I start to raise my voice. "*This* is *important*!" I wave the card from the first murder attempt.

"Well, you were too busy rejecting me, that's why."

"Then you should've told me about this first before anything else!" I shout.

Seriously, this guy always knows how to raise my blood pressure so high.

The mortal enemy to my mind, body, and soul.

I hate this guy to the bone.

I close my eyes, inhale, then exhale, before I open them again.

I *needed* that short few seconds of peace. So desperately.

"Anyway, you need to leave now. I have company," I say rudely.

"Who? *Florian*?" he asks not so seriously. I even sense a bit of snorting coming out.

"As a matter of fact, it *is* him," I shrug my shoulders.

"WHAT?" His eyes baffle. And then, he starts screaming. "I was just kidding, Seraphine! Where is he now?"

"We were just reading in the library. So can you please just go, now? I want to get back to my reading."

"Well, what a coincidence because I feel like reading too. Yves, guards, I'm going to her library."

"WHAT?" I'm the one who screams this time. "Wait, Gregorius!"

In return, he sticks out his tongue like a child then runs into the library as if he owns the property. I mean, I guess technically he *does*. But anyway, that's not the point!

Leon, Reon, and Florian are very shocked to see Gregorius and Yves standing before them. As the Crown Prince strides towards the long table, the others force themselves to bow with respect. Probably because of Yves, not because they actually respect him.

Gregorius walks around the table first, but then he stops when his attention lingers on the book I'm reading, *Murder on the Hill*. He grins and then chooses to sit on the empty seat next to mine. I can't help but roll my eyes.

"Would you kindly recommend a book for me to read, Seraphine?" Gregorius relaxes himself on the seat cushion. His elbow rests on top of the chair frame and his head moves around the space.

"I don't think they have a book called *The Idiot Crown Prince* around here," I blurt.

Leon, Reon, and Florian can't help but giggle. I think even Yves accidentally bursts out a soft chuckle too.

Gregorius returns the gesture by glaring at them in motion until they turn quiet again. "Anyway, I don't mind reading something you like." He turns around the book I was reading in the air. "Now I see why you're so good at being a detective. You know, if you marry me, I can easily get you your own library ten times bigger than this with all the murder mystery books you want in the world. How's *that* for a proposal?"

"Still a no," I answer rather lazily. I hear the others giggle again and Gregorius stares at them ferociously once more in return. "So can you please just go?"

"No," Gregorius insists. "Well, if you don't want to pick a book for me, I'll just have to get it myself."

I roll my eyes – for the millionth time whenever he's around. I may need to start putting tapes around my eyeballs if he's going to hang out here any longer.

Gregorius walks around the shelves and then sets his eyes on a book.

"*The Ice Princess*. Perfect. I think I'm going to read this one. I need to see if there's a way to melt just her heart," he smirks.

I have no choice but to roll my eyes again. See?

Gregorius eventually comes back into his seat next to me. As I finally give up, I return to my seat and continue my own reading.

Now, it feels so much more awkward than before. Gregorius on my left, Florian on my right, Yves by the door watching us, as well as Leon and Reon just basically everywhere all around nearest to my seat whenever possible.

As if that's not enough to make me feel uncomfortable, I notice that Gregorius is not even reading his book. He keeps on looking at me with his left elbow on the table while his palm supports the side of his head.

But I have no energy left, so I just choose to ignore him and go back to my book, trying to pretend that I don't even care.

What's even worse than worst, both Gregorius and Florian keep visiting my house for the next four weeks.

Every evening they would come over. Every night we would have dinner together in the library.

And because of this, I can't spend as much time with Reon anymore as we've always had before. Although, he now tries to make up for the lost time by persistently walking me to my bedroom door and bids me good night with a kiss on the back of my hand, regardless of what Leon thinks as he starts following me around the house too.

54

Before I've even realised, tonight is already the mid-term examination coming up.

The Crown Prince's Royal Coming-of-Age Ceremony.

I keep on thinking as I stare at the shelves where the secret passageway can open without reason. Should I just fail myself by not going? I think at this point, I'm sliding towards choosing that over being pressured to dance with Gregorius at his ceremony.

But when I think about how the killer will try to kill him again tonight, I find myself rushing to my bedroom to get prepared.

Just like last time, I've decided to bring over only three boxes to Ghyslaine's house plus one small one which includes the peculiar masquerade mask. But when the girls see me ready, everything they're holding in their hands immediately falls onto the floor.

They walk slowly towards me with their eyes

widened and their mouths wide open.

"The rarest and most expensive gemstone in the whole world. The *bluenite*," Ghyslaine says as she wraps her fingers around my necklace pendant and trembles in amazement.

"The rarest silky gauze dress dyed in sky blue and aquamarine," Melodie says as she strokes the fabrics with both hands altogether.

"The rarest white crystals glitter like the stars in the sky," Orianne adds as she strokes the other side of my dress.

"The rarest white glass molded into just the size of your feet," Coralie says as she bends and presses lightly on my heels.

"The rarest white diamonds filling each space like trees in the forest," Leonie says as she lightly scrapes the surface of the masquerade mask in my hand. She rarely sounds this poetic. "There's only two of these masquerade masks in this whole world. As rare as there's only one sun in our solar system."

And then everyone screams, "WHERE DID YOU GET THESE?"

"The shop?" I answer while raising my shoulders.

"*Please*," Ghyslaine says. "I'd definitely notice something like this if I came across it in the shop."

"And you definitely wouldn't notice since you were just buying whatever you were told," Coralie says.

"Did you really get these from the shops in town?" Leonie interrogates.

"But she did have two boxes with her in each of the first four stores we went to. One for each ceremony. I remember because I thought those were just too few compared to what we bought," Melodie argues.

"You know what? I know what's going on. Someone must have given these to you," Leonie cleverly deduces.

Everyone stares at me and shoves their heads very close to me.

"And it's pretty clear to me who the mysterious guy is," she adds. "It can only be… the Crown Prince."

"That's it," Coralie sighs. She then drowns herself into the chair and looks up to the ceiling. "He's clearly going to ask you for a dance."

"I thought that was pretty obvious since he kept proposing to her during class," Orianne says.

"And kept coming to her house," Melodie adds.

"Well, I think we're looking at the next Queen Consort, you girls," Leonie teases.

"Shut up," I say. "I'd rather fail this exam than marry that idiot prince."

He only wants me as a bodyguard anyway.

"Wait." Melodie re-reads the invitation and keeps on flipping it. "Do we even need a masquerade mask? It's not even written anywhere here."

"I guess we'll find out when we're there," Orianne

says.

"Or now," Coralie says.

Everyone's now looking at me again but then they shake their heads and laugh.

"If anything, Seraphine's the one that's going to get all the surprises," Ghyslaine says.

"It's so obvious she has no idea what's coming," Leonie says.

"Let's hurry so we can see her totally blown away," Melodie suggests excitedly.

The best thing about all these is that somehow, they've suddenly finished getting ready so much earlier than last time. Now, they're the ones rushing to get to the Crown Prince's castle.

Tonight, everyone else is going to find out what the inside looks like.

Just as we pass the giant front door, everyone stops to get their masquerade mask, except for me. They're in different colors and styles and sizes, and so it takes a while before one comes to a decision, such is the case with my best friends.

Surprisingly, the guards are required to wear a mask too. Leon complains, but I choose a random mask and put it on his face myself. He turns quiet afterward, and follows me silently from behind.

Coming into the Festivity Hall, I'm very surprised to see that the stars of the sky are all around us, even above.

All of our breaths are instantaneously taken away by the dark firmament that dims as vividly reflected from the outside, in the scent of fresh air. Almost feels like we're flying on the ground of the top of the world.

Doesn't make any sense with logic, but that's exactly what it feels like.

Every single thing in this hall.

When I look to my left and right, I've immediately realised that the girls are no longer near me. As it turns out, we've all now become scattered as we're perplexed by what's in front of us.

I mean, how can we not? No decorations are here but the stars, no wall but the window glass, and yet the black floor tiles are all lavishly sprinkled in diamonds as if mimicking the natural view. One cannot help but wander without direction in awe.

And beneath all these masks, no one can really tell who's who.

All of a sudden, I feel someone grasp my right elbow.

"Princess, is that you? Are you alright?" I hear Leon's voice.

"Yes, Leon, I'm okay."

"I have a feeling something's not right. It's too dark here. And with all these masks, anyone can do anything without a witness," he says. "What is the Crown Prince thinking? Is he trying to get himself killed?"

"I don't know," I mutter.

I don't even think we're talking about the same person here.

This… This reminds me too much of… someone else.

"Dear Princes and Princesses of the Kingdom of Oceastarasia," I hear Princess Prudence's voice coming through a microphone. Apparently, she's standing on the only balcony on the second floor of the hall, along with the other teachers. "Welcome to the Crown Prince's Royal Coming-of-Age Ceremony. Following the secret-masquerade theme as determined by His Royal Highness, this will form part of your mid-term examination, as you have all been told. The rule is simple. You must dance with a royal during this ceremony. Albeit the darkness and the masquerade masks, the teachers will still be watching from up here. And remember, that by the end of the night, we will be calling your names for grading. I wish you all the very best of luck."

Out of the blue, the dancing music starts, distracting all of us. But everyone's only looking to the left and right.

There's no mark of a dance floor. There's no platform to wish the Crown Prince a happy birthday.

Which reminds me.

Where in the world is he?

All of a sudden, the sound of royal trumpets ramble throughout the hall. First to arrive is the Crown Prince's royal knights doing the similar things the King's army did back when they got me my invitation to the academy, followed by Gregorius with his midnight-blue suit glittering in diamonds and a black masquerade mask on his face.

Gregorius is excited when he comes into the hall, but when he looks around, he becomes disappointed.

He definitely hasn't agreed to this theme.

Yves directs Gregorius to the other end of the hall, all the way across the entrance. Afterward, the rest of his men usher us to form a line in which we will bow and formally wish him a happy birthday personally. But there's neither throne seat nor stage set up, so that means he has to stand for the rest of the process with Yves on his side.

I've decided to skip the greetings and scatter myself with the rest who have just finished paying respect and gotten out of the line. Every time a princess presents herself before Gregorius, he always asks the same question. "Are you Seraphine?" And whenever they shake their head, he bobs his head down and then repeats the same thing all over again.

Exactly why I'm going to skip the courtesy this time.

If anything, I'm saving him and the monarch from utter embarrassment because there's no way I'm dancing with him in public.

Including myself, everyone looks and acts confused as the hall is quite dark. And beneath all these masks, it's quite hard to work out even the people you already know.

All of a sudden, I accidentally bump into someone wearing a green suit and chartreuse-coloured mask.

"Seraphine?" he confirms.

I look up and straight away notice the familiar gold earrings. "Florian?"

"Wow. You look stunning, Seraphine. Now, I must get you away from the *mummies*, in fear they're seeing you the way that I am and starting a sword fight again," he jokes.

"That's funny," I giggle. "Where should we go?"

"Take my hand," he says, and so I do.

Even as I'm holding onto Florian's palm, going wherever he guides me without any clue himself, we still look as confused as the others; though at least, we're not alone anymore.

"I was with Jerome, but when he found Ghyslaine, as his luck would have it, he immediately left me to the rest of the confusing crowd. This theme makes it so hard to find anyone you know," he says. "I feel so lucky that I bumped into you."

But when I'm about to respond, something – more like, someone – distracts me from the hall faraway across.

If there's only one figure who looks as contrastingly sure as everyone around him doesn't, it's only him.

Like he owns the place.

A strange figure in a striking white-and-gold suit

silently divides the sea of people as he saunters towards me. I can't see his face – nobody can – but I could somehow tell who's behind the mask from afar. But just when *I think* I've figured him out, he's already gone.

Where is he now?

"Seraphine," Florian shout-whispers.

"Here, Florian," I say. But my head still moves confusedly to the left and right.

"Don't let go of my hand. We need to stay together until the teacher calls our names." His palm grasps mine even tighter. "Let's keep going."

"Okay," I say.

At least, I don't have to worry about passing the exam now.

But suddenly, I feel a gentle touch wrap firmly around my other fingers, gradually pulling me away.

A familiar touch.

For a few short seconds, I feel like he's making me choose which hand to let go. Putting the burden of choice on me. But I almost didn't realise that I ended up not moving at all, and thus, letting go of Florian's hand by accident. Further, and further away from Florian, as he's now pulling me to the other side of the hall.

When we finally come to a stop, he bends his body to kiss the back of my hand, then gently moves both of my hands to begin our slow-dancing like we did the first time.

Too damn familiar.

I have no complaints. It's all too easy to tell, even beneath that masquerade mask. He's not even trying to hide it. More like, he spares no effort to not let me know – that it's him.

"Reon, it's you."

55

I stare at the emerald-green eyes enfolded by the masquerade mask that's slightly different in shape, but the only one that matches mine.

The only two in the whole world.

This is getting too obvious, too confusing, and too unbelievable.

"The Butler is here too, somewhere," he whispers.

"I don't understand. Why are you here? And how did you even get here without an invitation?"

"It's not hard when one knows this place like the back of his hand. Every mirror placed, every glass in between, every brick, and every stone."

I pause for a moment, but I don't look so surprised.

That's it. At last. One hundred percent.

It's not like I haven't thought of it.

"So, why are you here, Reon?" I ask again.

You thought I was the Crown Prince or something?

I knew it. I freaking knew it.

But he suddenly raises his eyebrows, like he's just perceived something in me.

"The stars always remind me of that night I was born in the woods." He now looks up and around. "I keep wondering if this was the first thing I saw as I came into this world, as it was the last for my mother." He tries to laugh quietly, but I sense tears building up in his emerald-green eyes, as it starts to shimmer like the mirrored stars at sea. But then, he pulls himself together and still tries to give me the biggest smile he can.

That smile always appears these days. The kind that mantles the pain, I've finally come to realise.

But all of a sudden, I feel something I've never really felt for anyone before. Strange. Like something's hurting inside of me too. I don't know what's in me, but I think it somehow pains me to see him so miserable, or when he's pretending not to be – which doesn't make any sense to me at all.

What's more, I start wondering what his life has been like for the past sixteen years. Born in the woods. Going around the kingdom. Living in fear. Hiding under multiple disguises. His freedom, taken away not so lightly.

I don't get it, and then I do. Simply said, my heart is aching for him.

"That reminds me," he interrupts my deep thoughts. "I'm glad that the secret keepers found you. You look as ravishing as you always are. Not any more beautiful than any other days, except everything on you matches your eyes perfectly tonight."

"You still haven't answered my question. Why are you here? You know how many people have been killed, Reon."

Poor Reon – and so I'm suddenly imagining it was *this* Reon who was falling from the sky and was burning. *My Reon*, I think.

I wince at the horrible vision. I can't even imagine if anything is to happen to him; if it happens right in front of me and I'm not quick enough to stop him, what would I do if– "You know what?" I shake my head. "You need to leave. It's too dangerous for you to be here. The killer knows about Gregorius. I've seen the cards. I've seen the murder pattern. And if they're onto you now–"

"Florian is over there." He points to the left, subtly making it as part of our dancing sequence with our hands still wrapped together. No more title address, as one royal normally addresses another. "Leon is over there." He gently dances our hands to the right. "Gregorius is here." He then twirls me and catches my back, our eyes return to stare so deeply at each other. We've done it again, so gracefully. "Should you have to make a decision with your heart tonight, what does it say? That's what I want to know. That's why I'm here." And now, we're back to slow dancing.

"I don't understand. You're here… because of me?"

"For the past few weeks, I could only wonder if it's about time someone's pulling you away from me. Just the image of you dancing with somebody else in my head…" His head is now the one that's shaking.

Unknowingly, I find my right hand wrapping his cheek to stop him from looking away. *What the hell?* I startle him as much as I startle myself, so I try to immediately let go, but he promptly stops me by embracing my hand with his like a pillow, then closes his eyes to rest.

"This is all I've ever wanted." He then opens his eyes. "I know you've been confused, Seraphine. Your mind can only focus on the case right now, I get it. Everyone else can see that too. But… this," he says as his fingers wrap tight and gently around mine, soft and warm. Not letting me go. "Does this mean you have figured out your heart?"

I'm still not entirely sure what he means, what I have meant, what this is. Heck, I don't even know why I'm doing the things I'm doing now. What I did for him definitely came about by instinct.

But would I do the same for Leon? And what about Florian?

I still don't know.

And so I respond with the only thing I can think of.

Let's just brush this topic off by talking about the case.

"From the last murder attempt, I figured the killer may have known about–"

"I *promise* you that I have loved you, and will always do so for the rest of my life."

What in the chunky-ice *hail* of thunderstorm *rain*?

I feel like a bolt of thunder has just struck me right in the heart. He… he didn't… he hasn't just said that.

"Reon, I think you've made a mistake." A *big* mistake, I swallow. "You said 'promise' and that you–"

"I know what I said," he utters in persuasion, staring at me just as though he's flooding himself with the blue ocean of my eyes, as I am now jumping into his emerald green of sea. "Do you want me to say it again?" *We're both drowning.*

But this is not the time we can afford. At least, not now.

"Reon, you don't understand. Maybe you have forgotten. But a promise– a *royal* promise–"

"I know what a *royal promise* is, and I have never forgotten it. And I perfectly know what I have just said, as much as you perfectly know who I really am."

Deeper, and deeper.

I can't help but swallow. By instinct, I turn my head to the left and right again, trying to make sure that no one else has heard his promise but me. That no one has figured the situation out yet.

I'd better make sure this stays between us. Right now, I'm the only one who can hold him accountable for the promise he's made, and I could pretend that I've never listened to any of that. His stupid mistake.

"Seraphine." He calls me by my name. Never like before. I guess he really means it this time.

Tonight, no more hiding.

When the time is right, you will know everything about me.

But, suddenly he asks, "Do you want me?"

Huh?

Forthwith, Reon's hands hauls slowly from my palms onto both of my cheeks. "I'm not asking if you love me back, and I will never force you to. It's my own consequence; this *promise* I've made, you don't have to deal with. And I know the way of your mind is not as simple as what love is to me, but I'm willing to follow your heart at your own pace – if you let me. You can accuse me all you want. You can forget about me all over again. I'll stay if you want me to stay. I'll go if you want me to go. So, I'm going to ask you again. One more time. Seraphine, even if it's only for tonight, *do you want me?*"

Too many words, and they're all loving and sweet and unselfish and brave.

And at the price of his life.

All in the wait, his head bends towards mine, which is now barely up to his nose thanks to these heels. His clench is rather soft, giving me the chance to descend from where his lips are getting close at a gradual pace. He takes it very, very slowly – giving me more than enough time to think, or run.

I could get away from this and he would let me go willingly. Run to my left or run to my right, he has laid out the options freely, so it will only come down to *my* choice. *Mine.*

My curious labyrinthine-mind. My recalcitrant beating-heart.

What does this all mean to me?

What does he mean to me?

The man I could never get away from, no matter the reason, no matter the consequences.

The perfect partner that is hard to find. Not everyone has read *Rigor Mortis* for ten times. *Ten. Times.* And most certainly, not every prince.

One who has guided me to love. Deeply, without boundaries.

Which one is it – if not all?

This should have not taken me this long to deduce. It should've been so obvious as it should've been quicker for me to realise. Less than the time one could tell a poison is from a cyanide. Less than the time one could determine the state of postmortem rigidity. Less than the time one could recite the whole periodic table.

What does it feel like to want someone?

How can I tell if I want him too?

But when I come back to my senses, our lips have joined together as one. It's soft. It's smooth. It's sweet. It's everything I could never imagine if I don't go through every edge of his lips now. When he pulls out slowly, I want it more. When I take the pause, he brings up the speed. I've never been so grateful for the darkness around me.

How long have our lips been planted to one another?

One minute? Two? Three? Maybe even more.

Regardless, desire has never made its name as clear as now.

At least for tonight, I want him too.

56

Reality strikes when I hear the sound of a buzzing mic coming from where the teachers are watching us. All of a sudden, all the lights are turned back on.

"Something's not right," I say. My eyes look around for clues by instinct.

"The lights are definitely supposed to be turned off throughout the ceremony," he says, sounding perplexed.

I survey a few meters nearby and suddenly notice a familiar figure whose hands I've accidentally let go. My focus unconsciously stays on Florian who keeps looking to his left and right.

"He's looking for you," Reon says, somehow notices too and sounds a bit irritated.

"Considering we were planning to pass this exam together, I guess that makes sense." Wait. "Oh, no! Maybe the teachers are about to start calling our names. That's why the lights are back on."

Reon looks and dresses like a prince, and if he's

the only one left and they realise he doesn't belong in the registry, with this mask… Oh, shit!

"We need to get you out of here, Reon. *Now!*" I start to panic. "Okay, let me think." My pointy finger unwittingly curves and taps on my lips as I do. "You know what? I've got it." I begin to plan aloud. "We find the Butler– Actually, nevermind." What was I even thinking? "We go to the exit. The Butler *finds* us." Now that sounds about right. "And then, he gets you out of here safely. Let's go!"

I try to pull him to move towards the exit, but for some reason, he doesn't even budge.

"What about me?" His right hand climbs to my arm.

"What about you?" My eyes still wander around the hall, looking for the least-crowded way in the meantime. I'm trying to be more productive with my head. "I don't understand."

His palms now ascend to both of my cheeks in vexation, seemingly trying to stop me from being distracted. I think I almost stopped breathing by accident. It's how crazily fast my heart is beating right now, even after all that *kiss*. "What if I reveal myself and ask you for a dance in front of everybody?"

What if he suddenly reveals himself and asks you for a dance in front of everybody?

"What if we pass this exam *together*?" he adds.

He's not smiling, his eyes only pressing.

Is he being serious right now?

"Wait, Reon," my voice low and quivers. *Poor Reon.* "You're not saying–" I shake my head. "But that means–"

"Let's just wait here in the hall. I have decided." His palms quickly slide back down to mine as he starts guiding us somewhere, purportedly the exact opposite way from where Florian stands. Not sure if that's intentional. "When the teacher calls *your* name, *I* will be the one to ask you for a dance."

"Reon, you can't possibly think that one night of this is worth your sixteen years of–"

"Seraphine, I've made up my mind. Perhaps, a long time ago." He stops every movement before he abruptly turns to face me. At once, his palms are back to my cheeks again. "It's going to be alright. It's going to be O-K."

No, it's not. It's *not*!

It's not going to be alright, and it's *not* going to be O-K.

What is wrong with him? What is he thinking? I don't understand him. It's his life that's on stake. *His* life, for God's sake.

But I think I've already cared too much about him that I'd rather play the bad guy if I have to. Even if it may hurt him, if it means it'll only keep him safe.

Even if it hurts me too.

"Reon." I brush his forbearing hands off my cheeks, he impetuously holds his breath at the abrupt release. "I could still say no. You know that." My eyes stare right into his as I dare him.

And that would be an embarrassment to the whole monarch, wouldn't it?

But to my complete shock, he only answers casually, "That's my problem, not yours," all the while he's looking right at me so endearingly in the eye.

How could he not even flinch?

Oh, shit. That can only mean that he's not only serious. He's *dead* serious.

You've got to be kidding me.

Straight after, Reon gently wraps my right palm around as he's back pulling me further into the crowd. "It's only the right time for me to proclaim my love for you, before somebody else does," he says under his breath.

We're now walking further and further away from where Florian is seemingly waiting for me, as we remain in silence – and me, still utterly confused.

What am I going to do?

But out of the blue, he stops the pace, and I notice his shoulders are taut with tension as he breathes, like he's been bottling up something and it's bursting to break out.

"I'm thinking sixteen years of hiding is worth one night of telling the world that my heart is yours. Forever. Even when you could still change your mind. But it's the risk that I'm willing to take. Would that be silly of me, or selfish of me?" He then lets out a pathetic laugh.

"Reon, just hang on a second here, please." Both of my palms gently shake him by the wrist. "You're not thinking this through." I draw my lips closer to his shoulder above my eyes. "You cannot be seen. At least, *not yet*," I whisper. "The killer is *here*, somewhere. I'm positive about that." My detective radar constantly tunes in to signal the warning. Repetitively. Desperately. "So let's just get you out of here safely. You know what? I'll come with you!" My eyes widen as they support my gleeful expression. "I never really care about passing this exam anyway," I say lightly. And tracking deep down in my heart, I think I'm telling the truth.

"Seraphine, I never want you to fail this exam. In fact, I *need* you to graduate. Do you understand?"

I wonder why he makes it sound like it's between life and death, but... "Okay? I'm not sure why, but if you really need me to, that's *easy*. Consider it done." I shrug my shoulders. "So now, let's get you out of here safely first. After that, I can just go to Florian and–"

"Seraphine, what do you think just happened between us?"

"What do you mean?" I ask confusedly.

The killer is here somewhere, *watching*. So it's only logical for me to pass this exam with Florian.

Reon only sighs before opening his mouth. "We kissed, Seraphine. Our lips touched and they collided," he further explains. "We *kissed*," he repeats, even. "So now, I don't think my heart can even take the thought of sharing your hand with another man, even when it's for my own benefit." His left palm remains on mine while the other comes up to my cheek. "Now, tell me. How can I leave you now if I can't even let go of your hand?"

His eyes fixated upon me like I'm the only one who knows the damn answer. I can feel his palms shiver on both, persistently squeezing into mine like there's no other way. Fingers locked with no key–

"Seraphine… Where are you?"

I suddenly feel my body recoil in horror as I suddenly hear Gregorius loud-whispering from afar.

"Seraphine, where are you?" He keeps repeating aloud.

Seriously, this guy always appears at the worst timing ever.

I look around in reflex and I can finally spot him strolling around the crowd, not yet realizing where I am. Yves is right behind him.

Stupid me forgetting about the light being back on, because Gregorius just happens to lock eyes into mine and lets out a very big grin. "Of course. I could never forget that look. Those gorgeous details of eyes and lips," he utters from afar.

He saunters directly towards me so quickly, I have to give a grunt of aggravation out of my system.

"Shit," I blunder quietly. "It's Gregorius. He saw

me," I whisper.

"*Shit!*" Reon blurts out, which actually startles me. I think this is the first time I've ever seen him this panicky. "We need to go." Reon pulls my hand in a hurry though still manages to wrap around my fingers as warm and gentle as a cashmere blanket.

"I've got you!" Gregorius is apparently quick enough to take my other hand.

Oh, shit.

Shit shit shit shit shit.

"Seraphine, where were you? You haven't even wished me a belated birthday." But then he immediately takes notice of where my other arm is. "Who is this? Florian?" He then goggles curiously upon Reon who's now trying to look the other way while covering part of his mask with one hand. But his ears still clearly show. No piece of jewelry on the lobe. "Wait. You're not Florian. And that mask… Who are you?"

Yves, on the other hand, looks very disturbed as he now stands on Gregorius' side. "You're not supposed to be here, Your Royal Highness."

But I feel like Yves is looking at Reon while saying it.

"I know," Gregorius responds to Yves instead, all the while his eyes are still staring at me, whereby Reon still keeps to his quietness. "But Seraphine's here now. Come with me, Seraphine. Let us dance so we can pass this exam together. Screw Florian. Screw this guy too."

Gregorius grasps my palm firmer than ever before and aims to move us towards the center of the crowd, but Reon is quick to stand right in front of me while pressing his other hand onto Gregorius' arm, completely blocking him.

"What are you doing? How *dare* you! Who are you?" Gregorius shouts.

But all of a sudden, a gun blazes towards the window wall nearest to us.

Everyone in the hall bends their knees towards the floor, including the three of us who are just right next to each other. The Butler and Leon come to cover Reon and me as fast as lightning, but to my own surprise, Yves acts to protect Reon first instead of Gregorius out of panic. After Yves realizes what he has done, he flinches in horror and migrates immediately to protect Gregorius.

I notice the Butler's giving Yves a murderous look for a split second. Gregorius, in turn, looks stunned but stays silent without complaint.

As everyone's now running frantically towards the exit to get out of the hall as soon as possible, I try to look at the shattered glasses and around the hall for more insights while Reon keeps on pulling me towards the same way hurriedly.

All the teachers seemingly have left their post as I can see some of them are now standing near the exit to make sure we're leaving the hall safely. In the meantime, I calmly scan for any missing figures among them.

"Seraphine, I'll make sure I'll never let go of your hands. We're leaving this hall *together*," Reon says.

Come to think of it, he has never even let go…

But all of a sudden, the Butler stops him by the shoulder. "This is not a good idea. You two need to go on your separate ways," the Butler whispers from behind, still covering Reon closely as we're walking.

"The Princess will be safe with me," Leon says to Reon and the Butler from behind me. Leon's arms and body suddenly wrap around me like a full-size blanket, body to body, and I notice Reon flinching at the sight.

For whatever reason, Reon puts his other hand on his face. It's like he's having a headache. But we're still holding hands.

"Reon," I whisper. "Are you okay?" My other palm moves to gently rest on his that's still holding me, and I tap the back of it gently. *You should probably let go.*

"I'm fine. I'm sorry, I'm just thinking." His palm sinks deeper into mine instead.

Reon turns his head to the Butler. "Just cover us from behind. I'm bringing her to the library, and then you two can take the carriage instead."

The Butler stares at Reon, completely puzzled. It's clear from his eyes that he disagrees with Reon's plan, but it also looks like he's still thinking carefully about his next choice of words. "But, Your Royal Highness–"

"I know what to do, Commander," Reon hastily snaps.

I knew it!

But anyway, now is not the time to be excited about being right.

Though somehow, Reon looks really different now. As may be his mind has been made up and he will accept no objection. Like he's giving a personal decree. *A royal command.*

He's never going to let go.

So in response, the Butler– Commander stares at him quietly and reluctantly agrees.

But now that we've arrived at the library's door, Leon keeps on insisting on coming with us. The Commander tells Leon to be quick on his feet and follow him, but he still doesn't want to listen.

He's still reluctant, and so my eyes glisten with the silent order. *Go, now.*

It's my royal command this time.

Soon enough, Leon comes to understand. He turns around and runs with the Commander as Reon has ordered.

I don't really know what to say to Reon now, so I just keep quiet as we saunter to wherever he wants to go in the library.

I notice that he immediately knows where the secret entrance is as he strides only towards and stretches himself onto the upper middle shelf.

After one particular book has been pulled down, we walk through the secret passageway which brings us into another side of the hill. Thereafter, we walk into the secret tunnel that brings us back into the run-down mansion. *Home.*

57

When the morning comes, I'm still wide awake. I haven't even slept for a second since Reon put me to bed himself last night and left me with Moyra.

The thing is, I just have this feeling that the repetitive gunshots where no one was killed meant something. Something else. Almost like a clarification, confirmation, or validation of some sort. There was no time to slip the card. There were too many witnesses. And yet, it was still theatrical.

But then, there was the Commander staring at Yves so tempestuously, and when Yves lost his cool, he knew it too.

This is now getting much too dangerous for Reon. Poor Reon. *My* Reon.

Consequently, I've been going through everything in my head and I've been devising plans in my head to catch the culprit. As long as they're not caught, Reon's life would still be in danger, and I can't let them rest.

I want him to be safe. I want him to be free.

I want him.

My Reon.

When Moyra comes into my room, she almost drops everything on her hand.

Apparently, I look like a zombie. My eyes are wide in red and blocked tears, and my skin is pale as a mouse.

But I say I'm fine. In fact, I shake her shoulders happily and say, "I think I've figured things out. I just need to go to school."

Get me ready so I can go to school. Now!

When Reon finds me just outside my bedroom, he looks at me in complete worry. He doesn't think it's a good idea for me to even leave the bed.

But I do to Reon what I did to Moyra. The exact same way.

"I just need to go to school." It's my royal command.

When Leon acts the same way as Reon, I give him the same treatment too.

"I just need to go to school."

There's something I desperately need to find out in school.

So desperately.

58

The whole school is now talking about what happened yesterday night and how it's just been announced that there will be no mid-term examination this year. So now, whether we will fail or not will depend almost in its entirety on our final exam.

As soon as I reach the class, my best friends come to me like I'm about to faint, but I keep on going in one direction.

Orianne.

I shake her shoulders and ask about her prince's lab. Only when she says it's ready, I rush to my seat to try to catch up on some sleep.

But I still cannot sleep, because I still cannot stop thinking.

After the afternoon class ends, we all head towards the back side of the Royal Prince Academy building. As expected, all the Diamond Princes – except for Gregorius – are already there, treating the place like it's their new, exclusive hangout spot.

"Seraphine, are you alright?" Florian asks. His arms stretch to wrap around my shoulders, making sure I don't fall from my seat.

"I just need to think," I say. "I'm O-K."

I pull my eyes up to keep myself attentive to what they're all saying. Both of my elbows rest on my thighs for support while I sit cross-legged on top of the seat cushion.

A thinking statue is what I've become.

"Alright. It's *smelling* time," Isaac announces while walking towards Orianne.

"You don't say that anywhere, Isaac," Humbert says, rolling his eyes in the process.

"That's none of your business, Humbert!" Isaac snaps. "Anyway, Orianne. Now is your time to shine like Phosphorus. Consider me your loyal subject whose only aim is to radiate your light."

I see Humbert rolling his eyes again.

Isaac excitedly directs Orianne to all parts of his lab like it's an exhibition show. From different test tube racks, petri dishes, incubators, microscopes, Erlenmeyer flasks, beakers, and even some desiccators. But none of those reminds Orianne of the distinct smell she thought there was.

And so I rub my hair in more exasperation. More frustration.

"Is there any chance that she could be forgetting

about how it smelled?" Jerome asks.

"I wouldn't say that's not a probability. But that should not be a concern. Perhaps I just need to mix a couple more different elements into the compound. Yes, I believe that would be a solution. Right. What should I mix now?" Isaac hums happily.

"Sounds to me like that's just an excuse. Are you sure you two are not working together just so that you have a reason to mix more elements up?" Humbert says.

"That is certainly not the case! Anyway, where's my glove? Ah, there it is—"

"Oh!" Orianne suddenly screams. "That's the one!"

Isaac looks at her confusedly as he's about to wear his other glove. Orianne then comes closer and sniffs on the glove on his left hand.

"This is the one. This is the smell," she says.

"Latex?" Isaac and I confirm at the same time. We stare at each other for five seconds, then back to Orianne again.

"I guess I've been overthinking the answer. Of course. Latex," Isaac says.

"Latex? Like… a balloon?" Jerome asks.

"But how come no one ever said anything about any balloon?" Florian asks.

"Nevertheless, it'd have to be so many balloons to release the scent as strongly," Humbert says. "Somebody should've seen it."

"Maybe they were painted to look like the sky," I say. "I remember a shop visitor saying something about a strange cloud moving in the opposite direction."

"But if they were to explode as the body dropped, the remains must have flown out somewhere, yes?" Humbert adds.

"Not to mention the mechanism to push out the air before releasing the body. Something like… a drone," Isaac says.

"And then dropped the evidence somewhere they could not be found," I say.

"With the scale and distance, the gusts of wind could only take the remains as far as somewhere in the hill to not ever be found," Isaac estimates.

"But that could be anywhere! The hill is like a really big forest. And who knows what's in there," Melodie says.

"I've never been to a forest. Even the sound of it scares me," Coralie says while shivering.

"The forest is not somewhere the royals would ever go. *Normally.*" I realise Leonie already suspects that I've been there as she sneaks a look at me.

"Well, the King himself was very familiar with the woods. We've learned it in class. Apparently, that's how he got to survive during that time in the war," Isaac says.

"Wait. How come we never learned that?" Ghyslaine asks.

"Actually, I've been curious. What subjects do you

learn in the academy?" Leonie asks.

"Well, they should be pretty much the same, except we also have *History* and *Politics* too," Kitburry says.

"No *Precious Jewelry Selection*?" Ghyslain asks.

Jerome laughs. "Mind you, my Queen, we don't wear jewelry. Well, except for Florian," Jerome winks at him.

I feel Florian sighing from my shoulder.

And I've just realised he's still keeping me wrapped under his arms.

"But you do have *Absolute Beauty Treatment* and *Ultimate Beauty Maintenance*, don't you?" I joke.

I already know they do. From the book *The Royal School Guide for Our Dear Daughter Princess Seraphine*.

"Yes, we do. I mean, you don't get this youth-fountain beauty without proper beauty treatment and maintenance." Jerome wraps his palms on his both cheeks proudly. "I mean, just look at this skin. We are men that *glow*."

Ghyslaine rolls her eyes, but now I slowly notice her trying to hide her laugh. I guess she really is in love with him. Whatever love means.

"Glad to know that you have *History* and *Politics*," I complain. "I wish we had lessons about surviving in the woods too. Who knows it's going to be necessary for the case." Now I think about Reon.

"Wait. Does that mean we need to check the woods

for evidence?" Leonie cleverly asks.

"But none of us knows about the woods," Melodie says.

"Why don't you let me worry about the woods?" I say. "There are other things that are important too." And I have to admit. I need help.

Everyone looks at me so peculiarly.

"You've already got plans in your head," Leonie quickly concludes.

"And suspects," Melodie adds.

"But you haven't got all the evidence," Isaac gathers.

"So you need help," Jerome gleans.

"I'm in!" Coralie shouts, followed by everyone.

I sigh. "But it could take at least another four months since we have to do it in a very subtle way. And that means at least three murder attempts before–"

"You mean I'll have to be on the brink of death at least three more times?"

Please don't tell me I'm dreaming, because I'm hearing *his* voice.

But everyone's looking so surprised at whatever– whoever is behind me, that I know I'm not. They quickly bow and show curtsy to him as he approaches my side. "And by the way, Seraphine, you look miserable. I think you need to get some sleep."

I'm not even surprised by his sudden presence

anymore.

"I can't, can't you see?" I rub my hair. I don't even bother to greet him.

"I see," Gregorius mutters as he shoos Florian from his seat next to me by waving his hand at poor Florian's face. Florian eventually stands up at the last minute out of consternation. "Of course, you worry about *him*. His Royal Highness. I get it," he sighs as he takes over Florian's seat without guilt.

I immediately look to my left. At him. Deeply startled.

He's now smiling cheekily at me.

Hang on.

"I've got a confession to make, especially for those of you who are still bowing to me. You see…" Gregorius rests his back to the chair, looks up to the ceiling, and wraps his arms behind his head while closing his eyes as if he's resting by the beach. "I'm not the *real* Crown Prince, you guys."

"WHAT?" Everyone screams, except for me.

"Well, technically, I'm Second-in-Line to the throne. And since I always lock myself in my arcade bedroom playing video games, no one really ever saw me too, just like the Crown Prince. I mean, if you think about it, I'm sort of a Crown Prince myself." He shrugs his shoulders while still acting just as though he's talking in his sleep.

"Still, you're not the *real* Crown Prince," I blurt out.

"But your *boyfriend* is," Gregorius says with a giant smirk that looks super annoying.

"WHAT?" Now everyone else but Gregorius screams at me.

"But… how did you know– did you always know?" I ask bewilderedly.

"Of course I didn't. Nobody was supposed to know, except for the King and the Royal Knight Commander. But I am *not* an *idiot,* especially when Yves had to make it so obvious that I'm less important than *that person*," he opens his eyes and shifts his face to me, "who was never letting go of your hands." Gregorius then turns his face towards the entrance of the lab. "You know, you can come out now, Your Royal Highness *The Mysterious Crown Prince.*"

Soon enough, Reon saunters towards all of us. *My* Reon. All the ladies hum while the other guys are shocked to stone.

Everyone now bows and drops a curtsy before Reon, except for me and the lazy guy next to me.

Reon's hands move in a gentle-wave motion, telling them to stop with the formal greeting. Next, he reaches towards my right hand and kisses the back of it, then drags on his own a chair to my right.

I hear the girls humming again.

"Hello, *Cousin*," Reon says to Gregorius as he sits.

"What? He? Your– WHAT?" I scream. My head shifts between left and right on repeat.

"Sorry I didn't recognise you the first time we met, *Cuz*." Gregorius swings his hands in relaxation. "My deep apology. I mean, the *real* Gregorius the Crown Prince."

"I never take it to heart, Theodorus," Reon replies. "And to be honest, I was actually quite relieved when you didn't."

So that's this annoying guy's real name. Theodorus.

"So, Seraphine," Reon continues, "Are you ready to go home? Because I'm really worried you're going to faint if I don't put you to bed real soon."

"Put you to bed?!" The girls scream.

"We're sorry, Your Royal Highness," Ghyslaine says while curtsying again. The others now follow her to curtsy too.

"Reon, why did you have to say it like that?" I glare at him. "It's not like that at all!" I object as I repeatedly shake my head at the others who are still gasping in total disbelief.

And I've just realised that I still call him Reon.

"I'm sorry, Seraphine. But I really did put you to bed last night, and you do really need to get some sleep," Reon says, his shining green eyes blinking innocently.

I can't even tell if he's just being simply naive or actually saying it on purpose.

Everyone else now gasps even wider, up to the point their mouths are comparable to that of an open door.

"Seriously, you get the throne, and you have to

get the girl too? This isn't fair! I was thinking of having Seraphine as my wife, since I'm a Sovereign Prince myself, but of course, I have to lose to you as well in that department. Just like my father," Theodorus retorts.

"For the record, my mother had a lot of contenders fighting for her hand in marriage. Not just your father," Reon retorts.

Theodorus turns his body back to sitting position and fixes his gaze upon me. "You know, Seraphine? If Gregorius dies, I will become the real Crown Prince. And since everyone thought he did, I really believed I was." Theodorus then moves his stare towards Reon. "*No offense*, Cuz. Since I never heard from you, and the serial killer has been wanting you dead since birth," he shrugs his shoulders.

My brain suddenly sends signals of goosebumps all over. Like the warning for an immediate retort is distinctly urgent. "For the record, Greg– Theodorus, even if you were the real Crown Prince, I'd still not marry you either. It's just you, that's all. *No offense*," I say while rolling my eyes. I hear the others chuckling.

"Right, right, I get it." Theodorus slouches back to his seat again. "Anyway, Florian, we should get a drink later. Maybe team up or something, since we have just been beaten by *the mysterious Crown Prince* himself."

"Can you please shut up?" I yell at Theodorus. "Anyway, we need to talk about the case. I don't like the idea of someone trying to murder my–" I immediately stop myself.

My… my… my what? What was I going to say? My Reon?

Reon comes out of his chair straight away and kneels before me, his right arm rests on his thigh. He looks really excited. "My what, Seraphine?" he grins. "What am I to you? You haven't really made it clear, have you? Even when I have promised you that I will always love you."

And then he has to declare it in front of everyone and collect witnesses for the promise, just when I already promised myself to bring it to my grave.

I really can't believe him sometimes. I mean, does he not get it? I could not even bring myself to imagine being a Queen Consort just yet.

That awfully sounds more like a burden to me somehow. And a lot of responsibilities.

But I still feel my heart beating so fast, I cannot even keep up with my breathing anymore. My cheeks rise in temperature and they've completely turned red.

Meanwhile, the princesses hum again, and I think Coralie almost falls for no reason.

But most importantly, I can't let him blurt out the word "promise" again. Not even by accident. So, "Anyway, back to the case," I immediately act to brush him off. The girls grunt from disappointment so loudly, I have to roll my eyes at them. "As I've said, we've only got four months.

I just want to get this over with, so Reon can have his life back. I mean Gregorius. I mean the Crown Prince. I mean–Wait. Do people really call you Reon? Because the servant boy's name is–"

"Reon, I know," he says, looking down. "But believe it or not, Reon has always been my nickname."

"Just like me, Theon." Theodorus winks at me straight after.

"I didn't ask," I blurt coldly.

Theodorus only rolls his eyes.

"So, was the other Reon really a servant boy too?" I ask Reon. *My* Reon.

"He was the real servant boy back in your mansion. We traded places where he was supposed to cover for me at school, just like Theon. I guess my father saw my cousin as a last resort. We're the same age after all. But I'm sick of seeing people die in my place. All those series of murders, there were too many of them. They have to stop."

"That's why you've been reading all of those books too – to help with the investigation," I deduce.

He nods. "In the process, I was hoping to do it with you."

"Why me?" I ask curiously.

"Well, I just always know that, if there's anyone who can catch the serial killer once and for all, it's going to be you," he smiles.

I unconsciously smile back.

"Okay, you two need to get a room," Theodorus complains. "Reon, Florian and I are still trying to move on here. *Have a heart.*"

In return, Reon and I can't help but look at each other and laugh. Now, it's Theodorus' turn to roll his eyes. Everyone else, except Florian, follows to chortle.

"For the record, my cousin Jerome would be perfect to cover for you too. He did it once," I say.

Ghyslaine stares ferociously at Jerome.

"Th-that's right, Your Royal Highness," Jerome lets out a cynical laugh. "Call me back-up!" he says.

But that suddenly reminds me of something.

I have an idea.

"Jerome, do you think I could borrow your skill to sneak into the office rooms in the Royal Princess Academy?" I ask. "Your super-spy skill, that is."

Jerome jumps in excitement.

"Hang on, Seraphine," Reon interrupts. "You don't mean that the culprit is one of the royal academy staff?"

"In our academy?" All my best friends shout at the same time.

"I do. A young woman, dressed in a prince suit, smelled like a royal." I should've thought of it sooner.

"But who? That doesn't sound like any of our teachers," Melodie says.

"And that's why we'll need a few more things done before we can close this case. I've made a plan in my head, and I will use my turn in the Royal Banquet assignment to lure and trap the serial killer in," I say.

"But Seraphine, the academy may fail you for not doing a proper royal banquet!" Orianne warns.

"What about your grade?" Coralie asks.

"I don't care about any of that," I say.

Because what I do care about now is Reon.

My Reon. My Prince.

The mysterious Crown Prince.

59

Four months have gone by so quickly. Everything during has formed part into another routine except for a few things we take as our *secret missions*.

Following my plan, we have divided ourselves into groups of two (sometimes three, because of Theodorus) since we need to make our investigation invisible from the rest.

When all the teachers, counselors, royal academy assistants, and the rest of the students and their royal guards arrive in my mansion with their own long robes as part of the dress code I've set for the last royal banquet of this school year, their eyes are baffled with shock and pity. The size of the house is even smaller than that of Class Bronze princesses, the decorations really come closer to a ghost-themed party, and the host is currently nowhere to be seen.

Nevertheless, Moyra has successfully given its ceilings and walls a touch of fantasy to bring out the magic of the house with its refurbishment and cleanliness. I'd say this is already better than what I'd imagined.

I have chosen a theme for my second assignment, which I title *Princess Seraphine's Royal Murder-Mystery Banquet* on the giant front banner on top of the stairs. So obviously, this is not going to be just another royal banquet in accordance with *The Only Guide for Preparing a Royal Banquet in the Most Acceptable Way* book. Not at all.

As planned, I turn the lights off across the whole mansion and sneak into the crowd without them realising that I'm now standing among them.

Following the next part of the plan, Moyra turns the light back on for only one of the hallways to their left. Let's just say, I'm taking them on a personal tour first before proceeding to the main event.

They've now come to realise that as they walk through, both sides of the wall are filled with printed papers of the actual serial murders that had happened within the past sixteen years in the Capital Region, which information was collected by Yves, Rainpard, and all of their men. The victims were all either crushed on the head or stabbed to the heart, just like what some of the town folks have heard and talked about, only without the fake Royal-Phantom cards.

As they turn into the second hallway, parts of the wall are now sheathed by two kinds of glossy cards, pink and white. Written on each side is either, *"The heart of the*

Crown Prince to replace the one you took from me," or, *"The heart of the real Crown Prince is what I really want."* The pink ones have the Royal Phantom's signature below the message whereas the white ones have none. Some of the letters are made *bold*, some are not.

My message for the real Royal Phantom.

I know you're here. Somewhere. I can feel it.

He wouldn't want to miss this party.

Arriving in the third hallway, two different maps are now laid out on the wall across from each other. To my left is the Capital Region and its surroundings, which include in a big red circle the King's castle, the woods, and the Royal Prince and Princess Academies. Meanwhile, the other side of the wall has the map of this island, where in circles are the town square, the academies, and the Crown Prince's castle.

As soon as they reach the mansion's Ballroom, which is a very small version of the Festivity Hall, Rainpard and Yves along with their men immediately take guard of the space on each edge. No one can get out without facing any of them first.

What's more, a spotlight now hovers towards only the stage with an empty table. Everyone holds their breath as they know the lights only dim for a show.

"Welcome, my dear royal guests and honourable town folks," I surprise everyone as I walk towards Princess Prudence with my cocktail dress in black and red.

"Commoners in the royal banquet?" Princess Prudence screams, as Lady Francoise would too. "What is the meaning of this, Princess Seraphine? Are you trying to fail your assignment on purpose?"

"On the contrary, Princess Prudence. I'm simply trying to do my best, my way," I say.

"What are you trying to achieve?" Princess Prudence asks.

"The truth," I reply. "I want to solve the case."

The spotlight now hovers among the academy staff and stays when it reaches certain three royals who are currently standing next to each other. Then I begin to explain the reason.

They had been invited to the Royal Birth Ceremony sixteen years ago. They had been living in the Capital Region. And they would have access to the cards from the real Royal Phantom.

Most notably, the serial murders in the Capital Region and its surroundings just happened to stop right after they first settled into the island – something Rainpard and his men had helped to verify within the last four months of my sleuthing plan.

Afterward, I bring my argument back to when the body fell back in the town square. These three figures in particular had been in desperate need of new clothes from the tailor shop on that Saturday afternoon, just a few hours before the body fell. And that's why during these past four months, Melodie and Kitburry had been hosting an all-chocolate pool party for all the students and the town folks, in which Coralie and Florian always attended, to perceive what they had noticed. And as the hosts just happened to be *big fans* of the three royal teachers who inspired them the most, their photos just happened to be hanging in the mansion in one of the hallways on the way to the all-chocolate fountain and swimming pool – the heart of the party.

What a curious thing when Melodie and Kitburry just happened to hear Prince Providence and Princess Prudence had been secretly going on a date and accidentally spilled wine on each other when a couple of students just happened to recognise them. And what a much more curious thing for Coralie and Florian to hear that a couple of town folks remember Prince Hugo buying an art supply and the others recognising he seemed to be missing a shirt under his jacket before going into the tailor shop, on the very same day.

And so at last, only a single spotlight remains, showering its light only at the appearing-slightly-confused Prince Hugo.

Glowing face with the long yellow hair of a young woman at a glance. Dressed in a prince suit. Smells like a prince. *A royal.*

"Princess Seraphine…" He snorts and lets out a soft chuckle. "What you have been saying is total nonsense. So you're telling me that you'd been investigating for the past three months and I didn't even notice?"

"Naturally, Prince Hugo, because it wasn't me who was doing the investigations. My best friends did," I say.

Prince Hugo starts laughing uncontrollably and insists that I'm just making up stories. So I close my eyes for about two seconds, then open them when I'm ready.

Inhale, then exhale.

First, I speak about how the Royal Phantom had revealed himself for the first time about three years ago. Shortly before moving, Prince Hugo who had been a teacher in the Royal Princess Academy slash serial killer in the Capital Region had just found out that Theodorus, of whom he had thought was the real Crown Prince, was a big fan of the Royal Phantom, and so he incorporated this into his next murder. The town square.

Prince Hugo had caught a glimpse of Reon, the servant boy, with the Crown Prince's royal knights when they had their meeting with Prince Providence, and so that's when he started to follow him around in the afternoon carrying a rope and a knife just in case. Reon was so excited to start his new role as the fake Crown Prince and so he started wearing the disguise outfit everywhere he went, including the town square.

It wouldn't be hard for Prince Hugo to convince Reon to come back into the academy on Sunday when there wasn't anyone around, except that there seemed to be sudden change of plans when the Crown Prince's royal knights started looking for him.

I had been thinking whether Reon had been killed somewhere in the town square or the academy. Prince Hugo was cleverly playing it safe by strangling the boy with a piano wire and only stabbing him after rigor mortis started to avoid spraying blood to his shirt, but when I heard he was missing his shirt, I knew something was going off the rail.

Then I remembered the knuckle. The bloody knuckle.

Once he'd realised he wasn't the real Crown Prince, he thought of getting the information before killing him so he must have tied him first and locked him somewhere while getting the art supply. Only he didn't realise Reon would hurt his hand so badly just to try to get out.

And that's when I got the idea to have Isaac make some luminol while Orianne putting it into empty small bottles of face mist.

So for the past four months, Leonie and Humbert had been spending time together exploring the town while secretly spraying luminol in any secluded places they could find. Big applause for team Leonie and Humbert, because they just happened to find a burnt spot where Prince Hugo had set fire to his shirt filled with blood and smudges of sky blue paint, plus what were smudges of blood on the door.

Even after being cornered with the facts, Prince

Hugo is still persistent about his innocence. Now, he's telling everyone that I'm just hallucinating and making everything up in my dream. So as expected, he then asks for evidence.

I let out a quiet chuckle.

I was waiting for this.

"What's so funny about?" Prince Hugo starts losing his cool.

Jerome comes to the stage with his fake counselor outfit on his left hand and the evidence on the other. All the counselors gasp.

"Look what I found in your office," Jerome says.

Jerome puts three sophisticated drones on top of the table.

"And look what we find in your house," Yves announces.

Yves walks to the stage with his three men behind him, each carrying a sniper rifle, a small bow, and a multiple-barrel firearm. These items stay in their arms instead.

"That doesn't prove anything. Those aren't even mine. Someone must have planted them to accuse me!" Prince Hugo screams. Still in denial.

"But they have your fingerprints all over. Princess Seraphine had them analysed too," Yves says.

For a short second there, I think Yves is smiling at me.

Prince Hugo is now telling non-stop a hundred different fantasy fictions aloud, explaining how his fingerprints could possibly be on any of those items. Mostly include me as the villain. He's damn creative, I can tell you that.

After about twenty minutes, I start yawning, and so I proceed to what's next on my bullet-point list.

"What about something with your DNA?" I say.

I walk up the stage with Theodorus carrying the remains of painted balloons inside an evidence bag.

"Jerome just so happened to get your DNA from one of your wine glasses. Then Rainpard and his men had these analysed. Turns out, it's a match," I say.

Theodorus and I now put the evidence bag on the table.

"A preposterous conclusion," Prince Hugo retaliates. He then faces his fellow colleagues and students around him. "You cannot possibly believe all of this nonsense. I'm a Prince. I'm part of the Sovereign House. There's no reason for me to kill anyone, let alone His Royal Highness The Crown Prince."

"Unfortunately, Seraphine had that figured out too. She told me I would find something like this. And this is what I found." Ghyslaine comes up the stage with her fake royal academy assistant outfit in her hand as well as a heart locket, then puts them on the table.

Jerome's perfect spy partner.

At the sight of the locket, Prince Hugo's knees fall onto the ground in an instant.

Seeing his face so despondent, I've decided to take the locket and go down the stage. I walk towards him, bend my knees in front of him, then hold up the lock in my hand.

When I open the locket, it reveals a picture of none other than the late Queen Consort Georgette. Reon's mother.

I put the locket on the floor right in front of him. Afterward, I bring my body to stand.

Seeing her face in the locket, Prince Hugo breaks down in tears.

Theodorus now comes off the stage and stands next to me. "You found out I'm not the real Crown Prince," about which everyone else gasps in response. "So why did you still try to kill me?"

"*The heart of the Crown Prince to replace the one you took from me*," Prince Hugo speaks quietly. "A sacrifice. His heart for her heart. A hundred, thousand stranger's hearts for her heart, but it's still not enough. Who knows. Perhaps, I'm just a monster." He starts laughing quietly, and then louder, louder, and louder until he can no longer breathe.

The Crown Prince's royal knights make their move to take Prince Hugo away. Unexpectedly, Prince Hugo requests to speak with me before they do. Yves is reluctant, but I tell him it's okay.

"Go on. Ask me now, before you regret it," he says.

"I know very well – the face of regrets. More than anyone in this room."

I swallow deeply before I talk. "You no longer tried to kill the Crown Prince after his ceremony. For the past four months, you didn't even try. *Why?* After you turned the lights on and fired off those gunshots, you still couldn't see him?"

"It's true that I never saw his face, but I had taken notice of him the second he came into the hall. Not as the Crown Prince at first, but as a fellow prince who's been truly and deeply in love. Even through the darkness, I recognised that gesture with harrowing clarity. Someone who only walked forward. Someone who knew exactly who he wanted to spend the rest of his life with. Someone who was about to make a royal promise of love, no matter the consequences. Someone… like *me*."

"He's *not* like you!" I immediately retort in deep aggravation. How *dare* he? "I would appreciate, if you don't talk as if you and the Crown Prince are the same people, especially after you had killed so many people because of him."

He even wanted to kill him too. *My* Reon.

"He's not me, you're right. He probably has a much better chance to spend the rest of his life with the person he loves, and I don't. That's what I noticed after the gunfight too. Whoever this guy was behind the mask I already had my eyes into turned out to be the real Crown Prince. He wasn't supposed to be there and yet he came for the girl of his dreams. His life was in danger but he was still never letting go of her hands. Maybe that's why I had lost the heart, but perhaps rather, that's when I got it back."

Afterward, Prince Hugo only cries and smiles. The royal knights of the Crown Prince's army then proceed to stride him away from my presence, but he furiously shakes them off. "I'm not quite finished," he says while glaring at them. But then he looks back at me with a different look. One with a devilish grin. "Perhaps if you'd break his heart, you might kill him for me." And then he bursts out a boisterous laughter and tears as he willingly trudges towards the door.

Without conscious thought, my nails engrave the middle of my palms with painless gore. Words can't describe how much I really despise him right now.

But then, another feeling comes through.

I begin to worry.

60

For the first and last time in our school year, Reon and I finally have the chance to go as students together. He insists on walking me to the front of the Royal Princess Academy building while holding hands, but I firmly express total disapproval of the idea.

"I want to make it clear, especially to the *mummies*, that you're off limits," Reon argues.

"Oh, please," I say. "I'm pretty sure everyone already has someone; otherwise, they're going to fail." And I'm honestly just glad that I don't have to worry about failing anymore, since being *the worst princess ever born* means getting one prince to choose me is already a giant miracle. Let alone the Crown Prince. "So can we please stop holding hands?"

We still do.

Just in time, all my friends arrive around the same time.

What comes as a surprise, Florian and Theodorus

ask to speak with Reon alone in private before the exam starts. But to me, I'm more confused as to why Theodorus is still here for the final exam.

"I'll be seeing you soon. I'll be standing right before you, I promise," Reon whispers to me before he leaves. A giant simper appears on his face, but quickly fades when he reluctantly lets go of my hands as my classmates push me to hurriedly go into the building while the others direct him to the Royal Prince Academy.

Arriving in the Festivity Hall, everything is set like a royal banquet. I don't really know what to expect during this final exam – and I don't really care – but the others seem to have very high anxiety about what's coming.

After the sound of a bunch of trumpets blaring throughout the hall, all the counselors direct us to stand with a huge amount of space in between each of us. Class Diamond right in the middle.

Soon after, the guard starts bellowing the name and royal status of the princes coming into the hall. One after another. After being announced, they are to walk and stand in front of their chosen princess, before the next prince is called.

The decision is clear as day when Jerome, Kitburry, and Humbert walk into the hall, but there's a lot of surprising moments when some of the princes and princesses just end up dropping out. Apparently, Melodie and Kitburry's weekly chocolate party caused a few of them to fall in love with some of the town folks here who look and act no different (some even better) than us royals anyway.

But the biggest bombshell for all of us is when Coralie turns out to be one of them. All of us gasp as her choice of man suddenly barges in with an enticingly arranged bunch of fresh fruits and vegetables, which sends her jumping hysterically and forgetting everything in the *Book of Manners for Princesses* and *Rules of Being a Princess* books.

"Girls, I'm going to become a farmer! I'm going to water fresh fruits and vegetables every day!" she screams excitedly before she walks out of the row to stand on the side with the others who have been chosen too.

I guess I should've expected Coralie would have fallen in love with a farmer here – especially one who grows vegetables, I suppose.

Naturally, Prince Providence and Princess Prudence look very distressed from all of this. Especially Princess Prudence after seeing more princesses choosing to fail their final exam by dating all these gorgeous humble commoners, as she constantly shakes her head and holds it with her hand.

Not that I'm not happy about my schoolmates, but I think this has caused five single mummies to be confused as they choose to stand in front of me instead, which makes me very unhappy. I don't even remember any of them, except for their bandages, and the similar color suits they wore to my Royal Coming-of-Age Ceremony. Yellow, green, blue, red, and black.

Taking his turn as one of the remaining two Diamond Princes, Florian is next announced. Everyone wonders where he will go, especially after that serious talk with Reon and Theodorus.

Florian calmly looks around the hall, but as soon as he sees the mummies, he saunters straight towards them.

Wait… *What?*

Now that he assuredly stands right before me, I can't help but be startled.

"Florian, what are you doing?" I whisper.

"*A royal-asscher rose, the most beautiful and rarest flower of all. One of its kind, of whom I desire to be with for the rest of my life.* Do you remember, Seraphine?"

"The first school assignment?"

"Yes, and to me, you're that of a *royal-asscher rose.* Even after these four months, I've decided. I'm not giving up on you just yet, Seraphine."

"Wait, Florian, just wait." I'm super confused. "I don't think we've talked about this."

"But the Crown Prince and I did," he says.

Soon enough, the guard alerts the hall for the next Diamond Prince to be called.

"Prince Gregorius of the Kingdom of Oceastarasia, the First in Line to the throne," the guard announces with utter respect. He also sounds slightly nervous.

Reon saunters confidently towards me. *His smile.* Every time I see that smile of his, it makes me want to not think about everything else. And as my eyes are locked on his, altogether they're like the last two pieces of the most beautiful puzzle.

While he's still making his way, I can see that he's constantly taking everyone's breath in the room. Everyone's whispering at each other. Everyone's choking each other. Everyone's pulling their hair, losing control from the excitement.

It's the mysterious Crown Prince's first appearance in public. *Ever.*

Shining yellow hair. Emerald-green eyes. The most beautiful prince anyone has ever seen, charming as ever. A gentleman of cosmic patience and intellect, who's read *Rigor Mortis* ten times. Ten. Times.

Gorgeous, in and out.

Reon should still be smiling, except now, he just looks really pissed as he's approaching the line in front of me.

Slowly but sturdily, he walks past the mummies and stands right next to Florian. He then sighs as if his cloud of breath spells the alphabets that make up the sentence: *I knew it.*

"For the record, I never agreed to this," Reon whispers to Florian, but they're not looking at each other as they speak.

"You did not, but I did inform you, and so did Theodorus," Florian whispers back. Still not looking at each other.

So did Theodorus, he said?

As if his mention is an act of bad enchantment, Theodorus barges into the door without even waiting for the guard to call his name.

"Prince Theodorus of the Kingdom of Oceastarasia, Second in Line to the Throne," Theodorus announces himself. The guard is now just staring at him, looking completely baffled.

Unexpected, but somehow, as expected of Theodorus.

As immediate as he can, almost running like, he prowls towards me. *Book of Manners for Princes* out the door.

"Seriously," I start yelling, "he doesn't even go here!" I point my fingers at Theodorus, furiously protesting at the whole row of head school cabinet.

"Prince Providence and Princess Prudence. I have come before you, though not as one of the Diamonds, but *still*, of Gold from the Royal Prince Academy in the Capital Region," Theodorus claims as he bows precisely at the two of them.

How in the hell could he even be a Gold by only playing video games? But, anyway.

"Prince Providence and Princess Prudence. Surely,

this is unacceptable," I complain, still.

What in the world is going on in my life right now? Eight princes before me? Give me a break.

"Well, there's no rule that says otherwise. Prince Theodorus is indeed still considered a student in the Royal Prince Academy," Prince Providence says firmly. Regardless, he still looks very shocked himself.

Everyone else is now panting for air as who the news has claimed to be *the worst princess ever born* has before her eight princes in line for her hand. Five confused princes who simply don't know where else to go. One whose heart and mind is as gentle and prickly as the rose he adores. One helpless, most annoying person on earth who I'd always come to protect instinctively in a heartbeat. And finally, the mysterious Crown Prince who'd rather risk his life just because he can't stand the image of me dancing with somebody else. *Mine.*

Damn it, I should've listened to Princess Prudence that day during orientation, I think. Only when I notice Princess Prudence frantically flipping a peculiar big book over and over, my heart sinks. I thought she'd have known what I'm supposed to do by now. But even *she* doesn't seem to know what to do with this, with *me.*

This is just too much. I mean, I have to admit, I had expected way less of me. I've never even considered this scenario at all. This is beyond my wildest deduction that I never even thought I'd ever need to think this through.

The worst princess ever born. Supposedly.

So, what's going to happen now? What am I going to do next? I mean, am I still going to pass? And what about them?

What's even the syllabus going to be like for us?

"I knew this was going to happen," Reon snaps without warning, unconsciously bringing me back to the present time. "Somehow, I could always feel it in my bones. Some men just don't know when to give up. Especially you, Theon."

"Please, Reon, we basically have the same genes," Theodorus retorts. "Exceptionally tall, bright green eyes, shining yellow hair. It's only about time before she realises that she's fallen for me instead. Besides, after these long four months of thinking, I've realised that you've said you love her all the time, but she's never really said it back, hasn't she?"

Reon appears fuddled. I unwittingly swallow at the fact, but that's when my brain suddenly jolts multiple kinesics.

Signal of a raw, recently-formed hypothesis.

"Hold," I say. "Did you just say, exceptionally tall, bright green eyes, and shining yellow hair are in your genes?"

"His father, the King," Theodorus says, "My father, the brother of the King."

Go on, kid.

"What's the matter, Seraphine?" Reon asks. "Wait."
Now, he gets it. "You don't think…"

Except, he knows exactly what I think. How I think.

This is only the end of my first year of high school…

The Mysterious Crown Prince (2025)

Nurtured Blood (2023)

The World with No Evil (2021)

PriscilaK.com